PRAISE FOR ST

"The Judas Blossom *is a tal*
assassins and long-forgotten magic. ....., ~~Stephen~~ *Aryan*
has depicted the brutal Mongol Empire by weaving history and fantasy
together. A must read!"

Shauna Lawless, author of *The Children of Gods & Fighting Men*

"*With* The Judas Blossom, *Stephen Aryan shows exactly why*
he's the 21st Century's David Gemmell. He transports you back in time
to when great Khans swept across the world, conquering all in a tale
that truly deserves to be called epic. Aryan deftly interweaves grandiose
battles with the intimate machinations of power politics as only a true
master can. The Game of Khans has begun and I can't wait to see what
happens next."

Mike Shackle, author of *We Are The Dead*

"The Judas Blossom *is relentless, unforgiving, and inescapable.*
Packed with ever expanding webs of intrigue, the story drags you kicking
and screaming from page to page. The burn starts off slow, but once the
stage is set the plot moves like a runaway train"

Ryan Cahill, author of *The Broken & The Bound* series

"*A delicious, blood soaked tale of power and duty. Aryan paints*
an unapologetically brutal picture of the Mongol invasion. A thrilling
and savage tale of family, imperialism and moralistic turmoil."

Stacey McEwan, bestselling author of *Ledge*

"*A fascinating and gorgeous historical fantasy that will tug at your*
heartstrings."

M.C. Frank, author of *No Ordinary Star*

Stephen Aryan

THE JUDAS BLOSSOM

THE NIGHTINGALE AND THE FALCON

BOOK I

ANGRY
ROBOT

ANGRY ROBOT
An imprint of Watkins Media Ltd

Unit 11, Shepperton House
89 Shepperton Road
London N1 3DF
UK

angryrobotbooks.com
twitter.com/angryrobotbooks
A Flame in History

An Angry Robot paperback original, 2023

Cover by Sarah O'Flaherty
Edited by Eleanor Teasdale, Robin Triggs
Map by Nicola Howell Hawley
Set in Meridien

ISBN 978 1 91520 219 2
Ebook ISBN 978 1 91520 252 9

Printed and bound in the United Kingdom by TJ Books Ltd.

9 8 7 6 5 4 3 2 1

MIX
Paper from
responsible sources
FSC® C013056
FSC
www.fsc.org

THE MONGOL EMPIRE

1260

Empire of the Great Khan
-Yuan Dynasty-

- XUNMALIN TADU (DADU)
- SHANGDU
- YONGZHOU
- XIANGYANG
- QUANZHOU

Khangai Mountains
Karakorum
Altay Mountains
Gobi Desert

East China Sea
South China Sea
Bay of Bengal

Chagatai Khanate
- BESH BALIQ
- BUKHARA
- SAMARQAND

Golden Horde
- SARAI

Aral Sea
Caspian Sea
Caucasus Mountains
Black Sea

- MERV
- NISHAPUR
- BALKH
- HERAT

Ilkhanate
- TABRIZ
- MARAGHA
- SULTANIYYA
- BAGHDAD
- ISFAHAN
- SHIRAZ

Persian Gulf
Arabian Sea
Indian Ocean

- KONYA
- DAMASCUS
- MEDINA
- CAIRO

Mediterranean Sea

HISTORICAL NOTE

The 13th century was an extremely tumultuous period, and the region in which this story is set was rife with complex political wrangling. The Ilkhanate, one of the four Mongol khanates, occupied parts, or all, of various countries in the Middle East including Iran, Iraq, Armenia, Georgia, Syria, Azerbaijan and others, as it expanded and contracted over the years.

Most of the major events in this novel are historically accurate, but the timings and who was involved have been changed, as some of the events happened years apart, and with different people. Likewise, some of the characters are based on historical figures, but others are fictional.

In the case of Princess Kokochin, little is known about her beyond a few mentions, the most well-known being in *The Travels of Marco Polo*, where she left China in 1291 intending to marry one Khan, but by the time she arrived in Persia two years later in 1293, she ended up marrying that man's son. She died three years later in 1296. Hers is just one story about which we know almost nothing.

Zurkhaneh, The House of Strength, is a real ancient athletic system, sport and martial art, which combines many elements including wrestling, music, philosophy, ethics and spirituality.

So while *The Judas Blossom* follows historic events, I have taken a number of liberties. The goal was to create a dramatic story, set in a part of the world many people know little or nothing about, while hopefully remaining true to the spirit of history.

PART ONE
Year of the Iron Monkey
(1260)

"EVERY MORTAL WILL TASTE DEATH.
BUT ONLY SOME WILL TASTE LIFE."
– RUMI

CHAPTER 1
Hulagu

On the summit of a ragged peak, in a secluded valley in northern Persia, stood the fortress of Alamut, stronghold of the Order of Assassins.

Hulagu, ruler of the Ilkhanate and brother of Möngke, the Great Khan and Emperor of the Mongol Empire, sneered at the thick stone walls. It would fall.

This was not his preferred way to wage war but, these days, it was how things were done. He would've preferred to be on horseback, taking heads with a blade.

Hulagu ducked back into his yurt to finish getting dressed. His wife, Doquz Khatun, held up his sword belt. He stepped forward and she wrapped her arms around his waist, bringing them face to face. His beard tickled her face and she smiled.

"Maybe today will be the day."

Hulagu grunted. "I hope so. I'm already sick of this place." His expression softened and he kissed his wife on the forehead. "I'm glad you're here."

"You always say that." Doquz stepped back and turned the mirror so he could see his reflection.

"Because it's true," he said, adjusting his belt to make it sit more comfortably.

She grounded him when he started to wallow. Gave him

sage advice and warmed his bed at night. He had nine wives and twice as many concubines at home, but none of them would travel with him when he went to war. They preferred to sleep behind walls, in luxurious rooms, with armed guards.

Despite the hardships of travel Doquz was still beautiful. Her skin was clear, her lips were soft and her touch was gentle.

"You're staring."

"I am, my autumn flower."

"Don't call me that. It makes me sound old," said Doquz, turning away to tidy up.

Hulagu grabbed her around the waist from behind and kissed her neck.

"You're not old. You're ripe! Like a delicious peach."

"Agh. You're obviously hungry." But she was smiling as she pushed him away and shoved a plate of food into his hands. "Eat and then leave me to rest."

"As you command." Hulagu stepped outside and sat down on a stool to eat breakfast. His stomach was rumbling. She knew the rhythms of his heart and his belly. While he ate Hulagu watched his men prepare for another day of fighting.

The blue sky above his head was vast, with only a few wispy grey clouds that ghosted by on a light breeze. Another good day for lighting fires and burning down the fortress, if Tengri favoured them.

Down in the valley, dozens of Chinese and Persian engineers were scurrying about like ants, making final checks to their engines of war. Hulagu didn't like the engines, but he needed them for this kind of battle. Working among them was Nasir, a Persian engineer and mathematician. Hulagu understood that Nasir's contribution to the siege was as critical as that of his warriors.

The Chinese engineers were po-faced. At least with the Persians he always knew where he stood. If he kicked one of them they would cry out and curse him. Hulagu appreciated their passion and direct attitude. If he kicked one of the Chinese engineers they would simply bow and say nothing, but the hate would be there, behind calm eyes and a placid expression.

A few more days and then it would be over. The fortress would be breached and he would end the Assassin scourge in Persia.

His old friend, General Kitbuqa, marched up the path towards him. As always he was ready for battle. His lamellar cuirass was clean, his face scrubbed and his expression grim. Behind him came two of Hulagu's sons, Abaqa, his first born, and Jumghur. Although Jumghur was the son of Guyuk, his first wife and Empress, he had not inherited any of her intelligence. He was brash and loud, but at least he was loyal and a good fighter.

"How does it look, General?" Hulagu wiped the crumbs from his hands and stood, towering over them all. Most Mongol warriors came up to his shoulder. The only exceptions were his three brothers, all of them big men, with big appetites. Many believed that his grandfather, the great Genghis Khan, had been a tall man. In spirit and vision he had been a giant, but in the flesh he had been average in height. Everyone remembered the great deeds, but few had known the real man.

"My Khan." Kitbuqa bowed and the others followed suit. "The engineers are nearly ready. The flames from yesterday have gone out, but they're confident the walls will catch fire again today."

"Is today the day?" said Hulagu as he picked a bit of meat from between his teeth.

Kitbuqa, never a man to shirk responsibility, just shrugged. "God willing," he said, sketching the Christian sign of the cross on his chest.

"We will crush them, father!" Jumghur pounded his fist into his empty palm.

"None shall escape," said Abaqa.

Hulagu hoped that was true. The Assassins had been a thorn in his arse for many years. Most recently, forty Assassins had made the long journey to the Mongol capital, Karakorum.

They had tried to murder his brother in the palace. It was that attempt that had sealed their fate.

Hulagu grunted. "All right. Let's make a start."

"Fire!"

The arm of the catapult sprang forward, hurling a massive boulder at the walls of the fortress. The impact was deafening and the sound echoed around the valley. Hulagu heard a crack and his men cheered. The end was near. They could feel it.

The battlements were an array of fractured stone, smeared with blood and stained with pitch. With shields raised above their heads for protection, his warriors slammed the ram into the gate but it barely moved. Something was blocking it on the other side. A rockslide or blocks of stone.

"Give them some more fire. Let them choke on it," said Hulagu.

General Kitbuqa signalled the engineer. "More fire."

Nasir bobbed his head and scurried back to the catapults to confer with the others. The next two boulders were carefully doused with pitch. The angles of the arms were changed slightly to accommodate the wind, and then a spark was struck.

The dull rhythmic booming of the battering ram continued.

Crackling with flames, like a pair of falling stars, the boulders hammered into the walls of the fortress. The pitch splashed everywhere. Men inside screamed and the sticky substance trickled down the walls, seeping into joints, breaking down the mortar. A huge crack ran up one section of the wall. Flaming men threw themselves from the battlements, braining themselves on the ground to escape their suffering. Somehow a few survived the fall and they continued to thrash around.

"Leave them," said Hulagu, waving back his warriors. "Let them burn."

The sight would inspire fear in the hearts of the enemy. The smell of cooking flesh was not something that easily forgotten.

"Again?" asked Kitbuqa.

Nasir stood ready, awaiting his command.

"Wait." Hulagu stared at the closest point of impact. The crack had slowed and then stopped, but he could feel something, deep in his bones. Eventually the others felt it as well. Even the ram slowed and then stopped. A peculiar silence gripped the valley, broken only by the whimpering of dying men. Although the flames were low, a section of the wall was still on fire. Black smoke blotted the sky above. Wisps of it were carried away by the wind, but the bulk remained, hanging over them like an angry cloud.

"There!" said Abaqa, pointing at the wall. A crack had appeared running parallel to the gates.

"Get them back!" shouted Hulagu.

The message was relayed to those at the front. They dropped the ram and ran for their lives. The fractures continued to spread across the wall. A low grinding sound began deep underground. It built and spread, gaining volume. A huge slab of stone, about the size of a horse, broke off and fell away from the wall.

"Get ready," said Hulagu, pulling on his helmet.

Much like the other strongholds he had destroyed, Alamut had been well made. It had withstood a barrage for days, but the end had never been in doubt. This was also the last Assassin stronghold in Persia. With the death of the last grand master, Rukn al-Din Khurshah, anyone who escaped would have nowhere to hide. Everything had a season and theirs had come to an end.

Large sections of the wall broke apart, more cracks appeared and one of the gates came off its hinges. The noise was horrendous but before it fell silent Hulagu heard cheers from his warriors.

"Charge!" he bellowed, and ten thousand warriors poured into the fortress.

Hulagu slammed his shoulder into the face of one man, bloodying his nose, then kicked out at another, catching him in the stomach. Before the first could recover Hulagu slashed him across the belly, disembowelling the Assassin. The second man screamed as Jumghur's mace hammered into his shoulder. It cracked, shattering bones, and the man dropped to his knees.

"Fucking die!" shouted Jumghur, bringing his weapon down with both hands. The man's head was smashed into a bloody pulp. He didn't even have time to beg.

Remnants of black smoke drifted through the air, obscuring Hulagu's vision for more than a few steps in every direction. It didn't matter. His men were methodically working their way through the streets, smashing in every door in their search. Any Assassin who escaped the slaughter could run, but they were deep in the mountains, far from civilisation.

Jumghur cackled with delight as he smashed another man to the ground. He was good at killing, but little else. Jumghur had inherited Hulagu's anger, but it was a wild thing that could not be controlled, only carefully managed. Hulagu gestured at a squad to follow Jumghur and keep him out of serious trouble. They understood their duty and the consequences if they failed.

"My Khan." Kitbuqa had a smear of blood across his face and yet he was smiling. "We've found him."

The fortress was a lot bigger than Hulagu had realised. As his squad marched up the road towards the castle, they spotted a group of six Assassins. Disliking the odds, the Assassins ran for the safety of the castle. His men set off in pursuit, screaming war cries. Four Assassins managed to get inside before his men caught up with them. They cut down the last two and then hurled themselves at the side door. Their combined body weight threw it open and his squad stumbled inside. Hulagu swung his sword with precision, hemmed in on either side by the narrow walls. His men followed, baying for blood as the Assassins fled.

Kitbuqa stayed behind and called for more men because the castle was a warren of corridors. The grand master could be hiding anywhere. Hulagu didn't want to spend the rest of the day trying to dig him out like a tick. More Mongol warriors flooded into the castle and soon the air rang with the sound of fighting.

Hulagu came to a paved courtyard where a single pomegranate tree had been planted in the centre. There were four entrances and he gestured for his men to spread out in all directions. The clash of steel grew louder until fighting spilled into the courtyard.

Half a dozen Assassins were being pursued by Mongol warriors. By design, the tight spaces made it difficult to fight side by side, making greater numbers mostly irrelevant. But his men were relentless and all of the Assassins were bleeding. Hiding in the middle of the fleeing group was the grand master. When the Assassins realised they were surrounded they stopped in the centre of the courtyard.

"Surrender him to me," said Hulagu, pointing at the leader.

"Never," spat one of the men. A second later he fell to his knees with an arrow buried in his chest. Archers stood on a balcony, fresh arrows at the ready.

"Stand back," commanded the grand master. The Assassins reluctantly allowed him to step forward. Hulagu and Rukn al-Din Khurshah finally came face to face for the first time. The famed Old Man of the Mountain wasn't much to look at. Rukn was a small wiry man, with a touch of grey in his dark hair and beard. His brown eyes were hooded with heavy folds of skin, making them cavernous.

"You don't look that old," said Hulagu.

"Reputation and misdirection." Rukn lifted his shoulders. "If I come with you, will you spare my men?"

"Why should I?" asked Hulagu. "The fortress is lost and your people are either dying or dead."

"Why did you come here?" asked Rukn.

"Who paid you to kill the Great Khan?"

It galled Hulagu that forty Assassins had made it all the way into the capital without being detected. These days, security was much tighter but they should not have been able to get that close to his brother.

"No one. It was my decision to remove him. He was dangerous and a menace."

If Jumghur were present he would be screaming at the grand master. An ember of that same anger flickered in Hulagu's gut and it threatened to swell into a blaze.

"Step away from the others," said Hulagu, beckoning Rukn towards him.

When he didn't move Hulagu gestured at the archers. Two more Assassins fell, arrows punched through their throats.

"Enough. Please!" begged the grand master.

"Gag him and kill the rest," said Hulagu, turning away from the Assassins.

Silence engulfed the courtyard and from there it spread throughout the castle. The fire in the library continued to rage but otherwise the fighting was done. Once the grand master was dead and their library turned to ash, this would be the end of the Assassins. No one else would be taught their foul methods.

As Hulagu walked towards the front gate his men cheered, raising their weapons to the sky.

Apart from the grand master, every man and woman in the fortress had been butchered and sent on their way to whatever came next. If the Buddhists were right, then the Assassins would be reborn in another time. Given all that they had done Hulagu hoped their future lives were full of suffering.

His men dragged the grand master into the valley where the rest of his army waited. At the sight of their Khan a cheer went up from the throat of every warrior. Hulagu saluted them with his sword, adding his voice to the clamour, thanking Tengri and the old gods, the Christian god and whoever else was listening for victory.

"There." Hulagu pointed at a spot in front of him and Rukn was made to kneel down on the ground. Hulagu loosened his gag and then stepped back. Despite the destruction of the fortress and the death of every Assassin, the Old Man remained proud.

"Do you have anything to say before the end?" asked Hulagu.

As Rukn opened his mouth to speak Hulagu brought his sword down on the Old Man's neck. The blade bit deep, severing the Assassin's head from his body. Hulagu's warriors cheered he held up his gory blade. Now, it was over.

Later that evening, as Hulagu sat in his tent with Doquz, his thoughts turned again to what lay ahead. There was still so much to do.

A shadow fell over the entrance of the yurt and someone cleared their throat outside.

"My Khan."

"Come," he bellowed.

The rider was red-faced and stank of horse. His hands shook as he held out a message. Hulagu accepted the paper and sent the man on his way. He read the contents twice and then put it aside.

"What is it, my love?" asked Doquz, sensing his distress.

It had been many years since he'd cried. Hulagu thought the last time had been when he was a young boy. His father had killed his favourite hunting falcon in front of him to teach him a lesson.

"My brother, Möngke, is gone."

The Great Khan of the Mongol Empire was dead.

CHAPTER 2
Temujin

In the city of Shiraz, in the Fars province of Persia, Temujin cleared his plate with relish. As ever, the food was delicious. The tomatoes were ripe and juicy. The meat was so tender that it melted, and the rice was fluffy, doused with butter and herbs. He'd even grown accustomed to the sour milk drink, which was refreshing in the heat.

Golnar's tea room was his favourite place to eat and the owner always gave him a large portion. Temujin liked to believe that it was because she knew how much he enjoyed her cooking and that it had nothing to do with him being the youngest son of Hulagu Khan. Sadly, his illusions were shattered when he tried to pay.

"Please, madam," he said, counting out the coins.

"No, no. It's my pleasure. An honour to serve you."

"I insist," said Temujin, shoving the money across the counter.

"No, I cannot," said Golnar, refusing to touch the coins. "When people know that you have eaten here, it will bring great fortune to my business."

Temujin didn't believe that but it was nice of her to say it.

"Please," he insisted. He could feel other people in the room staring and they had probably caught sight of his masked bodyguard, Mahmud.

"Very well," she relented.

"Thank you." Temujin added a few extra coins to the pile before she swept them off the counter.

The threat of indirectly upsetting Hulagu Khan, however tenuous, followed Temujin around, day and night.

His stomach bumped into other patrons as he tried to squeeze between the tables but none of them complained and all of his apologies were ignored. Everyone ate their food methodically, with heads bent towards their plates, as if it wasn't delicious. The moment he set foot outside, blinking at the brightness of the noonday sun, Temujin heard conversations start up again behind him.

With a long sigh he set off towards his office, doing his best to ignore the silent shadow that trailed after him. He'd tried talking to his Kheshig on many occasions, but Mahmud had no sense of humour, no appreciation for food or wine, and he refused to eat a meal with Temujin. After a few weeks of refusals he'd stopped asking. Then he'd stopped talking to his bodyguard altogether. Now he did his best to pretend that he was alone and not being followed around by a silent man in a creepy leather mask.

There were times when a bodyguard was useful, but it didn't stop people from whispering when they thought he was out of earshot. Even now people stared at him. It didn't matter. He knew what they were saying.

Half breed.

Latin.

Round-Eye was the most common, because he had one brown eye and one bright blue.

People also made fun of his weight. While heavier than most people it wasn't as if he ate five meals a day. He just liked his food. People had mocked him all his life for one thing or another.

In Shiraz, far away from the disappointment of his father, Temujin was building a new life. There was a long line of people waiting outside the office. He smiled and waved but none of them returned his greetings. Most refused to make eye contact. A burly pair of local men glared at him, but that was as far as it went. After what had happened to their country, Temujin didn't blame them. They were a proud but conquered people.

Inside the main room a dozen tables had been set out and all but one were occupied. Most of the census takers were local men and women. All of them were exceptional at maths, but were also good at getting to the truth.

This far south there had been limited damage to the city and surrounding areas. It was a different story in the north. Whole towns and cities had been destroyed. Every building burned to the ground or reduced to rubble. Populations decimated or sold into slavery. His father's army had smashed against the Persian forces and crushed them. Many of the southern provinces had surrendered before the Mongolian horde swept over them and they suffered the same fate as the north.

"Late again I see," said Hamed, the chief census taker. He was an officious little toad who delighted in pointing out the smallest of errors. He wielded his tiny bit of power like a shovel. He was determined to remind them of their place.

"Big lunch was it?" said Hamed.

Temujin ignored him and sat down at his desk. "I am on time."

He waited for Hamed to disagree but he just sniffed and went to irritate someone else.

"Next in line," said Temujin as he refilled his nib with ink. A middle-aged woman with luscious black hair sat down. She had a kind but worried face and, although she gave a start at his eyes, it was obvious she didn't know who he was.

"Name?"

"Shohreh Alipour." Her voice was like warm butter with a gravelly undertone. She wrung her hands and couldn't sit still.

"Do you have a husband?"

"No." She swallowed and lowered her voice. "He died in the fighting."

"Any children?"

"Three. No, two," she said, correcting herself.

Temujin looked up from the page. The census was the best way to understand the population and how much they could be taxed. His father needed the money to expand the Mongol Empire.

This was vitally important work. It was also not the first job he'd tried. Every time he started a new one, it was with the hope that he would find somewhere to belong.

Temujin was also determined to show his father that, although he wasn't a warrior, he was useful and someone to be valued. Not every problem could be solved with a sword. He'd much prefer to use his intellect. Some of his sisters were cherished, and they were captains of industry. Hopefully, in time, his father would respect him for similar accomplishments.

"Why did you say three children?"

Shohreh frowned. "I recently lost my youngest daughter. She died giving birth to my grandson."

He had a notion of how she felt. His mother had died shortly after giving birth to him. It was something for which his father had never forgiven him. Guyuk, his father's first wife, had been his surrogate mother, and she had protected him from the worst of Hulagu's wrath. She had made a promise to his mother before her death to look after him and she continued to honour it.

"I'm sorry," he said. Temujin thought about sharing his story but changed his mind. "What do you do for work?"

"I own a small carpet shop," she said. "It used to belong to my husband."

Temujin tried to swallow the lump in his throat but couldn't.

"Is there anyone else in your house?" he croaked.

"My mother. She's too old to work," she said with a shrug. "What is this for?"

"So that we know who is living in the city."

"Are you going to sell me into slavery?" she asked.

"No. This is about taxes."

"I see," said Shohreh, pursing her lips. "First you conquer and kill us, and now you want to take all our money."

"No. That's not it," he said, but she'd stopped listening. Anything else he said would fall on deaf ears. "Thank you. You can go," said Temujin, filing away her paperwork.

The rest of the afternoon passed slowly. Almost every person he spoke to had been affected by the invasion and occupation. A semblance of normal life had returned across Persia, but it was clear everyone resented his presence. He represented the conqueror. If they had known his true identity, Temujin suspected their reactions would have been significantly worse.

Outside he could see a gathering of about a dozen local men and women. They weren't doing anything suspicious, but they made him feel uneasy. At first he thought it was nothing more than paranoia, but as their number grew he noticed Mahmud watching them.

Putting them from his mind Temujin called the next person forward. It was a young mother with two small children. They were hot, tired, and had been standing in line for a long time. The children were crying, fidgeting and desperate to play but she held on to both boys with an iron grip. Keen to make it as painless as possible, Temujin rattled through the standard questions.

When he next looked up the group on the street had tripled in number. Mahmud was standing in the doorway with his hand resting on his sword. Temujin spotted one man on the street distributing cloth wrapped bundles to others. The Kheshig grabbed Hamed by the neck and the chief squeaked like a little girl.

"Send someone to bring the guards. A child with fast legs."

"I don't have anyone like that," spluttered Hamed.

"Then you do it. But go now. Right now." Mahmud's voice

brooked no argument. Hamed wasn't astute but even he understood something was about to happen. Perhaps deciding it was safer to be elsewhere, Hamed ran, his sandals slapping on the ground.

The mob let him go. Their eyes were focused on the building. The other census takers realised something was wrong and began to panic, many of them running out the back. Those waiting in line scattered when the mob unveiled their weapons, an array of daggers, curved swords and short spears.

"Get in the far corner of the room and don't move," said Mahmud, drawing his sword. Temujin did as he was told while Mahmud piled the desks in front of him, creating a barrier across the open doorway. It wasn't much protection but it was better than nothing.

"Are they here for me?" he asked.

"No. They don't care about you. It's this place." Like Shohreh, they probably thought the census was a precursor to more violence and slavery. "If they make it past me, run out the back door," said Mahmud.

Temujin was about to argue when he heard a scream. A local woman stumbled about with an arrow in her throat. She dropped her knife and was trying to pull the shaft out of her neck. More arrows peppered the mob and half a dozen more people fell to the street.

Hamed must have run very fast or he'd been lucky. A squad of Mongolian warriors came down the street. The first six were armed with horn bows and a second volley fell on the crowd. Instead of running the mob split into five groups. Four of them ran towards the warriors in a zig-zag pattern. Peering through the doorway Temujin couldn't see where the others went. The sounds of battle echoed around the building as steel clashed on the street and men and women screamed in pain. Mahmud made no attempt to get involved and simply watched from behind the barrier.

Temujin was about to leave his corner for a better view when he heard the back door open. The fifth group of rebels poured into the room but then stopped in surprise when they found it empty. His bodyguard turned to face them and, despite being outnumbered six to one, he ran at the rebels. One of them dashed towards Temujin while Mahmud battled against the others.

A long time ago Temujin had trained to fight and ride a horse, but he'd not done either in a long time. He'd not carried a sword in years, but now wished he had something to defend himself with. With a hefty kick Temujin snapped a desk leg and held up his makeshift club. With no one else to attack, the rebel stalked him, armed with a dagger.

"Die slaver!" screamed the rebel. Temujin swung with his club and managed to clip the man on the shoulder. Despite wincing in pain he came forward, swinging wildly. Temujin tried to block with the club, but his opponent ripped it from his fingers and cast it aside.

When the rebel tried to stab him, Temujin grabbed the man's wrist and they wrestled for control of the blade.

The thing Temujin loathed most about his father was buried somewhere deep inside him. In his fury and frustration he felt it coming to the surface. Heat rose in Temujin's chest and something monstrous fluttered just beneath the surface. He could feel it fighting for release.

Temujin and the rebel had their wrists locked together. Even with his muscles strained to the limit, the blade crept closer to Temujin's face. He imagined it splitting his skin. He wondered if anyone would mourn him. He wasn't ready. He didn't want to die.

The heat rose until it filled his arms and then his hands. The look of triumph on the rebel's face turned to pain. The smell of burning meat filled the air and smoke rose from his skin. With a scream he stumbled back, staring at the burns on his wrists.

Something collided with the rebel's back. It took Temujin

a moment to realise it was a severed arm. The rebel flicked it away with horror and stumbled back. Cradling his burned arms, he ran out the back door.

Mahmud was bleeding from a wound in his side and another on his left leg. There was also a lot of blood splashed around the room and Temujin knew it wasn't all his. Two of the rebels were already dead and a third was fatally wounded. She dropped to her knees clutching the stump of her missing arm. Her dagger lay forgotten beside his foot.

As he bent down to pick up the blade the remaining rebels coordinated their attack, coming at Mahmud from opposite directions. He took a spear in the side but that didn't stop him from tearing open a man's throat. The wound sprayed blood across the ceiling and Temujin knew the rebel would be dead in seconds. Temujin tried to stab the other man in the back, but he turned at the last moment. The blade only skimmed the meat of his shoulder, doing little damage. A shadow fell over the rebel and Mahmud cut him down with a slash across the body.

Silence gripped the room. Mahmud took two faltering steps towards the front door and then stumbled to his knees. Temujin caught him before he could fall over. His bodyguard was bleeding from a number of wounds but Temujin didn't know what to do.

"Help! We need help!" he shouted.

Someone on the street pushed the desks to one side that were blocking the front door. Temujin didn't care who it was. He wasn't going to leave Mahmud. He managed to ease the mask off and was shocked by how pale he was underneath. His beard was matted with blood and one of his eyes was bloodshot and already bruised.

"Tell me what to do," he pleaded. Mahmud didn't hear him or had no advice to give. "How can I help?"

Temujin tried to stop the bleeding, pressing his hands into the wound on Mahmud's side but it had slowed by itself.

Temujin had no idea if that was good or not. There had to be something he could do to save the man's life.

The remaining desks were shoved aside and several warriors came into the room. Temujin was relieved to see a group of Mongolian warriors.

"Help me. He needs a doctor," said Temujin.

One of the warriors checked on the rebels while another squatted down beside him. He surveyed Mahmud's wounds and then shook his head.

"Help him!" he shouted, but the warrior's expression didn't change.

"It's too late. He's already dead."

Looking down he realised Mahmud's eyes were still open but he'd stopped blinking. He was gone.

CHAPTER 3
Kaivon

Kaivon watched in horror as the last of his people was cut down in the street by the Mongol warriors.

"We have to go. Now," said his brother, Karveh, pulling him by the shoulders.

A dying woman reached towards Kaivon, pleading for help. When the Mongol stabbed her through the heart Kaivon was sure he saw relief in her eyes. Just to be free of her suffering.

Karveh shoved him and then both of them were running, ducking between buildings, racing through gardens and hurdling over walls. The city of Shiraz was a beautiful place and it had been home his entire life, but it no longer felt safe. Kaivon ran until his lungs burned.

The plan had been simple. Wait until the end of the day and then kill everyone in the census office. By that time the workers inside would be tired, distracted and there would be fewer people waiting on the street. Some of those working for the Mongols were Persian, but in Kaivon's mind they were traitors.

He'd really wanted to kill the fat Mongol. There was a rumour that he was related to Hulagu Khan. Kaivon didn't know if that was true but the Mongol was important enough to have a bodyguard, which made him a valuable target.

"I have to stop," said Karveh, one hand pressed against his side.

"Keep walking," gasped Kaivon, taking in their surroundings. "Just a little further."

Up ahead was a monument dedicated to Rumi, the popular poet and scholar. The statue was a crude representation, but the sculptor had captured something majestic in his expression. The statue was at the centre of a small public garden, surrounded by benches and fruit trees. It was a quiet oasis in the middle of the city. A place where people came to read and relax with their families.

Kaivon sat down on a stone bench with his brother. Both of them did their best not to look suspicious, which was difficult given the circumstances. There were a couple of other people, reading or talking, but they paid no attention to the brothers.

"I don't understand what happened," said Karveh.

"It was the masked bodyguard. We took too long before attacking. We should have gone in sooner," said Kaivon.

"There were too many innocent bystanders on the street. They could have been hurt."

"Our people were hurt," hissed Kaivon, trying to keep his voice down. "They're dead. They're all dead."

Karveh shushed him, watching as an old couple tottered past, arm in arm. Kaivon stayed silent until they were alone in the gardens.

"If we had attacked sooner, innocents would have died." Karveh preached as if he was the one who had experience of war.

"Innocents always die in war." Kaivon fixed his brother with a glare until he looked away.

"Of course, General," sneered Karveh.

Kaivon grabbed his brother by the collar. "Are you mocking me?"

"Let go."

"If you'd seen what they did in the north." Kaivon's eyes

glazed over and he saw the horrors again. "Mountains of bodies. Young and old, men and women. Dead. Slaughtered like cattle. And the children."

The army had fought bravely in defence of their country, but it the end, it hadn't mattered. They had been filled with rage and righteous fury, which gave strength to their weary limbs. Unfortunately, even that had run out before the battle was done. Kaivon had killed and maimed until he was covered in blood, climbing over the dead to find the living. But there had been too many, like raindrops in a storm.

The punishment for failing to beat the Mongols had been severe. He'd watched as ancient monuments to their ancestors were torn down. Buildings, full of history and culture, smashed and broken apart. Libraries full of knowledge and accumulated wisdom sent up in flames. Millions of words lost, for all time.

The smell had been overpowering. The air thick with choking black smoke and the stench of charred meat. Kaivon wished it had ended when night had fallen but, in the darkness, the vermin had gathered. Rats and carrion birds and dogs had swarmed over the bodies.

So many of his friends had been killed that after a while it became easier to ask who was still alive. Great leaders were cut down. Other generals led brave charges that ended in agonised screams. Junior officers took huge risks to turn the battle and their lives ended abruptly. The noises had been barely human. Kaivon hadn't known a person could make such sounds.

He had wanted to stay and fight. To see it through to the end. Against his wishes, he fled south so that his people could fight another day.

"I'm sorry," said Karveh, bringing him back to the present. "I know you've suffered."

"You should pray for the dead. They need it more than me."

"I'm not so sure," said his brother.

"After the first day, we knew that we couldn't win. Did you know that our leaders surrendered? Hulagu Khan refused and the slaughter continued. For days, Karveh. Not hours. Days. Until nothing remained. How can you rebuild a city if all that's left is rubble and ash?"

Kaivon left his brother beside the statue and began to walk away.

"Where are you going?" called Karveh.

"I want to be alone. I need time to think."

"Don't do anything rash," said Karveh, as if he were the eldest.

Kaivon walked through the streets until he lost himself in the rhythm of the city. He let the familiar sights, smells and sounds overwhelm his senses until he felt at home and his equilibrium returned.

He passed through a busy market, admiring the bolts of beautiful cloth and the colourful rugs with their intricate designs. The mix of glorious spices and fresh fruit created a heady aroma that bordered on cloying. For a time he stood off to one side, watching people going about their daily lives. Buying and selling. Bartering and laughing with apparent good cheer. At first glance they were oblivious to the truth, but after a while he spotted signs of underlying tension. The furtive glances. The snatches of hushed conversations. A patrol of Mongol warriors walked past the edge of the market, further souring his bad mood. In search of cleaner air, away from the outsiders, Kaivon walked on.

As Kaivon passed through the streets many people recognised him, but no one made an overt greeting. With so many Mongol patrols they didn't want to take the risk. But that didn't stop them from offering him a sign of respect for all that he'd done. Several placed a hand over their heart and slightly bowed their head. They didn't blame him for losing in the north and, despite his own guilt, he was buoyed up by their warmth and admiration.

As darkness fell Kaivon made the long walk home. His legs ached and his heart was still heavy about what had happened. The pain would fade but the regret would remain, driving him on, forcing him to try again.

The basket shop was a modest business and a long way from being a general in the army. It had belonged to his late father and was now his brother's business.

Letting himself in through the back door he wasn't surprised to find a candle burning in the store room. Karveh was sat in the corner dozing in a chair, but he came awake as the door squeaked. Kaivon's brother reached for a dagger but then relaxed and sat back.

"It's late," said Karveh. "I was expecting you hours ago."

"I needed time to clear my head."

"Do you feel better?"

Kaivon dragged a chair across the room and sat down opposite his brother. "A little."

At Karvch's elbow was a pot of tea. He filled a second glass, added a slice of lemon and passed it across. "I'm glad to hear that."

"What are people saying about the attack?"

"Very little. The Mongols are pretending it didn't happen. The bodies are gone and the street has been washed clean."

"It must have something to do with the fat one." Kaivon began to wonder if the rumours had been true. It would explain the response. Normally such an attack would result in a disproportionate retaliation. Dozens would be killed, whether innocent or guilty. Their homes burned to the ground. A total cleanse to send a clear message about what would happen if anyone else tried.

"Perhaps." Karveh sat back in his chair, his face wreathed in shadow.

"You think it's something else?"

"What I think doesn't matter," said his brother.

"Of course it does. We're in this together."

"Are we? Really, brother?"

"What are you saying, Karveh?"

For a time he said nothing, just stared into the shadows. "While you were out walking, I met with the other rebels." The last word came out with a sneer but Kaivon couldn't blame him.

There was no organised resistance. No network of groups trying to repel the invaders. Not yet at least. Everything had to start somewhere and so too would the resistance. At the moment they had only a few dozen people who were interested in the idea of fighting back. None of them were soldiers but, in Kaivon's mind, that made them braver. They were willing to risk everything for their country. They were true patriots.

"What did they say?" said Kaivon, putting the wedge of lemon in his mouth before taking a drink.

Karveh sipped at his tea. He had a sour expression but Kaivon knew it wasn't because of the tea.

"After today, they're done. They're out."

"Who? Who said that?"

"All of them, brother." Karveh leaned towards him so that Kaivon could clearly see his eyes and the fear behind them. "The resistance is dead."

"I know today was horrible, and I deeply regret every life that was lost, but it was inevitable that some would die."

Kaivon had told them, over and over, that this was not a game. They were not noble heroes from ancient legend, slaying white demons and capturing golden crowns. Their war would be fought in the gutters and the alleys, not riding horses on a battlefield. It would be won in the dark, with the knife and the garrotte. It would be slow, painful and difficult.

"It doesn't matter. It's over."

"We've only just begun," said Kaivon.

Karveh gripped his hand tightly. "Listen to me. Please. It's over."

"I know you're afraid, but we can't give up now. We must show them that we're not a broken people."

"But we are!" yelled Karveh. "The war is over and we lost. Persia doesn't exist anymore. Now, there is only the Ilkhanate of the Mongol Empire."

Kaivon pulled his brother out of his chair and shoved him up against the wall. "Never say that. Never!"

"We are a conquered people. You've always been braver than me. That was why you became a soldier and I stayed at home. I'm tired, Kaivon. We are all. We don't have the heart to fight. Not today."

"And tomorrow?"

"I don't know."

"So that's it. You're going to live like a dog, for the rest of your life, on a Mongol leash." Kaivon felt sick to his stomach. The air in the room was stifling.

"Of course not," spat Karveh, raising his voice. "We all want to be free, but now is not the right moment. We need to bide our time, rebuild our strength and then attack."

"And what should I do until then? Sell baskets with you?"

Karveh shrugged. "There are worse ways to make a living. It has fed my family for many years."

The Mongolians had pacified the people with low taxes, the freedom to worship and a semblance of law and order, but their peace had been bought with desecration, destruction and the murder of thousands.

"I cannot stop. I will not." Kaivon took a deep breath and found that the air tasted bitter. It wasn't just the house. It was the whole city. This was no longer his home.

"What will you do?" said Karveh.

"Cut the head off the snake. Hulagu Khan must die."

"That's impossible. He's surrounded by an army, guarded day and night. Even if, by some miracle, you succeeded, they would just replace him with someone else. Maybe someone worse."

Kaivon shrugged. "What else can I do?"

The muscles in Karveh's jaw twitched but he didn't argue.

He knew it would be pointless. It had been this way ever since they were boys. Kaivon would relentlessly pursue his goal with single-minded focus. Either he would accomplish it, or would die in the process. There was nothing in between.

"Then I wish you good luck," said Karveh, embracing him tightly, "and I will see you again soon."

It was a lie. They both knew it. Kaivon would not be returning from his trip to the north. Not this time. He'd beaten the odds so many times, but this was different. He had no allies. No strategy. Not even a vague plan, just a strong desire for vengeance.

Kaivon's only wish, before he closed his eyes for the last time, was to see Hulagu Khan dead at his feet.

CHAPTER 4
Hulagu

In the Orkhon valley, in central Mongolia, was the capital city Karakorum. It had been a long time since Hulagu's last visit and it had grown significantly. The outer stone wall barely contained the thriving metropolis. Standing watch, alongside the guards at the gate, was a huge stone turtle. One sat at each of the city's four corners, marking the boundary, offering their protection. A nod to the old ways as the new marched past without looking back.

As he rode through the gates Hulagu could see the palace in the distance on a hill, surrounded by its own wall. Immediately in front were hundreds, perhaps thousands, of houses and stone buildings, familiar and strange in design.

Rising up above the streets were great storehouses, exquisite stone temples, and churches dedicated to several religions.

Hulagu saw the Christian cross on a steeple, the bell-shaped tower of a Buddhist temple, and a dome covered with geometric patterns belonging to a Muslim mosque.

Beside the gate were a dozen large buildings swarming with men and women in a hurry, each carrying an armload of papers. A small army of bureaucrats, translators, scribes and tax people managed the empire's affairs. It was tedious work, but vitally important and best suited to those who preferred the pen to the sword.

Next on the street were law courts for special cases. People from across the world were standing outside waiting for their turn. As well as Mongol faces he saw Chinese, Persians, Georgians, Armenians, Indians, a few Europeans, Latins and even some Franks. The array of clothing was as diverse as the nationalities waiting in line. Some wore bright silk garments made from multiple layers. Others were dressed as if for war, in leather armour edged with grey fur. Tall and short. Fat and thin. Pale skinned and dark. Minor foreign nobles rubbed shoulders with merchants, peasants, foreign dignitaries and scribes, all of them demanding justice.

A few people gave Hulagu's party curious glances but most of them were busy with their own affairs. Beyond the administration buildings were rows of workshops where skilled men and women fashioned items that ranged from the practical to the decadent. Weapons, armour, paintings, fine wines and spirits, ceramics, clothing, boots and exquisite jewellery. The array of items for sale was without limit and it came from all four corners of the world.

Where the rows of shops and businesses ended, he was pleased to see a large section of the city laid out in the traditional style. Hundreds of yurts were spaced out on an empty meadow that covered one third of the land inside the city's wall. In the time of his grandfather, there had been no permanent structures. The city had moved from place to place as needed, depending on the weather and grazing. Now there were more buildings made of stone than hide.

"You're brooding," said Doquz, noting his expression.

"I was just thinking about how much the city has changed." Hulagu wondered if his grandfather would have been delighted or ashamed.

"It was inevitable. No one could have stopped it. Not even the great Genghis Khan."

Hulagu raised an eyebrow. "You can read minds?"

"Only yours," she said, patting his hand.

Following the worn stone path, they crossed an empty section of grassland before reaching the palace. Looking back down the gentle hill, Hulagu was again amazed at how big the city had become. How long would it be before the houses and businesses were crowding up against the palace walls? He wished that his brother Möngke was here. As they had done so many times in the past, they would sit together with a drink and talk long into the night. But his brother was dead and they would never speak again.

As he stepped down from his horse and threw the reins to a stable boy, Hulagu tried not to dwell on the past. It could not be changed and he was here for only one reason. The future was what mattered and over the next few days the kurultai would decide who led them into tomorrow.

"Will you put your name forward, father?" asked Jumghur.

On the journey Hulagu had spent a lot of time discussing that topic with Doquz. He had come to a decision but was not ready to share it.

Ignoring Jumghur he marched towards the guardhouse, flanked by General Kitbuqa on one side and Abaqa on the other. Behind them came Jumghur, six of his daughters, who had business in the city, and an army of servants.

In a huge courtyard at the entrance to the palace was the famous silver drinking tree. Built by a man named William the Parisian, for Ogedei Khan, second Great Khan of the Empire, the monstrous thing was a blending of wood and metal, topped off with an angelic figure carrying a trumpet. At the base of the tree sat four lions made from silver and at the top there were several metal pipes crafted into fantastic shapes. Day and night, different alcoholic drinks fell from a great height into huge bowls which never overflowed. It was an ingenious device but it worried him a great deal. Ogedei had been extremely fond of his drink and in the end it had cost him his life. If he had been more moderate in his appetites, the rest of western Europe would already be part of the Empire. It was a lesson that Hulagu had taken to heart. He drank often, but less than people realised, and rarely to excess.

"Until later," said Doquz, giving his hand a squeeze. The majority of his entourage went towards the private apartments to rest from the journey while his sons and General Kitbuqa followed him.

The tiled floor of the palace rang out as their boots drummed across its polished surface. Forcing a smile Hulagu heard the crowd long before he saw them in the feast hall. Almost fifty men were drinking, talking, shouting and laughing with one another, standing in groups or sitting on benches scattered around the room. All of the visitors were honoured. All of them brave warriors, military leaders, or men of learning. Hulagu was related to many via blood or marriage, and the rest were significant for their accomplishments. Together they would decide who would be the next Great Khan and Emperor of the Mongol Empire.

The discussion had been going on for hours. In addition to deciding who would lead them there was much to agree upon in terms of strategy. As darkness fell Hulagu knew it was only the first day of many, but for him the decision had already been made.

Tomorrow the games would begin, but for the rest of the night conversation would be relaxed. The hall was full of mangled conversations as people were talking around their food, laughing and drinking, while an army of servants refilled their bowls with airag and wine. Several sheep and goats were roasting over spits and Hulagu saw some people eating pork and beef. The city, like much of the Empire, had become a melting pot of the cultures it had absorbed.

A shadow fell over his table. "Brother," said Hulagu, standing to embrace Kublai.

"It's good to see you. It has been too long."

"Sit, sit," said Hulagu, creating space on the bench. "You look well. How is Chabi?"

"In good health. She sends her regards. She wants to bend your ear later. One of your daughters has been cut-throat with some of her business deals."

Hulagu laughed. "When it comes to business I find it's best not to get involved."

"Wise council, brother." Kublai's eyes roamed the room. "I didn't want this moment to arrive so quickly."

"Nor did I, but here we are."

They drank in silence for a while, listening to the conversation of others. "Have you come to a decision yet?"

"I'm not putting my name forward," said Hulagu. "There is much work to be done and I have made my home in the north of Persia. My family is there and my daughters perform magic, turning air into money."

"Truly, they are wizards." Kublai wiped the airag from his moustache and grinned.

"You have my support, brother," said Hulagu, clapping him on the shoulder.

Kublai let out a long sigh. "I hoped you would say that."

"You are the right choice," said Hulagu. "Where is Ariq?"

"There's been no word."

From an early age Kublai had always been in conflict with Ariq. As brothers they fought often, rolling around in the mud like dogs, but it had often gone beyond play. Ariq was quick to anger and Kublai prone to mocking their youngest brother. Hulagu had played the role of peacemaker and when that didn't work he would drag them apart. He had expected their rivalry to end when they became men, but instead it had festered into jealousy and hatred.

"Messages were sent," said Kublai.

"Then for now we must put him from our minds."

"Always the peacemaker," said Kublai with a smile. "What of Berke?"

Across the room, Berke, their cousin and Khan of the Golden Horde, was entertaining a group of generals. He was an accomplished warrior and had won a number of significant battles, most recently against Lithuania.

"I don't think he will be a problem. He has asked for several concessions regarding his Muslim brothers." Kublai gestured at a passing serving girl.

Hulagu grunted. "I didn't realise he was devout."

"Islam will soon be the official religion throughout the Golden Horde." Kublai accepted the bowl of stew from the servant and began to eat with relish.

Hulagu watched Jumghur drain his cup for the second time in as many minutes. He was already drunk and it was still early. "And what of the other faiths in his territory?"

Kublai shrugged. "They are free to pray to whoever they want. For now."

Freedom of religion was something they encouraged in every territory. Limiting people to one faith would cause problems, but that was a problem for another day.

Buqa-Temur, ruler of the Chagatai Khanate, was the latest in a line of many. The region had a complicated history and, although their borders were expanding, progress was slow. It was unlikely anyone would nominate him.

"How goes your expansion?" asked Kublai.

"Slow. I am rid of the Assassins, but there's trouble with the Mamluks in Egypt. I sent letters to the Pope in Rome and the King of France for support to reclaim their Holy Land, but nothing has come of it."

Kublai smiled and then started to laugh so hard he thumped the table with his fists.

Hulagu raised an eyebrow. "What's so funny?"

"Do you remember when we were boys? How many times

did we hear grandfather speak about his dream of ruling the world? And now look at us." Kublai gestured at his fine clothes and the palace. Genghis had united them into one tribe, and they had conquered a huge portion of the world. And every day more nations fell under Mongol rule.

"It's a different world."

Kublai lowered his voice and leaned close. "We have accomplished more than grandfather ever dreamed. There is much to do, but for tonight, we should just enjoy ourselves."

"Come then, brother. Tonight, we will celebrate. Everything else can wait until tomorrow."

They raised their bowls and drained them in several large gulps. They were the first of many and all thoughts of staying sober were forgotten.

By the fifth day of talks the decision was made. Kublai would be the next Great Khan.

After overdoing it on the first night, Hulagu had drunk in moderation. Nevertheless, there was a tightness at the back of his skull which he put down to not enough sleep. Determined to get some rest before the official announcement in the morning, Hulagu left the feast early.

"Wait," said Kublai, catching him at the door.

"Enough, brother," said Hulagu. "I'm tired and need my bed."

"I wanted to offer my thanks for your support."

"No thanks are needed, Kublai. You would have won without me."

"Perhaps, but it would've been a longer fight. Come, I'll walk with you. I need some air."

They left the palace and, taking a lantern each from beside the front door, crossed the meadow towards the private apartments. Spread out below them was an endless sea of lights. It reminded Hulagu of past campaigns with hundreds of campfires. The air was rich with the smells of wood smoke and cooking meat. Warriors playing instruments, singing, laughing and joking.

The palace apartments were far larger than Hulagu needed, capable of housing five times his entourage, but such was the way in Karakorum. Excess and splendour were commonplace.

"I have left a gift in your room," said Kublai with a smirk.

"What sort of gift?"

"A new wife."

"I don't need a new wife, Kublai, I barely have time for all of those I have. Then there are the concubines as well." Hulagu knew that while some would be happy to see a new face, several of his wives would not.

"Have you lost your passion? Do you need help getting hard?" said Kublai, fumbling at Hulagu's crotch.

Hulagu slapped his hands away and shoved him for good measure. "I have no problems there."

Kublai laughed. "She is young, pretty, and still a virgin."

"Then you take her."

"She is too precious a flower for someone like me," said Kublai. "She needs a delicate soul."

"Do you want me to add to your scars?" asked Hulagu, raising a fist.

"I'm sorry," said Kublai, sounding genuine. "It's being back here. Normally I would trade jibes with Ariq. At least look at her."

"Very well."

"Good. Then I will leave you to your rest," said Kublai.

Hulagu watched as Kublai's lantern bobbed up the path towards the palace.

"Are you coming inside, husband?" said Doquz.

"I'm trying to work up the courage."

"Why do you say that?" Her sweet tone of voice made him wince. When he turned around her face was as sour as if she'd chewed a lemon.

"Show me," he said.

Doquz led the way to one of the bedrooms at the far end of the building. Candles had been lit within and waiting on the bed was a young woman with pale skin and a lithe figure. She was beautiful and ethereal, dressed in a blue silk robe that clung to her body.

"This is Kokochin, the Blue Princess. She is from the Bayaut tribe," said Doquz.

No wonder Kublai wanted to be rid of her. His brother had killed most of the Bayaut when they'd rebelled. As a rule, Mongols did not kill Mongols, but how could they hope to rule the world if they couldn't unite their own people.

If Kokochin was left in Karakorum she would serve a constant reminder of what Kublai had done. There was also the possibility she would generate sympathy and stir unrest. It would be better for everyone if she were far from Mongolia.

"I am honoured to serve you, husband," said Kokochin with a deep bow. Her voice was light and melodious. Her accent slight and alluring and there wasn't a hint of ire or hatred. Perhaps she didn't know.

Hulagu raised an eyebrow at Doquz who lifted one shoulder in reply.

"It is a long road back to Tabriz," he said, rubbing the small of Doquz's back with one hand. She leaned against his shoulders and one of her hands began to creep up the back of his leg. "It would be nice to have someone new to warm the bed."

"I was thinking that too," said Doquz.

Hulagu feigned distress. "Have you grown bored of me?"

"Of course not. But it does take a lot to satisfy you and it would be nice to have some help."

Hulagu laughed and gripped her arse which made her jump. After all of the miles, all of the campaigns and all of the years, she could still set a fire in his loins.

"How can I serve you?" asked Kokochin. "Should I disrobe?"

"There will be plenty of time for you to learn what pleases me. We will be returning to Tabriz in a day or two. Prepare yourself for the journey."

With luck they could be back on the road in three days. Before that he had letters to prepare.

"I will see to her needs until we leave," said Doquz, seeing that he was distracted.

"I will wait for you in my bed chamber," he said, swatting her backside. It was good to know that he could still surprise her. The letters could wait until the morning.

The following afternoon the decision was made official. Kublai would be the fifth Great Khan and Emperor of the Mongol Empire.

The celebrations began in earnest. An endless stream of drinks flowed from the silver tree fountain and many important guests and their families gathered in the palace. The festivities would continue for several days, but Hulagu intended to leave for Persia in the morning.

A disturbance at the palace gates began with a murmur of voices that quickly spread. The sea of bodies parted to reveal Ariq. He was dusty from travel and behind him came half a dozen generals, all of them battered from a recent fight.

Ariq stared at their brother Kublai with hatred.

"Welcome brother," said Kublai, into that gulf of silence. "We are celebrating the end of the kurultai."

"The end?" Ariq whispered but his voice carried. "Why was I not informed?"

All eyes were on Kublai but rather than wilt under pressure, he grew in stature. He had been born to lead. "Messages were sent." He spoke with the utmost certainty and none had any reason to doubt him. Except Ariq.

"I had to find out about the death of Möngke from a passing merchant."

"Come, Ariq," said Kublai. "You must be tired from your journey. We can discuss this inside."

Ariq looked as if he would refuse what had been couched as a request, but Hulagu knew that it was not. Kublai was now the Great Khan and when he spoke, people obeyed. Those who refused were not long for this world.

The crowd waited. Kublai remained open, smiling and a welcoming host to his newly arrived brother. Ariq resembled an ungracious guest and a bitter sibling. With so many watching he had no choice. He gestured for his generals to remain while he followed Kublai inside.

Hulagu went after them and before the front door had closed the shouting began.

"You are a liar and a cheat!" said Ariq, pacing back and forth. "You have stolen the kurultai."

"I sent several messengers. Möngke's vizier sent three. No one would dare interfere with them."

But Ariq would not be appeased. "You arranged this. Somehow you had them diverted or killed."

"Ariq." There was a warning note in Kublai's voice which was ignored.

"How did you do it?"

"Enough," barked Hulagu, drawing their attention. A servant came walking down the hall but quickly scuttled away. There was noise from the festivities outside but inside the palace was silent and cold.

"We are no longer children, Hulagu. You cannot settle this dispute with a calm word or a story about grandfather."

"Ariq, hear me," stressed Hulagu. "I also sent you a messenger. Are you now calling both of us liars?"

Ariq stared at them with eyes that were cold and without passion. He started to say something but then turned and stormed away.

"Let him go," said Kublai, when Hulagu went to follow. "For once in his life, he must learn that he can't always get what he wants. Eventually he will calm down."

Hulagu hoped that would happen but this rift went far deeper than any in the past between his brothers.

CHAPTER 5
The Twelve

The room was bright and warm sunlight poured in through the open windows. Everything smelled of bread and turmeric. The woman known as One immediately closed the blinds, blocking out the heat, filling the space with shadows. Anonymity wasn't necessary. They all knew each other's real names, but it was critical that no one saw them together.

The twelve of them had no reason to know each other. Anyone witnessing such a meeting might remark on it and they wanted to avoid that at all costs. The House of Grace had not existed for such a long time by taking huge risks.

By pure chance, not because it was pre-arranged, Two limped into the room. They exchanged a nod but Two didn't speak. She sat down at the table and waited. Two never said much at the meetings, unlike Seven who never stopped talking. One heard Seven approaching long before she pushed open the door.

"Hello, my sweethearts," she burbled, flicking a loose strand of blonde hair out of her eyes. As usual her make-up was impeccable and outrageously expensive. "How are we today? Are you happy? I will make you happy," said Seven, not waiting for an answer to any of her questions.

"Sit down, please," said One, starting to feel a headache

building up behind her eyes. Seven raised a delicately crafted eyebrow but took her place. The silence in the room was heavy, but One was happy to let it stretch on. Before Seven could spoil it, the others began to arrive, never with someone else. The last to arrive was Twelve. She was the oldest member and had held her position for a long time.

One rapped her knuckles on the table and the conversations stopped.

"As ever we need to be brief. What news from the north?"

"It's not good," said Three, twisting her wedding ring around. "The last Assassin stronghold has been destroyed. Now that Persia is secure, Hulagu Khan will continue his campaign in the west."

"Where is he now?" asked One.

Five cleared her throat. "Karakorum. They're electing a new Great Khan."

"Fucking Mongols," muttered Eleven. She hawked and was about to spit on the floor when One gave her a look. With a sour twist of her mouth Eleven swallowed instead. One was lenient with her because she was new. Four of the Twelve were replacements for those they had lost during the invasion.

They all hated the Mongols but for some the wounds were still raw. When the north of Persia had been conquered, many of their friends and families were murdered or had disappeared, most likely sold into slavery. One had lost her sister. As well as being her only living relative, she'd been one of their number. It was another reason she was so lenient with Eleven. It had been her sister's number.

"Three, send word to all of your contacts in Baghdad. Warn them about Hulagu Khan. They need to ready their defences and stockpile food."

"Of course," said Three.

"Are the Assassins truly gone?" asked Ten.

One glanced at Twelve for her insight but she merely shrugged, then made a quick gesture.

"*Maybe,*" signed Twelve, speaking with her hands. As ever she wore a colourful scarf around her neck, concealing the old wound that most believed had robbed her of speech. Twelve could speak, but only quietly, which is why some in the House referred to her as the Queen of Whispers. The other reason, known only to One, was Twelve's network of contacts was more extensive than anyone realised. It was the main reason why the House still existed after the invasion and occupation.

"There's a rumour some of them fled Persia before Alamut was destroyed. I'll try to find out," said Three.

"What other news?" asked One.

"The rebellion in the south of Persia has failed," said Six.

"Survivors?"

"Only a handful."

Everyone took a moment of silence to reflect. Since the occupation there had been few organised attempts. This group had been the largest and it had been led by a former soldier.

I don't think the group will try again," said Six. "Their spirit has been broken."

"Keep an eye on them," said One. "In time they may change their mind."

"So where does that leave us?" asked Seven. "How are we going to get rid of them if we don't have any contacts in the south?"

"My network is growing," protested Six, but Seven just rolled her eyes.

"We've been here before," said Ten, silencing the muttering that had sprung up. Ten could always be relied on to quash histrionics. "We set out breadcrumbs. We see who bites and we pick up little birds. We watch and we listen. We recruit with care and we regrow our network. This isn't the first loss and it won't be the last."

"*Slow and steady,*" signed Twelve. "*This is not a race.*"

"She's right. It's going to be a long and difficult road to get rid of the Mongols," said One, making eye contact with Seven.

"I want all of you to talk to your people. Remind your contacts that they are not alone."

"I should kill Hulagu Khan when he returns to Persia," said Nine. "I could do it. Sooner or later he always comes to visit one of my girls."

The man had many wives and concubines, yet he still made regular visits to the pleasure houses.

One clenched her hands into tight fists. "You know how I feel about him. I want to rip out his throat with my teeth." The anger surged through her head until her vision swam. One felt someone put a hand on her shoulder. Twelve gave her a brief squeeze and One felt the rage ebb away. "But we can't. Not yet."

"But one day?" said Eleven.

"One day," promised One.

"I have news from Europe," said Four. "My contacts in Paris and Rome continue to circulate stories about the horrors committed by the Mongols. Privately, both the Vatican and King Louis loathe the barbarians. Publicly, they're being civil but remaining aloof. Both Berke Khan and Hulagu Khan have proposed an alliance, but neither has received a response."

"Finally some good news," said Seven.

"For now," said One. "Keep the pressure on. The more we can do to isolate and weaken the Ilkhanate, the better. I've been talking to contacts in Georgia and across the Caucasus. They're scared."

"And rightly so," said Seven. "They saw what Hulagu did to our people."

"Progress is slow," said One, refusing to be interrupted. "I'm growing a network of contacts in the Caucasus, but it's difficult with so much paranoia. They think every new face is a Mongol spy. It will take time to gain their trust."

There had been less good news than One had hoped for, but at least nothing disastrous had happened since their last meeting.

"That's all for today. Please, be careful," said One, making eye contact with each woman around the table.

One by one they left the room, returning to their lives where friends, colleagues and even their family didn't know about their real job.

The House of Grace would make the Mongols regret invading Persia. One day their nation would be free. Of that she had no doubt, it was only a matter of time.

CHAPTER 6
Kokochin

Kokochin came awake with a start. It was the seventh night in a row she'd been having nightmares. Someone had been suffocating her. The images faded quickly, making them difficult to recall, but she was left disorientated and nauseous. As she stared around at the unfamiliar bedroom it took her a while to remember where she was.

Her rooms in the palace of Tabriz were spacious and well appointed. Upon arrival she'd been measured by a tailor and three days later a dozen beautiful dresses had appeared. The silk was incredibly soft against her skin, the colours bright and although the geometric patterns were unfamiliar, blue was a dominant colour. Slippers, jewellery, shoes, perfumes, make-up and other items had appeared in her rooms. She didn't want for anything and all of it was designed to make her beautiful for her husband.

With the death of her tribe she had been left without a home, land or money. Kokochin had feared she would end up as a beggar, but instead had been made a guest in the palace at Karakorum. However, it had been made abundantly clear by those who had schooled her that all of it could be taken away.

Over and over again she had been told she was nothing but an empty vessel. All independent thoughts and desires were to be squashed. Her purpose was to serve her husband. For months Kokochin was taught how to walk and even talk. How to play the erhu, how to read and write, and how to please a man without ever touching one. And now she was married to someone she barely knew and lived in a country she'd never visited.

This was the seventh night in a row she'd fallen asleep on top of her bed, waiting for her husband. Since their arrival in Tabriz he'd not paid her a visit but she didn't know why.

After washing off the dried make-up, Kokochin changed out of her wrinkled clothes and went in search of breakfast. As soon as she opened her door a servant approached bearing a letter.

"My lady. I have a message from Empress Guyuk," said the man, bowing low.

"Thank you," said Kokochin.

The message was a simple request to join the Empress for breakfast.

The eastern wing of the palace caught the sun early in the morning. In a spacious room with large windows she found the Empress drinking tea. Dressed in an aquamarine dress that showed off her lithe figure, Guyuk was the epitome of grace and beauty.

The table was on a slightly raised dais in the centre of the room. Surrounding it were several tall trees with huge green leaves that provided shade from the worst of the heat. The air was moist and had a slightly floral aroma coming from colourful shrubs at the far end of the room. An open door looked out onto a veranda and beyond that were the lush palace gardens.

Half a dozen servants stood around the edge of the room bearing drinks or simply waiting for a task. One of them guided her to the table, easing her chair in behind her.

"Welcome," said Guyuk, pouring her a glass of tea. The table was laden with cheese, warm bread, fresh herbs, fruit, nuts, boiled eggs and slices of cooked meat. "Please eat. Or would you prefer something else?" she asked, holding up a hand.

One of the servants eagerly stepped forward.

"No, this is more than enough, thank you."

Guyuk waved her hand and the servant stepped back. "How have you been sleeping?"

"I've been sleeping well, thank you," she lied. The Empress was the most powerful woman in the Ilkhanate and she had her husband's ear. A wrong word from her and Kokochin would find herself in the gutter or sold to one of the pleasure houses.

"Now that you've been here for a few days, I thought we should get to know one another."

"I would like that, Empress." Kokochin helped herself to a small portion of breakfast. The bread was soft and tasty so she dared pull a second piece onto her plate.

"Tell me, what have been doing since your arrival?" asked Guyuk, nibbling at some bread.

"I've been making myself available for our husband," she said.

Guyuk wasn't impressed. "Anything else?"

"No, Empress."

"I see." Guyuk beckoned a servant forward and whispered something in his ear. With a clap of his hands the others hurried out of the room. The last servant closed the doors behind him but Kokochin could see him standing on the other side.

"Did you make yourself available to our husband on the journey from Karakorum?"

"I did," she said.

"And did he come to your bed?" asked the Empress.

"Yes."

It had been painful and she'd bled the first time. Hulagu had grown angry when she'd cried and had stormed out. The next time it had hurt less, but he'd complained that she was like a lump of wood.

The following night Doquz Khatun, who many called his War Wife, had come to Kokochin's bed to show her what would please their husband. She had been gentle and patient with her demonstrations and unflinching in her explanations, despite Kokochin's blushes. Several times that night she had found release from Doquz. Thereafter when Hulagu had visited her, Kokochin had been able to satisfy him. On three occasions Doquz had joined them in bed, and on those nights Kokochin had gained even more experience.

"Has Hulagu visited since your arrival in Tabriz?" asked Guyuk.

"No, Empress."

"As I thought. My child, let me explain something to you. Hulagu is a man of great appetites and great passion. In addition to you, he has seven wives and thirteen concubines. He also has twenty-one children, so he doesn't need you to give him an heir. Do you understand?"

"Yes, Empress," she said. She'd known about his other wives but hadn't thought about the possibility of other children. "May I ask a question?"

Guyuk wiped her mouth with a cloth. "I see that no one has told you anything, so let me speak plainly. You don't need permission to ask a question, of me, or anyone else. You are the Khan's wife. That means you have power and supreme authority. You give commands. They will give way before you or will feel the Khan's displeasure and suffer. Do you understand?"

"Yes, Empress."

"Ask your question."

"If I'm not to wait on our husband, what should I do?"

Guyuk rolled her eyes and took a long deep breath. "Many years ago, I was like you. Young and naïve. I also found myself wed to a man I barely knew. One day the Mongol Empire will cover the entire world, but for that to happen, it requires great men of vision. Hulagu is such a man. Even now, our warriors fight in the south, and in a few days our husband will join them. He will be gone for months. You must find your own path," said Guyuk. "This city is a wonder. A frontier between east and west. Splendours from all corners of the known world come through the city gates. There is much to explore within its boundaries. I suggest you go into the streets and find something to fill your time. Something that gives you pleasure."

"Can I ask…" she said, then changed her mind at Guyuk's frown. "What do his other wives do?"

"That's a good question," said the Empress with a smile. "I work closely with Rashid, the Khan's vizier, to run the city and keep the army provisioned. One of his wives has a passion for horses, which is also critical to the war. Another enjoys the theatre and is a patron of many artists and playwrights. A third is a scholar. She works closely with the scribes who are recording a detailed history of the Empire. In a thousand years, people will be able to read about our husband's exploits. So, what do you want to do?" asked Guyuk.

"I don't know," admitted Kokochin.

"Explore the city," said Guyuk. "When you find your place, come and tell me."

"I will," promised Kokochin.

With a pair of Kheshig bodyguards walking behind her at all times, Kokochin left the palace for the first time. To begin with she was worried about approaching people, but quickly realised they were just as apprehensive. She saw the nervous glances when she walked towards them and assumed it was normal. Once they realised who she was the people became generous and welcoming. They couldn't do enough to please her.

Kokochin ate fresh fish and caviar from the Caspian Sea. She drank red wine from Europe and bitter Turkish coffee sweetened with cream. She spoke with poets about the beauty of nature and the silence of death. She cried at a play about forbidden love and laughed at a puppet show from Persia about a clumsy hero. She drank tea with Buddhist monks, discussed philosophy with a Muslim Imam and listened to a Christian priest tell her about his god that was three men and one.

For four days she submerged herself in the heart of the city. Walking miles through its streets she explored the dark corners, savouring the cultures and customs. Kokochin witnessed a hundred miracles of creativity and genius as people turned the most mundane of items into wonders. Lumps of metal and rough stone into glorious pieces of glittering jewellery. Hot sand into glassware so beautiful it deserved to be on display in the palace.

On the fifth day she realised why everyone was so accommodating. Her bodyguards meant she was a member of the royal family and therefore someone to be feared.

By the end of the week Kokochin resented her bodyguards. There were some places they refused to let her explore. Some things she was forbidden from sampling. The reason given was for her safety, but she had her doubts. Many unusual delights were kept from her, but after talking to so many people, she was aware of them. The version of the city she came to know was real, but only up to a point.

On the seventh night, after studying the palace grounds and its guards, Kokochin was ready to explore the city by herself. There were several gates in and out of the palace and all of them were locked at night. Some were used by visitors and others by servants who came and went at all hours. Only a handful of the most trusted people were allowed keys. Once she'd learned the guards' shift patterns Kokochin found several gaps to exploit. After generously bribing Maya, one of her retainers, she obtained a key for the servants' gate.

As dusk fell Kokochin managed to slip out of the palace without being seen.

Almost immediately Kokochin noticed the difference. Dressed in plain clothes, borrowed from Maya, people no longer stared at her. For the most part they were still friendly, but they no longer looked at her because they were terrified.

In a tea room Kokochin sat in a corner, eating roasted pistachios, while people talked without fear of reprisal. She had never felt so free in her life.

Behind her at another table two women were gossiping about a friend who was spending time with two suitors. Both men were vying for her hand in marriage and neither of them knew about the other. To her left an old man was lecturing his son on responsibility, to God and his family, but not always in that order.

When a burly drunk man stumbled into the tea room, knocking over a table and chairs in the process, she was pleased when several customers stood up to him. They drove the drunk onto the street with threats and fists, until he ran off in a panic. The drunk had knocked an old woman out of her chair and she'd banged her head on the floor. She had a shallow cut on her forehead, but it bled profusely.

"Is she all right?" asked Kokochin.

The owner, a local woman with greying hair, nodded without looking around. She held a cloth to the old woman's head to stop the bleeding. "There will be a bump tomorrow, but it's not bad."

"I'm sorry, grandmother," said Kokochin, placing a couple of coins on the table. "Let me buy you a drink."

"Thank you, child," said the old woman with a smile, but then her eyes widened when she saw Kokochin's pale skin.

As more people noticed her Kokochin was afraid she might be recognised. Before anyone had the chance to ask her any questions she slipped away. To make sure she wasn't being followed, Kokochin took a winding route through the city before heading back towards the palace. By sticking to the shadows and taking her time, she made it to her rooms without being seen.

That night, as she lay down in bed, Kokochin was bursting with so much energy it took her a long time to fall asleep. She had seen the true face of the city and, although there had been some unpleasantness, she was still excited. The worry she'd felt about finding a place and purpose began to ease. There were so many possibilities.

Her daily trips into the city continued but they became more focused. She spent time studying craftsmen and women while they were at work. One morning she sat in the corner of a forge, sweating alongside a lanky smith as he beat a glowing piece of metal into an intricate design. Another day she watched a trio of basket weavers sitting on the floor of a shop with hundreds of wiry threads spread out around them. Their hands and feet almost moved of their own accord as they chatted and bent the willow into shape. Kokochin spent a short amount of time at a stable but the intimidating size of the animals was enough to drive her out.

And while she searched during the day her nights were equally busy, delving into the darker side of the city. In an opium den she watched erotic dancers on stage but was too scared to take her turn on the pipe. She drank exotic alcohol from faraway lands, some of which delighted and others made her sick.

The next night, as she wandered the city in search of distraction, Kokochin spotted a pale-skinned European woman. She was boldly standing outside the front door of her shop. There were arcane symbols painted on the windows and she was dressed in an array of colourful beads and shawls.

"You're searching for something, girl," she said, calling out to Kokochin from across the street. "Come inside and I'll read your fortune."

When Kokochin didn't respond the woman shrugged and retreated back inside. Kokochin was tempted, even though she didn't believe in the occult, but something worried her about going alone into the shop. As she reached the end of the street she looked back and noticed two men had started following. They were also pale Europeans and Kokochin didn't think it was a coincidence. To be safe she walked faster, heading towards a busier part of the city. The two men behind her started to run.

Kokochin's first thought was to lose them in a crowd. She'd barely gone a dozen steps when her foot slipped. Kokochin stumbled but managed to stay upright, skidding around a corner. She wobbled and righted herself by pushing off the wall with one hand. Her left palm scraped against the stone but she ignored the pain and kept running.

They were getting closing. She could hear their laboured breathing. One of the men was already out of breath, the other muttering a litany of abuse. Promises of what he was going to do if she didn't stop.

Kokochin was about to turn down an alley when something hit her between the shoulders, spinning her about. The taller of the two men had something in his left hand and she instinctively darted to the right. Something crashed into the wall, narrowly missing her head. Kokochin ran in the opposite direction, taking her away from the safety of a crowd.

The street ahead was narrow and winding. It was an unfamiliar part of the city she'd not explored during the day or night. There were houses on either side but no shops and everyone here was in their bed.

It was where she should have been. Safe in the palace surrounded by armed guards and high walls. It was safe and comfortable, but it wasn't real. It was still a prison.

Gritting her teeth against the ache in her lungs, Kokochin pushed herself harder. Pain blossomed in her right side and she was gasping for air, but refused to stop.

Sweat poured down the inside of her dress and the scrape on her left hand burned. She needed to head west to a busy area. The street ahead was winding, preventing her from seeing the far end. At the end of the road was a junction and she immediately turned left. Risking a look behind, Kokochin saw the two men were still chasing her. One held up a dagger which he waved at her in a threatening manner.

Kokochin ran.

The threat of being stabbed and left to die in an alley pushed everything from her mind. She had to survive. It was the only thing that mattered.

She raced past a group of prostitutes lurking on a street corner. They called after her and a moment later squawked as the men ran into them. Abuse followed the men but they pursued her relentlessly. After all of their effort they were determined to get something. She saw several people with unfriendly stares watching from the shadows. Drug dealers or criminals. They wouldn't help her and were just as likely to rob her.

Her thighs began to ache. The pain in her side was getting worse. Kokochin started to slow down and then she stumbled, tripped and fell. She rolled forward over one shoulder and came back upright but twisted her right ankle in the process. The pain was sharp. Putting weight on it hurt but she kept going, right foot scraping along.

Up ahead she saw a familiar sight. The cross that sat on top of the Christian church she'd visited. Using it as a point of reference she stumbled down the road, navigating towards a civilised part of the city.

The buildings around her looked familiar. Not much further to go. She was going to make it.

A hand clamped on her shoulder, yanking her to one side. Kokochin flew through the air before her shoulder slammed into a wall.

"You're mine," said a voice. A pair of rough hands seized her and she lashed out, raking her nails across the man's face. She'd accidentally hooked his mouth with one finger and he screamed. Using all of her strength she shoved him backwards. The thug tripped over his own feet and fell, banging his head on the ground. As blood began to well from the back of his skull, the other man pinned her to the wall by her throat.

"Give me your money." His breath was rank. His hands roamed all over her, searching, violating her body. She was struggling to breathe. Kokochin tried to force him backwards but he barely moved. He was too strong.

She was going to choke to death.

When he found her money pouch the pressure eased as he needed both hands to open it. Gasping for air she stayed put until the black spots dancing in front of her eyes had faded. The other man was sitting up, one hand pressed to the back of his head. As blood ran between his fingers she knew this wasn't over.

Seeing a chance to escape she ducked under the thug's arm and tried to run. His hand clamped around her wrist and with a scream she yanked her arm free, ripping the sleeve from her coat. Kokochin didn't look back. Keeping her eyes on the church she ignored the pain in her ankle. One more step. Just one more.

Any moment he was going to stab her in the back. She didn't want to die alone.

One more step. Almost there.

The brightness of the busy street was overwhelming. The sound of the crowd slammed into her like a wave. Kokochin received a few peculiar looks as she stumbled along, bloody and bruised, but she didn't stop. She couldn't risk it. They were right behind her.

Weaving through the crowd she navigated down familiar streets, wheezing like a tired donkey, uncaring of her appearance. The press of bodies blocked her from view. She flowed with the press of bodies down one street, cut down a side street, and shuffled west, always west. Confident that she'd lost them in the crowd she finally headed for home.

When the wall of the palace came into view she sighed with relief. Kokochin watched the guards carefully, waiting for them to move out of sight before she approached the servants' gate and slipped inside.

Kokochin was so worried about being spotted that she moved slowly through the hallways, listening every few paces before moving on. When she rounded a corner Kokochin had to bite her lip to stop herself from screaming. One of the Kheshig lay on floor, asleep or dead. She couldn't see any wounds and there was no blood. Worried that she might be blamed for whatever was happening, she limped on. She found two more guards on the floor before she reached the door to her rooms.

She was safe. All she had to do was go inside and pretend not to know anything.

Morbid curiosity made her turn away from her door and follow the line of bodies. Touching one of the Kheshig on the wrist she was relieved to find his skin was still warm. Someone had disabled several guards quickly and quietly and with little sign of a struggle.

A short distance ahead was a small courtyard with a stone fountain in the middle. The sound of bubbling water was incredibly loud in the still air. Something brushed against her cheek and looking up Kokochin noticed one of the high windows was open. Hanging from the window was a knotted rope which trailed down to the floor. The bulk of it had been tucked away behind the plants around the edge of the courtyard.

In the distance she heard someone shouting. Kokochin moved to the edge of the courtyard and hid behind a tall leafy plant. A masked woman raced down the hallway, pursued by a pair of Kheshig. Both of them carried swords and were laden with armour. She wore only light clothes and didn't even have a dagger. The bodyguards were much slower on their feet, but they caught up to her as she unhooked the rope.

The man on the left tried to stab her through the back but she flowed around the blade like a dancer. Sweeping under his arm she closed the distance until they were almost nose to nose. Before he had a chance to react she hit him twice in the chest and he stumbled back, gasping for air. The other Kheshig attacked, trying to take off a leg with his blade, but she dodged and spun away. With a whoop of surprise the warrior went flying through the air as she swept his legs out from under him. His head struck the ground and he groaned but was still conscious. The first warrior attacked again with a wild slash. The masked woman moved back and back, maintaining the distance between them. With a roar of frustration the bodyguard charged. The woman grabbed him by the collar, spun around and, using his momentum against him, threw the Kheshig over her hip. He landed badly, driving the air from his lungs and cracking his hips against the floor. With two sharp punches to his head she rendered him unconscious. The other man was still groaning and had made it to one knee.

The woman stepped up behind him, tilted his head to one side and stabbed two fingers into his collar. The bodyguard slid to the ground in a boneless heap and silence returned.

The fight had lasted barely a minute. Barely using her legs, the woman shimmied up the rope. Feeling that the danger had passed Kokochin stepped out of her hiding place. She approached the fountain and glanced up.

The woman was still there. She'd taken off her mask and was closing the window. As their eyes met Kokochin studied her face. She'd never seen the woman before but Kokochin knew she'd be able to recognise her.

Someone began shouting down the hallway. The bodies had been discovered. Looking up she realised the woman had disappeared.

Kokochin ran, hissing in pain at her twisted ankle. Somehow she made it back to her rooms without being seen. She quietly closed her door and slumped down on the floor.

She was safe.

CHAPTER 7
Temujin

Temujin was sweating. He mopped his brow and tried really hard not to look nervous but it was a bit difficult with sweat trickling down the sides of his face. His armpits were damp and the collar of his shirt was starting to itch. He was desperate to make a good impression and was already failing.

The silence in Farshad's office was deafening. In the other room he could hear the scratching of pens, the clink of money and the rattle of abacuses. Farshad was one of four most senior tax collectors in Tabriz. He had a reputation for being firm but fair. As Hulagu Khan's son, Temujin knew he would receive no special treatment. He didn't even have a bodyguard anymore. The reason given by his adopted mother, Guyuk, was that he didn't need one because the city was safe. If that were true all members of the royal family would be without, but he'd seen Kheshig following them around all day. He suspected his father was responsible for the change but couldn't prove it.

His mind strayed back to what had happened in the census office and Mahmud's death. He'd seen people die before. His father had made all of his children watch executions from a young age. Temujin had seen traitors, thieves and enemies of the Mongol Empire die. Many wept and begged. A few were silent. But he'd never had anyone die in his arms before. Mahmud hadn't liked him and yet he had sacrificed his life for Temujin.

Staring at his hands Temujin wondered again what had happened with the rebel. Somehow the rising heat inside his body had burned the man's flesh. He's seen the marks on his wrists, red and swollen. Nothing like that had ever happened before. With no way to explain it he'd kept it to himself.

The job. He had to focus on the new job. Collecting taxes. It was important work. It was also his last chance. Guyuk had told him that if he failed his father would step in and then Temujin would have to become a warrior in the army. More than ever he was determined to prove that he was good at something and make his father proud.

"I'm glad to see you're on time," said Farshad, bustling into the office. He was in his fifties with thick black hair that was streaked with grey, and his long strides were deliberate, like a soldier. Farshad had a stack of papers in his hands which he laid out on the desk and began to read.

"I'm ready to help," said Temujin.

When he reached the end of the page Farshad looked up. "Did you say something?"

"What do you need me to do?"

"Ah, yes. Sohrab!" he bellowed. A portly balding man with a goatee waddled into the room. "Take the boy out."

"Am I not working with you?" asked Temujin, glancing between the two men.

Farshad frowned. "No one starts at the top of the ladder. You must climb the rungs like everyone else. Sohrab will show what to do. Any more stupid questions?"

Sohrab pulled his arm and led Temujin out of the office. The little tax man kept a tight grip until they were outside.

"Not very clever on your first day," said Sohrab, stuffing a felt cap onto his shiny head. "Don't worry, he doesn't hold a grudge. He probably won't even remember your name by tomorrow."

"Really?"

Sohrab laughed. "Numbers, he never forgets. Faces, he's not so good at. Come. Let me show you the life of a humble tax collector."

He followed the little man down the street to a battered cart that was hitched to a weary donkey. The cart bed was littered with a collection of random items including rolled carpets, silverware, paintings, an intricate glass vase in a wooden crate and two ivory tusks.

Sohrab appeared happy, so his life couldn't be that tedious. Perhaps this was the right place for Temujin after all.

"Hop on," said Sohrab, creating room for him on the seat. "That's peculiar," he said, pointing at Temujin's eyes. "I bet people stare a lot."

"Sometimes."

"Don't worry. The people we're going to visit won't notice. They won't even look at your face." He clicked his tongue and the donkey began to walk.

"Why?"

"Because we're tax men. No one likes us!" said Sohrab with a cackle.

The first day was long and tedious. As they went from business to business, knocking on doors, the response was always the same. People stammered, sweated, and kept their eyes averted as Sohrab went over their books. He laughed and made jokes, but when the time came to reviewing finance, his demeanour became serious.

After a week of following Sohrab around, Temujin was allowed to take the lead on a couple of businesses. Sohrab stayed with him to make sure all of his figures were correct. When a business couldn't pay the full amount Sohrab would take something from the individual and cover the shortfall himself. It explained his growing collection of items in the cart which he then sold on for a profit.

On the tenth day of being a tax man, Temujin was allowed to go into a shop by himself. By that point he was already numb and struggled to fake any enthusiasm.

Temujin glanced at the shop, noting a sparse display of herbs and spices in the window. Inside, the shopkeeper, a skinny man with a greying goatee, came out from the back room. His clothes were threadbare but he had a welcoming smile. The interior of the shop was not much better than the window. More than half of the shelves were empty and what remained looked poor quality.

"Hello, how can I help you today?" he asked.

"I'm here to inspect your books."

"Of course," said the shopkeeper, reaching under his counter. "Please, see for yourself."

Temujin pulled up a stool and began to pour over the books. Unlike many he had seen, the shopkeeper's notes were neat and the writing was legible. The sales showed a steady decline, with the occasional spike, that quickly trailed off. There was no way he would be able to pay what he owed.

"How much do you have?" asked Temujin.

The shopkeeper produced seven silver pieces, but he owed fifteen. "I'm sorry, it has been a bad month for spices. My supplier let me down, so people have gone elsewhere."

There wasn't enough on the shelves for Temujin to resell to make up the shortfall.

"Tell me your name?"

"Javeed."

"How long do you need to make up the rest?"

Javeed sighed and scratched an elbow through a hole in his robe. "Maybe three weeks."

"I will be back in two weeks' time to collect," promised Temujin. "Please don't make me regret this."

"Thank you. You are most gracious," said Javeed, shaking his hand with enthusiasm. "Thank you."

Uncomfortable with praise Temujin smiled and hurried out

of the shop. He knew Sohrab wouldn't like it, but there wasn't anything else he could have done.

When he turned up empty handed his mentor's smile faded.

"He doesn't have it," said Temujin.

Sohrab ground his teeth. "Are you sure about his books?"

"You're welcome to inspect them yourself if you don't believe me. I'll wait." Temujin folded his arms and raised his chin. He was getting tired of people assuming he was incompetent.

"This is going in my report to Farshad. I'm not going to take the blame." It was the first time Sohrab had shown any signs of genuine fear. A worm of doubt made its way into Temujin's stomach.

"He doesn't have the money," he insisted.

"We'll see," said Sohrab.

The following morning Temujin had barely finished getting dressed when someone hammered on his bedroom door. He was staying in a small suite of rooms in the palace, as far away as possible from his father. So far Temujin hadn't seen him since his return to Tabriz. In less than a week his father would be leaving. Once he was gone Temujin would be able to relax and he could stop tiptoeing around.

"Wake up," said a familiar voice.

Temujin opened the door to see Sohrab. "What are you doing here?"

He was wringing his felt cap, twisting it into a knot between his hands. "Come with me. I was ordered to bring you at once."

"Who sent you?"

"Your brother. Please," said Sohrab, tugging on his sleeve. "If you don't come soon he's going to kill my family."

"Lead the way," said Temujin.

The tax man was almost running, his feet skipping along the tiled floor. Temujin had seven brothers but most of them were not in the city. They were fighting in battles on behalf of their father, claiming territory for the Ilkhanate.

"Was it Jumghur who threatened you?" he asked.

"Yes, yes. Please, this way," said Sohrab, leading him down a corridor he'd not visited before. Temujin had never spent any time in this part of the building, but he knew its purpose.

At the top of a wide set of stairs two masked Kheshig were on duty. The air was noticeably cooler and an unpleasant smell wafted up from below.

"Hurry," urged Sohrab, nearly tripping in his haste. The corridor at the bottom of the stairs was dusty, damp and the walls slick with water. Patches of green mould clung to the low ceiling and even though it was far above his head, Temujin realised he was hunching over. The cell doors on either side were made from wood with iron bands. A tiny window at head height could be opened to peer inside each cell. All of them were closed which was a small mercy. The smell of damp became secondary to the stench of rot and human filth. It seared Temujin's nostrils and he walked faster in a vain attempt to get away from it.

At the end of the corridor was a guardroom but Sohrab didn't stop, leading him down a side corridor to a large room filled with light. Several lanterns were set in alcoves around the walls, banishing all shadows. When he realised they were in a torture chamber Temujin wished it wasn't so bright.

Hanging from the ceiling by his wrists was a naked man. His body was criss-crossed with a series of red stripes from a blade or whip. The wounds were shallow, but there were many across his chest and legs. His toes barely touched the floor and his wrists were already bleeding and bruised.

Standing off to one side, wearing a big grin, was his brother Jumghur. In one hand he held a bloody knife that dripped gore. On the far side of the room, sitting at a desk, was Rashid, the Khan's vizier. The awful heat began to rise in Temujin's chest but he quickly pushed it down. Now was not the time to get angry and lash out like his idiot brother.

"I brought him as fast as I could," said Sohrab. "Please don't kill my family. Please!"

Jumghur laughed and patted him on the shoulder. "Don't worry, little man, they're safe. I was only joking."

Sohrab was torn between relief and horror that Jumghur would play such a cruel trick for his own amusement. Ignoring his bloodthirsty brother Temujin approached Rashid, who was studying a book.

"Rashid, why was I summoned?"

At first Rashid said nothing, but then he turned the book around and shoved it across the desk. "Do you recognise this?"

Temujin inspected the book and quickly realised it was the spice merchant's accounts. Glancing over his shoulder he realised the prisoner was the same man.

"Normally such things are dealt with by other people. However, because it was you, I was kept appraised. Better me than someone else."

Temujin had always thought of Rashid as a kindly uncle, but today there was nothing friendly in his eyes. "He couldn't pay. I checked the books."

"Sohrab, come here," said Rashid.

Despite the rancid air in the cells Temujin could smell the tax man. He reeked of fear.

"Yes, master," he said.

"Tell him what you discovered," said Rashid.

"I checked ten other spice shops in the area and all of them have seen an increase in profits. When I spoke to some of his neighbours, I found out that Javeed was seen buying expensive clothes for his wife and daughters. He is flush with money."

Rashid produced a second notebook which he laid on top of the first. It showed a much healthier income and a significant rise in sales over the last six months.

"You have done well, Sohrab. You may go," said Rashid, dismissing the tax man.

"Thank you, master," he said, bowing as he backed out of the room.

"Everyone lies," said Jumghur, approaching the spice merchant. "Especially this one." He slashed Javeed across the chest and the merchant screamed, his voice bouncing off the stone walls.

"An example needs to be made. We must send a clear message that no one can cheat the Khan." Rashid spoke calmly, but his tone of voice sent a shiver down Temujin's spine.

The others looked at him expectantly. "What sort of example?"

"All of his money and belongings have been seized and someone else now owns his shop. In addition, his wife and daughters have been killed," said Rashid.

Javeed sobbed and made a half-hearted attempt to pull his wrists free of the shackles. Jumghur laughed and cut him again, this time across the ribs. The spice merchant seemed to barely feel it. Temujin was certain the cry of anguish was for his family.

"He is all that remains to be dealt with." Rashid showed no signs of discomfort. It made Temujin wonder how many times the vizier had done something like this before.

"So let Jumghur kill him and be done," said Temujin. The spice merchant was not getting out of this room alive. There was no point in torturing the man any further. With the news that his family was dead all remaining strength had leached from his body. He hung, practically lifeless by his wrists. Waiting for the inevitable.

"Normally I would agree. However, this was your mistake and is therefore your responsibility," said Rashid.

Jumghur drew his sword and before he could argue he slapped it in Temujin's hand, closing his fingers over the hilt.

"Kill him," said his brother, grinning like they were playing a game. "He lied to you. He knew you were soft and used it against you."

Temujin shook his head. "I can't kill him."

"This job was your last chance. And you failed." The disappointment in Rashid's eyes burned more than Temujin had expected. "If you kill him, then all of this goes away, and you go back to your job."

"And if I refuse?"

Rashid bit his lower lip but it was Jumghur who leaned close to whisper in Temujin's ear.

"Then father will find out. Prove that you're not a fat, useless coward. Do something right for once in your life. Kill this cheating liar."

Jumghur grabbed him by the arm and dragged him across the room until they were standing in front of the prisoner. He mimed stabbing Javeed and even tapped him on the chest. "Right here. One quick thrust through the heart. Then we can get out of this dungeon and have some breakfast."

Food was the last thing on Temujin's mind and his stomach clenched with revulsion. Javeed raised his head and their eyes met. His lips were bleeding but his words were still clear.

"Kill me," he croaked.

"See! He wants to die," said Jumghur.

Temujin stared at the sword in his hand and then up at the pale, scarred flesh of the doomed man. It wouldn't take much. A quick push and it would be over. His problems would disappear. He could go back to being a tax collector and his father would never know about any of this. And all he had to do was kill a defenceless man.

Temujin dropped the sword. "I won't do it."

"Fucking coward," sneered Jumghur.

"Are you sure?" asked Rashid. "You understand what will happen if you refuse?"

"I'm not afraid," said Temujin and his brother laughed. They both knew it was a lie.

Nevertheless he turned around and marched out of the torture chamber. Behind him there was a brief yelp of pain from the dying man and then silence returned.

All thoughts of breakfast were banished as Temujin returned to his rooms to contemplate his future. There was no going back. He would have to face his father's wrath and there was nothing anyone could do to save him.

CHAPTER 8
Hulagu

As Hulagu strode down the corridors of the palace, Rashid and Guyuk struggled to keep up with his angry strides.

"As you anticipated, my Khan," Rashid was saying. "Your forces have taken Kermanshah. Your warriors and allies are now gathering in the south. Warriors from the Golden Horde are also on the way. Once you and Berke Khan arrive, the army will be ready to march deeper into Iraq."

It was good news. In a week he would be able to put aside matters of state and get back to the war. Then they would march on Baghdad and begin their assault.

"Have terms been sent to the rulers of Baghdad?" asked Guyuk.

"Yes, Empress. As with the others, the same offer was made. If they submit to the rule of the Ilkhanate, and pay tribute, then no harm will come to anyone."

Servants passing them in the hallways saw Hulagu's mood and quickly scattered in case his wrath fell on them.

"Do you think they'll agree?" asked Guyuk.

"Unlikely. Even with the fall of Kermanshah, there is the promise of support from the Mamluks."

"Fucking Mamluks," spat Hulagu. Their time was coming.

He shoved open the doors to the throne room and stomped

inside. Normally he found the throne comfortable but today, no matter how he positioned his arse, it ached. On his left was a plate of fresh dates and nuts. Sitting beside it was a jug of airag but he ignored it. Picking up a shelled walnut Hulagu rolled it between his palms.

"Their time will come," said Guyuk, mirroring his thoughts.

"Yes, Empress," said Rashid, with a nervous smile. They both knew something was wrong but had not asked.

"Have spies been sent ahead into Baghdad?" asked Hulagu.

"A dozen are already in the city, gathering information. By the time you arrive there will be reports on troop numbers, city defences and food stores."

Unless those in charge surrendered another siege was inevitable. Once his forces cut off supplies going in and out, it wouldn't take long for the food to run out. The people would turn quickly on their masters when the alternative was starvation, or to start eating rats and dogs.

"Explain something to me," said Hulagu. "Why is it that I had to hear about Temujin, days after the event, from Jumghur?" Guyuk and Rashid exchanged a look. "Talk to me!" roared Hulagu, spittle flying from his mouth.

"I didn't want to upset you," said Guyuk. "I didn't think it was important."

"And you?" he asked, turning towards Rashid.

His vizier swallowed hard. "I thought it was under control. I can only apologise–"

"Get out." Hulagu's voice echoed around the room. Part of him was tempted to throw the jug at Rashid's head. His hand moved towards it but then stopped. Control. He had to regain control. He was not a savage dog.

His vizier bowed and backed out of the room, leaving him alone with his wife. The Kheshig also melted away and although they were in earshot, he knew they wouldn't repeat a word.

"How many times have you saved the boy?" he asked. "How much is a promise worth?"

"He seemed to be doing well," said Guyuk, moving to sit below him on the steps. He knew it was a ploy, having her look up at him with her big brown eyes. He'd fallen for it in the past but not today.

"Enough," said Hulagu. "We've tried it your way for long enough. Once again he's proven to be an embarrassment and a disgrace."

"You can't–"

"Can't?" said Hulagu, cutting her off. That was not a word he heard from anyone. "Send him in." It wasn't often he gave her a command but today she didn't refuse.

A short time later she returned with Temujin in tow. He looked scared, which only made Hulagu angrier.

"You're even fatter than the last time I saw you," he said. Temujin didn't reply but he stood close to Guyuk, as if she could protect him.

"Why did you refuse to kill the thief?" asked Hulagu.

"I knew Jumghur would enjoy it," came the evasive reply.

"That isn't what I asked."

"I didn't hate him."

Hulagu leaned forward. "He hoarded money and lived like a king. He stole from me."

"His family didn't deserve to share his fate," said Temujin. He risked eye contact but quickly looked away, disappointing Hulagu with his tame attitude.

"They were happy to benefit from his stolen wealth. A message needed to be sent. One that would not be forgotten."

"No one will forget," said Temujin.

For a moment Hulagu thought it was a threat, but the boy withered and the words became hollow. "You are responsible. Your weakness cost the lives of four people." Temujin clenched his fists and Hulagu willed him to argue, but instead he remained silent. "I wish you'd died instead of your mother."

Guyuk looked horrified but he ignored her.

Mercifully his son didn't cry. "Why am I here?" he asked.

"Because, despite your incompetence, you're still my son. So I am going to make a man of you. When I leave the city, you will be coming with me to Baghdad."

"No!" said Guyuk, but he ignored her.

"You will serve as a warrior in the army and if you die, then at least it will be in service of the Empire. I have eight sons and thirteen daughters. All of your brothers and sisters are productive and useful. From today, until the moment we leave Tabriz, you will train with a sword. All day, every day, from the moment you wake up until nightfall. If nothing else, I will be able to use you as a human shield, and the next time someone tries to kill me, you will die in my place. Now get out of my sight!"

Temujin's whole body was trembling. Hulagu thought he was shaking with fright and looked ready to piss himself. Sickened by the sight of his son Hulagu turned away until he was gone. When he turned back Guyuk had left the room, leaving him alone to wallow.

Frustrated and annoyed, Hulagu left the palace to walk the streets and clear his head. A pair of Kheshig trailed behind, doing their best to remain inconspicuous. It was a difficult task when they were dressed in armour from head to toe. Out of habit Hulagu wore a blade on his hip but he wasn't in any danger.

As he wandered through the streets Hulagu cast an eye over the crowds. The city was thriving. The number of people swelled in number every time he returned from being away. In the heart of the city was the historic Bazaar of Tabriz. The massive indoor market was unlike anything he'd seen. It was another example of the local people's ingenuity. The huge vaulted ceiling was covered in thousands of colourful tiles. Light filtered in through high windows in the cathedral-like structure, and every few paces there was a lantern on the wall so it remained bright, day or night. The air was rich with pungent smells and dozens of overlapping conversations blurred together creating a sound which echoed off the walls. Each row of the bazaar was dedicated to one item; jewellery, spices, shoes, rugs. The best from across the world was on display, and each shop owner worked hard to compete with their neighbours.

At first Hulagu's presence went unnoticed, but eventually people began to realise he was in their midst. The conversations petered away until the atmosphere was tense. For a moment he'd enjoyed being just another nameless person in the crowd.

Leaving the bazaar, Hulagu went in search of something to eat. He passed several places he'd previously visited but wanted to try something different. Eventually he stopped at a tea room that served local Persian cuisine. Half of the tables were occupied but at his arrival the customers quickly finished their food and left.

As Hulagu took his seat the owner came bustling out from the back. He was a short chubby man with a goatee beard and a bald head.

"Lord Khan, you honour me," he said, wringing his hands.

"Do you prepare the food?" asked Hulagu.

"Yes, with my brother and nephew," babbled the man.

"Do you have a special dish?"

The owner considered it for a moment. "My kebab is very popular." The smells coming from the kitchen made Hulagu's stomach rumble.

"Bring me two."

While he waited for his kebab, a teenage boy brought him a plate of bread, cheese and herbs and a cold glass of milk. It was flavoured with spices and tasted salty, but it was refreshing in the heat.

By the time his food arrived a few other patrons had risked grabbing a table to eat. The food, a golden plate of rice and two skewers of lamb kebab flavoured with herbs, proved to be as good as the owner's promise. The tender meat melted in his mouth and it tasted delicious. After a pot of tea and some honey pastries, Hulagu felt sated. Once word spread that the Khan had dined at the tea room it would become incredibly popular. He liked to see hard work rewarded and this place deserved more attention.

For almost two hours he'd managed to keep his mind away from thoughts of his family, but now disappointment about Temujin crept back.

Hulagu gestured and the owner raced over. "It was excellent."

"My pleasure, great Khan," said the man, beaming with pride.

He paid far more than was required for the meal and walked away before the owner could argue. Hulagu wondered if Temujin would have been more successful if he'd doted on him. Then again, all of his other children had thrived. Some of his daughters ran powerful business empires. His sons were senior officers in the army, rulers of districts and titans of industry.

The answer was clear. The blame lay with his son. There was something in him that was weak. The only explanation was that it must have come from his mother. Perhaps it was a good thing that she had died. The shame at seeing her son grow up to be so useless would have broken her heart. Becoming a warrior would either kill Temujin or it would expunge the weakness inside him.

Just as Hulagu was crossing the street the bodyguard in front of him stumbled. He dropped to one knee but quickly came upright, as if he'd caught his foot on something. The Kheshig managed three more steps before he slumped to the ground. When Hulagu rolled him over he saw a dagger sticking out of the man's neck.

In the time it took Hulagu to draw his sword something flashed past his face in a silver blur. It sailed past him and was buried in the shoulder of his other bodyguard.

A woman ran towards them, dressed in normal clothes, but she carried a pair of daggers. They were exquisitely made with distinctively shaped blades.

She was an Assassin.

The Kheshig stepped in front of Hulagu and slashed at the woman with his sword. When she tried to skirt around him, the bodyguard went on the offensive, forcing her back. The wound in his left shoulder was bleeding quite badly, but he didn't need to beat his opponent. All he had to do was keep her at a distance.

It became a race against time. Someone would have noticed the attack and word would quickly spread. More bodyguards or a patrol would soon arrive. Realising that her chance of success was growing short, the Assassin took a risk.

Whirling her daggers she attacked, feinted left and attacked right, just in time for Hulagu to bring his sword down on her shoulder. It went through the meat of her body, breaking her collarbone in the process. With a scream she dropped to the street as pain became her entire world. The Kheshig ended it quickly, putting his sword through her throat and she gurgled a final breath.

"In my city," spat Hulagu. "How is the shoulder?"

"I will live, my Khan," said the Kheshig between gritted teeth. He pulled off his mask and Hulagu saw the strain on his face. "We should return to the palace."

No sooner had he finished speaking when a dagger blossomed in his eye. Something flitted towards Hulagu and he ducked as another blade went sailing by, barely missing his head. The Kheshig was dead by the time his body hit the ground.

A second Assassin slowly walked towards him. He was out of daggers but he picked up a sword from the street. "She was my sister," he said, sparing a glance for the woman on the street. "You will pay for her, and those you murdered at Alamut."

"Come and get me," snarled Hulagu, raising his sword.

The Assassin was skilled with a blade and incredibly strong.

Despite his obvious despair, he moved with precision. The tip of his blade skimmed across Hulagu's thigh when he was too slow in stepping back, but thankfully the wound was shallow. A moment later Hulagu was bleeding from a cut on his left arm.

"I will take you apart, piece by piece," promised the Assassin. "You're weak. Just like your sister."

Somehow the Assassin stayed calm and would not be taunted into being reckless. It quickly became apparent that for all of his skill with a sword, Hulagu was outmatched.

Hulagu was sweating and using all of his skill to stay alive, but he barely kept his enemy at bay. He knew help was on its way, but he no longer felt confident that it would arrive in time. He needed an edge to survive.

When the Assassin came for him, rather than turn and run, Hulagu stood his ground. He used every trick to delay the inevitable, turning to one side or stepping back to create space between them. He tried to make his opponent trip over the dead bodies and retrieved a dagger to use as a secondary weapon. Despite everything it wasn't enough.

Hulagu saw the attack coming that would end his life. He heard the blade whistling towards his head. He blocked and immediately riposted, but his opponent wasn't there anymore. Something slammed into Hulagu's forearm and he watched in horror as his sword tumbled to the ground from numb fingers. Moving on instinct he stabbed downwards with the stolen dagger. It bit into the Assassin's thigh and he stepped back.

Something hard slammed into the centre of Hulagu's chest and he tumbled backwards, gasping for breath, wincing at the pain. As he stared up at the sky, he muttered a brief prayer to Tengri. A shadow fell across him, blocking his view. The Assassin stared down at him with a mix of contempt and hatred. Hulagu expected some words. Insults or a final message.

As the Assassin raised his sword something nudged him from behind and he gasped in surprise. As he turned his head to see what had happened the point of a sword erupted from the centre of his chest. Blood trickled from the Assassin's mouth and he dropped his blade.

Hulagu rolled out of the way and scrambled to his feet. A Persian man stood behind the Assassin, still holding onto the sword. With a huge wrench the stranger dragged his sword free. The Assassin's sword dropped from useless fingers to the ground. His legs went next and he collapsed before rolling over onto his back.

Hulagu knelt down beside the Assassin. Only now, as the end neared, did he speak.

"You will never find us all. The Order of Assassins will forever be lurking in the shadows." He gagged and coughed up blood and phlegm. "One day, we will kill you."

"Perhaps," conceded Hulagu, kneeling on the man's throat. "But not today."

He watched the Assassin thrash about, desperately trying to breathe. But he was too weak and his attempts became slower until they stopped.

Raised voices and the rattle of armour announced the arrival of a dozen warriors, far too late to have been useful. Hulagu stared at the face of his saviour and wondered what kind of a man he was.

CHAPTER 9
Kaivon

Kaivon had always known it would end this way, locked in a cell awaiting execution.

The rebellion in the south had failed. Apathy, exhaustion and the death of countless friends and relatives had sapped the people's collective will to fight. He understood their reasons but it still made him angry. Eventually the people of Persia would rise again, but for now they needed time to heal. For Kaivon there was no more time. He could not rest and barely slept. All food tasted bitter and his mind was consumed with endless thoughts of revenge.

His plan to murder Hulagu Khan had been a foolish one. Even if he had been successful, the Khan would just be replaced by another Mongol overlord. And the subjugation of nations would continue, with more countries either surrendering or being destroyed by the relentless Mongol horde.

Killing Hulagu wasn't sensible or rational, but revenge was all he had. It was a way to honour all of those who had died fighting to protect their homeland.

Somehow Kaivon had found himself in the right place at the right time. He'd been idly browsing in the bazaar when Hulagu Khan had walked through the front door. When the

Khan sat down at the tea room he'd lurked around the corner, trying to come up with a plan of attack.

The two Kheshig had been a serious problem that could not be brushed aside. They wore toughened black leather armour from head to toe, in addition to a lamellar cuirass. Even their faces were covered with a flexible leather mask, providing few weak points. The armpit and the groin were susceptible to a blade, but getting close enough to try was an enormous risk. Every bodyguard was a skilled warrior. Only the best were chosen to protect royalty and their training never stopped.

When the Assassins attacked the Khan's bodyguards, it felt as if someone had listened to Kaivon's prayer. First one and then the other bodyguard were disabled, leaving Hulagu vulnerable. The Kheshig were accomplished fighters but the Assassins were relentless killers. They did not train to fight in wars. They did not protect people. Their sole purpose was murder and they were masters of their craft. It was why it cost a small fortune to hire them and the death of their target was usually a given.

Hulagu had fought well but the end had been inevitable. And all Kaivon had to do was do nothing.

It had come as a surprise to himself when he'd picked up the Kheshig's fallen blade and stabbed the Assassin through the back. Despite saving the Khan's life he'd been manhandled and locked in a cell. At least it had given him time to think it through and try to understand his reasons.

His brother had been right. Murdering Hulagu would only have made matters worse. The Persian people would have been punished and more innocents would have died for his crime. There had to be better way to destroy the Ilkhanate.

The door to the cell block opened and two masked Kheshig came into the corridor. The other cells were empty but the air still stank of shit, decay and mould. A gust of fresh air allowed Kaivon to take his first deep breath in hours.

Hulagu strode into the room, the top of his head almost

scraping the doorframe. He was a tall man but also broad across the shoulders and chest. A formidable leader, a savage ruler and as Kaivon had seen, a competent fighter. He could see why so many were inspired by the Khan.

One of the bodyguards brought in a chair which he put down in front of the bars. The Kheshig retreated leaving him alone with Hulagu. Kaivon was not a threat, but the door to the cell block stayed open. His bodyguards were not willing to take any chances.

Kaivon felt the Khan studying him and he met Hulagu's gaze without fear.

"It took some time," said Hulagu, settling into his chair, "but we determined you were not working with the Assassins. You recently came from the south, yes?"

"Yes." At this point there was little point in lying.

"I had thought, with the destruction of their stronghold at Alamut, that the Assassin threat was over," said Hulagu.

Kaivon felt no sympathy for him. When he looked at the Khan, all he saw was a figure drenched in the blood of his people. All of those who had fought and died to protect their homeland from a ruthless invader.

"Is it true you work as a butcher?"

"Yes." Kaivon had come to the north weeks ago with few skills that made him useful. A long time ago, before he'd been a soldier, he'd learned the basics as an apprentice.

"But you were not always one." Hulagu said it with confidence.

Perhaps he knew more than he pretended. Perhaps he'd seen Kaivon's bearing and recognised that he was a soldier. Or perhaps he merely wished that his life had been saved by someone remarkable. It added an exciting twist to the saga that was being written about Hulagu's life.

"I was a soldier," said Kaivon, proud of his accomplishments. "My name is Kaivon Dehnavi. I am the last living General of the Persian army."

He expected gloating or mockery, but Hulagu merely nodded, deep in thought. "Tell me, Kaivon. What do the people in the south think of me?"

"They're afraid of what you might do to them."

"But you're not afraid."

"No."

"Because you have nothing to lose."

Kaivon thought of his brother and his family but kept his face blank. "I have nothing."

"Are the people safe?" asked Hulagu, catching him off balance.

"What?"

"Is there law and order across Persia? Are the people prospering as part of the Mongol Empire?"

Kaivon wanted to deny him but he could not. "Yes."

Hulagu sighed. "Is there peace?"

"Yes, but only because those who could fight were slaughtered. By you."

"True." It had not been his hand, but the Khan had given the orders.

"Many of my people lost their entire families," said Kaivon. "Others lost fathers and sons, all of them brave warriors. Men who defended their country. The wounds run deep and it will take a long time for this nation to heal. We will never forget and cannot forgive you."

Hulagu Khan leaned back in his chair, as if to consider Kaivon's fate. Two young men entered the cell block who bore a resemblance to the Khan. One was broad and walked with a swagger. His eyes were full of wicked malice. The other was more slender but no less fierce.

"He doesn't look like much," said the braggart. Kaivon noticed that although he was smiling it never reached his eyes.

"What would you do if I let you out of this cell?" asked Hulagu.

"Kill you." Despite knowing it would not change anything,

Kaivon could not repress the urge. "Stab you to death until you choked on your own blood."

The atmosphere became tense. The air buzzed with the promise of violence. Kaivon's hands curled into fists. He was ready to fight until the very end. Until the last breath left his body. It was the only way they would stop him.

"Let me kill him," said the one on the left, drawing his sword. "Jailor. Bring me the key!"

"Hold, Jumghur," said the Khan.

"No one speaks to you like that," said the other son.

"You're right." And much to everyone's surprise Hulagu laughed. "I find his honesty refreshing."

"At least let me take his tongue," wheedled Jumghur.

Hulagu ignored his zealous son. "I offer you thanks for saving my life. In return you will go free, but you now have two choices. Either you can go back to your mundane job and spend the rest of your days cutting up meat."

"What is my other choice?" he asked, struggling to speak.

"Work with me and fight at my side. Help me expand the Empire and bring peace to the world."

Kaivon's mocking laugh drew a scowl from both sons. "Why would I help you conquer other nations?"

Hulagu got up from his chair and approached the bars. "You said it yourself. We bring peace and prosperity."

"At the point of a sword. How many have you killed? Do you even know?"

"I always offer them a choice," insisted Hulagu.

"Surrender or die is not a choice."

"You are not a naïve child. You know the world is a dark and dangerous place. If not us, then someone else will come. Someone less forgiving and more cruel. Maybe the Mamluks and their Muslim brothers. Bow to their god or die." The Khan gripped the bars with both hands until his knuckles turned white. "We treat people with fairness. Look at the city around us. There are law courts and places of worship for all faiths. Do you think the Mamluks would offer you a choice? Or the Pope and his Crusaders?" Hulagu shook his shaggy head and leaned forward, looming over Kaivon.

"What are you asking me to do?"

"I have military experts and advisors from all over the world. Much of my army comprises of warriors from across the Empire, including your countrymen. Even my chief engineer is Persian. I could use someone with your skills and a clear head to advise me. Someone who isn't afraid and will be honest."

Kaivon shook his head in despair. "You are asking me to betray my people."

"Your people are not suffering. They're not slaves or starving. They're free to live as they did before, and pray to whichever god they choose. Tell me I am lying."

Kaivon bowed his head. "I cannot."

He knew that once the fighting was done life had returned to a semblance of normality. Other nations, like Georgia, had seen what was coming and had chosen to surrender rather than endure the same fate. Now they were a vassal state. They mostly governed themselves, but in return for such freedom they paid their due to the Khan and supported him with the expansion.

"Come with me," said Hulagu. "And if there is a better way to bring peace, help me find it. You can do nothing to change the path ahead, if you're not part of the story."

Hulagu was twisting the truth. Making it sound as if he were a kind neighbour that politely knocked at the door and asked to be let inside. As if his only wish was to improve the lives of everyone for the better.

Although the city of Tabriz had only suffered minor damage, most of the scars from the war had been painted over. Walls rebuilt, new homes erected, all to give the impression that it hadn't happened. Kaivon knew there were other towns and villages that had been obliterated. The inhabitants butchered and those who survived had fled or had been sold into slavery.

All buildings had been razed and all signs of habitation removed so that nothing remained. The names of such places would soon be lost. Thousands had died and many more had been wounded.

And now the Khan wanted Kaivon to pretend that none of it had happened. That it had all been for the greater good.

"It's not an easy decision to make. Think on it. I will return in the morning for your answer," said Hulagu, walking from the cell block.

Alone with his thoughts, Kaivon considered his future.

Trying to stand up to the Mongols head on had failed. It was painful to admit but there was no avoiding the truth. If he wanted to be a part of the Empire's downfall, it required a new approach. The only way to destroy it was from within. Before that could happen, he needed to understand his enemy. Then he would begin to erode what had been built. It would take patience and time. Perhaps he would not live to see the end and others would continue the work, but someone needed to make a start.

After being escorted to private rooms in the palace, Kaivon was bathed, given a haircut and his beard was trimmed. He was measured for new clothes, dressed in custom armour and given a splendid new sword. The slightly curved blade was sharp along one edge and, although lighter than anticipated, it was beautifully balanced. Staring at himself in the mirror Kaivon saw only his fear. Once he had been a General and someone who mattered. He tried to project that image and conceal his nerves.

After a day of being pampered and lazing around, eating wonderful food that left him satisfied and sleepy, he was summoned to the throne room. Two silent Kheshig walked behind him. Kaivon was under no illusions that they were there for his protection. He had merely exchanged one cell for another. He would have to prove his loyalty before the shackles were removed.

The Khan was sat atop his throne, a surprisingly modest seat, on a raised platform. Surrounding him were several of his military figures. Mongols, Armenians, Georgians, two local men, and two of Hulagu's sons, who Kaivon had met before; Abaqa and Jumghur. Spread across a wide table was a large detailed map of Persia and the surrounding nations. It was covered with lots of tiny markers and notations. Standing off to one side was the Khan's vizier, Rashid, a small man with no military rank, but Kaivon understood that he wielded significant power. He observed that when the vizier spoke all of the others listened. Without his efforts they would have no food, horses, weapons, and there would be no war.

"General Kaivon, join us," said Hulagu Khan, waving him over.

"My Khan," said Kaivon, giving a short bow.

Jumghur glared at him and some of the others sniffed, offended by his presence, but they didn't say anything out loud.

"We were discussing our plans for the next assault."

"Why is he here?" asked Jumghur.

The Khan ignored his loud-mouthed son and jabbed a finger at the map. "Baghdad. That's our next target."

"Father, I agree with Jumghur," said Abaqa. "He has sworn no oath. He admitted wanting to kill you."

"Enough!" roared the Khan, slamming his hand down on the map. Everyone leaned back from the power of his voice. One or two of the Generals took a step back as Hulagu's gaze fell upon them, but his sons bore the brunt. Abaqa had enough intelligence to look worried but Jumghur remained puzzled. The rasp of steel around the room echoed loudly in the silence that followed as the Kheshig drew their swords.

"He saved my life when my own fucking Kheshig failed," said Hulagu, daring anyone to interrupt. "All of you came to me as vassals and I gave you my trust. Now, you stand around this table as my inner council, and I rely on your wisdom. When you speak, I will listen. I offer him the same chance that all of you received. If anyone breaks my trust, they will not live very long. Is that understood?"

A chorus of agreement followed from a circle of chastised faces.

They were all scared and with good reason. Hulagu could kill anyone in the room with his bare hands and no one would move to prevent it. There would be no consequences for such a rash act and Kaivon suspected it wouldn't play on the Khan's conscience.

"Good. Now, back to business. We leave in a few days." As quickly as it had arrived Hulagu's anger was gone. Their collective attention returned to the map and Kaivon listened intently, soaking up details about what was planned. He was called on, from time to time, to offer his opinion and with each opportunity he held nothing back. Some of his answers shocked the others but Hulagu just grinned, pleased to have someone who pointed out the flaws.

"How many started out like me?" wondered Kaivon, glancing at the others. Defiant. Determined to erode the Ilkhanate from within. Now, without exception, all of them were obedient dogs.

When their business was nearly concluded Kaivon glanced up as he felt someone's eyes resting on him. On the other side of the table the Khan's sons were staring. Jumghur was full of hatred and had all of the subtlety of a rock. Abaqa was more intelligent than his brother but his distrust was clear.

Their hostility served as a good reminder that although he was part of the inner circle, it would take a long time before anyone trusted him. Which made Kaivon ask himself, how far was he willing to go and how much blood was he willing to spill in order to serve his people?

CHAPTER 10
The Twelve

The twelve women had arranged to gather in a different room in the city of Tabriz. They arrived one by one until eight of them were assembled around a long table in the back room of a restaurant. It was early in the day, so the restaurant was abandoned and the kitchen was empty. Even so, One's nose twitched. The whole building was soaked with layer upon layer of heady and tantalising aromas. Part of her had been tempted to find something to eat, but she'd moved through the kitchen without stopping. Time was of the essence and they couldn't afford to be discovered.

One sat at the head of the table to conduct the meeting.

"Ladies. Let's begin," said One. "Twelve is currently in the east, so she couldn't make it."

"Seven, Two and Nine also send their apologies," said Three. "As you know, Hulagu Khan is in the city, and they cannot get away without it looking suspicious."

"Understandable," said One. "Is there something else?" she said, noting Three's excitement.

"Yes. The Order of the Assassins has not been destroyed. I have a small, but reliable network in Cairo. The surviving Assassins fled there and are now working for the Sultan."

"Allah be praised," said Six. "That is good news."

"I wouldn't get too excited just yet," said Three. "Even though the Assassins did make an attempt on the life of Hulagu Khan."

"I'm assuming it was unsuccessful," said Eleven, running a hand across her shaven scalp.

"Sadly, yes. They're still angry about Alamut and they lashed out."

"They need guidance," said One.

"I'm working on it," said Three.

"Do what you can."

"There's something related that we need to discuss," said Ten. One already knew what she was about to say, but everyone needed to hear the news. "The reason Hulagu is still alive. He was saved by a former Persian soldier. The same one who was a rebel in the south and now he's in service to the Khan."

"Traitorous bastard," spat Eleven. "We should kill him."

"Should we?" asked One, putting the question to Ten. "Is he a traitor?"

Ten shrugged. "It's too early to tell."

"He wouldn't be the first Persian to end up working for Hulagu Khan," said Eight.

"True," said One, "but most of them start off as slaves. Their choices were 'serve or die'. This man, Kaivon, he saved the Khan's life of his own free will."

"It is unusual," said Ten.

"So, do we kill him?" asked Eleven.

Ten raised an eyebrow ever so slightly. It was only because of their long association that One knew what Ten meant by it.

"Not yet. I suggest we have someone watch him," said One. "We need to know where his loyalty truly lies. If he proves to be an enemy, then we can leak information about his connection to the rebels. But if he's loyal to Persia, he could be extremely useful." One glanced around the table and all but Eleven nodded in agreement. "Three, send word to the others in the north. See if they can get someone close to him."

"Of course," said Three. "Two also wanted me to convey a message. The job in the palace went off without a hitch. We now have another agent within the finance system."

"Excellent, and I have news from the east," said One. "Ariq Khan has refused to withdraw his claim. He still believes the kurultai was a sham and that Kublai stole the vote. My networks in China and Mongolia are continuing to spread stories that he was cheated by his brothers."

"Does Ariq have any supporters?" asked Four.

"More than you would imagine," said One. "Several Generals and senior officers are unhappy with Kublai becoming the Great Khan. They think he's too influenced by his Chinese wife, Chabi. There are even rumours that he wants to move the capital city away from Karakorum to the east."

"Did we start the rumours?" asked Four.

"No, those ones are genuine," said One.

"There are also grumblings in the north," said Five. Most of her contacts were in the Golden Horde, the northernmost khanate. "Berke Khan made a number of concessions during the kurultai. If they were not met then a rift could develop between the four khanates."

"Where is he now?"

"Bringing warriors south. He's joining forces with Hulagu to invade Iraq."

"That presents us with a lot of opportunities," said One.

With such a large gathering, it would be easy to have some of their people join the army. A few more Persian faces among the crowd would not be noticed. The Mongol horde needed a lot of people to support it. The baggage train alone stretched for miles, and that didn't include all of the engineers and their equipment.

"How many do we think? A dozen?" suggested One, and the others agreed. This would be the first time since Hulagu Khan had conquered Persia that he'd gathered together so many men. Allies and vassal states across the Caucasus would send men. If they didn't it would be noticed and remarked upon to the Khan. With such a large gathering it would be easy to gather information, but also to plant stories and see how they spread among the campfires. They could do a great deal of damage without killing or blackmailing a single person.

"The tide may be turning in our favour," said Eleven, eager for victory. She still thought it would be a fast rather than a gradual erosion of the Mongol Empire.

"It's early days," said One. She didn't want to crush any enthusiasm, just temper it with patience. She and some of the others had been here before. Even so, she did feel a flutter of excitement.

It was a good start, but there was still a lot of work to be done.

CHAPTER 11
Kokochin

The morning after the attack in the palace, Kokochin slept in late. She had nowhere to be, so no one paid any attention to her schedule. When she tried to get out of bed, her muscles ached from her flight. Her ankle was swollen and sore, but her hand was already beginning to scab over. After applying face paint and dressing in gloves, she concealed the worst of her injuries. The ankle was more difficult. She bound it tight, to limit movement, and picked out a pair of sturdy shoes to provide additional support. She could ask a servant for something to manage the pain, but word might spread and that could lead to questions she didn't want to answer. Until she could get out of the palace Kokochin knew she would have to manage the pain by herself.

She ate breakfast in her rooms and then carefully strolled towards the palace gardens. Along the way she saw more Kheshig in the corridors than ever before. There was an atmosphere around them and she didn't linger.

Turning a corner Kokochin came face to face with a pair of bodyguards. A few paces behind them was her husband, Hulagu Khan. This was the first time they'd been face to face since she'd arrived in Tabriz.

Hulagu was in discussion with his vizier, Rashid, but the

conversation trailed off and the corridor filled with a peculiar silence. Hulagu was lost for words. With so many wives he'd probably forgotten she existed.

Remembering what Guyuk had said, Kokochin boldly looked him in the eye. Rashid raised an eyebrow while Hulagu fidgeted.

"Are you settling in?" he finally asked.

"Yes, thank you. The Empress has been most helpful."

"Good. That's good," said Hulagu, which exhausted their conversation.

"We are already late, my Khan," said Rashid, saving everyone from further embarrassment.

"Yes, you're right," said Hulagu. He opened his mouth to say something else but then changed his mind. They swept past and she inclined her head but didn't bow. Hulagu glanced back once and then he was gone.

Her heart was racing and her palms sweaty. Another minute and he might have noticed her bruises. Kokochin hurried to the gardens before she ran into anyone else.

Kokochin had been dozing and reading for an hour when Guyuk found her. Out of respect Kokochin started to rise but the Empress waved her back, which was a relief. It would have been difficult to mask the pain in her ankle.

"How are you?"

"I am well, thank you, Empress. Just enjoying the sunshine," said Kokochin.

"Good," said Guyuk, taking a seat. "Did you sleep well?"

"Yes, thank you." Kokochin rested a hand on the other woman's leg which drew Guyuk's focus. "Are you ill, Empress? You look distressed."

Guyuk's suspicion eased into a motherly smile. "I'm fine, dear. Tell me, did you hear any strange noises in the night?"

"No, nothing." Kokochin leaned closer to whisper, even though they were alone. "But I did see more bodyguards in the hallways. Should I be worried?"

"Hmm, yes." Guyuk paused, mulling something over. "Someone was attacked, but don't let it worry you. Measures have been taken. You're perfectly safe."

"That's good to hear."

"I'll leave you to your reading," said Guyuk.

Kokochin smiled, delighted that she knew more than the Empress. Despite the walls, the locked doors and the guards, someone had made it into the palace. It was unthinkable and unprecedented. It was thrilling.

As Guyuk left Kokochin noticed a bodyguard lurking nearby. She'd need to take extra precautions when leaving the palace at night.

The first thing she wanted to do was find the woman who'd broken into the palace. She had been fearless against some of the best warriors in the Mongol Empire. To become one of the Kheshig was not easy and it was an honour to be chosen. And yet the intruder had taken down at least half a dozen without a weapon. That was real power and Kokochin wanted to understand it.

Every day for the next week Kokochin went into the city after breakfast to search for the mysterious woman. She had a clear picture of the stranger in her mind, but at the end of each day without any sighting, doubt began to creep in about her recollection.

After a few days a more worrying thought occurred. Tabriz was a busy city. There was a constant stream of people coming and going with the merchants. What if the woman had immediately left after the attack? From listening to gossip, Kokochin knew that was how the Order of Assassins operated.

On the seventh day she began to lose hope and dragged her feet. At first her progress had been slow and painful, so that her ankle could recover, but now malaise made her aimlessly wander about.

Gazing around the streets, not really caring where she was going, Kokochin drifted over to a jewellery store. Her silent bodyguard trailed after her, watching the crowd for any danger. As she stared at the ornate necklaces in the window, Kokochin realised her search had been futile. It had been a ridiculous and childish notion.

Something caught her attention, and peering inside the shop she saw the owner wrapping up a package for a customer. At first Kokochin was convinced her eyes were playing tricks on her as she was desperate. But as the woman moved around the shop, Kokochin saw something familiar in the owner's graceful movements. Staring at the woman's face she thought back to that moment seven nights ago when their eyes had met. Startling brown eyes. A heart shaped face and black hair so glossy it was like a wave of silk. It was her. She was certain.

Kokochin pretended to be browsing but actually she was waiting for the customer to leave. Once the shop was empty she went inside, knowing that her bodyguard would stay on the street.

A little bell tinkled above Kokochin's head as she entered the shop and the owner came out to meet her from the back. The woman's smile was welcoming and she showed no signs of recognition.

"Can I help you?" she asked and then gestured at her wares. "Are you searching for something in particular?"

The jewellery on offer was more stylised than what Kokochin had seen in other shops. There was also a lot less gold. The gemstones, in a myriad of colourful hues, were arranged into specific patterns; constellations, the outline of animals and geometric shapes. All of the pieces were loosely connected and spoke to a single mind that had created them.

"Is this your work?" asked Kokochin.

"Yes. All of it," said the woman with pride. "I'm Layla."

"Kokochin. I live at the palace," she said, waiting to see

her reaction, but Layla's expression didn't change. "Is this everything?"

"I have a few pieces that are not quite finished."

"I'd really like to see them," pressed Kokochin, knowing her position would make it hard for Layla to refuse.

"Of course," said Layla, gesturing towards the rear door.

The back room was larger than she'd expected, with a work bench against the left wall and rows of shelves against the other. In the centre was a small furnace and hanging from the ceiling, racks of moulds and heavy tools. Layla picked up a piece from the bench that was still in progress. It was an elegant pendant of a crane with its wings spread in flight.

"You're very talented," said Kokochin. "But surely, you can't spend all your time here."

Layla cocked her head to one side but didn't reply. Her dark eyes watched Kokochin, searching for something. A heavy silence settled in the room but eventually she spoke, breaking the hush. "What are you asking me?"

"I know who you really are. I saw you at the palace."

Layla didn't reply and carefully put down the pendant she was holding. Kokochin had barely blinked when the jeweller was in front of her, a knife in her hand. Before Kokochin could say a word she was flipped upside down. The world tilted and she landed on her back. The air was driven from her lungs and Layla's bodyweight pressed down on her chest, making it difficult to breathe. When the cold steel touched her throat Kokochin froze.

"Why are you here?" asked Layla, in a calm voice.

"I saw you take down six Kheshig," gasped Kokochin, "without any weapons."

"It was eight, but yes," admitted Layla. "You still haven't answered my question. Speak quickly or prepare to meet your god."

"You can't kill me," said Kokochin. "I'm the Khan's wife. If I go missing they will tear the city apart looking for me."

Layla shrugged. "Not if they can't find your body. They'll think you ran off with a handsome stranger. It happens all the time."

"My bodyguard is outside," she said. The jeweller eased back, giving her space to breathe but her blade was still in hand. "Are you an Assassin?" asked Kokochin.

Layla hissed like an angry cat. "I'm not a filthy rat and I do not kill for money."

"Then why do you kill?" asked Kokochin.

"If you were going to turn me in, you would have done it already. So it's something else." Layla leaned closer staring into Kokochin eyes. "Something happened to you."

Layla backed up slowly and hunkered down on the far side of the room. She had her back against a wall and kept one eye on the door. She was in the perfect position to surprise anyone who came in. They wouldn't see her until it was too late.

"I went into the city at night without a bodyguard. I wanted to see what it was really like."

At first Kokochin wasn't sure why she telling her, but the answer was simple. She didn't have any friends. She needed to talk about what had happened without fear of reprisal. So she told Layla about her nightly trips, the wonders she'd seen and being chased and attacked.

"I didn't know what to do. I was powerless, so I ran. I was sure they were going to kill me." The fear was still there, buried deep.

Layla had barely moved, but as Kokochin finished she stood up and stretched her back. "After chasing you for so long, it would have ended badly."

"Teach me," said Kokochin, blurting it out.

"What?"

"Show me how to fight."

Layla shook her head. "You don't know what you're asking."

"Why do you do it?" asked Kokochin, changing her approach. "Is it for the thrill of the hunt? Do you enjoy it?"

Layla didn't react until the last question. "I do not revel in death, nor am I her disciple. I simply do what must be done."

"My family were murdered by Kublai Khan. Then I was trained to serve as a wife to his brother." Kokochin shook her head, full of self-loathing. "I have nothing in my life that is my own."

"You're alone," said Layla.

"Yes, but you also showed me the palace isn't impregnable and that scared me."

"That was never my intention."

"I never want to feel powerless again. I need to take control. Will you teach me?"

"Even if it were possible, how would you explain your presence here?" asked Layla, gesturing at the shop.

"I'm supposed to find something. A skill or craft to occupy my time. Why not making jewellery?" she said with a shrug. "I could be your apprentice."

Layla leaned back against the wall and briefly closed her eyes. "You're asking more than you realise."

"If it's about money—"

"It's not."

"Then what is it?" asked Kokochin.

"It's more than just a way of fighting." Layla's expression was grave. "This will bind us to one another."

Kokochin felt a chill at the words but she shrugged, trying to act nonchalant. "I have nothing else," she said, knowing how sad that sounded.

Layla studied her in silence for a long time.

"Be here early tomorrow morning," said Layla.

"Thank you," said Kokochin.

"But you must come alone. Your bodyguard scares my customers."

It would be difficult, but Kokochin was confident she could find a way. "I'll see you tomorrow."

When she re-emerged onto the street her bodyguard was

still there. He looked bored. For him everything was exactly the same as when she'd gone inside. For Kokochin it felt as if she'd stepped into a new world.

As she walked back to the palace, her mind whirled with possibilities. For the first time since her family's murder, she was in charge of her destiny. Hope blossomed in her chest and looking around at the city, Kokochin thought that perhaps, one day, it could become her home.

CHAPTER 12
Hulagu

Hulagu's army descended upon the city of Baghdad in three columns.

From the north, under the leadership of Berke Khan of the Golden Horde, the army crossed the Tigris River near Mosul. From the west, his old friend General Kitbuqa led warriors into battle. And in the centre, down the banks of the Alwand River, Hulagu led the third column. Arranging the assault had taken a great deal of time but, finally, the day had arrived.

Sixty kilometres from the walls Hulagu's column were attacked by a small army of Muslim foot soldiers, amidst the irrigation fields. The battle was short and bloody, ending in the wholesale slaughter of the enemy.

Hulagu made sure a few were spared and sent back to their masters to spread word of what they had seen. Terror was a powerful weapon that could weaken hearts, erode courage, change stubborn minds and even prevent a battle. When the future was a choice between surrender or death, it was simple.

However, by the time they met up with the other columns no word had been received from Baghdad.

"Nothing?" asked Berke.

"No."

Berke's smile was grim. He did not relish wholesale slaughter like some. Jumghur was practically bouncing in his saddle, delighted at the thought of what lay ahead. Abaqa was less enthusiastic but determined to see it through, which was a good sign. One day he would be ruler of the Ilkhanate and a bloodthirsty nature would not serve anyone well.

Watching everything with great interest was Kaivon, the Persian General. He had acquitted himself well in battle, fighting with skill against the enemy, but Hulagu was not ready to trust him. Either he would prove his loyalty in the days ahead or he would die.

Doquz was keeping a close eye on Kaivon. The Persian General made her uncomfortable but, unlike her sons, she had not voiced her complaint. Instead she'd doubled the number of Kheshig around him, and had personally chosen the two warriors who acted as Kaivon's bodyguards. Hulagu was truly blessed to have such a thoughtful wife.

"Onwards," said Hulagu, urging the army forward. At over a hundred thousand warriors strong, it was the largest he had led into battle. The assembly included warriors from across Mongolia and the Ilkhanate, as well as surrounding vassal states and allies. There were soldiers from Persia, the Golden Horde and Armenian soldiers from the Kingdom of Cilicia, under the leadership of King Hethum. Buqa-Temur had arrived with warriors from the Chagatai Khanate, bringing together forces from three of the four khanates.

King David of Georgia had also insisted on personally taking part in the battle. There was bad blood between his people and the Iraqis for past sins, and he was determined to see that the scales were balanced. Against such a vast horde, Hulagu knew the defenders of Baghdad did not stand a chance.

Despite their slow progress, the walls of the great city came into view. Sitting upon the mighty Tigris River, Hulagu could admit that it was an impressive sight. The crenellated walls extended around the perimeter and, even from a distance, he could see numerous warriors. The city's ruler, the Caliph, had been given sufficient time to ready the city for a siege, but he could not prepare for every eventuality.

A few hours later Hulagu called the army to a halt. In no time his yurt was assembled and the command tent was raised. At midday he gathered together his commanders, while a messenger was sent for the Caliph's answer.

Over the past few weeks his scouts and spies in the city had gathered intelligence. A huge map of the city and surrounding areas was covered with scribbled notes and figures. Several of his spies stood at the edge of the tent, ready to be called upon to explain any details that were not readily understood.

"Where do we start?" asked King David of Georgia.

"We must cut off their access to supplies," said Hulagu, stabbing the map with one meaty finger. The river almost split the city in two, which made it easy to transport goods via the water. "We must block the river upstream with a barrier that's heavily protected to prevent even small boats from slipping through."

Nasir, his chief engineer, lurked at the edge of the gathering. Hulagu gestured for him to approach and his commanders made room around the table. "It can be done with floating pontoons."

"What about downstream?" asked Hulagu, glancing around the table for ideas.

"The current is too strong. They can't bring goods in that way, but they might try to run," said Kaivon, mirroring what Hulagu was thinking. "I would station a large number of cavalry to stop them from escaping."

"I agree," said General Kitbuqa.

They discussed tactics for several hours, firming up what had been sketched out. Some of their plans had to be adjusted, but on the whole they were ready.

As they were finishing up a nervous messenger arrived. Even before he spoke Hulagu knew what the Caliph's response had been. He could have read the message in private but the others needed to hear it, to fire up their blood. As Hulagu read the letter all conversations in the tent dwindled until silence enveloped it.

"The end is known. The city will fall." Hulagu spoke with confidence so that each man would be instilled with the same certainty. "I offered the Caliph a choice and he has refused. Instead of agreeing to peace, he sent insults. This was his decision," he said, staring at Kaivon. "He will receive no mercy. There will be no negotiation from this point forward. Ready your men. We go to war!"

The Generals cheered and Jumghur whooped, his face flushed. Standing out from the crowd, because they were perfectly still, were Abaqa and Kaivon. Both were studying the map, not the men, their attention focused on the details. They were more alike than Hulagu had realised. Perhaps the Persian General could become a mentor to his eldest son, but first he had to prove himself and, in the days ahead, there would be plenty of opportunities.

The next few days were filled with the complex arrangements of establishing the army. A sea of yurts was erected, while the tail end of the supply train finally caught up, bringing with it much needed equipment for the engineers.

The army set up camp on both banks of the Tigris, trapping it in a pincer so that no one could escape. Nasir and a few of his engineers went upstream to erect their floating barrier, while others began to assemble the newly arrived engines of war. The catapults were powerful weapons, but they were also heavy and difficult to transport. The Persian and Chinese engineers worked long into the night, carefully piecing together and testing their weapons for the assault.

The Iraqi people must have wondered why the invaders did not immediately attack. With each passing day their fear would grow. Doubt would flourish and terror would rear its head as they saw the full might of the Mongol forces arrayed against them. Many would begin to question the Caliph's wisdom and might even turn on him, but the time for talk was over. His men wanted a battle to remember and Hulagu intended to deliver.

While all eyes were focused on the siege engines his sappers went unnoticed. Dozens of warriors were ordered to dig trenches close to the city. To keep the enemy looking in the wrong place, Hulagu went to inspect the siege engines. It was early in the afternoon and the sky was clear. He caught the tell tale glint of lenses from those on the wall watching his movements.

Three nights later, on the eve of the attack, Hulagu hosted a feast for his officers. The airag flowed and the tables groaned under the weight of the food. A trio of musicians performed and their voices overlapped to create a sound reminiscent of home.

There was laughter and lots of bragging about the battle, but the jokes were not as raucous when he was nearby, as they feared what he might do if they caused offence. There were few who would talk to him honestly. Hulagu moved through the crowd, laughing and clapping warriors on the shoulder, but he never stayed long. He refilled his plate with meat and bread before returning to his fire where his old friend, General Kitbuqa, waited.

"My Khan," he said, giving a seated bow.

"Eat, be at peace," said Hulagu. They ate in companionable silence for a while, listening to the party around them. "Do you think the Caliph will call for aid from the Mamluks?"

As Muslims, the Egyptian Mamluks were bound by a fellowship of faith, but Hulagu didn't know if that would be enough. His army was vast and the cost of interference would be severe.

Kitbuqa shrugged. "Perhaps. We have scouts keeping watch in the west, but I think it's unlikely."

"Why?"

"They have seen what your army has done. The cities and territory it has taken. God is on our side. If I were in their place, I would be fortifying my own defences, not rushing to help a city that is already lost."

Hulagu grunted. He was about to ask another question when King David of Georgia approached. Although he was a king he waited until Hulagu granted him permission to sit. Georgia had seen the fate of other nations and had wisely agreed to serve. The kingdom was untouched by destruction and the people unscathed. For now, at least. The threat of violence was always there.

"My Khan, I have a request," said David, getting straight to the point.

"This is about Tbilsi," said Hulagu. Decades ago, the Muslim Abbasids in Baghdad had sacked the Georgian capital. The scars were gone but the people, and their ruler, had not forgotten.

"Yes, it is."

"I promise you will have your revenge. The leaders will not be spared."

"Thank you, my Khan," said David, giving him a bow before leaving alone.

A short time later it was Hethum's turn. And so it went. One after another, men came to him with requests. Even Nasir, his chief engineer, was bold enough to seek an audience. Given all that he had done during previous campaigns, Hulagu allowed it and agreed to consider the request.

Kaivon was the only one not to seek him out. Instead Hulagu sent someone to fetch the former General.

"Do you need something, my Khan?"

"I was going to ask you that. You've seen the others," said Hulagu, pretending to grumble about granting favours. More than being a necessary manipulation it was also useful. It told him how each man could be controlled.

Kaivon shook his head. "I don't need anything."

"Are you sure? How about some company in your tent. Girl? Boy?"

"No."

"Ah, you want to pick your own," said Hulagu. "Once we get into the city, you'll have plenty to choose from."

"I did have a question," said Kaivon, changing the subject.

"Speak."

"Where will we go after Baghdad?"

Kitbuqa raised an eyebrow but didn't comment. He'd asked the same question not an hour before. His old friend was always looking ahead to what came next. Most of his commanders were intelligent, but they tended to be shortsighted. Having someone else who focused on the big picture could be useful, especially as they expanded the Ilkhanate.

Hulagu leaned back in his chair. "We will push west into Syria. After that, we will take the Christian Holy Land of Jerusalem."

"God willing," said Kitbuqa, making the sign of the cross on his chest. Sometimes he forgot his old friend was a Christian.

"Then we will head for Egypt and the capital, Cairo. Do you think it's possible?" asked Hulagu, testing him.

"With this army," said Kaivon, gesturing at the sprawling camp. "How could we fail?"

Later that night, Hulagu lay face down on his bed, Doquz astride his back. The scented oils were pleasant, but the way she dug her thumbs into his shoulders was agonising.

"Are you trying to cripple me?" he gasped, feeling as another knot shifted.

Doquz ignored his complaints and kept going. If anything he thought she'd started to press even harder. "You're so tense. You need to relax."

"There is much to do, and many requests I must deal with."

Her fingers began to gently massage his temples and for a time Hulagu dozed. The tension headache that had started to form eased away. Her touch was soothing and he let his mind drift.

"Your lower back still needs work," she said, moving to sit across his hips. After applying fresh oil she began to work her fingers up and down his spine.

Hulagu grunted in discomfort but didn't complain. "Tonight, even Nasir asked me for a favour."

"What did he want?" asked Doquz.

"The central library in Baghdad has thousands of books and scrolls, some of them about advanced weapons. He thinks it's possible to develop more powerful engines."

"It's a reasonable request and the end result would be of benefit," said Doquz. Her fingers found a sore spot and Hulagu hissed in pain. She kissed his cheek and whispered in his ear while her hands kept working.

"All of them will become loyal. Everyone wants something, except for Kaivon." Doquz's hands stopped moving for a moment.

"I don't trust him," she said. "And neither should you."

"He reminds me of Kitbuqa and, at times, Abaqa."

"Don't make the mistake of believing that fear is the same as loyalty."

"I don't trust him. Not yet."

"That's good," said Doquz.

A pleasant silence filled the yurt. Hulagu's mind wandered before it latched onto something unpleasant he'd seen earlier.

"You're tensing up again. What is it?" she asked.

"I saw him today in the trenches." Temujin. He'd assigned him to a unit and made sure the officer in charge understood that Temujin was to receive no special privileges.

By chance, his unit had been given one of the most tiring jobs. Digging trenches for the sappers. The final part of their job was tricky, but the bulk of it required a lot of manual labour.

The warriors didn't complain because they understood the importance of the task. He doubted Temujin had such awareness.

"You can't be distracted by him. Not now," said Doquz.

"You're right." Tomorrow was the first day of what would be a lengthy siege. The blockades on the river were in place. No one was getting out of the city without him noticing. There was no escape for the city's inhabitants.

"Turn over," said Doquz and he complied, rolling onto his back. Standing over him she continued to massage his shoulder and chest, easing the muscles. It was unlikely he would actually wield a sword tomorrow, but he needed to be ready, just in case. The moment would come.

"Husband, I have a request," said Doquz. Her roaming hands moved lower, down to his stomach. "It's important to me."

"Hmm, I wondered." Kitbuqa had been hinting at something, but he'd not asked. Hulagu had suspected he would leave it up to Doquz. "What is it?"

"There are some ancient churches in the city. Could you spare them from being destroyed?"

"We will be bombarding the city. I cannot tell my engineers to avoid them."

"I'm not asking for that," said Doquz, her hands questing lower. "Once the city is yours, I merely ask to you to spare them from further destruction."

"As you wish," he said.

Doquz smiled and he felt himself stiffen at her caress. "Yes, but also for the future. Once the city is yours, and you move west, you will need allies to take the Holy Land."

Hulagu scoffed. "The Pope and his Crusaders have promised much, but have yet to deliver."

"Once they see the might of your army and they understand your relentless power," she said, gripping him tightly enough to make him wince. "They will come, or they will lose out, and the glory will be yours alone. Send new messages to Paris and Rome."

Her reasoning was sound, even if she wasn't doing it for wholly unselfish reasons.

"You ask for a great deal," said Hulagu as his breathing began to quicken.

"I'm sure I can find a way to persuade you," said Doquz, slipping out of her robe. She guided him into her and he sighed with pleasure. As she began to ride him, he seized her hips and rose to meet her with every thrust. As much as he'd enjoyed a massage, she knew the best way to help him relax before a battle. Tomorrow would be the start of something glorious, but tonight was all about pleasure.

CHAPTER 13
The Twelve

Two waited until the woman had finished eating her evening meal before she knocked on the front door. After all, everyone was entitled to a last meal.

The woman, tall and slender like a willow, cautiously peered out through a gap. "Yes?"

"Darya, I'm here with news about your husband."

"Oh please, come in," she said, and then gestured for Two to enter while she peered up and down the street. Two limped inside and briefly glanced around the small and immaculate home. There wasn't a speck of dust. Everything was incredibly neat, from the jars of spices with the labels facing out in a uniform row, to the plates and bowls. The only mess was the pan she'd used for cooking, and a plate with a few crumbs.

"Please," said Darya, gesturing towards the main room. "I'll make tea."

Two made herself comfortable on a padded chair, shifting about the collection of tasselled cushions. There was an odd painting on the far wall that looked faded. She could make out a few blocky shapes, something blue and green, but had no idea what it was supposed to be. It was the only peculiarity in an otherwise orderly home.

As the host, Darya poured tea into two glasses and pushed a

plate of honey cakes across the table. "Help yourself," she said, with a faint smile.

"What is that?" Two said, gesturing at the painting.

"Oh, it was something of an experiment," said Darya. "It's supposed to represent controlled chaos."

"What does that mean?"

Darya waved it away. "It was nonsense. A childish fancy. You can't control chaos. I keep it as a reminder."

"Your home is very tidy," noted Two, sipping her tea.

Darya beamed but then her proud smile faded. "You have news?"

"Yes, it's about Reza. Unfortunately, he's dead."

"What? How?" gasped Darya, her hand shaking so badly her glass rattled against the saucer.

"His body was found in a canal by a local fisherman. It must have been there for a few days. It was very bloated and had been nibbled on."

Silence filled the room. Darya stared out the window into the darkness. Her eyes were wet with tears and Two could see her throat moving as she swallowed tears.

"Do you know who did it?" she asked in a hoarse whisper.

"We have a few suspects, but the more important question is why." Two helped herself to a cake and took her time, chewing it before sipping more tea. "He was a miller, yes?"

"Yes. He supplied several of the local bakeries," said Darya, her hand fluttering in a vague gesture.

"That must have been nice."

"Nice?" said Darya, and a crack appeared in her grief.

"To have him come home smelling of fresh bread."

"Oh, yes." She was distracted, which was to be expected.

"Did he ever track flour into the house?"

"Once or twice." Darya's right eyelid twitched.

"That must have been annoying, especially in such a neat home."

"Who did you say you worked for?" asked Darya.

"I didn't. I just told you I had news and you invited me into your home."

"Who are you?" said Darya, suddenly wary.

Two finished her tea and set down her glass. "Delicious, thank you."

"You should leave."

"I tried to work out what he might have done that was so horrible. All of his friends spoke well of him. I visited a dozen bakeries, and no one had a bad word to say. Reza was friendly, kind, and generous to his customers. Everyone loved him. How could a man like that have enemies?"

"Get out of my home," said Darya, pointing at the door.

"And then I realised, it wasn't a stranger. It was you," said Two. Darya lowered her arm and sat perfectly still. "Most people would be desperate for information, but you made tea first, because you already knew what had happened. You poisoned him and then dumped his body. I was going to ask why, but looking at your home, I think it's obvious."

"You have no idea what kind of a monster he was," said Darya. "Bringing flour into the house, day after day, month after month. I'd get it clean and then it would be back. Another cloud of white. Inside a cup. Inside a locked cupboard. On the bed. On my clothes, even in my make-up. I couldn't bear it. Not for one more day."

"I'm going to share a secret with you," said Two. "Over the years I've killed a lot of people but, without a doubt, you are the craziest one I've ever met."

Darya smiled and then laughed, her voice echoing off the sparse walls. "Then let me share a secret in return. I knew why you were here, so I put some poison in your tea. Very soon you'll start to feel the effects. A tightness in your chest and then you'll fall asleep. You'll be dead in an hour."

Two stared at her empty glass then back at Darya. "This is a surprise."

"You really are quite stupid," said Darya with a smile, but

then it faded. She coughed, cleared her throat and put a hand against her chest.

"Oh. I forgot to mention. I switched our glasses," said Two. "When I saw there were no wounds on his body, I knew it was poison."

The colour drained from Darya's face. She tried to stand up but the strength had gone from her legs. She flopped onto the floor, sending her glass flying. Her eyes were still open but she couldn't speak. Both of her hands were pressed against her chest.

Two sat in contemplative silence, drinking her tea and nibbling on the cakes until they were gone. When she had finished eating, Darya was dead.

An hour later, Two was sitting in her kitchen when there was a knock at the door. She picked up a knife from the counter and moved to the window. Seeing Layla alone in the street, she opened the door.

"What are you doing here?"

"I needed to speak with you. It's urgent." Layla was flustered, which was a surprise.

"Sit. Tell me what's happened."

Instead Layla paced back and forth, trying to find the words. Two sat down, knowing this could take a while.

"I've done something reckless."

Two sat back in her chair but kept the knife within reach. "Go on."

"I've started training someone. She's young and naïve, but could be extremely useful. She's well-connected and the Mongols have taken everything from her."

"It sounds like she could be useful."

"That's my point," said Layla, finally stopping her back and forth. "If we could harness that rage, I think it's worth the risk."

A cold prickle ran down Two's spine. "What aren't you telling me?"

"She's connected to some of the most powerful people in the Ilkhanate."

"Layla…"

"We'd have unprecedented access to vital information."

"Who is she?"

Layla took a deep breath and sat down, placing a hand over the knife. "Her name is Kokochin. She's the Khan's new wife."

Two rocked back in her chair and would have toppled over if Layla hadn't caught her. "Do you have any idea what you've done?"

"She's an innocent young woman."

"She's a Mongol," spat Two. "Her kind murdered thousands of our people!"

"She hasn't killed anyone. She's alone, in a foreign country, with no friends and no family. Most of the time her husband will be away at war. She's bored and lonely. She needs friends and focus."

"How did this happen?"

"She saw me as I was leaving the palace. She sought me out and I had to make a decision."

Two felt sweat trickling down her neck and tasted bile in the back of her throat. "I should kill her, and you."

"That would cause a ripple and I know you don't like them," said Layla with a smile.

One or two could be ignored. More than that and someone might notice a pattern. The House had not remained secret for so long by rushing into decisions.

"What about the Inner Circle?"

"What about them?" asked Two.

"Will you tell your superior about this?"

As far as Layla, and everyone else in Two's network knew, she reported to someone in the Inner Circle. It was safer that way.

"I think we should keep this to ourselves. If it becomes necessary, then I'll talk to someone."

"Thank you," said Layla.

"Don't thank me. If she becomes a liability you may have to kill her."

There would be reprisals for killing the Khan's wife, but at least the House would be safe. She hoped that Layla understood it wasn't just Kokochin's life hanging in the balance.

"I can do this," said Layla.

"I really hope so," said Two, glancing at the knife.

CHAPTER 14
Temujin

For over a week the only thing Temujin had done was dig, eat and sleep. Even in his dreams he was in a ditch, ankle deep in water, straining tired muscles to their breaking point.

At first, his days had been consumed with erecting a defensive earthen wall, so that if the enemy sallied out of the city, the camp was defensible. Then his time had been filled with cutting wooden stakes to build a palisade. It had been a brief change, but not a respite as the work has been as tough. Once that was done he'd gone back to digging, this time under the supervision of the Khan's sappers. To make matters worse, for part of it they had been close to the city wall, leaving them susceptible to enemy archers. Thankfully, the defenders were distracted by the vast catapults that began to dominate the sky. His unit's work mostly went unnoticed, for which he was grateful. They were up to their shoulders in mud with no way to defend themselves. It would have been a bloodbath.

Temujin had tried to stay positive but his optimism had quickly been eroded by the mind-numbing, back-breaking work. After that, he tried to come up with a list of things for which he was grateful. The difficulty was that every night when he lay down to sleep, weary to the bone, he didn't have the energy. However, when he woke up on the seventh morning, he realised he had his list.

Food. He was grateful for food. It was the only thing that kept him going. It wasn't what he was used to eating, but it gave him enough energy to make it through the day. Although he ate exactly the same as everyone else in his unit, they still made jokes about his weight, or called him Round Eye, but it was in good humour. He was with them from the moment they jumped into the trench until the end of the day. There were countless times when he wanted to quit or complain, but no one else complained about the conditions so neither could he. It was probably his silence that eventually earned their respect.

His unit. He was grateful for them and even his superior officer, Captain Ganbold. He was tough but fair. Temujin received no special treatment but also no extra duties because of who he was.

His bed. Dry boots. A warm blanket. These were the things that actually mattered. Beyond that he was glad for his health. Every day he was getting stronger.

Far from the palace and the cities he'd lived in, Temujin's life had become simpler. And for the first time in years, he felt a sense of freedom. Among the men his name and status meant nothing.

"What are you smiling about?" asked Arban, one of the men in his unit.

"Nothing."

"He's thinking of all the concubines he's bedded," said Batu, on the other side of him. He had a dirty mind and often told dubious stories about his sexual exploits. "Have you ever been with a French woman? I hear they're very good with their tongues."

"He was thinking about his next meal," said Hexa, jabbing a finger at Temujin's side. Hexa was big, loud and stupid, but he was also very strong. His spade dug deep into the earth and he worked tirelessly. Temujin said nothing and focused only on the next cut. The next shovel full of earth. The chatter of the men faded away with the rest of the world. If there were any more jibes he didn't hear them.

"Stop!" shouted Ganbold, his voice loud enough to penetrate the fog in Temujin's mind. "Take a short rest."

Looking up Temujin saw how much progress they'd made. They were almost done. One of the Persian engineers and two sappers were walking along the top of the trench. They were deep in conversation and Temujin barely understood what they were saying. The trenches were not particularly close to the city, so they weren't designed to destroy the walls. They were not deep and no support beams had been used. They were wide at eight paces, but no one had told them why. When he'd asked a few men in his unit they'd simply shrugged. Most didn't care. They just wanted the job done, so they could get back to the real battle. They wanted to plunder the city. Several had already spent the money they expected to receive.

Ganbold conferred with the sappers and then approached his men. "Everyone out. We're done. Return your tools to the quartermaster."

"What's happening, sir?" asked Temujin.

Ganbold glanced at the sappers and shook his head, unwilling or unable to tell them what was going on. The others didn't notice that he was worried about something.

"Be ready," was all Ganbold said. "Gather your armour and weapons," he yelled as everyone scrambled up the muddy bank. Even with a wooden board at an angle, it was a precarious balancing exercise. A couple of men tumbled off their boards and people jeered when they resurfaced, covered head to toe in mud. Temujin held his breath as he walked up the board and when he reached the top Hexa spat at his feet.

"You just lost me a bet," he said, passing some coins to a smug man beside him. "I was certain you'd fall off."

Temujin didn't acknowledge him as he walked away.

Back in the tent he shared with five others, he stripped out of his muddy wet clothes. His other set was dry and, although spattered with mud, most of it came off when he shook them. Dressed once more in leather armour, with a sword around his waist, he felt uneasy. This was the part he enjoyed the least about being in the Khan's army.

An hour later Temujin and the rest of his unit were summoned. He returned to the trenches but, by the time they arrived, something had changed. The bottom of the trench had been littered with hundreds of boot prints. Now they had been erased and the mud swirled around, as if to conceal something.

Feeling a prickle of unease, Temujin thought someone was watching him. He turned this way and that, searching for the observer. Eventually he looked up and saw dozens of archers staring down from the city walls.

Trying not to draw attention to himself, Temujin walked at a leisurely pace until he was standing beside Captain Ganbold. He was frowning at the back of the two sappers.

"Sir, we're being watched."

Ganbold slowly raised his eyes. "Fall back," he shouted.

Temujin didn't think they were in range of the archers, but better safe than sorry.

Behind the walls of Baghdad, Temujin heard a deep grinding sound. The city gates began to open.

"Riders! Riders!" someone shouted.

In response the Mongol cavalry began to amass. Hundreds and then thousands of riders readied themselves for the first battle. Temujin had expected panic or chaos in the camp, but there was none. The organisation in the camp was remarkable. His father had planned for this.

He wondered if digging the trench had been nothing more than a pointless exercise designed to draw out the enemy. Whether the work had been genuine or not, Temujin knew the risk to his life would not have concerned the Khan. Taking the city was all that mattered.

A gap appeared between the gates and beyond Temujin could see hundreds of warriors on horseback, ready to ride out. But this was where the Mongols ruled. From the beginning, on the steppes of Mongolia, they learned to ride and fight on horseback. It was deeply engrained in their blood and bones.

Temujin watched the stationary line of Mongol riders without envy, but he wasn't allowed to go far. Once the cavalry had charged they were expected to follow and engage the enemy on foot. His hands were sweaty, his heart raced and he desperately needed a piss. Maybe there was still time to go. Several men had the same idea, relieving themselves where they were. He couldn't. His hands were shaking too badly and Temujin didn't want to end up with piss all over his clothes.

In the distance he saw dozens of men run out of the gates, carrying a temporary bridge which they used to ford the trench. Layer upon layer of roughly-cut tree trunks, lashed together into rafts, were dropped on top of one another until there was a solid crossing, strong enough to sustain the weight of many riders. The men quickly scrambled out of the way and a moment later the city's cavalry rode out to meet the Mongol army.

The ground began to shake as if there were an earthquake. Temujin stumbled a couple of steps before righting himself. A war cry went up from the mouth of one Mongol warrior and it was repeated, echoing up and down the line until it vibrated deep in his chest.

And then the Mongol cavalry charged. Thousands of riders hurtled towards the enemy. A deadly, screaming, thrashing wave of horse flesh, armour and swords, glinting in the sunlight.

"Steady," said Ganbold, somewhere to his left. He sounded nervous but maybe he was excited. It was hard to tell as Temujin was terrified. "Forward, slow walk," said Ganbold, leading his unit. On either side of Temujin officers repeated the same order. Several thousand warriors on foot trailed after the riders, giving them plenty of space.

The two mounted forces drew near and Temujin braced himself for what was to come. His teeth rattled together. His bladder felt tight. He should have relieved himself when he had the chance.

Even though he was quite far back, the moment of impact made him stagger. Tremors ran through the earth. Many warriors fell or tripped while others wobbled on their feet.

The sound was unlike anything he'd ever heard in his life. Thousands of men and horses slamming together in a cacophony of screeching metal and cries of pain. The horizon was full of thrashing bodies, riders moving this way and that, sprays of blood and riderless horses aimlessly wandering about.

The order was given to pick up the pace. Temujin and the others began to jog forward. With every step the volume of battle significantly increased. The ringing of steel thrummed in his temples. Hundreds of horses were whinnying, many on the ground with thrashing limbs kicking at the air. Temujin saw a horse rear in fright, its rider dead on the ground. Its front legs caved in a man's skull and he fell over dead.

They outnumbered the Iraqi cavalry many times. Even before the riders came within range he saw dozens cut down, maimed and kicked from the saddle where they were trampled to death or slashed open by Mongol blades.

And in the heart of the battle, surrounded by generals, royal allies and two of his sons, was Temujin's father, Hulagu Khan. Astride a horse it was easy to pick him out from the crowd as he towered over everyone else. His sword rose and fell, slicing open bodies, lopping off heads and limbs. Pleas for mercy went unanswered. The injured and maimed were forgotten. Trampled into the mud. Ground underfoot by boots and hooves. Left to die or fend for themselves. A few attempted to escape by crawling away but there was nowhere to go. No one made it to safety.

Howling like a madman Jumghur lay into the enemy with his mace, smashing the skulls of anyone who came too close. A dazed Mongol rider, knocked from his horse, wandered past and was beaten down with the rest. In the heat of the battle no one saw that Jumghur had killed another Mongol. The pain he caused spurred him on to inflict greater misery.

The two lines had broken apart and the coordinated battle had become a thousand skirmishes. There was little room to manoeuvre on horseback and no space to charge. Riders walked their mounts forward with their knees while they swung at each other, trying to avoid trampling their own men. Many had been knocked to the ground and dozens of horses ran past Temujin, desperate to escape the chaos. The Mongol army would kill every Iraqi rider but they would never, knowingly, hurt one of the animals. Horses were cherished and it was upon their backs that the Empire had grown.

Temujin stepped to one side, creating an opening large enough for three horses to trot past, their flanks heaving and their noses spattered with blood. Once they were gone he moved back into position.

The battle was not done, but even he could see the defenders had already lost. For every Mongol they managed to kill, ten or eleven of their warriors were cut down. But the chance to retreat had been taken away from them.

The trenches that Temujin and the others had spent days digging had been flooded. Parts of the Tigris River had been diverted, creating a swampy quagmire that could not be jumped and the horses would be reluctant to swim. The temporary bridge they'd built had been destroyed, the wooden pieces swept away or broken apart with axes. In addition the city gates were closing. The Caliph had fallen into the Khan's trap and had decided to sacrifice the men outside to protect those who remained inside the walls.

While the outcome was inevitable, the danger wasn't over as Temujin finally reached the front line of the battle.

A horse slammed into his shoulder hard enough to numb his arm. He managed to hang on to his sword even though he couldn't feel his fingers. A moment later an Iraqi warrior appeared directly in front of him. Other members of Temujin's unit were nearby, but he knew that in such a fractured battle he was on his own.

The Iraqi was blood spattered and his left arm dangled at his side, but he was snarling like a dog. Temujin lashed out, moving on instinct, swinging at the man's head. The warrior stepped to one side and made a clumsy overhand riposte. Their swords scraped together and the sound of screeching metal tore at Temujin's ears. His opponent was injured but not out of the fight. They grappled and shoved, trying to trip or unbalance the other. For once, Temujin's weight acted in his favour as he became an immovable object. No matter how hard his opponent shoved, he didn't budge. With a snarl of his own, Temujin slammed his fist into his enemy's injured arm. The man reared back in pain and Temujin tried to run him through but he twisted aside.

As fear mixed with adrenaline, he felt heat rising up from somewhere deep in his chest. He remembered burning the rebel in the census office and the smell of cooking meat. The memory made him gag, the hidden fire vanished and Temujin tried not to panic as the Iraqi soldier came towards him again. Their swords clashed together. The metal screeched and then the Iraqi's blade shattered like glass.

Instead of trying to escape, the man tried to rip Temujin's sword away and they wrestled for control. Spitting and swearing the soldier tried to bite him. As the man's hot breath drew closer to his neck Temujin screamed and slashed wildly at his opponent.

A torrent of blood gushed down the man's leg from his groin. He tried to speak but didn't have any breath. With a final gurgle he toppled backwards into the mud. Temujin stared at the blood on his sword with a mix of horror and shame.

Someone clipped him from behind. This time Temujin dropped his weapon and fell forward onto his knees. A dead body fell onto the ground beside him, his throat ripped open, eyes staring. A horse screamed on his left making his ears ring. A heavy thump behind announced another body landing. A hand grasped at his ankle and he instinctively kicked out, shaking them off. Something nudged Temujin in the ribs so hard he was certain something had cracked.

As he searched for his blade in the muck, a horse nearly stepped on his hands. Scrambling backwards he banged into something and turning around saw it was another enemy warrior. Only this one was not injured. He sneered at Temujin and raised his sword for a killing blow.

Just before the blade came down a shadow fell over him. A second later his head exploded in a shower of gore from Jumghur's mace. Temujin was sprayed with blood and bits of brains. He spat and wiped the worst from his face, but he couldn't dislodge the taste.

"Get up! Fight!" shouted Jumghur. He moved off in search of another victim and Temujin continued raking the mud for his weapon.

"What are you doing on your hands and knees?" said a familiar voice.

"Trying to find my sword," said Temujin.

"Here, use this," said Abaqa, throwing a sword down beside him. "Get out of the mud."

With a sigh Temujin picked up the borrowed weapon. When he turned around to thank his brother, he was rewarded with another spray of blood. Abaqa had stabbed a man through the throat to save his life. That was twice he'd been saved by his brothers.

Temujin knew word of what had happened would get back to their father. It would be yet another embarrassing anecdote to add to the list.

It shouldn't matter, but he still wanted his father's approval.

Annoyed at himself, he waded back into the battle, using anger to fuel his limbs. A furious melee had developed where dozens of warriors on either side were caught up in a fight. Most of them were up to their knees in churned mud, making it difficult for anyone to move quickly. Not far away he spotted one of his unit struggling against a tall warrior. Screaming in rage, Temujin slashed at the enemy, catching him across the face. The Iraqi screeched, pressing a hand to his bloody cheek. He grunted a second later as Arban stabbed him in the stomach.

"Thank you," he gasped, leaning on his sword to stay upright. Working together they fought as one against the remaining enemy soldiers. On his left, Temujin spotted his father battling with an Iraqi officer. His armour was considerably better than those around him and his skill was apparent, so much so that he managed to unhorse the Khan. Instead of staying in the saddle, and using the higher ground to his advantage, the officer slid from his horse to finish off Hulagu. His generals, allies and bodyguards were elsewhere, engaged in battles of their own. The Khan was on his own and struggling to climb back to his feet. The weight of his armour and the uneven ground made it difficult.

Before the officer had a chance to kill Hulagu, a thunder of hooves filled the air. A Persian warrior launched himself from the saddle, colliding with the Iraqi officer. They went down in a tangled knot of limbs, clawing at one another. Both of them were snarling and biting, then fighting over a dagger. The Persian warrior slammed his elbow into the side of the officer's throat which made him gag. Using his bodyweight, the Persian warrior drove the dagger into the Iraqi's chest up to the hilt. Blood fountained from the officer's mouth and he choked to death on his own blood. Offering a hand, the Persian warrior pulled Hulagu to his feet. With barely a nod of thanks, the Khan waded back into the battle, as if he hadn't been a heartbeat away from death.

Several defenders attempted to escape, throwing down their weapons and pulling off armour, in the hope of being able to swim across the muddy inlet. Many drowned, dragged down by the mud, but a few made it across, only to find the gates sealed. The water turned from a muddy brown to a dark red from the blood flowing into it. Dozens of bodies floated on the surface. The stench of death filled Temujin's nose. Overhead the carrion birds had gathered, ready for their grisly feast.

Soon, only a handful of enemy warriors remained, and none of them were willing to surrender. Perhaps they understood no mercy would be granted and it was better to die on their feet than on their knees.

Archers were called forward and those hoping to get back into the city were cut down. Every single one of them was killed until only one defender remained.

Hulagu Khan stood behind the kneeling man, facing the city where grim-faced defenders lined the walls. A terrible hush swept the battlefield, moving among the men, like a living thing until it had engulfed them all. The joking and laughing stopped. All conversations stopped. Even the cries of pain from the injured became muffled and distant. The ringing in Temujin's ears faded until all eyes were focused on his father.

Holding a dagger in one hand Hulagu raised it above his head and then waited, extending the agony of the final man. With a grunt of effort he jabbed the dagger into the top of the man's skull.

The warrior didn't die straight away. He wheezed and choked, sputtered and burbled like a child learning their words. His fingers clawed at the air, searching for purchase. Hulagu held him up by the collar, unwilling to let him topple forward, so that all of those on the walls could see the man's suffering. The awful noises seemed to go forever, but in reality only lasted a few seconds. Finally, the warrior fell silent and the Khan let him drop to the muddy field.

"Look at what your Caliph has done!" shouted Hulagu,

his voice carrying across the battlefield. "Look at what his arrogance has cost your people."

Spread out, in all directions from the Khan, lay the bodies of the city's fallen. Looking at the sky, Temujin realised that in less than an hour, thousands of men had been killed.

"I offered him a peaceful solution and he threw it away." Hulagu sounded genuinely angry, as if the death of so many had personally injured him. It was nothing more than a performance for the crowd. "Tonight, when your homes are empty, when your fathers and sons rot in the mud, remember who is responsible."

On the city walls a figure pushed their way to the front, a tall handsome man with a flowing beard who had to be the Caliph. "You would have killed us all!" he shouted.

"I am not talking to you," said Hulagu. "I am speaking to your generals and officers, those who possess some intelligence, for it is clear that you have none."

"You filthy liar–" said the Caliph, but Hulagu spoke over him. The Khan's powerful voice silenced the other.

"He has no voice in this final decision. Make no mistake, after this moment, there will be nothing but carnage and death. Open the gates, spare your people, and we can end this today. Test me and everyone in Baghdad will suffer. I will raze the city to the ground and burn it to ash. Your city will die."

Hulagu's voice echoed over and over, bouncing off the stones. It was not an idle threat. He had done it before. The Caliph had gambled and now all of his cavalry were dead. Thousands of warriors were gone, while the Mongol army was barely bloodied. Temujin had seen the engines of war and knew of their power. The end was inevitable.

"Throw him from the walls and end this." Hulagu said, studying the faces of the men on the battlements.

Temujin waited, hoping for some movement. A frantic struggle as the Caliph pleaded with his own men, but no one moved.

Hulagu gave them a little longer and when nothing happened he smiled, pleased at the city's defiance. If they surrendered, his father would have accepted it, but this was what he wanted. To break their spirits, and give his men a battle that would be remembered for a long time for its savagery. Family, wealth, even being the Khan. None of it was what his father truly desired, or cherished. He was never more alive than when he was murdering others in battle. It nourished him like nothing else.

Staring at the city, Temujin felt pity for the people trapped inside and what was to come.

CHAPTER 15
Kaivon

After the battle, Kaivon had a few hours to rest before he was due to meet with the Khan and his advisors.

After cleaning his sword and armour, and then scrubbing his skin, he tried to sleep. Despite the luxury of his own yurt and a soft bed, he couldn't get comfortable. His mind whirled with images, and he ran through scenarios where he hadn't saved Hulagu's life during the battle.

Letting the Khan die would have changed little, but that didn't stop him from feeling guilty, especially after seeing so many friends die during the invasion. After an hour of tossing and turning, Kaivon realised he'd made the right decision. Saving Hulagu would also stand him in good stead for the future. He needed to earn the Khan's trust, and those closest to him, if he was to be given any real power and responsibility.

Even now he could see the shadow of two men standing guard outside his tent. When he was no longer followed, day and night, Kaivon would know the situation had changed. Without trust it would be impossible for him to undermine the Khan. At the moment Kaivon's life was completely at the whim of a murderous maniac.

Shaking off his melancholy he stepped out of his yurt and came face to face with Abaqa, the Khan's first son and heir.

"I saw you, during the battle," said Abaqa. It sounded like an accusation.

Kaivon glanced past Abaqa's shoulder, but thankfully he was without his idiot brother. "What of it?"

"You fought well."

"Thank you, Prince Abaqa."

"But I still don't trust you. Before you charged at the enemy, you hesitated."

"You're mistaken," said Kaivon, staring him straight in the eye.

"One day you'll step out of line," said the Prince, "and when that happens, I'll give you to my brother, Jumghur."

Without waiting for permission Kaivon stepped around Abaqa and went directly to the command tent.

Many of the Khan's senior figures had already gathered but there was no sign of Hulagu himself. Kaivon exchanged nods with Berke Khan and King David of Georgia. Both had fought well during the battle, although the King's zeal had rivalled Jumghur's. Perhaps he also had something to prove to the Khan.

Hulagu entered the tent and went directly to the map at the centre. They all gathered around and Kaivon was pleased when the others made space for him. The story of how he had saved the Khan's life must have spread throughout the camp. Abaqa might not trust him yet but his efforts in battle had not gone unnoticed. Kaivon was pleased when General Kitbuqa favoured him with a smile.

"How long before the catapults are ready?" asked Hulagu, looking at Nasir.

The engineer grinned. "We can begin the bombardment immediately. Just give the order, Lord Khan."

It was late in the afternoon. The men would not attack the wall today, but it was possible the battery could start. Raining fire and boulders on the inhabitants throughout the night would leave them fragile and disheartened come first light. It was the same tactic Hulagu had used against Persia. As the remembered screams of his people filled his ears, Kaivon focused on staying calm and breathing slowly.

"Start at first light," said Hulagu, which came as a surprise. "How long do you think it will take to breach the walls?"

Nasir's smile faded. "I won't know how well the walls are built until we see how much damage they can endure. After an hour's barrage I will have a better idea."

"Give me your best guess," said the Khan.

"Four days," said Nasir. "Six at most."

Hulagu grunted, giving nothing away. A messenger arrived and immediately held out a note towards the Khan. He moved to the other side of the tent to read it in private but quickly returned to the table.

"Nasir, make your preparations for the morning."

"Yes, my Khan."

When the engineer was gone Hulagu glanced around the table at those assembled. "Before I left Tabriz, I asked my brother, the Great Khan, for some black powder. Sadly he cannot send any to aid us. He's having problems with the Song dynasty and now Ariq is contesting the results of the kurultai."

An awkward silence filled the tent. No one was really sure how to respond to the news. Hulagu stared at the map without really seeing it. Eventually the hush was broken by General Kitbuqa, clearing his throat.

"Then we will take the walls in the traditional way, my Khan. As we have done, many times before."

"Yes we will, old friend," said Hulagu, coming out of his reverie. "With a hundred thousand men at my back, the city will be mine."

His words sounded final and Kaivon knew they spelled death for many of Baghdad's inhabitants.

* * *

Kaivon watched with a mix of terror and excitement as the catapults began their assault. The monstrous arms hurled forward and six massive boulders were flung through the air at the city's walls. All six hit, four of them striking the outer wall while two went over, causing destruction within. He was too far away to hear the screams but Kaivon knew there would be some as buildings collapsed and tonnes of rubble came down.

The arms of the catapults were slowly pulled back, minute adjustments made to their trajectories, and then they fired again. The sheer power of the weapons was immense and yet the city's walls stood. One boulder had struck the top of the outer wall, shearing off the battlements. Kaivon watched as men were killed in an instant while others were hurled into the air like toys. More tumbled down the wall, falling to their deaths outside the city. And yet the wall was unbroken.

Nasir and the other engineers weren't discouraged. Staring at the city through a telescope the engineer and his colleagues talked among themselves then ordered the next load. He'd estimated four to six days before the wall broke. Kaivon wondered if the city would make it to the end of the night before relenting.

Slowly, the silhouette of several siege towers came into view. The sappers had been kept busy, sending the Tigris River back on its normal course. The trench had been drained and now several sturdy bridges had been built across the muddy remains. The tall wooden towers were doused with chemicals and the door at the top covered with a heavy layer of material. The stench was vile and it would be difficult to breathe when inside, but the alternative was being burned alive.

By absorbing many nations and their armies, the Mongols had learned a great deal about war. It was one of the things that made them unstoppable.

As Kaivon stared at the city a disturbance drew his attention. Hulagu moved through the assembled men, smiling and offering encouragement without ever stopping. Warriors stood taller when he approached and their fear melted away in his presence.

Another boulder struck the wall where the battlements were already damaged. Even at this distance Kaivon felt the impact in his bones.

"Are you ready?" asked the Khan, stepping up beside Kaivon to survey the city.

It had been decided that Kaivon would lead a unit of one hundred men into battle. "Yes, my Khan."

"Prove that you are loyal." Hulagu's good mood had evaporated. It had been nothing more than a show for the other warriors. Kaivon found himself staring at the face of a conqueror who had destroyed nations. "Convince me that you're worthy of a place at my side."

Before Kaivon could reply Hulagu had turned away. General Kitbuqa gave him a tight smile and made the sign of the cross on his chest before following the Khan.

Once the towers were in place, the battle would begin.

A heavy thumping announced another barrage from the catapults and a second later a shadow passed overhead. A boulder the size of a horse flew through the air like a pebble being skimmed across the surface of a lake. It hammered into the wall with bone-crunching force. The impact sent men tumbling from the battlements. Flaming stones, doused with naphtha, flew into the city. In half a dozen places smoke began to rise as buildings caught fire.

The trajectory of the catapults had been adjusted. At least Kaivon wouldn't have to worry about being crushed. Of course he still worried about being stabbed to death by the defenders.

As the siege towers came close to their destination, pushed by teams of oxen and men, the archers loosed their deadly rain upon the defenders. A second volley followed and then a third as hundreds of arrows arched overhead. Many defenders were killed or maimed but others took their place, holding fast against the invaders. Kaivon pitied them. He knew what they were going through and they were as powerless as his people had been during the invasion of Persia.

"Forward!" came the order. Kaivon drew his sword and led his men towards the nearest tower. Holding his shield firmly against his shoulder, Kaivon peered over the rim as he jogged forward. He kept one eye on the tower and the other on the defenders. He'd barely counted to ten in his head when he saw dozens of bows poke over the battlements.

"Cover!" he bellowed, crouching down between two of his men, their shields overlapping. The temporary barrier wasn't impenetrable and several men screeched in pain as arrows found their mark, going through legs, arms, shoulders and heads. The man on his left grunted as an arrow bounced off his shield. On his right the arrowhead had punched through the wood, bringing the point within a hair's breadth of the warrior's eye. Much to Kaivon's surprise the man laughed, delighted at his close call with death.

"Forward," shouted Kaivon, getting to his feet. He risked a glance over his shield and quickly ducked back as more arrows fell. A few more of his men were killed or injured but soon enough, he was standing in the shadow of the tower. Those who had fallen were left to fend for themselves. Going back for them would be a death sentence. The injured were crawling for cover, but he knew few would make it.

Once Kaivon was inside the tower, with men behind him and in front, he found it difficult to breathe. There wasn't much light as the front was covered and, with so many bodies pressed together, he couldn't see the door below. Kaivon had no choice but to shuffle up the steps. He was desperate to escape what felt like a death trap.

The stench of the chemicals filled his nose, overwhelming the smell of leather, steel and mud. The tower magnified sounds, and outside he heard cries of pain as more archers found their targets. He caught a whiff of smoke and heard the thud as flaming arrows struck the outside of the structure.

With enough arrows it was possible the towers would catch fire, but not yet. At least, that was what he hoped.

Kaivon was three rows back from the front when the door was thrown open. Light flooded the tower and he had to shield his eyes. Bodies pushed from behind and Kaivon found himself carried forward, his toes barely touching the ground.

He burst out into the light, wobbled across the drawbridge and found himself standing on the battlements in the midst of battle. More flaming boulders flew overhead before plummeting down to strike buildings. As the smoke cleared he saw the extent of the fighting on the wall. Hundreds of Mongol warriors and their allies were surging onto the battlements like water poured from a glass. Although the Iraqi warriors were hard pressed, they stood firm against the tide of bodies.

All other thoughts were driven from Kaivon's mind as his world was reduced to a primal function; the need to survive. Energy coursed through his body and he charged into the fray. Ducking a clumsy swing he riposted with a stab to the enemy's throat, catching the warrior under his helmet. He spat blood, dropped his sword and Kaivon was past him, shoving him off the wall with his shoulder. He traded blows with the next man but it was difficult in tight quarters.

For a time, Kaivon lost himself in the battle. He stabbed and slashed at the enemy until his sword arm was red to the elbow. His face and armour were splattered with blood and he could taste it. When a space opened up in front of him Kaivon was initially confused, but then he saw what lay ahead.

A solid wall of Iraqis waited, their shields locked together. These were fresh warriors and reinforcements were coming up the stairs. Hundreds and hundreds of warriors eager to defend their homes.

They wouldn't take the city today.

Kaivon knew it, but those around him hadn't realised. While he hesitated the rest of his unit charged the line of shields, confident of victory. Several died in seconds, stabbed to death with spears while the defenders hunkered down behind their shields. Moving as one they stepped forward, driving the Mongols back.

The first rank fell dead and then the second. Elsewhere he could see other units were struggling to hold their ground. The Mongols had superior numbers, and on an open field they would be victorious. But here, on the walls of Baghdad, they were being funnelled through the siege towers.

"Pull back," shouted Kaivon, pulling the man next to him by the shoulder. The Mongol snarled at him until an arrow hammered into his shield. "Run!" shouted Kaivon, shoving the men behind him.

It was taking too long. Arrows still found their mark in the men around him. There was no time for friendship or helping the injured. They were left for the enemy and their pleas were ignored.

A full rout of the Mongols' forces began.

Men streamed from the walls. The lucky ones were already at the bottom of the walls and Kaivon saw them running towards the camp. There were hundreds of men between Kaivon and escape. The chance of seeing tomorrow was slim.

"Steady!" he shouted, trying to conceal his fear. "Hold your shields tight." Behind him the tower shook as the Mongol warriors shoved and stepped on one another in their attempt to escape. But there was little space inside and the press of bodies slowed everything to a crawl.

He needed to buy some time.

When Kaivon reached the nearest tower he bullied about twenty men into position. "We hold here. Shields tight."

The circle of men protecting the entrance locked their shields together. If they fell everyone inside would be slaughtered. Kaivon and the others had to wait until the tower was clear if they were going to have a chance to escape.

Flaming arrows hammered into the sides of the tower

behind him. More arrows followed and the wood began to smoulder and turn black as it caught fire.

"Any archers?" he yelled. Four men had bows and he pulled them off to one side. "If the tower burns we all die. Take out their archers."

Raising their bows to the sky, the Mongol archers rained arrows down upon the enemy. Inside the tower, the men were less than a third of the way down.

The Iraqis formed their own shield wall, spears and swords poking out between the gaps.

"Keep them back or we all die!" he bellowed. Risking a glance inside the tower Kaivon saw Mongols streaming out the bottom, but it was still half full.

The two shield walls collided and the fighting devolved into a scrum of shoving and stabbing. Men went down on both sides with grievous wounds, bleeding from arms, legs and faces. One Mongol stumbled back into Kaivon, hands pressed to his face where a spear had gone through both cheeks.

"Heave!" shouted Kaivon, lending his weight to the shield wall. Despite their combined efforts the Mongols were driven back one step and then another. The men they were facing were fresh reinforcements. Kaivon didn't know how long he'd been fighting but just holding onto his sword was an effort. In the end he sheathed it so he could grip his shield with both hands.

More defenders were coming up the walls to reinforce the others. His archers were still firing but only a few arrows were hitting their targets. More flaming arrows hammered into the side of the siege tower in an attempt to cut off their line of retreat. Smoke began to curl around the outside of the tower.

They were out of time. He gave the enemy one final heave with his shield to create some space and then fell back.

"Retreat!"

The whole tower shook as men ran for their lives. When most of them were clear, Kaivon grabbed the man beside him and pulled back. Holding his shield above his head he ran, down and down, round and around, until he ran into the back of someone. Kaivon shouted at him to move faster. Toxic black smoke filled the tower and everyone started to cough and splutter. Above his head Kaivon heard the sound of fighting and men screaming in agony.

Warriors pressed against his back until he was wedged between bodies. He couldn't see if he was close to the door but he kept shuffling down, one step at a time. More smoke filled the tower until it was impossible to see his hand in front of his face. He choked and coughed until breathing became a challenge. His vision narrowed, his head spun and he felt himself starting to teeter on the edge of consciousness.

With a final stumble he stepped forward and the smoke cleared. He was outside. Taking a deep breath he desperately inhaled the clean air. Staying by the entrance he pulled men from the tower as they were as blind and disoriented as he'd been. The flames spread and the heat began to rise. Kaivon stayed there as long as he could, pulling men out, urging them to follow the sound of his voice until the fire engulfed the bottom steps.

There were still men trapped inside. He could hear them moaning and crying out.

"Sir, we have to go," said someone at his shoulder, pulling him back. Flames wreathed the tower and the smell of burning meat filled his nose. He couldn't save those trapped inside.

Kaivon stumbled after the other survivors while the city's defenders jeered at them from the wall. Holding each other up, the remains of his unit eventually made it back to the outskirts of the Mongol camp. He walked another dozen paces before collapsing face down on the grass. Someone rolled him onto his back and Kaivon lay staring up at the sky. His throat burned and his lungs ached from nearly choking to death.

Despite all that he'd done it hadn't been enough. He'd failed the Khan and would have to face the consequences.

Once his breathing had eased, Kaivon struggled to his feet. His chest ached with every breath and his throat was raw, but there was no point delaying the inevitable. Caked in blood and stained with soot, he walked through the camp to the command tent. Men gave way when they saw him coming. They knew he was condemned and wanted nothing to do with him.

With the last of his remaining strength Kaivon stumbled into the tent. He wasn't sure if he tripped or his legs finally gave out, but he found himself on hands and knees. Determined to look his executioner in the eye, he forced himself back onto his heels.

Self-loathing filled his gut. When he looked at Hulagu all he saw was a blood-soaked invader. Now, Kaivon had become the very thing he hated. He'd killed people who had done nothing more than protect their home from an invader.

Dying would be a relief. He wouldn't have to live with this pain anymore.

Hulagu regarded him with an impassive expression. The Khan had killed thousands of men, women and children. Ordering the death of one more would make no difference to him.

"We failed," said Kaivon in a harsh rasp. Hulagu came forward until he loomed over Kaivon. "Baghdad remains in the hands of its people."

Kaivon waited, refusing to break eye contact. He would face down his enemy until the final moment. He would not cower and ask for mercy.

Hulagu should be on his knees, begging forgiveness for all of the death and destruction he had wrought. Kaivon felt light-headed and sick, but he gritted his teeth and forced himself to hold on.

"I saw what you did on the wall. We were all watching," said Hulagu. "You saved the lives of many warriors."

"I don't think he can hear you," said General Kitbuqa, stepping forward. "His ears are probably ringing."

Kaivon had heard, but he didn't know how to react. He was barely holding on to consciousness.

"You fought bravely," said Hulagu, annunciating his words. "You have earned your place at my side."

Kaivon's head was reeling and he swayed. To his disgust Hulagu steadied him with one hand.

"See to him," said the Khan.

Firm but gentle hands lifted Kaivon to his feet. His eyes were streaming and his head was tight and swollen at the same time.

Fresh air brushed his skin and he took deep breaths of clean air. Someone guided him through the camp until they arrived at a familiar yurt. With warm scented water, gentle hands wiped the soot and blood from his hands and face. Kaivon was eased from his armour and wrapped in a blanket. Staying awake was impossible and, for a time, he fell into the darkness.

Hours or perhaps days later, he awoke in darkness, sore, hungry and still tired. He tried to speak, but barely any sound emerged. Nevertheless, someone moved towards him in the gloom and they eased him back to the floor. Cold water, sweeter than any he'd tasted, was dribbled down his throat a small gulp at a time. It soothed the burning pain and eased the terrible ache in his head. Next he was fed warm soup, swimming with meat and vegetables, one spoonful at a time. With his hunger and thirst sated he fell asleep again.

Kaivon was cared for by a Persian woman he'd never seen before. He drifted in and out of consciousness. He talked to his dead parents. Sometimes the Khan tried to attack him and Kaivon cried out. Throughout his ordeal the woman stayed with him. Washing his skin, feeding him and tending his wounds. On the third day, his chest ached less and his throat wasn't as sore.

"Who are you?" he asked.

"Try not to talk," she said, offering him a mug of tea with honey and lemon. "Your throat and lungs are still damaged. You inhaled a lot of smoke."

"What is your name?"

She rolled her eyes. "You're just going to keep talking, aren't you?"

"Yes."

"Then I'll talk and you listen," she said. He sipped his tea, enjoying the sweetness. "My name is Esme. I lived in the north of Persia. My parents were killed when the Mongols invaded. My sister is gone, but I was spared because of my knowledge of medicine. I was useful." The bitterness was apparent but, even though they were alone, she kept her voice low.

"How long have you been here?" asked Kaivon.

"I'm not sure. Two years. Maybe three. I haven't been home in a long time." Esme leaned forward and spoke in a whisper. "Do you need anything else?" she asked, running a hand up his thigh.

Kaivon leaned backwards. "He sent you, didn't he?"

Esme's smile slipped, revealing the anger beneath. "Of course."

"You don't have to do anything."

"I have no choice. I'm a slave, like you."

Kaivon gripped her hand before it moved even further up his leg. "If they ask, tell them I was satisfied, and I will do the same."

"You're not what I was expecting," admitted Esme, sitting back on her haunches. "Who are you?"

"I'm just a soldier," he said.

"No, you're not," she said. "For him to order me to do this, that means you're important."

"I used to be someone."

Esme shook her head. "I know why you're really here."

"What do you mean?" said Kaivon, starting to sweat.

"You talked in your sleep about destroying the Ilkhanate," said Esme, starting to gather her things.

Kaivon tried to swallow the lump in his throat. "I was delirious."

"Do you think I serve the Mongols by choice?" said Esme. "I'm only alive because I'm useful. They will slit my throat the second I refuse. You should remember that."

"I have no illusions," said Kaivon. "As an advisor, I thought I was safe, but then he sent me to die on the walls."

"But you survived and now you are favoured by the Khan."

"For the time being. If we are being honest then tell me, what is it that you want?" asked Kaivon.

It didn't take long for Esme to answer. "I want to live long enough to see Hulagu's face when his dreams turn to ash. I want to see hope die in his eyes."

"You're serious."

"Deadly serious. One day our nation will be free, and I'm going to help you or die trying." She gave him a fierce kiss. Before he could reply Esme hurried from the yurt.

Outside he heard the rhythmic pounding of the catapults. The distant cry and clash of steel. The faint screams as men fought and died.

Despite being told he had earned his place, Kaivon knew he was nothing more than a pawn. He would do everything he could to destroy Hulagu and the Ilkhanate, but doing it alone had always been impossible. He would need help. And if there was one person like Esme, working for the Khan, then perhaps there were others.

CHAPTER 16
Kokochin

For five days Kokochin had been training with Layla, but it felt as if she'd learned little. The only things she knew for definite were that she was unfit and her body was weak.

Staring at herself in the mirror Kokochin knew she was lithe, but until she'd begun stretching, she hadn't realised how little she understood about her own body.

Layla had instructed her to eat more at every meal to help build muscle. Kokochin stuffed herself with rice, chicken and heaps of vegetables. She enjoyed the occasional pastry, but after such filling meals, she rarely wanted anything sweet. She began to gain weight and slowly she unlocked the joints of her body, as well as waking up muscles that had been asleep.

"You're still too skinny," said Layla, poking her in the side. "Are you practising your stretching?"

"First thing in the morning and again before going to sleep." Her shoulders ached less and she had more movement, but little else was different.

Layla grunted, unsatisfied.

Kokochin had been warned this would be difficult, but hadn't realised the size of the challenge.

"Let's work on your hips," said Layla, gesturing for Kokochin to lie down on the floor.

They were in the back room of the shop, which also served as Layla's workshop. All of the equipment and benches had been pushed against the walls to create enough space for them to move around. As Layla leaned her weight against Kokochin's left ankle, bending her in two, she focused on her breathing and tried to relax.

"Flexibility is key. You need to bend like the willow in the storm. If you are too tight," said Layla, easing back slightly when Kokochin hissed in discomfort. "You will snap. You need to learn how to flow."

Layla had been talking like that since the first day. Kokochin was beginning to realise this was more than a martial art.

"Do you understand?" asked Layla, switching legs.

"Not really," admitted Kokochin. "So far all we've done is stretches. I haven't learned a single move."

Layla sat back on her heels, biting her bottom lip as she often did when deep in thought. It softened her features and Kokochin thought it was endearing. "Get dressed. I want to show you something."

To avoid getting their clothes dusty they exercised in plain black garments that Layla had provided. The cotton hugged Kokochin's skin in a flattering manner, but it also accentuated her bony limbs, whereas Layla's showed off the strength in her firm legs and shoulders. It would take her months, even years, to have a similar physique.

Feeling self-conscious, Kokochin changed into her own clothes, facing away from Layla. At one point she risked a glance over her shoulder and caught sight of pale flesh that made her bite her bottom lip.

When they were dressed, Layla closed the shop then led her to a busy part of the city. A large crowd of people lined one of the streets, so it took them a while to find a spot at the front.

"Is there a parade?" asked Kokochin. Sometimes the leader of a temple or church led processions to celebrate special days from their religious calendar. The birth of saints, special feasts or hallowed days, most of which came with a parade and a party atmosphere. Today the crowd was a mix with faces from both east and west, but there were more local people than anyone else.

"Yes, but not for a church. In Persia there's an ancient martial art. It's a form of wrestling, which is exclusively taught to boys and men. They train in a *zurkhaneh*, a House of Strength. This style of wrestling makes them strong, but it's more than that." At the far end of the street a murmur of excitement ran through the crowd. Kokochin strained her neck, trying to see who was approaching, but they were too far away. In the distance she heard the rhythmic thump of a drum and men's voices raised in song.

"This is a procession for the local House of Strength. The men who train there are putting on a show and asking for donations."

"What do they do in a House of Strength?" asked Kokochin.

"They train the body, but the martial art combines sport with ethics, spirituality, morality and philosophy. It's not just about strength of the body. It's also about the spirit."

Layla spoke with passion, and looking at the crowd Kokochin saw the same pride reflected in their faces. "A month ago, a woman lost her husband in an accident. The *zurkhaneh* made sure she had enough food, until she was ready to start work again. A local tailor was robbed and beaten up. They ran the business until he had recovered, and they found the person responsible. They look after their local community. They serve."

The singing was getting louder as the procession drew near. Several men with deep voices were singing together in Farsi. Although she didn't understand the words, Kokochin knew the song was a celebration. Finally they came into view at the far end of the street. Two dozen burly men marched down the road, their shirts cut short to show off their muscled arms. Most of them carried a bulky wooden club in either hand, which they whirled around in precise movements like a dance. They looked like heavy and quite dangerous implements, but their purpose appeared ceremonial.

Riding behind them on a horse was a drummer who kept the beat. The men sang and whirled their clubs, flexed their muscles and made a few impromptu demonstrations.

"The man playing the drum is the leader. He is the heart and the captain. He is the greatest in spirit," said Layla. Many people waved or greeted the drummer. It was as if he knew everyone on the street. "He has done much for his community and yet he lives a humble life. It is not about reward or recognition. It is about caring for others and enriching the spirit."

One man in the procession picked up a woman from the crowd who he lifted overhead with ease. She shrieked and then laughed while her neighbours cheered. Another bearded man with huge shoulders picked up a pair of boys by their belts. He lifted the boys above his head and they whooped in delight. When the boys returned to the ground they asked to be lifted again, but the procession had to move on.

At the back of the procession was a group of teenage boys, all of them carrying baskets. People tossed them coins and they thanked or blessed the individuals.

Kokochin watched the procession with interest, noting how beloved the men were and how many women stared at their muscles with interest. When the teenagers were abreast of her, Layla tossed a few coins and received a blessing.

"Come," said Layla, leading her away by the hand. Some of the crowd were following the procession, but they went in the opposite direction towards the shop. When they were clear of the crowd Layla let go and Kokochin wished she'd held on a little while longer. "The martial art has its history in ancient warfare, but over the years, its movements have become ritualised."

In the back room of the shop they changed back into their black garments. This time she fought the urge to look over her shoulder. As instructed Kokochin sat on the floor opposite Layla. "Can a woman enter a House of Strength?"

"No. It's forbidden." There was anger in Layla's voice, but no real heat. The decision had been made a long time ago. "What I am teaching you is almost as old. In secret, women created the House of Grace. We cannot have processions to raise money, and we do not own or train in special buildings. Welcome to a House of Grace," she said with a wry smile, gesturing at the workshop.

"You will never be as big or strong as a man, but strength isn't everything. They are the mace, blunt and powerful. We are the knife, subtle and quiet. We have always trained in secret, small spaces. That is why we do not travel far with our bodies. Why our movements are precise, and why we use the strength of others against them. First, you must learn how to evade an attack and then the counter. Everything begins with these basic pairings. Once you have those, we will start to build up the flow. I will then teach you to improvise and, over time, it becomes like a dance.

"But, like the House of Strength, this is about more than learning how to fight. It is a way of being," said Layla.

Taking one of Kokochin's hands Layla placed it on her heart. Then she put a hand on Kokochin's chest until they mirrored one another. Kokochin could feel Layla's strong heartbeat through her fingers. A tremor ran through her at Layla's touch. She tried to ignore it and focus on what Layla was saying.

"This is not a game. If you commit to this, it must be with your whole self." Layla's heart remained slow and even, while Kokochin knew hers was racing with excitement and fear. "The House of Strength serves the people of Persia, and so do we. Like them, we don't do this for riches or recognition. They operate in plain sight, and we operate in secret. I can teach you how to protect yourself, but is that all you want?" asked Layla.

Thoughts of revenge stirred in Kokochin's mind.

"What else can you tell me about the House of Grace?"

"We're governed by an Inner Circle of twelve. They have the most experience and knowledge. Each has their own network of people, but it is all for one purpose; to see Persia prosper. In times of peace, we grease the axle to keep the cart moving. In the last few years, our goal has changed to one of freedom from our oppressors. We had to become more proactive."

"Have you met any of the Inner Circle?" asked Kokochin.

"No, and I only know a handful of other members within the House. That way if any of us are ever tortured, we can't betray everyone. Occasionally I've been paired with someone, but if I ever see them again, we act as strangers."

"What else can you tell me?" asked Kokochin.

"Many in the House have more subtle roles than mine. Some gently guide and coerce. Some people are bribed, some blackmailed and others removed, but only if necessary. Some people work for us and never know. They take the money and do as they are told."

With so many people operating in secret, in different areas of society, it made Kokochin wonder if she'd already met other members of the House and not realise.

"This is your last chance to turn back," said Layla. "This will change your body and your mind. It will also change your self," she said. "Think carefully before you answer."

"The person you killed in the palace. Did you know him?"

"No. I had no personal feelings for him and we had never met. We are instruments of change, not filthy Assassins. They kill for money. Taking a life is the last resort when other avenues have failed. It can never be for selfish reasons. The man I killed was for a specific purpose."

Kokochin considered her options carefully, but in the end there was only one choice. She wanted to build a new life, and first of all, that meant feeling safe.

"Teach me," she said.

* * *

After another hearty breakfast, where Kokochin forced herself to eat every mouthful, she headed back to her room in the palace to change. Her current outfit was snug around the waist and legs which she took as a sign that she was gaining weight.

She'd barely gone a dozen paces down the corridor when Tuqtani, one of the Khan's many concubines, stepped out of an alcove directly in front of her.

"Oh, you startled me," said Kokochin with a laugh, but Tuqtani continued to glare. She was a tall Mongol woman with rounded hips and a full bust, giving her an hourglass shape. Her outfits often accentuated her figure, and she walked around the palace as if she were the Empress. Up to now, Kokochin had done her best to avoid Tuqtani as she had a reputation for being pretty but unpleasant.

"I saw you at breakfast," said Tuqtani, looking Kokochin up and down, assessing her somehow. "Didn't they feed you wherever you came from?"

Kokochin ignored the sneer and the question. "Did you need something?"

"From you? No," said Tuqtani, stepping around her as if Kokochin smelled. Doing her best not to roll her eyes, Kokochin went on her way, ignoring the daggers she could feel in her back. Whatever Tuqtani was upset about wouldn't be important and didn't concern her.

By the time she had changed clothes and walked to Layla's shop, Kokochin had put the concubine from her mind. Layla smiled when she entered the shop and Kokochin instinctively found herself smiling back.

As part of her pretence at becoming a jeweller, Layla spent the morning teaching her the basics about the equipment she used. Kokochin struggled to remember the names for all the different tools, but Layla reassured her it would come with time. Although the back room was smelly, even with all the windows thrown open, Kokochin enjoyed watching Layla turn a lumpy block of silver into hot metal. Using thick gloves, she poured the glowing liquid into a number of crucibles, which Kokochin helped seal. Once or twice she noticed Layla glancing at her and Kokochin did her best impression of someone paying attention.

"Now, we let the metal cool, and tomorrow we can start to polish and shape what's inside." This time when Layla smiled at her Kokochin felt her heart quicken.

They went out for lunch at a local tea room and when they had finished eating, Kokochin offered to pay. It took some time for Layla to agree, as Persian etiquette required she refuse, but eventually she relented. "How did you become a jeweller?" asked Kokochin, trying to distract her.

"It was my father's trade. I spent a large portion of my childhood at his shop. I loved watching him work. He had big, strong hands," said Layla, her eyes distant. "But he could be very delicate and precise."

"And your mother?"

"She was equally strong-willed."

"That explains it," said Kokochin with a smirk. "Were you always this confident?"

"No," admitted Layla. "Some of it came with age and some with experience, both good and bad. I'm glad for all of it."

"Even the bad things that happened?"

"Not all, but some. Think of what happened to you. If those men had not chased you, would you have sought me out? Would we be sitting here together?"

It was feeling so helpless that had forced her to change. Kokochin didn't believe that everything happened for a reason, but a part of her was glad it had happened.

That afternoon several customers came into the shop, so Kokochin stayed in the back room while Layla conducted her business. Dressed once more in black, Kokochin ran through the series of stretches she'd been given. She kept exercising until her joints felt more supple, and her skin was covered with a layer of sweat.

When it went quiet Layla closed the shop then joined her in the store room. Mirroring her instructor, Kokochin attempted to copy the slow, flowing movements. The gliding of limbs and arms with such precision was like one of the many dances she'd been taught, but each gesture had significance beyond the aesthetic.

When Kokochin put a hand or foot wrong, Layla would carefully correct her, tilting her foot, shaping her hand, or even squaring her hips. Despite making many mistakes Layla never shouted at her or lost her temper. It was a far cry from her singing teacher who had used a broom handle on the palm of her hands when she missed a note.

"Practise in private, if you can. Don't worry about getting every position right, you need to get your body used to these movements," said Layla, raising Kokochin's left elbow. "We need to build up your muscle memory. Later we can work on your form."

After another hour of practise Kokochin was red-faced and sweating more heavily.

"Can you show me what all of this is for?" she asked when they took a break.

"I don't want to hurt you," said Layla.

"I trust you," said Kokochin. When she was around Guyuk, or any of the Khan's other wives, there was always a frisson of tension. Even though they were not in competition with one another for his affection, Kokochin was always on edge, waiting for them to do or say something unpleasant. With Layla, she could be real true self, not the closed-off façade she presented to others in the palace.

"All right," said Layla. "Come at me with an attack at chest height, as if you're trying to stab me."

Kokochin jabbed at her with one hand thrust out in front. As her arm reached its full extension she felt herself pulled forward. Her legs were swept out from under her and the world turned upside down as she was tossed over Layla's hip. She landed awkwardly on the ground and knew there would be a bruise on her rear. Layla had a hand against her neck, applying gentle pressure, but not enough to do any real damage. From this position, it would have been easy for her to crush Kokochin's throat. With Layla's fingers so close to her throat, Kokochin could feel her pulse. It was strong and steady.

"Are you all right?" asked Layla, helping her upright.

"Fine," she said, surreptitiously trying to rub her bruised arse.

"I used *Salmon Leaps* to pull you off balance, and *Bear Feasts* as the counter. Remember the pairing. Let's try that again, but this time I'll move slower," promised Layla.

"All right."

"Give it time," said Layla with a smile. "It will come."

The next three days blurred together. Kokochin seemed to spend all of her time eating, stretching and being thrown around by Layla in the House of Grace. They practised grappling and ground work and then more stretching. She also began to learn some of the names of the forms, which mirrored the way animals moved in nature. When Kokochin seized Layla around the waist, her teacher used *Leopard's Breath* to spin her about, and *Hyena Laughs* as the countermove to finish her off.

The first move was always defensive, designed to disentangle an individual from their attacker. The countermove always ended the fight decisively. Many could be used as deadly strikes, but Layla mostly showed her how to disable her opponent, no matter their size or strength.

When she tried to attack Layla from behind, *Squirrel Climbs* turned the tables. Suddenly she was in front of Layla, and *Fox's Bark* sent her flying across the room. She narrowly missed smashing her face into the floor. She would have had a bloody nose if Layla hadn't pulled her punch.

"*Fox's Bark* is very dangerous," warned Layla, guiding Kokochin's hand to a very specific point on her lower back. "If you hit someone too hard, you will do more than incapacitate them. You could crush their spinal column and cripple them for life. Maybe even kill them if the strike is too high or low."

Kokochin understood what they were doing was not for fun, but when she heard it in those terms it focused her mind. On the fourth morning Kokochin was surprised when Layla asked her to sit on the floor instead of warming up with stretches.

"Has something happened?" asked Kokochin.

"Everything is fine. We've begun the work on your body, but now we need to expand your training to include the mind. Do you trust me?" asked Layla.

"Yes." Kokochin didn't even need to think about it.

"I need you to focus on a moment from your past when you were genuinely afraid. You don't need to tell me what it is, but I want you to hold the memory in the front of your mind."

There were a few to choose from, mostly recently being chased through the city. "Why?" asked Kokochin, reluctant to begin.

"Here, in the quiet and peace of the House, we can practise without interruption. But outside, everything around you will be chaotic. You need to master the fear inside, so that you are like the eye of the storm, silent and calm. You need to carry the peace within."

"How?"

"First, we will start with your breath, and then focus on the bad memory."

With some effort, Kokochin swallowed the lump in her throat. "I'm afraid," she admitted.

Layla gripped her hand tightly, lending Kokochin her strength. "You're not alone."

By the time she returned to the palace that evening, Kokochin was exhausted. Her muscles were sore, but she felt emotionally drained as well. Keeping something unpleasant in her mind for a long time had taken a toll. She was on the verge of tears, but also wild hysterics. Her skin felt unusually thin and she was certain that the slightest provocation would set her off. All she wanted to do was be alone.

Kokochin was almost back to her rooms when she turned a corner and found Tuqtani waiting outside her door.

The concubine walked towards Kokochin with a smile, but there was something vicious in her eyes. "I know what you're doing."

"I don't know—"

"Don't lie to me!" shrieked Tuqtani, right in her face.

Kokochin tried to find inner calm but her pulse was racing and icy fingers of fear crept down her spine at the concubine's words.

"What do you want?" she managed to ask.

"Nothing from you. It's too late," gloated Tuqtani. "I've already spoken to Guyuk and she's going to deal with you!"

With a throaty chuckle she sauntered away. Kokochin managed to make it into her rooms before she collapsed on the bed. A terrible gnawing pain gripped her stomach which bent her double. She'd finally made a friend and was discovering her own place in the world, and now, all of it was going to be taken away.

CHAPTER 17
Hulagu

For three days the catapults had pounded the city of Baghdad.

On the fourth day Hulagu had ordered another assault with siege towers but it had ended almost as badly as the first attempt. It had taken a heavy toll on the defenders, but it wasn't enough. Sections of the city continued to burn, day and night. A black pallor of smoke hung over everything. The wind brought clouds of ash into camp and Hulagu watched as black bitter rain fell, dusting everything with a grey cloak.

As dawn broke on the fifth day Nasir, and the rest of his engineers, began their assault with catapults. Shortly after a cheer went up from thousands of men. The sound spread throughout the camp until everyone was shouting. Hulagu stumbled out of his yurt to see what had caused the commotion.

The city wall had been breached.

Numerous parts of the battlements had already been broken off, but this went beyond minor damage. Focusing the immense power of the engines on two spots had finally yielded devastating results. There were two gaping holes punched through the wall, enough to show daylight on the other side. As he watched a section of the wall collapsed, and even from so far away he heard screams as men were crushed by tonnes of rubble.

By midday the breaches were significantly larger. It was more than sufficient for his army to enter the city, but Hulagu held them back. He let the catapults do the work for him. By now the enemy would be on edge, full of raw nervous energy. And with every hour that passed without an attack, the more difficult it would be for them to remain focused and battle ready.

Hulagu invited Berke Khan to join him for a private lunch. As soon as Berke sat down it was clear that he had something on his mind.

"A messenger just arrived from Karakorum," said Berke. He was practically bouncing in his seat. "Ariq has said the kurultai was a sham. He's declared himself the rightful successor to the throne."

Up to that point Hulagu had been enjoying his food, but now he pushed his plate away. "There is little that we can do about it from here. By the time we arrive in Karakorum the situation could have been resolved."

"True, but we could show our support," said Berke.

"We chose Kublai as the Great Khan."

Berke grimaced. "I wonder if we were too hasty with our decision. I think Ariq would be a better choice."

"It's too late. He had plenty of time, but didn't show up." Hulagu held up a hand, forestalling whatever Berke was about to say. "Regardless of who sits on the throne in Karakorum, we have work to do. Baghdad is ripe and the spoils will soon be ours, cousin."

That mollified Berke and he smiled. "Do you believe in Allah?" he asked.

"You know I favour the old ways and the Heavenly Father. Tengri is my god. Why?"

"I want to ask you for a favour. Spare the Caliph's life. He is a holy man."

"You know I cannot do that," said Hulagu, keeping a firm hold on his anger. "Twice I gave him a chance to surrender. Twice."

"It was unwise of him to refuse, but he is proud. All great leaders are the same."

"He aligns himself with the Mamluks of Egypt. Do you also think they are holy and deserving of clemency?"

Berke's loyalty to Islam was blinding him. Hulagu waited in silence, gritting his teeth to prevent an outburst. He was used to buying the loyalty of the others with favours, but he'd not expected it from his family.

"The Mamluks must be destroyed," Berke said eventually.

"The city will be ours and the Caliph must die. The Georgian King wants his head on a spike, and I need to keep our allies happy."

"Am I not your ally?" asked Berke.

"You are my cousin. We are family," said Hulagu. Even Berke didn't seem to understand how reliant they were on their allies. With every nation that they conquered, Mongols had to be left in charge to establish and then maintain order.

"Ask me for another boon and I will grant it, but not this," said Hulagu. "The Caliph must die, so that hope of his return dies in the heart of the people. Baghdad is an important step in expanding into the west. Do you not share in the dream of our grandfather?"

"You know that I do," said Berke, although he said it without enthusiasm. "One day the whole world will be one, under Mongol rule."

"I will try to spare what I can, holy temples and the like," said Hulagu, trying to placate his cousin.

Berke pushed his plate away and stood. "I must see to my men." He gave a brief bow and left in a hurry.

As Hulagu was pouring himself a bowl of airag Kaivon came into the tent.

"My Khan," he said, bowing deeply. The Persian warrior had done well on the first day of the siege. He'd earned the respect of many, for his prowess in battle, but also for saving lives. Doquz still didn't trust him, but Hulagu thought the former General had a future as part of the Mongol Empire.

"How much of that did you hear?" he asked.

"Just the last part," admitted Kaivon.

"Is there something you want me to spare in the city? Maybe a special fountain or an ancient church?"

"I don't need anything," said Kaivon.

So far Esme had not reported anything suspicious. He had no reason to doubt Kaivon, but Doquz urged caution. "Is it time?" asked Hulagu.

"Yes, my Khan."

He followed Kaivon out of the tent towards the front lines. His Generals and advisors had gathered to hear him speak, but they already knew what to do. Nevertheless they looked towards him for inspiration. Looking at each face in turn, Hulagu saw trust reflected in the eyes of every man. He had led them to victory again.

"This will be a great day. One that will long be remembered in history." Hulagu's voice carried far and many heads turned to listen. "We will make them bleed for their insolence, for their mockery, and for daring to stand in our way. We are unstoppable and today, we will punish them for their arrogance. One day soon, the whole blue sky will be ours. As Tengri decreed!"

The men cheered and hammered weapons against their shields. He gestured at his generals and they moved off, shouting orders at their officers. Shortly after, the army began to divide up into battalions of a thousand men each.

Some of his inner circle had asked to lead a battalion and he'd been happy to give them permission. The Georgian King gave a nod of thanks as he tightened his shield, then went to prepare his men. Half of his men were from Georgia and the rest a mix of Mongols and Kurds. They would carve a bloody path through the defenders in an attempt to settle old scores. Blood called out to blood.

Jumghur had asked for his own unit, but Hulagu turned him down. The atrocities he would commit would be bad enough without a thousand men following his lead. Instead he was part of his brother's battalion. Although Abaqa would not be able to totally restrain his brother, he might be able to distract him from his darkest urges.

Berke led his own men from the Golden Horde. Unlike those around him, Berke was grim-faced rather than excited about the battle. No doubt he was still smarting from their earlier conversation. King Hethum, Buqa-Temur and his old friend General Kitbuqa also had units of their own. Spies had told him about the number of defenders in the city, and Hulagu knew it would not be a short battle.

He was mentally preparing himself for what lay ahead when Doquz approached carrying his shield. "You will need this, husband," she said, helping him secure it to his left arm.

"Thank you, wife," he replied, just as formally. Last night she had been far less disciplined. He still had scratch marks on his back. She was always like this the night before a battle. As if it would be the last time they were together.

"Don't forget—"

"Yes, yes, your precious churches."

Doquz raised an eyebrow. "I was going to say, don't forget to come back safe."

Hulagu considered apologising but didn't want to appear weak in front of the men.

"I will try," he said.

Before a battle Doquz never asked him to make promises that he couldn't keep. She understood him better than anyone, and knew that a warrior's heart beat in his chest. One day he would die in battle, not fat and old in bed. It could even be today, but looking at the broken walls of the city, he didn't think so. They'd already won. All that remained was the bloodletting.

* * *

The catapults had finally fallen silent, but a cloud of smoke still hung over the city as fires continued to burn. As he approached one of the vast breaches in the outer wall, Hulagu stared in amazement at the thickness of the stonework. As he studied the magnitude of the damage caused by the engines of war, he thought Nasir's request was fair. If possible, the main library of Baghdad would be preserved. He suspected there were many books that would be of interest to his inner circle, and bestowing them as gifts would strengthen the bonds of loyalty. Thoughts of favours were brushed aside as he clambered over the rubble into the adjoining street.

Twelve thousand warriors had already entered and more were waiting behind him. All of them were eager to fight and plunder the city of its riches. Kaivon marched two steps behind Hulagu, his eyes darting around the streets for trouble.

As they rounded a corner, Hulagu saw a group of Mongols breaking down a door with a makeshift ram. The door broke off its hinges and the warriors raced inside, bellowing for blood. A few seconds later a man was thrown from the second-floor window. Hulagu heard high-pitched screams coming from inside and a clash of steel.

At the far end of a wide street, a dozen warriors were engaged in a savage battle with twice as many Iraqis. The Mongols locked their shields together and gave ground, stabbing and slashing to keep the enemy at bay. Hulagu was ready to lend them his aid, but he saw that it was a trap. Thirty more Mongol warriors burst from the mouth of alleyways, surrounding the enemy on three sides. A massacre followed where every defender was cut down until all that remained were silent bodies, their warm innards steaming in the cool air.

The further they went from the wall, the more chaotic and savage the streets became. Bodies were strewn everywhere. They lay in the street where they had died, mouths and eyes open, many already gathering flies. Fires burned in windows and glass shattered as the pressure built.

Everywhere they went Mongol warriors fought Iraqi soldiers in groups. Archers picked off targets from high windows, while men scrambled for cover, only to be shot in the back or legs.

Families and clumps of local people cowered in dark corners and doorways, hoping to be ignored, begging for mercy and often receiving none. Men were beheaded or their bodies torn open in front of their families. Children were butchered and women ravaged while their relatives watched in horror, unable to do anything. A few residents tried to fight, wielding swords and wooden clubs in defence of their families. A mob of a dozen tried to protect their people, and examples were made of them in front of witnesses. Their bodies were opened up, their innards were torn out or tied in knots and they were left to die, hanging upside down or nailed to wooden poles.

Everywhere Hulagu went the ground was awash with rivers of blood. The stench of death was strong, but he knew it would get worse over the next few days as the bodies began to rot.

Some families had barricaded themselves inside their homes and nothing drew them out. Not the screams of their neighbours and not the clash of steel. A little further on, Hulagu came across an entire row of houses that had been set ablaze. If left unchecked it could spread and engulf an entire neighbourhood.

"Take down that building," said Hulagu, doing nothing to curtail the violence of his men. It was far too early to try and control them. They needed to sate their indulgences, but Hulagu was determined to limit the amount of destruction. He left a hundred men to create a firebreak and the rest went with him deeper into the heart of the city.

He had to find the Caliph and his Generals. There was no power, divine or earthly, that would prevent their deaths.

Hulagu was surprised that the defence had been so disorganised. A short time later, when they came across the first barrier, he realised what the enemy had done. In order to slow down the Mongols' advance through the streets, they had sacrificed all of the people in the outer districts. It was brutal, unexpected and not something he was used to seeing from his enemies. It was the sort of tactic they would accuse him of deploying.

The barrier was poorly made, fashioned from rubble, barrels and wooden carts, but it blocked the entire street. Archers stood on a raised platform, and they caught a few of his warriors through luck rather than skill. Hulagu and the rest of his thousand withdrew to a safe distance to plan their next move. A scout was sent to explore the surrounding area and it didn't take him long to report back.

"The barrier covers this street, and two more on either side. Several others have been completely blocked with rubble. They look unguarded and you could scramble over but–"

"They smell like a trap," said Hulagu.

"They are wide enough for only two or three abreast, and there are a lot of windows."

Hulagu grunted. "Then we punch through here."

Orders were sent to other units, until nearly two thousand men were gathered in the street behind him. Coordinated attacks would shortly take place in three other positions along the barrier.

"What's the signal to attack?" asked Kaivon.

"You will know it," said Hulagu, drawing his sword.

A collective shout went up from nearby, with dozens of voices chanting in unison. It was an old song, something every Mongol child had been taught about honouring their ancestors. Even with the sounds of battle elsewhere in the city, Hulagu heard when the song was taken up by other units. After taking a deep breath Hulagu added his voice to the throng.

As he charged towards the barrier, with two thousand warriors at his back, Hulagu felt invincible. This was why he had been born. To lead men into battle and conquer his enemies. There was no greater feeling in the world.

Roaring at the cowering Iraqis, Hulagu slammed his shield into the barrier. The impact and collective weight of his warriors sent men tumbling back. Stabbing and spitting, Hulagu tried to push through, but was rebuffed. Someone tried to stab him through the face, forcing him to deflect a series of blows from a burly warrior. Something flickered past on his right. Turning his head slightly, Hulagu saw Kaivon cutting into the enemy. With only two men at his back, he had gone through the barrier and was now laying into the enemy, fighting like a hero from legend. Those he faced had talent, but Kaivon shamed them with his skill, cutting down one after another, his movements precise and deadly. As others broke through the barrier in Kaivon's wake, the enemy saw their chances of victory begin to fade.

Hulagu kicked a man in the knee, slammed the pommel of his sword into the warrior's face and dispatched him with a stab to the chest.

The defenders were driven back from the relative safety of the barrier, only to be overwhelmed by sheer numbers. Countless warriors were cut down, maimed and bludgeoned to death. The trickle of blood running across the street became a river. Men howled like wounded animals, cried out for their mothers and whispered final prayers to their gods as they lay dying in street.

The moment arrived.

Despite fighting for their homes and loved ones. Despite the anger and fire in their veins at the invaders, it still happened. Hope died in the eyes of the Iraqi soldiers.

They had fought bravely but the inevitability of being conquered swelled in the mind of every defender. From here the message would spread. Faster and more dangerous than a plague, surrender would become the only choice in the hope that there would be a tomorrow. It was the end of Iraqi rule in Baghdad.

The city belonged to him.

CHAPTER 18
Temujin

Despite it being early in the evening, the sky was a deep murky grey and the light was poor. A thick pall of black smoke hung over everything, blotting out the sun. The camp was awash with campfires and lanterns, but it did little to chase away the depressing gloom. The air stank of burning wood and burning meat. There were other unsavoury smells mixed in, things Temujin didn't want to investigate, which immediately turned him off the idea of food. His stomach growled, putting up a weak protest, but he ignored it. Yesterday he'd been forced to tighten his trousers another notch. Although the life of a warrior in the army was not one he would've chosen, there were some benefits. He had more energy. He slept better at night, although that was mostly due to exhaustion.

Temujin stamped his feet and sighed for the hundredth time. Today he was on sentry duty, although why he was guarding the camp was a mystery. But it was required, so he obeyed his orders like a good soldier.

It was the fifth morning since they'd breached the walls. All day there had been screams from inside. Despite the distance he'd been able to hear them. It spoke of the numbers being slaughtered and the savagery of their deaths.

More than anything, he wished that the sacking was over

so that the rebuilding could begin. Although no one in his unit had been inside the walls yet, many had shared stories of things they'd seen. While others laughed and joked about the atrocities, Temujin had clamped his teeth shut so that he didn't lose his lunch. To his shame, he'd smiled but said nothing.

It was one thing to fight enemy soldiers. Murdering defenceless and unarmed civilians was something else. There was no glory or honour in such cruel deeds. They were innocent. Temujin felt utterly alone with such feelings, so he buried them deep.

Far above the city, wheeling in huge flocks amidst the smoke, were carrion birds. Many more waddled along the ground, or sat upon the city walls, bloated from feasting on the dead.

Somewhere in the distance Temujin heard a child crying. At least he thought it was a child. The high-pitched keening spoke of pain and prolonged suffering. It tore at his ears and clawed at his heart, but he didn't dare show any of his feelings. At best, he would be laughed at and mocked. At worst, he might end up being branded a traitor and simply disappear. No one would notice one more dead body among the others lying in the streets.

So far the Caliph had not been found. The city was ringed with warriors and the river was blocked to all vessels, which meant he was in hiding, while his city was torn apart. Temujin wanted to believe that the brutality over the last few days was spurred on by the hunt, but deep inside he knew that wasn't the case. Many of those around him were eager to have their turn inside the city so they could indulge the darkness within. As much as he found his current assignment boring, Temujin preferred it to the alternative.

As Ganbold approached, Temujin did his best not to look weary of his current duty.

"Anything?"

"Nothing," said Temujin.

Ganbold grunted and spat, annoyed by something. He

hadn't said anything, but Temujin knew he didn't like being given such a meaningless task. "You should check the river. Feel like a walk?"

"I'd be happy to, sir," said Temujin, pleased with the opportunity to stretch his legs.

"I'll take your post," said Ganbold.

There were men spaced out along both banks, and the blockade would stop even a rowboat from getting through, but Ganbold had received orders to guard the riverbank, so that's what his men were doing.

Temujin walked up and then back down a large stretch of the nearest bank. It took him almost two hours to complete, during which time he saw no signs of life. However there were many bodies floating in the river. Several were face-up and staring, although he saw some were without their eyes. The water hid most of the wounds, but he could see all of them had suffered. Temujin did his best not to stare at the small bodies. The water had been stained a dark red from all of the blood and the muddy banks were black. Breathing through his mouth did little to diminish the stench of swollen dead flesh and decay.

By the time he'd made it back to camp it was pitch black. He returned to his post and found a messenger waiting for him instead of Captain Ganbold. As instructed, Temujin changed into clean clothes and then reported to the senior officers' tent, where a feast was underway.

The Kheshig at the entrance waved him inside before he had a chance to speak. At the far end of the huge tent was a high table, where his father sat with his most senior officers. Temujin recognised many of them, but there were some new faces whom he identified by their clothing and regal features. Kings and generals from other nations that had bent the knee rather than suffer the Khan's wrath.

All of the tables were groaning under the weight of the food and drink, but Temujin had no appetite. The sights and smells of the last few hours were lodged in his mind. Abaqa and Jumghur were seated close to the high table, surrounded by lackeys and those seeking to curry favour in the hope of impressing their father. Despite being invited to attend the feast, Temujin was unsure of where he should sit. He settled at a quiet table towards the rear where he hoped to go unnoticed for the duration.

In order to avoid unwanted attention he filled a plate with food, but only ate a few mouthfuls. The bodies in the river had robbed him of any appetite. After an hour, Temujin began to doze in his seat. Men were celebrating and laughing in voices that were too loud to be sober. Dozens of conversations mixed together, creating a cacophony that washed over him. It had already been a long day and tomorrow would be as tiring. Just when he was thinking of sneaking out and getting some sleep, people at the high table began to mingle with the crowd.

From the corner of his eye Temujin watched his father move with purpose around the room. Even now, in spite of everything that had happened over the years, Temujin still wanted his father's approval, which made him feel sick and ashamed.

Eventually the Khan moved to stand beside Temujin, but instead of talking to him directly, Hulagu faced outward, surveying the room. Temujin did his best to ignore his father, picking at the cold food on his plate.

"I'm told by Captain Ganbold you've been performing your duties well," said Hulagu, speaking from the side of his mouth, as if embarrassed to be seen with his son. Temujin waited in silence, not seeing any reason to respond.

Much to Temujin's surprise his father sat down beside him. "I'm saying that you've been doing well. You've surprised me," said Hulagu.

Temujin bit back a comment about not wanting to be an embarrassment. A few people were watching, noting that the Khan was favouring his youngest son.

"Tomorrow, as a reward, you will accompany me into the city," declared Hulagu.

"I'd rather stay with my unit."

Hulagu glared at him. "What makes you think this was a request?"

"Because I'm your son," said Temujin.

"Others would see it as a great honour."

"I'm sorry to disappoint you again, Father."

"This was supposed to be a good thing. I want us to hunt the Caliph together." When Temujin didn't reply Hulagu stood up to leave. "Be ready to leave early in the morning."

"As you command," said Temujin, giving a seated bow.

Hulagu's shoulders stiffened, but he said nothing and walked away.

Temujin slept poorly and woke many times during the night. His dreams were full of images of the drowned reaching out towards him with bloated limbs, their eyes bulging from swollen faces. Towards dawn he gave up, crept out of his tent and had plenty of time for a long wash. He considered skipping breakfast because he was worried about seeing it again later in the day, but in the end he ate something to help him endure what lay ahead.

Dressed in slightly mud-spattered armour, he reported to his father's tent. The Kheshig barred his entry as the Khan had not yet risen from his bed. With nowhere to go, Temujin was forced to stand outside for almost an hour. Eventually Doquz left the tent in a hurry without saying a word, but there was still no sign of the Khan. Eventually his father emerged, dressed in his armour and grim-faced.

"Come," was all Hulagu said. He led Temujin to the command tent where orders were given, but everyone already knew what was expected of them. Any sightings of the Caliph were to be reported directly to Hulagu.

Outside a thousand men were waiting for the Khan to lead them and Temujin took his place among their ranks. They entered the city through one of the breaches and his senses were immediately assaulted by a revolting stench. The smell from the river had been bad at a distance. Here, the dead and decay was all around and often underfoot. Bodies were scattered in the streets in various states of decay. Some were missing limbs and some their heads. Some were torn open, their faces ripped apart making it difficult to tell man from woman. Packs of feral dogs fought over chunks of meat. They ran when the warriors approached, but Temujin could see them lurking nearby, eyes gleaming with hunger, muzzles painted red.

Huge clouds of flies created a constant background hum. Swarms rose from the dead as the warriors passed and then resettled, continuing with their feast.

This close to the walls the buildings had suffered severe damage. Some had been reduced to rubble. Others were standing, but their roofs had been ripped off which created hollow chimneys.

Much to Temujin's surprise, a procession of prisoners was heading out of the city, led by General Kitbuqa and Doquz. All of the men and women wore rags or loose robes, and they had been daubed with a red cross on their clothing, marking them as Christians.

Hulagu said nothing, but Temujin saw him exchange a significant look with his war wife. Behind the prisoners was a cart laden with an assortment of furniture and religious items. Temujin spotted statues, paintings, a large metal cross on a chain and dozens of books. An old bald man dressed in purple silk sat among the relics. There was a large purple bruise over one eye, and he glared at each Mongol as if they had been personally responsible for his injuries.

They moved deeper into the heart of city and began to search every building for the Caliph. If a front door was not immediately opened, the Mongols broke it down, often killing the occupants for being slow. Sometimes they were killed simply because the warrior felt like it. Wailing women and children cowered in doorways, clutching the bodies of their husbands and fathers. Many more were taken away in chains to become slaves. Temujin felt bile rise in his throat as he witnessed a warrior negligently smash a woman's head apart with his mace. Moments earlier, she'd dared to scream at him for murdering her husband. The two small children were left crying amidst the bodies of their parents.

"My Khan," said a runner, approaching from down the street. He was out of breath but managed to gasp out a message. "Resistance. Soldiers. That way," he said, pointing to the east.

"It is the Caliph?" asked Hulagu.

"We don't know. They're protecting something."

They left the house search to another unit and ran towards the disturbance. The sounds of battle reached Temujin's ears long before he saw it. A few hundred men were engaged in a savage fight in the middle of what must have once been a beautiful tree-lined street. Now they had been reduced to blackened stumps. Every building had broken windows and shattered doors and many had been looted. Halfway down the street, several carts had been turned on their side to create a temporary barrier which protected the Iraqis. A few archers were picking off targets, but they were not well organised. The whole defence was badly planned.

With Hulagu at the head of the spear, his thousand men waded into the fight. The enemy were severely outnumbered and the outcome was not in doubt. Temujin had no choice but to draw his sword and try to keep up. Men with longer legs and more bloodthirsty hearts streamed ahead of him on either side.

The sound of the two forces smashing together was so loud Temujin's ears rang. By the time he reached the fight, men were already dead and injured. An Iraqi warrior stumbled towards him, bleeding from the shoulder, his sword dragging along the ground. Before he could raise it, Temujin stabbed the man in the heart. At least he could make it quick.

The man dropped to his knees, almost dragging Temujin's sword with him. He'd barely managed to wrench it free when someone swung an axe at his head. It clipped him on the shoulder, spun him around, and Temujin kept going, swinging his sword in a wide arc. The blade hammered into the soldier's side and lifted him off his feet with the momentum.

Off balance, Temujin slipped and fell to his hands and knees, putting him face to face with the dying man. He spat and tried to strangle Temujin, despite the blade buried in his side. Even though the man was dying, he was determined to take Temujin with him. Using his fist like a club Temujin hammered the man's face, over and over again, bouncing his head off the ground. Eventually, the dying man's strength faded and he fell back, waiting for whatever came next.

It felt as if the fight had been raging for hours, but by the time Temujin had retrieved his sword and got back to his feet, he realised barely a minute had passed. He found himself at the rear of the melee with a few stragglers who were finishing off the injured who cried out for mercy. A Mongol who had lost his hand grabbed Temujin and demanded help with securing a strap around his wrist. By the time he'd tied off the belt, Temujin's hands were slick with blood. Others mistook him for a healer and called for aid. Feeling compelled to do something, he did the best he could, binding wounds and sometimes just sitting with the dying in their final moments.

Eventually, the sounds of battle faded and a tall shadow fell over Temujin. Hulagu's sword and armour were splattered with blood and his expression was a mix of anger and embarrassment.

"What are you doing? Get up," said the Khan, apparently horrified that his son had tried to help others. Temujin left the injured behind and followed his father to the front.

A dozen enemy soldiers were all that had survived the battle.

With hands tied behind their backs, and heads bent forward, they awaited their fate. Taking a heavy dagger from his belt Hulagu slapped it into Temujin's hand.

"Use it," said Hulagu, his words ringing out. With so many watching, Temujin knew that refusing the order would result in dire consequences. As Temujin approached the first kneeling soldier his legs wobbled and threatened to give way.

Knowing that the end was near, the man looked up to the sky and muttered a short prayer to his god. Temujin wished he hadn't, because now he'd seen the man's face. Before he had been a faceless enemy soldier. Now he was an individual, with a name, and probably a family that was waiting for him to come home.

Sweat ran down the sides of Temujin's face. His hand trembled as he raised the dagger and tucked it under the man's chin. He'd killed pigs and goats before. This was no different. That's what he tried to tell himself, but no part of him believed it. Hulagu had disappointment stamped into his features. He was waiting for Temujin to fail.

With one quick jerk from left to right, he slit the soldier's throat. The choking and gurgling went on for a long time. Eventually the man toppled forward onto his face as a pool of red spread out from under his body. With hands still covered with warm blood, Temujin approached his father to return the grisly blade.

He wasn't sure what he'd been expecting. Relief. Maybe even a touch of pride. Instead Hulagu glanced at the blade and then at the line of kneeling men. "Why did you stop? Kill them all."

Temujin's heart dropped.

This was supposed to be a turning point in his life. To make him into a warrior or a son that his father could be proud of. Jumghur would have killed them without hesitation and asked for more. Abaqa would have understood the reasons and gone through with it, even if he didn't like it. His sisters would have asked about the potential loss of earning, but it wouldn't have stopped them getting blood on their hands.

For a brief moment Temujin thought about stabbing his father in the neck. No one could stop him. Then it would be over for both of them. The crowd would tear him apart in seconds, so at least it would be fast. Somehow, his father knew what Temujin was thinking. Hulagu moved his hand away from his sword and raised his chin, daring Temujin to do it.

The rest of the world faded away and they stared at one another in silence for a long time. Temujin was the first one to break eye contact. Even this failure to act disappointed his father as he muttered the word *weak* under his breath.

Without thinking what he was really doing Temujin went down the line, slitting throats until all seventeen men were dead. When he was done he dropped the blade and walked away.

For a time Temujin drifted through the city, not knowing where he was going. Captain Ganbold found him sitting on an empty beer barrel outside a burned-out building.

"The Khan has new orders for you. Come with me." Ganbold said nothing about Temujin's blood covered hands, but it was clear he knew what had happened. He followed the Captain across the city until they came to a huge stone building with massive iron-studded doors. It was fairly plain in comparison to some in terms of architecture, but the scale was impressive.

"What is this place?"

"The central library of Baghdad."

"What are we doing here? Guarding books?" It was another insulting duty from his father.

"The Khan waits inside," said Ganbold, heading up the stairs.

Temujin didn't want to see or speak to his father.

It was early in the afternoon, but he immediately noticed the change in light inside the building. Despite the presence of many lanterns spaced out along the walls, they were in deep recesses. The air was utterly still and deep shadows gathered in corners.

Six Kheshig stood at the far end of a corridor but they gave way as Ganbold approached. Beyond them was Nasir, the Khan's chief engineer and one of the geniuses behind the destructive catapults. Temujin had never seen him so animated before.

He stood on the threshold of a cavernous room that was filled to the brim with rows and rows of shelves, all of them stuffed with leather-bound books. Nasir lovingly ran his hand down the spines of several before cackling with delight.

"What have you found?" said Hulagu, approaching from deep within the library.

"My Khan," said Nasir, sketching a bow. "Books on history, astronomy and mathematics. There's so much to learn. All of this knowledge can be useful."

"What about the books on ancient weapons?" asked Hulagu.

"I haven't found them yet. I'll need help," said Nasir, gesturing at the vast space around him.

"Keep looking, then take whatever you need. Ganbold, bring half a dozen men to carry the books. Temujin, come with me." Without waiting for a reply, Hulagu marched deeper into the stacks.

Temujin hesitated but, with no other choice, he followed his father. He passed through room after room full of scrolls and books. The amount of knowledge stored here was immense. Like so many other buildings, it could have been destroyed and all of this would have been lost.

His father stopped when they came to a rotunda. Four tables sat around the edge and several lanterns had been gathered, creating a rich pool of yellow light amidst the gloomy shelves. Another Kheshig warrior waited beside a slight man with greying hair and long delicate hands.

"This is Reyhan, the chief librarian," said the Khan. The

librarian cowered away from them, terrified for his life. Temujin wondered why until he saw someone's foot sticking out beside the nearest bookshelf. Several young men and women had already been killed. "He will tell where to find the books on weapons and sieges. If he doesn't, he'll die like the others."

"Of course. Whatever you need," said Reyhan, briefly raising his head. When he spotted Temujin his eyes widened in alarm and a peculiar expression of wonder crossed his face.

"Spare me, Wise One," he said, dropping to his knees before shuffling forward to grip Temujin's hand. "I am your humble servant. Please, Kozan."

"What are you doing?" asked Temujin, yanking his hand away. The librarian sat back on his haunches, daring to make eye contact.

"Forgive me," said Reyhan. "I didn't mean to offend you, Wise One."

Hulagu laughed. "He's not wise."

"He bears the marks. His eyes," said Reyhan.

"It's a clever ruse to spare your life," said Hulagu, "but it won't make a difference if you can't find those books."

"My lord. I speak the truth," said the librarian, slowly getting to his feet. He stepped over the bodies and then scuttled down the shelves, disappearing into the gloom.

"There's nowhere to run," said the Khan. "All of the doors are barred."

A short time later Reyhan returned with three old books clutched to his chest. He laid them out on the desk and quickly flicked through one of them. The paper was yellowed and the book written in a language Temujin didn't recognise.

"What is that?" he asked.

"Ancient Greek," muttered Reyhan, scanning the page for something before his finger stopped at a particular passage. "Few in number, but powerful within, the Kozan stand above all. Capable of wielding power beyond the knowing of mortal men. They stride through the world and time."

The second book was much newer and the language more familiar. He could pick out a few words, but some of it was unreadable. Temujin guessed it was some form of archaic Farsi. Reyhan flipped through the pages, searching for something in particular.

"Here, another passage, but this one also talks about 'the Knowledge of Power.' There's also something about the 'inner fire and the knowing' but it's been translated several times." Despite what his father had said Reyhan stared at Temujin with awe. "He is one of the Kozan. A powerful and wise warrior with gifts from the Father of Time."

"Superstitious nonsense," muttered Hulagu.

At the mention of inner fire, Temujin felt the hairs lift on the back of his neck. He remembered the heat inside him and the rebel he'd burned. He wasn't sure what it meant, but the librarian was the first person who might have some answers.

"Why would he make it up?" said Temujin, breaking the silence. "He already knows he's a dead man if he doesn't find the books you want. What does he gain from this?"

Hulagu remained sceptical. "How does it work?"

"I don't know, Lord Khan. But there are other books and ancient scrolls in the stacks," said Reyhan.

"How convenient."

"Isn't it worth investigating, Father? Knowledge is power. Isn't that what Nasir said?" Temujin didn't know if there was anything to what the elderly librarian had said, but he would not watch another innocent being murdered. Hulagu waited for him to back down but Temujin refused to look away.

"Find the books on warfare. Then, if you have time, you can indulge in this nonsense," said Hulagu, making it sound as if it had been his idea. "But I want to see some evidence. His life is now in your hands and, when he fails, you will have to kill him."

"I understand," said Temujin.

He waited until the Khan was out of sight before sagging

against the table. It was the first time in his life that he'd
stood up to his father. Saving one life amidst the slaughter in
Baghdad was a small victory, but it still felt good.

After what Temujin had been made to do, he swore never
again to seek his father's approval. Today would mark a change
in his life. It just wouldn't be the one his father expected.

CHAPTER 19
Kaivon

After several days of witnessing horrors being committed against the people of Baghdad, Kaivon had thought he would become immune. Instead he had a permanent taste of bile in the back of his mouth, and his jaw ached from clenching it so tight.

Most of the wanton destruction had stopped. Now the Mongols were focused on pillaging the city. There were still a few murders, but it was less frequent now that all organised defence in the city had been crushed. Every enemy soldier had been killed or imprisoned, and if any remained they had cast off their armour and now pretended to be civilians. Occasionally there was an insolent glare, or flutter of a hand towards a weapon that wasn't there, but Kaivon pretended not to notice.

The city had been taken, but the people's spirit had not been crushed. While the Caliph remained free, there was hope in the heart of every Iraqi. Eventually there would be a rebellion, but first they needed time to heal, and get used to being occupied by an enemy that pretended it wanted peace. It was very familiar, and Kaivon wished them luck in reclaiming their home.

He wondered if, in the future, he would find an Iraqi general standing beside him in the command tent, serving the Khan.

Every day Esme paid him a visit to check on his wounds. She was efficient and good at her job, but she always stayed longer than necessary to talk. Kaivon's thoughts drifted back to that kiss but then he put it from his mind. It had been nothing more than a declaration of her intent to destroy the Mongols.

When he shared his thoughts about an Iraqi officer working for the Khan she snorted. "Of course he will. He's like a leech, but instead of blood he draws out knowledge from those he's conquered. I've thought about killing Nasir many times, but I realised it was pointless." Nasir was important, but not irreplaceable.

"You'd have to kill all the engineers to make a difference, and there's no way to make that many deaths look like an accident."

"It's possible," said Esme with a shrug. "A bad batch of meat. Certain herbs are tasteless."

"And it only kills engineers?" he said.

She shrugged, unwilling to admit that it was a bad plan. Every time they spoke, she had a new idea of how to cripple the army. Kaivon had the impression she had been bottling up her feelings for a long time, and talking with him came as an enormous relief. It felt good not having to pretend. Around each other they could relax and be themselves.

"I asked around about you," said Kaivon.

"Oh?" said Esme, suddenly unwilling to look him in the eye.

"I came across several warriors with broken arms and wrists. All of them claimed to have been injured in battle."

"There's nothing strange about that. I treat all kinds of injuries."

"Yes," agreed Kaivon, "but apparently these happened after they came to you for treatment."

"How strange," said Esme, studiously sorting her supplies.

Kaivon briefly rested a hand on her shoulder. "I'm glad you can take care of yourself."

"There's more to me than healing people," she said with a grin.

"So I see. I should be going. They're still desperate to find the Caliph."

"Wait," said Esme, resting a hand on his leg. "You should stay awhile."

"Why?"

"The Khan believes you're bedding me, remember?" They both noticed her hand was still resting on his leg. Esme quickly pulled it away and Kaivon cleared his throat.

"All right. Tell me about your life before all of this," said Kaivon, to fill some time. "Where did you learn how to fight?"

"How do you know it wasn't part of my medical training?" she asked, raising an eyebrow.

"None of the men were drunks or fools."

"You're half right," said Esme which made him laugh. "Before being captured, I was part of an organisation that's designed to protect Persia. My fighting skills were just part of my training."

"Can you tell me about it?"

"Maybe another day," said Esme. "I need you to do something for me."

"What's that?"

"When the Khan asks, tell him that you need me."

"I need you?"

"You've seen how he treats his vassals. Hulagu won't give you his complete trust, unless he thinks he can control you. Make him believe you're satisfied and then I'll be made off-limits to others."

"I'll tell him," promised Kaivon.

"Thank you. That should be enough time."

Esme loosened her clothes and then left the tent. Kaivon counted to fifty and then followed her outside.

* * *

Now that the city belonged to the Mongols, a house-to-house search was in effect. Every cellar, cupboard and attic was being thoroughly checked. The Mongol army would not leave until the Caliph had been found and executed.

Although Kaivon held no rank, he'd been given command of eleven men. They were currently searching what used to be a bank. A short time later they emerged with grim expressions. "Nothing," one of them said.

"Let's try down there," said Kaivon. They headed down a wide street that must have been beautiful in the past. Many of the buildings were decorated with intricate mosaics, made from tens of thousands of colourful tiles. Most had been damaged. Faces with missing teeth and eyes stared at him. Phrases from poets and religious figures now had missing words, their deeper meaning lost to those passing in the street. Fountains had been smashed, and what once must have been a small park burned until all that remained was scorched grass and churned earth.

Kaivon spotted a disturbance and directed his men to follow him towards the fray. A woman was screaming as a Mongol warrior dragged her out of a building by the hair. A man followed, being clubbed and kicked by more warriors. The agonised wails of horrified children came from within the home. Seven or eight men were involved in assaulting the adults and another dozen looked on, bored with what had become commonplace. Several warriors were kicking the man as he lay on the ground, with his arms wrapped around his head and knees drawn up to his chest. When the woman tried to shield him from the worst, the Mongols targeted her as well.

"What's happening?" asked Kaivon.

The Mongol officer glanced at him in annoyance. "Nothing."

"What did they do?" he said, trying another approach.

"Tried to stop us from searching their house." The officer turned his back on Kaivon and gestured at two of his men. "Block the front door and burn it down."

Kaivon tapped him on the shoulder which the officer

ignored until he did it again. "What do you want?" he snarled, getting in Kaivon's face.

The men behind him bristled and he heard the scrape of steel.

"We've already won," said Kaivon, fighting to stay calm. "Stop this."

"I know you're one of the Khan's pets," said the Mongol dismissively. "You have no rank. You're nothing but a yowling mutt. What will you do, dog?" he asked, stepping close until they were almost nose to nose.

The question hung in the air between them. Just as Kaivon was about to headbutt the officer, someone new spoke up.

"Stand down," said a commanding voice. Prince Abaqa marched towards the Mongol officer and behind him came a hundred men. All of them were grim-faced veterans, and each one held a naked blade. "There has been enough bloodshed, and we do not kill our own."

Abaqa cocked his head to one side, waiting for the officer to contradict him. As a rule Mongols didn't kill Mongols, but they all knew Kaivon wasn't one of them. The moment stretched on. The officer tested the limit of Prince Abaqa's patience before he finally stepped back.

"Let's go," he said, refusing to make eye contact with anyone. The torches were extinguished and the surly group of men went elsewhere. After he had taken a few deep breaths Kaivon approached the Prince.

"Search the street," said Abaqa, gesturing at the buildings that surrounded them. Kaivon's men made themselves busy, adding their numbers to the search. Abaqa waited until they were alone before speaking.

"Do not think this makes us friends," he spat. Anger passed over his face but it quickly faded, reminding Kaivon of the Khan.

"Nevertheless, Highness, I am thankful," said Kaivon.

Abaqa waved it away. "Come. Let's search in there."

Kaivon followed the Prince to a narrow shop that had previously been looted. The shelves had been broken and the contents scattered across the floor. From the rich herbal and heady aroma, he guessed that it had once been a tea shop. The back room was empty, but a set of narrow stairs led to the upper floor. Abaqa drew his sword and working together they searched the entire building, but found no secret rooms or hiding places.

The street was still empty, but Kaivon could hear warriors moving around in nearby shops and homes. Several local people squawked in protest, but no one else was dragged out.

"I heard what you did on the wall," said Abaqa. "You should be rewarded."

Kaivon said nothing, waiting to see where this was going.

"He was right, you know," said Abaqa, gesturing after the Mongols officer. "You have no rank, but that could change. I could ask my father to make you a general again. Or give you command of a thousand men."

"That's very generous," said Kaivon, "but some men will have a problem following me."

"If it was made formal, it wouldn't be an issue. You've seen the army. We have vassal soldiers from all over, even some Persians. You could even lead some of your own people."

"I miss being in command," admitted Kaivon. He had not asked for anything yet, and being in command would come with a lot of benefits, including more freedom.

Since there was no one around he sheathed his sword. "Where do you see me serving?"

"Why not here?" said Abaqa. "The city will be rebuilt under the rule of a governor. He will need a strong right hand to guide him and keep it secure. I think it could be you."

Kaivon could think of no legitimate reason to refuse without it looking suspicious.

"I would be honoured," he said, realising that Abaqa had outmanoeuvred him.

"The Mamluks are a fierce and dangerous enemy," said Abaqa, moving to search another building. "They know my father marches towards their territory. Very soon they will push back, and Baghdad will become the frontier of our war with them."

And if Kaivon was killed while defending the city, then it wouldn't look suspicious. On the other hand, the Mamluks had become a powerful enemy through strength and ingenuity. They would have spies and contacts of their own in Baghdad. There might be a way for him to work with them to destabilise the Ilkhanate. By putting him in a position of power, Abaqa could help to bring about the downfall of his father.

"It would be an interesting challenge," said Kaivon, warming to the idea.

They searched three more buildings together and found no sign of the Caliph. The Prince's men and his own moved down the street. The two of them waited in the shade of a building out of the sun for the others to emerge.

A short time later Hulagu Khan came marching down the street.

"Father, I was just talking about a reward for Kaivon's efforts during the siege," said Prince Abaqa. "I think he could be given the rank of general again. With his knowledge and skills, he could be of great use to the new governor of Baghdad."

"A generous offer," mused Hulagu.

"He deserves it, Father. He's saved your life twice."

"I remember," said the Khan.

"Earlier, you asked me what I wanted. I want the woman, Esme, and this," said Kaivon, hoping he could help sway the decision.

"No, your place is at my side," said Hulagu, crushing the spark of hope in his chest. "But restoring your rank to general seems fitting. And you can keep the healer. I hear she's a wildcat."

"Thank you, my Khan," said Kaivon, forcing a smile.

He was saved from further conversation when a runner approached.

"The Caliph," he gasped. "They've found him."

"Show me," said Hulagu.

In a large home, that had already been sacked, they discovered a secret room concealed behind a bookcase. It could only be opened from inside, but a ram had been used to smash it open, and now the Caliph was revealed.

In what had once been a lavish room, Kaivon noticed bloodstains on the floor, the walls and even the ceiling. The bodies had been removed but there was still a whiff of death in the air.

Hulagu approached the shattered doorway and after seeing what was inside, he took a step back in surprise. As he peered over his shoulder, Kaivon's mouth fell open. The Caliph was surrounded by a king's ransom. A dozen chests were overflowing with coins. There were solid gold cups, crowns, religious icons, a pile of glittering jewels and that was only what Kaivon could see. There was enough wealth to ransom a dozen kings.

Cowering on the floor amidst the gold and jewels was the Caliph. Although he was a handsome man in the prime of his life, he had seen better days. His clothes were fraying and filthy, and they looked too big on his skinny frame. His face was thin from a lack of food, and the stench coming from inside the room suggested he'd been holed up for days.

"And here you are," said Hulagu, speaking to the Caliph, but also the Mongols crowded into the room. "Hiding like a rat, surrounded by your wealth. Did you weep when your countrymen were slaughtered?" asked the Khan, gesturing at the bloody room behind him. "Were you tempted to come out and help them?"

The Caliph licked his cracked lips but didn't speak. There

was a murmur of voices through the crowd before Berke Khan came into the room. Hulagu made space so that Berke could see the Caliph.

"Here is your holy man, cousin," he said. "Hoarding wealth while his people suffered."

"What will you do to him?" asked Berke.

"We will gather up all of his coins and gems, and then he will pull it through the streets on a cart."

Hulagu was the most hated man in Baghdad. But when the people saw what their glorious leader had been doing while they suffered, it would turn many against him.

Kaivon was ordered to bring people forth to witness the spectacle. His dozen men knocked on doors and shouted for attention. The locals were reluctant at first, but slowly, when they realised it wasn't another massacre, they came to windows and doors. Harried along by a Mongol with a whip, the Caliph pulled a cart through the bloody streets of Baghdad like an old mule. The people stared at the man who had refused to surrender and spare them from the Khan's wrath.

By the time they reached the gates of the city, the Caliph was splattered with rotten food, and his back was bloody from the whip. When he stumbled the people laughed, and when the whip touched his flesh, they cheered.

Eventually the Caliph was taken away, under heavy guard, to await his execution. Finally, Kaivon was dismissed and allowed to return to his tent. A short time later Esme joined him.

He tried to say something, to explain what had happened, but she already knew. Grief and hopelessness threatened to overwhelm him.

"Today, the people might hate the Caliph, but in the years to come, it will be the Mongols they remember." In the wake of a desolate future, the Caliph's greed would be forgiven, if not forgotten.

"It's happening all over again," said Esme, her voice choked with despair. "Just like it was at home."

Kaivon held her tightly in his arms, trying to lend her strength, but the truth was he felt untethered. He wasn't sure if she was holding him up or vice versa.

"I had stupid dreams of making a difference. Of tearing the Ilkhanate apart from the inside," said Kaivon, shaking his head. "I'm a fool."

It was ridiculous. Two people could not change the world. It took armies and a force greater than their combined determination. Grief, for the future of his people and his country, threatened to swallow him whole. Kaivon wanted to lie down and sleep forever. Sink into darkness and just give up.

Esme's body shook, waves of emotion making her shudder. Tears ran from his eyes as the only thing he could see ahead was more death and destruction. His knees almost buckled and she squeezed him tight, helping to steady his legs.

"You're not a fool. I share that dream," she said, whispering in his ear. The warmth of her breath made his skin tingle. "One day we will free."

"I want to believe, truly I do, but the road ahead is so long."

Much to his surprise, Esme's mouth pressed against his. Kaivon's arms instinctively encircled her waist, drawing her closer.

"Then we'll face it together," said Esme. "You're not alone anymore."

While the Mongols celebrated the capture of the Caliph, the two of them cast off their loneliness and despair about the future. And for a time, they found peace in each other's company.

CHAPTER 20
The Twelve

One stared down with envy at the people in the street as they browsed through the busy market. They were happy and totally oblivious to the dangers all around. The colourful awnings on the stalls flapped in the breeze, bringing with it the smell of spices and fish from Lake Urmia. It was late morning, and drifting on the air One could hear the hawkers in the fish market, selling off the last of today's catch to any latecomers.

Behind her the others began to file into the room. Instead of a single table, a double row of small desks had been shoved together in the middle. Once this had been a classroom for children, but now it was mostly used for storage. Crates and stacks of bottles crowded the space.

Instead of trying to squeeze into one of the tiny chairs, One stood at the end of the table and the others followed suit. When they were all assembled she cleared her throat, pleased to see that, this time, everyone had made it to the meeting.

"Thank you all for coming. I know it's not easy for some of you to get away," said One, wincing at the fresh scar on Nine's face. "I have good news from the east. Bolstered by supporters and the promise of men, Ariq Khan has publicly declared that Kublai stole the kurultai. Ariq believes he should be the Great Khan."

"Does this mean civil war?" asked Five.

"Not yet but, God willing, we can hope," said One. "Although I'm sure attempts will be made to calm the waters."

"*They will attempt it,*" signed Twelve. "*But we must make sure that they fail.*"

"Hulagu is normally the peacemaker, but he cannot make the long journey. He's still laying waste to Baghdad," said Ten. She bowed her head and sketched the cross on her chest. "Berke Khan is with them," she said looking at Five.

"There are rumours that he favours Ariq," said Five. She had an extensive network among the Golden Horde that constantly fed her information. "As a Muslim, Hulagu's fair-handed approach to all religions disturbs him. Most of the north has already converted to Islam."

"Did they have a choice?" asked One.

"Not really," said Five.

"What of the atrocities committed against the people of Iraq?" said Three. "Many towns were decimated on the way to Baghdad."

"I have made sure the court of King Louis is flush with the latest stories about the Horde," said Eight.

"True stories," pressed Three.

"No colourful fabrication was needed," said Eight. "Their savage butchery, rape and enslavement speaks for itself. An alliance with France is impossible."

"And Rome?" asked One, turning towards Four. Once she had been flamboyant, but after spending years in Europe amongst the devout, her clothing had become demure.

"My contacts have made sure the Pontiff has been apprised of the latest atrocities. He believes Hulagu and his ilk are barbarian devils. He will never form an alliance with them."

"Not even for the promise of reclaiming the Holy Land?" asked Ten, drawing all eyes towards her. "If Hulagu continues to march west, he will reach Jerusalem."

"He would not be unopposed," said Four. "There are many standing in the Khan's way."

"Can any of Hulagu's allies in the Caucasus be persuaded to turn against him?" asked One.

Two had contacts in Georgia, Cilicia and Armenia. Not as nimble as she once was, Two leaned heavily on the desks. Even with the limp, she was still an attractive woman who could turn heads. It was a weapon she had used many times in the past.

"They're too terrified or entrenched in old blood feuds," said Two, shaking her head sadly. "They will not take the risk. If Hulagu were to lose support from other quarters, then perhaps."

The kingdoms in the north had seen what had befallen their neighbours and had bent the knee in service. It was safer than being invaded and brutalised like many others.

"I have news," said Seven. She had been unusually withdrawn since her arrival. Glancing across the table she exchanged an unreadable look with Nine. "As discussed, we infiltrated Hulagu's army before it left Tabriz. We have a dozen people in the camp."

"You look worried. Has something happened?" asked One.

Seven shook her head but didn't answer.

Nine took up the explanation. "During the siege of Baghdad, a lot of Mongol warriors were injured. We thought it prudent to have at least one contact in the field hospital. Many secrets are divulged in a man's last hours."

"Stop stalling, Samira. What's happened?" said One.

"We found her," said Seven. "Your sister is alive, Kimya."

One stared at the two women. "Are you sure it's her?"

"We have two people watching the Persian General, Kaivon. He was injured and a healer was sent to tend his wounds. It was her. It was Esme."

One was appalled. "She's been alive all this time?"

"As far as we can tell, when the north fell, she was taken prisoner," said Nine. "Instead of being sold as a slave, her skills as a healer made her useful. She's been a part of Hulagu's army for almost two years, moving from one place to another."

One wanted to be angry, but she had no one to blame. Like everyone else she'd assumed her sister had been killed. During in the invasion she'd searched for Esme, in case she'd been sold as a slave, but now felt guilty for not doing enough.

"Did you say she was with the Persian General?" said Ten, her voice cutting across the whispers.

"We believe so, yes," said Nine.

"*With him, how?*" asked Twelve, raising an eyebrow.

"Are they working together?" said One.

"We're not sure, but we have four people watching them," said Seven. "When we're certain it's safe, someone will speak with Esme."

One was speechless. Her sister was alive. After all this time.

"That is wonderful news," said Six. "If they are working together against the Khan, we would have access to information at the highest level."

"I will not put my sister at risk," said One. "Not now."

"Any information we receive would be carefully judged, so that neither of them were put in danger," said Ten. "We would not risk exposing either of them."

"We're getting ahead of ourselves," said Two. "First we must make contact."

"If nothing else, Esme needs to know she's not alone," said One.

"Just make sure it's done carefully," said Ten, and the others agreed. With nothing else to say, the women filed out of the room.

As One she was the first to arrive and the last to leave. Her position as leader required that she maintain a confident façade, but with the others gone she reverted to her true self.

As Kimya, she wept with relief that her sister was alive. One day soon, they would be reunited.

CHAPTER 21
Kokochin

Kokochin had barely slept. Almost every hour she'd woken from a nightmare, shaking and clawing at the sheets. Her face was wet, her muscles ached and her back was sore. Eventually she'd just lay there, staring at the ceiling. When daylight filtered in through the windows she got up. The room spun and she fell into bed, dizzy and sick. Her eyes were sandy, her throat was dry, and it took a while to find her equilibrium.

The nightmares weren't difficult to interpret. Many of them had involved her being chased. In others she'd been locked in her rooms, unable to escape. In one she'd been sent back to Mongolia, where she'd been forced to marry a withered old man. When she refused to carry out her duties as his wife, she'd been beaten and then blinded with a hot poker. She'd woken up screaming, clutching at her face.

Gritting her teeth against the dizziness, Kokochin forced herself to stand, resting one hand on the wall for balance until it passed. She washed and dressed, felt better for it and then applied her make-up. But when she sat down for breakfast, all of her fears welled up inside. She was finally able to make decisions and had started to find a place in the world. To have it all taken away filled her with a gnawing sense of dread.

There was no sign of Tuqtani or Guyuk. She'd hoped to be able to speak with one or both this morning, but after making enquiries with the servants, she discovered both women were indisposed. Neither would return to the palace until this evening.

Kokochin made herself eat, although she had no appetite. Layla had instilled in her the importance of food as fuel. But on her way out of the palace, she felt a quiver in her stomach and had to race back to her rooms. She managed to lock the door before vomiting every mouthful back up, all over the floor. After changing into fresh clothes and washing again, she made it out of the palace without any more problems.

The fresh air cleared her head a little, but she was still tired and now her ribs and throat were sore from being sick. By the time she had walked to the jewellery shop, Kokochin felt unsteady on her feet again and close to tears. She'd barely made it through the door before she was forced to rest a hand on the wall to stay upright. The fear swelling inside threatened to suffocate her.

Layla was talking. Kokochin could see her mouth moving, but she couldn't hear the words. The world tilted to one side and then everything went black.

When she woke up Kokochin was lying on the floor in the back room. As she tried to sit up, Layla appeared at her side, cradling her head.

"Drink," she said, holding a cup to Kokochin's lips. The water was cool and refreshing.

"What happened?"

"You fainted."

"I lost my breakfast," said Kokochin. The fear tried to swallow her whole again. Tears welled up in her eyes and this time she let them fall.

"What's wrong?"

"They know. I'm going to lose everything."

"Take a deep breath and then tell me what happened," said Layla.

Kokochin took a moment to settle before she told Layla what had happened with Tuqtani.

"No wonder you're so drained. Stay put," said Layla, pressing her down when she tried to sit up. She covered Kokochin with a blanket and left the room. When she returned, she had a steaming cup in each hand. The room spun, so Layla supported Kokochin with a hand against her back.

The tea was spicy and sweet. She smelled cinnamon and tasted honey. When she tried to put it down, Layla shook her head. "Drink all of it. You need the energy."

"I need to leave. The Kheshig could be here any moment."

"What can they know?" asked Layla. "We always train in the back room, out of sight. As far as they know, you're learning to be a jeweller."

"But what if someone peered in through the window? What if they saw us?"

"The door to the front is always closed, and the inner door is locked." Layla spoke in a calm voice, but Kokochin wasn't soothed. Tears ran from her eyes again as the pain welled up inside.

"It's too risky. It doesn't matter if I'm imprisoned in the palace–"

"Of course it does," said Layla, but Kokochin ignored her.

"I couldn't bear the thought of something happening to you."

Layla stopped her talking by kissing her. When she sat back, Kokochin was so surprised she could only stare.

"I'm sorry," said Layla, starting to pull away.

"No. Don't go. You just caught me off guard," said Kokochin. The fear was still there, but other pleasant feelings had pushed it aside. This time Kokochin moved towards her, savouring the feel and taste of honey on Layla's lips. "I've been hoping you'd do that for some time."

"I felt your heart racing whenever we touched."

They sat with their foreheads pressed together for some time.

The plan for her life had been laid out by other people. Kokochin had not been an active participant in deciding her fate. Being married to Hulagu and brought to Persia had seemed like a cruel decision. In truth, it had set her free in ways she couldn't have imagined, but in others she remained a prisoner. Her life was not her own. But with time to think, only now was she starting to realise what she wanted. That included who she wanted to spend time with.

"It's too dangerous. I'm putting you at risk," said Kokochin, trying to pull away, but Layla stopped her by resting a hand against her cheek.

"That's not only your decision to make."

"You're right, I'm sorry. Can we just work on the jewellery today?"

"Of course," said Layla. "I need to open up the shop, but rest here as long as you need."

An hour later, Kokochin felt strong enough to move around. She even ate a little bread and cheese, which her stomach didn't reject. Layla mostly stayed in the front of the shop, serving customers, but she would regularly come into the back to check on Kokochin. Her current task was to carefully take apart a piece that had been brought in. A gold necklace, crafted to resemble a simplified spider-web had broken, and it no longer held the four diamonds. Layla was confident she could recreate the original shape. Kokochin had been tasked with rearranging the pieces into their original design, and then sketching it. Once that was done, the gold would be melted down and the gems reset in the new web.

The fear of losing everything was still there, but over the course of the day it ebbed away until it became a subtle murmur. As the afternoon drew on, and her return to the palace came closer, the tension in her body increased. By simply resting a hand on her shoulder, or smiling at her from across the room, Layla held it in check.

Unable to delay it any longer, she kissed Layla again,

hopefully not for one last time, and then set off for the palace. With every step Kokochin became more determined that she was not going to give up without a fight. There had to be a way to keep all that she had gained.

As she passed through the palace gates, Kokochin casually studied the guards but none of them paid her any attention. There were more of them stationed in the hallways than when she had first arrived, but that had become the norm ever since the attack. Perhaps Tuqtani had been bluffing, and she'd not spoken to anyone about Kokochin's trips into the city at night. Maybe no one knew about Layla.

Just as she was starting to feel foolish, she rounded a corner to her rooms and found a servant waiting.

"Princess," said the servant with a bow. "Empress Guyuk requests that you join her for a meal this evening, at your earliest convenience."

The taste of bile rose in the back of her throat, but Kokochin gritted her teeth and swallowed it. "Tell her I will be there shortly."

The servant hurried away and Kokochin dashed into her rooms. How much did Guyuk know and what was she going to do? Kokochin considered running. Gathering up her clothes and whatever money she could find and fleeing the city. She could wake Layla and together they could run away. Kokochin knew it was foolish and could never work. The Mongol Empire was vast. There would be nowhere that was safe.

Her only real choice was to face up to Guyuk. To accept the consequences and try to minimise the damage, then she would go after Tuqtani. Find whatever she loved and destroy it. As the rage built up inside, the fear receded. It was a mask for her pain, but it was better than being afraid.

Once she'd changed clothes and touched up her make-up, Kokochin strode down the hallways of the palace with confidence, daring Tuqtani to make an appearance. Sadly the concubine didn't show and she was escorted into a private dining room by a servant.

Guyuk was sat reading a note at the table, but she put it to one side to give Kokochin her full attention. Her smile was warm, but there was definitely an edge to it.

"How are you, my dear?"

"I'm well, thank you Empress."

"You look healthy," said Guyuk, casting an eye over her figure. "In fact, I think you've gained weight."

"You've spoken to Tuqtani," said Kokochin, phrasing it as a statement. It was better to face this head on than dance around the subject.

"I have, but if I were you, I would ignore that vapid idiot." Guyuk's venom took her by surprise. She smiled at catching Kokochin off balance. "Do my words shock you?"

"A little. I don't know much about Tuqtani, but she was very aggressive."

Guyuk dismissed the concubine with a wave, as if getting rid of an annoying fly. "She thinks the reason you're putting on weight is to make yourself more attractive. Our husband prefers a woman with curves."

"I wasn't doing it on purpose."

"I know that, but, as I said, she's an idiot."

"I've been exploring the city and taking many long walks. All of the exercise made me hungry." It was a partial lie, but she hoped Guyuk wouldn't notice.

"And what have you discovered in this wonderful city?" asked the Empress. There was that subtle note in her voice again.

"I think you already know," said Kokochin.

Their conversation halted while servants filled the table with many small plates of food. There was a large bowl of rice, a variety of local stews, salads, skewered meat and a plate of salted fish. The smells were tantalising and, despite the situation, Kokochin realised she was hungry.

"Go ahead," said Guyuk, serving herself a scoop of rice. The servants closed the doors behind them, leaving the two of them to talk in private. Kokochin filled her plate with a bit of everything, marvelling at the rich flavours of the Persian cuisine. It was extremely filling, but she was determined to taste every dish.

After they'd been eating in silence for a while, Guyuk set her fork aside and dabbed at the corners of her mouth.

"You're right. I do know what you've been doing." Kokochin felt her heart skip a beat at Guyuk's words. "How is the jewellery apprenticeship coming along?"

She had a mouthful of food, so she took her time chewing, buying a few seconds to consider her answer. Layla had been right. They only knew that she had frequently been visiting the shop, not what went on inside.

"It's more delicate work than I realised, and more difficult. I'm not sure I'll ever be any good at it."

"A pity. I was hoping you would make something for me," said Guyuk.

"In a few years' time I would be able, but not before. I must master the basics before I can move on to something more complex."

"And is that what you want to focus your time on? Making jewellery?" Although it didn't show on her face, Kokochin thought Guyuk was disappointed.

"No, but before I can manage the jewellery trade, I need to understand the value of something and how it's made."

It was Kokochin's turn to catch Guyuk by surprise. One delicate eyebrow slowly crept up her forehead. "Manage the trade?"

"You told me to find something for myself and now I have." Kokochin spoke boldly, maintaining eye contact. Her hands began to tremble so badly she put them in her lap to hide her nerves.

"And does this new pursuit give you pleasure?" asked Guyuk, her face giving nothing away.

"Yes," said Kokochin, thinking of the time she spent with Layla.

"You've surprised me, Princess," said the Empress. "When we first met I thought you were nothing more than a wide-eyed girl. Just another pretty face, like Tuqtani and some of the others."

The Empress resumed eating and Kokochin followed suit until she was replete. Once the plates had been cleared away, they moved to comfortable chairs and sipped tea.

"Tell me what you've discovered about jewellery," asked Guyuk. "I only know a little."

Kokochin doubted that was true, but she played along. "You said this city is a crossroads, and that's absolutely true. Gemstones come in from both east and west. This area is rich in gold, so a lot of women wear jewellery made from it. Gold is a very soft metal to work with, so you can make very delicate items, but they're also easily broken."

After weeks of exploring the city and listening to Layla, Kokochin had picked up a fairly good understanding which she shared. Guyuk listened in silence, nodding on occasion but giving nothing away.

"It would take me more than ten years to become competent in crafting jewellery," said Kokochin, plucking a random number from the air.

"Ten years?"

"At least, but I don't plan on doing that. My teacher is a master, so I'm learning as much from talking to her as making things with my own hands."

"I'm impressed," said Guyuk, smiling with genuine warmth. "But you'll also need to study the supply. The merchants, the mines, the smelters and the gemstone cutters."

"Yes, of course," said Kokochin, although she hadn't thought about all of that.

Guyuk leaned across and rested a hand on Kokochin's shoulder, even giving it a friendly squeeze. "It's good to hear that you have ambition. We are not normal women, and should not act or think like others. I'm pleased that you're finding your place."

"I listen carefully when you speak and take it very seriously."

"I can see that. Don't worry about Tuqtani, I'll take care of her."

"Thank you, Empress."

"We should do this more often. Eat meals together and talk."

"I would like that very much," said Kokochin, lying through her teeth.

It was late when Kokochin snuck out of the palace. She was so excited she knew that sleep would be impossible until she had told Layla the good news. No one knew the whole story and, even better, she been given the Empress's blessing to continue with her current pursuit.

As excited as she was, it still took Kokochin a long time to avoid all the palace guards roaming the hallways. Full of nervous energy, she wanted to run through the streets to expend some of it, but restrained herself. It would draw too much attention and she had to be extremely careful. To that end, she took a winding route back to Layla's shop, pausing regularly to listen for anyone who might be following. Finally, satisfied that she was alone, she cut down a side street and then down an alley that led to the rear of the shop. Layla lived above in a small apartment, and Kokochin was pleased to see a light in one of the windows.

To her surprise she found the back door open, and when she touched the handle her fingers came away sticky and wet. Easing the door open slowly she crept inside, alert for danger, but the apartment was silent and cold. On the floor was a trail of dark splotches and in the light from the candles she could see that it was blood.

"Layla? Are you here?"

Moving from the main room to the bedroom, she tracked the bloody path until she found its origin.

Layla lay on the ground in a pool of blood. Her face was pale and her eyes were closed.

CHAPTER 22
Hulagu

It was the morning after they had captured the Caliph and yet
Hulagu couldn't rest. Even though it was early, Hulagu sat up
in bed, leaving Doquz to sleep.

"I'm awake," she murmured. "You were grinding your teeth
again."

"That explains the headache."

Kneeling behind him, Doquz began to rub the sides of his
head with her fingers, slowly easing the aching muscles. "What
were you thinking about?"

Hulagu laughed. "Easier to say what isn't on my mind."

"You can only do so much. You need to rest."

"Soon," he said, patting her hand.

"You always say that."

"And I always mean it. Come, help me get dressed," said
Hulagu, offering Doquz a hand up.

"What needs to be done first?" she asked.

"Rebuilding the city. Now that we have the Caliph, I can
install a governor and restore order. We'll need to leave at least
ten thousand men and someone to lead them."

It was a significant number of warriors, but experience had
proven that it was necessary to squash rebellions and make
the people understand this was a permanent change. Over

time, once they were used to their new lives, he could reduce the number of warriors in the city and return them to the frontlines.

Doquz turned him around so she could tie his shirt closed around his back. "What about the Persian? I heard Abaqa put his name forward for a promotion."

"Kaivon is capable, but it's Abaqa I'm worried about."

"Why? What's wrong?"

Hulagu sighed and lowered his arms so she could fasten the wrists. "One day, he will be ruler of the Ilkhanate. Mercifully, he's more intelligent than Jumghur, but he's not learned the importance of leadership and timing. There are unspoken rules."

Doquz gestured at his cuirass which he lifted over his head. "What sort of rules?" she asked, helping him settle it on his shoulders.

"Abaqa should have spoken to me in private about Kaivon. I do not expect him to consult me on every decision, but this is not a small thing." Hulagu had someone in mind to act as Governor, and three possibilities for leader of the military. "It pains me to say it, but Abaqa has not been tested like Temujin."

Doquz was so surprised she dropped his boots. "That almost sounds like you paid him a compliment."

"For all of his flaws, Temujin always gets back up after being knocked down. This latest notion of his is nonsense but, when it fails, he will try again."

"I never thought I would see the day," said Doquz, shoving on his first boot. "But we were talking of Abaqa."

"He's not been challenged in the same way. Steel is heated over and over again, to get rid of the impurities, and at the end it is stronger. Abaqa needs to struggle, fail and then rise again. He will not be ready to lead until he has tasted the bitterness of defeat."

"It sounds as if you have something in mind," said Doquz, holding out his sword belt.

"I do and he will not like it, but it must be done." It was risky, but his son would learn a great deal. It would push him like never before and make him stronger. Today, they were victorious, but Hulagu knew there would be difficult days ahead as they moved west.

"I will see you later, wife," he said, bending down to kiss her.

"Take care, husband," she said, resting a hand against his cheek.

That afternoon, on the tallest hill in camp, tens of thousands of Mongols gathered to witness the execution of the Caliph. Everyone important was in attendance, from Nasir the senior engineer, to generals, royalty from vassal nations, and Hulagu's sons. Berke Khan and all senior officers from the Golden Horde were also present. His cousin wasn't happy, as he had refused Berke's latest request, to kill the Caliph without spilling any blood. It was traditional to roll up enemies into a carpet and trample them to death with horses. Hulagu had considered it, but such a death would not be much of a spectacle. A clear message needed to be sent to all of those watching on the walls.

Temujin was absent from the execution, but Hulagu paid it no mind. The boy was still holed up among the books, desperately trying to find something that would prevent him from having to kill the librarian.

A small wooden stage had been erected and, as Hulagu stepped onto it, the men cheered. He raised his arms, saluting them and then the blue sky above before gesturing for quiet.

"Today, we send a clear message to our enemies. To stand in the way of the Mongol Empire means defeat, disaster and death." The men stamped their feet and roared in feral voices. Hulagu let the noise spread until his ears rang.

"Bring him forward," said Hulagu. The Caliph had been a striking and powerful man, but now he resembled a beggar.

Stripped of all finery, his head and beard shaved, and dressed only in filthy clothing, even his pride was gone. With head bowed he stared at nothing, waiting for the inevitable.

Hulagu beckoned and King David of Georgia mounted the platform. His men roared loudest of all, adding their voices to the din that rolled out across the army. Every single warrior was cheering, except for Berke who stood with a sour expression and his arms folded. Once King David had taken the Caliph's life it would solidify his loyalty, and that of Georgia. The favour cost Hulagu little, as the Caliph had to die anyway. Georgia was a useful buffer between the Ilkhanate and the Golden Horde on the western side of the Caspian Sea. Anyone that travelled from the north to the south, or vice versa, was seen and noted.

At this critical stage of expanding into the west, information was vitally important. Hulagu had many men, but there was much he didn't know about the surrounding nations, their landscape, armies and shifting loyalties.

"Make him squeal!" shouted a warrior from Cilicia. Next to him, King Hethum laughed and cheered along with the rest. Buqa-Temur and his men from the Chagatai Khanate celebrated as well. This moment had been a long time coming. The death of the Caliph and the fall of Baghdad marked the beginning of a shift of power in the Muslim-dominated peninsula. This was the first step to destabilising it and stripping away allies from the Mamluks in Egypt.

The crowd fell silent as King David raised his sword with both hands. The blade had been polished until it shone. The wispy clouds broke apart and the entire army was momentarily bathed in sunlight. It was a good omen from Tengri, that what they were doing here today was right. Hulagu imagined that in years to come, there would be many paintings of this moment.

The sword came down in a blur, and the Caliph's head rolled away from his body. Holding his bloody sword aloft, King David yelled in triumph and the entire army shouted back, echoing his joy.

* * *

Early that evening, before the grand feast, Hulagu gathered together all generals and senior officials. Altogether there were over a hundred men, including the new Persian General, Kaivon. As well as the title, he had been given a personal aide and Esme. She still tended to injured men, but everyone knew where she spent her nights. For once, Kaivon was smiling. It wasn't power he'd coveted, it was a place to belong. Now he had it all, and Hulagu knew how to control him.

Berke Khan's absence had been noted, as had that of his men. He was already heading north, back to his capital city, Sarai. His absence was an inconvenience, but it was more frustrating that he'd taken his men with him. They would need to be replaced, but that was a task for tomorrow.

"My friends," said Hulagu, bringing them to order. Everyone in the huge tent had a drink in their hand, but all servants had been dismissed. Those whose cup was empty would not find it refreshed until the feast began. He needed them awake and alert. "Today was a great day, and the start of something important. A change of power in the region. Now we must rebuild Baghdad, but the work has already begun."

The pyres had started that morning, burning the dead to prevent the spread of disease. Burying them in huge pits was easier, but Hulagu had learned the hard way how it could poison the land and the water.

"Rebuilding will be a great challenge, as the Mamluks are close by, watching our every move. They have spies in the city, however, today there are twenty less." The discovery had been a stroke of luck rather than skill, but his men didn't need to know that.

Jumghur cheered and raised his cup. No one else joined in with his son's enthusiasm.

"I need someone with a wise head to lead the city. Someone with intelligence to rebuild. Ten thousand men will be left here under the direct command of the city's new governor and his general, my old friend, General Kitbuqa."

The veteran warrior raised his cup. Hulagu noted he was stone-cold sober. All of the others returned the salute, as the General was well-liked by everyone.

"I can think of no one better to take on this difficult challenge than my son and heir, Prince Abaqa." Hulagu was looking directly at his son, so he saw the look of surprise that passed over his face. With so many watching he forced a smile, feigning delight. "Enough talk, now we feast!"

The feast had been going on for several hours. As had happened in the past, many of the senior figures in the army came to speak to him individually, pledging their continued support and loyalty. Hulagu accepted all of them with grace, knowing that such promises were easy to make after a decisive victory.

Some would remain loyal, but others needed to be watched. Now more than ever, he needed their strength and numbers to expand the Ilkhanate. His disagreement with Berke could not have come at a worse time.

As the night wore on, most of his men became drunk. Even Jumghur, whose capacity was legendary, was swaying in his seat. By comparison, Abaqa was sober and deep in discussions with Kitbuqa. The future of the Ilkhanate depended on him being reliable and level-headed, not prone to pride or personal grudges. He stayed for another couple of hours and then retired to bed, leaving the younger men to drain the barrels.

In the morning Hulagu was awake early but Doquz had already left. When she returned he was sitting outside eating breakfast.

"Where have you been?"

"Dealing with the Christian prisoners and their religious artefacts," she said, helping herself to some tea from the pot. "There are some remarkable items."

"Valuable?"

"Only for their religious significance. Some of them were stolen a long time ago."

"I wanted to speak to you about the Christians."

"You said their lives would be spared."

"And they will be, but we cannot keep them here or take them with us."

"Then what do you propose?" she asked.

"With Berke taking his men back north, we need new allies in Europe."

"Who are you thinking about?"

"I will send a letter to King Louis of France and tell him of our victory here."

"That will worry him," said Doquz.

"As it should, but I will also send him a warning about a possible alliance between the Syrians and the Mamluks in Egypt."

"Is that true?"

Hulagu shrugged. "Perhaps. If they had any sense it would happen. Regardless, fear is not enough to make an ally of France. We are going to reclaim Jerusalem from the Muslims and regift it to Rome and their church."

"It would mean a great deal if we could recapture the Holy Land," said Doquz, touching the gold crucifix around her neck.

"Which is why I'm also going to send another letter to the Pope, asking for his support."

"He doesn't like you," said his wife.

"He may think me a heathen and want me dead, but he's smart enough to see the bigger picture. To convince the Pope that I'm sincere, I want to send him the Christian prisoners and some of the artefacts you recovered."

Doquz considered his plan. "It might be enough to convince him. Even so, the Pope may still try to kill you," she said.

"As long as he and King Louis send soldiers, that's all that matters. Next spring will be the time to attack Jerusalem. There is little of the year remaining for us to take land in Syria, so the Christian Holy Land will have to wait. At least by then, I will have a better idea if they are going to lend me their support or not."

Hulagu had asked for aid in the past but, despite exchanging a few letters, no soldiers or Crusaders had ever appeared. If Berke did not send warriors in the spring, and he could not secure men from Buqa-Temur from the Chagatai Khanate, it would be difficult to grow the Ilkhanate.

"You will need to send guards to keep the prisoners safe, and the artefacts."

"Will you deal with it?"

"Of course," said Doquz, kissing him on the forehead.

"Thank you."

"My Khan," said a voice, and a moment later a messenger entered the tent.

Hulagu accepted the letter and sent the man on his way. Even before he read what was inside, there was a nasty pain in his stomach. He read the letter twice and then put it down. Doquz waited in silence until he was ready to speak.

"What has happened?"

"It's Ariq. He's gathering warriors to his banner. He's demanding that Kublai step down and that they hold a new kurultai."

It was less than a year since Kublai had been chosen as the next Great Khan and already there were problems. It did not bode well for the future.

"What will Kublai do?"

"He will not step down, but he cannot let this go unanswered. Ariq is impulsive and he lacks foresight. Even if his request was legitimate, he would be a poor choice to lead."

At times, Hulagu thought Jumghur had inherited many traits from his uncle. Both were useful in a fight, when death was close. But when the battle was over, and careful decisions were required, people needed a politician not a warrior.

"Kublai will seek a peaceful solution."

"And if that fails?" asked Doquz.

The next few years were critical for the expansion of the Empire. They could ill afford squabbling and infighting. Each Mongol victory brought his grandfather's dream closer to reality, but it also served as a rallying cry to those in opposition. Old enmities were set aside, and alliances formed to repel the oncoming horde. If the Mongol Empire was in disarray, then it would send a message to their enemies that they were weak and ripe for attack.

If negotiation between his brothers failed, it could be catastrophic for the Empire.

CHAPTER 23
Temujin

While others sacked and looted the city, Temujin stayed inside the library with Reyhan. As promised, all books relating to ancient weapons, black powder and battlefield tactics had been located before anything else. In total, they found twenty books. Temujin couldn't recall seeing Nasir look so happy. The engineer carefully opened the first book and his eyes greedily drank in the contents. Once he'd taken the books back to camp for study, Temujin was left to investigate the mystery of the Kozan.

The walls of the library were extremely thick and they muffled most of the noises outside. Even so, there were days when he saw the golden flicker of flames through the glass. The sky was always black or grey, and the air reeked of decay and smoke as the dead were burned.

At first Temujin had been going back and forth to camp each night, but on the third day he decided to stay at the library. Food was brought to them and there were modest living quarters in the basement.

Bored of watching them read books and discuss the contents, the Kheshig retreated to the main entrance, leaving the two of them alone.

To begin with Temujin enjoyed the hunt. It felt as if he

was searching for hidden treasure buried somewhere in the bookshelves. The idea of discovering something that no one else knew in the whole world was appealing. However, unlike the books on warfare, there was not a single volume dedicated to the mysterious Kozan. All of the scraps they found were in other books on a wide variety of subjects.

With every day that passed, the thrill of the hunt faded and Temujin became more nervous. He could feel the grains of sand trickling through the hourglass. Unless they found something practical, his father would order him to kill Reyhan. Even worse, he didn't know if he could do it.

"Let's go through what we have," said Temujin after breakfast on the fifth day. "Try and put it all together."

Without further violence, Reyhan's fear had faded and a waspish, professorial attitude emerged. The librarian rearranged the papers on the table between them. "The earliest mention of the Kozan is from ancient Greece, but it didn't originate there. I've found two short passages about a cult called the Arzai, dedicated to the Father of Time, although the word isn't actually gendered."

"And he was a god?"

"No. Not in the same way as other religions. Some faiths have multiple gods and the Arzai believed all of them were the children of a primordial deity. This is the Father of Time."

"So, were the Kozan priests?" asked Temujin.

"There are no mentions of any churches or temples. My best guess is the Kozan were followers of a rare faith. As few people could walk the path, it didn't spread like other religions."

Reyhan must have been frustrated by the scarcity of information, but it didn't show. To him this was nothing more than an academic exercise. Perhaps he had forgotten that his life was forfeit if they didn't produce tangible results. After spending a few days with him, Temujin had found Reyhan to be thoughtful, patient and kind, the exact opposite of his father.

"So, what does it mean to be a Kozan?" asked Temujin.

"By communing with the Father of Time, and achieving inner stillness, a Kozan can summon the Eternal Fire," said the librarian. They had only discovered that last part the previous evening. Given the task that lay ahead, Temujin had shared with Reyhan his experiences of the rising heat in his body, and burning the rebel with his hands. It had provided them with some reassurance that they were on the right path. It suggested his different-coloured eyes were not just a random occurrence.

"There are fire worshippers here in Persia and in other countries. Could this faith be related?" asked Temujin, hoping they might be able to provide some answers.

Reyhan shook his head. "No, the Kozan do not pray to the fire and they predate those who do. From what I can gather, the Eternal Fire is a by-product of achieving inner peace."

There were a dozen scraps of paper on the table, all of them notes copied from books on the floor. Each gave a tantalising hint at something greater.

"Meditation then," said Temujin with a sigh. He'd spoken to several Buddhists in the past, and many of them had discussed the notion of inner calm.

"I would start there. Focus on calming your mind, clearing it of all thoughts and thinking of nothing but stillness. Start with a candle, but not here," said Reyhan, gesturing at the flammable books. "Do it in the basement. I'll keep digging in the meantime."

"Do you have any advice?" he asked.

The old librarian sat back and rubbed his forehead. Some of the vitality he'd exhibited as part of the hunt had faded. Temujin saw the fear lurking beneath his normally calm façade. So, he did understand that their time was limited and the consequences if they failed. "Try to see the flame in your mind. Apparently, once you can do that, a Kozan can summon the Eternal Fire."

"How?"

"You need to find a calm place inside. Tell me of a good memory from your childhood. Something that makes you smile."

Most of his childhood memories were tinged with regret from the death of his mother, or fear of his father. Competition between siblings was encouraged, and Temujin had sustained many beatings from his older brothers. It took Temujin a while to find something that fit.

"Once, when I was eight, my father took me hunting. We both carried falcons on our arm." It had been a cool day with a gentle wind blowing across the grasslands. Away from the brutal jibes and fists of his brothers, Temujin had been able to relax for the first time in weeks.

"My bird caught a rabbit and my father was so proud. He cheered and laughed, showing me off to all of his men. I was happy for the first time in years." Temujin wiped away tears, not realising how much he'd been affected by the memory.

"It's a good memory," said Reyhan with a smile. "Focus on it, and try to stay calm for the count of ten in your mind. When you achieve that, try a hundred and then a thousand."

"That could take a long time," said Temujin.

"I know. In the meantime I'll keep searching for more clues."

After two days of meditating, Temujin felt as if he'd achieved little. He was able to concentrate for longer than at the beginning, but he was still easily distracted by stray thoughts. The silence of the library and the candle helped, but worries about the future kept intruding.

When he wasn't trying to meditate, Temujin did his best to understand the Kozan. More buried clues explained that by achieving inner calm, and channelling the Eternal Fire, it granted wisdom. Literally translated, the Kozan name meant Wise One, although Temujin felt no wiser. It also became clear that the Fire was not a weapon but a conduit to the Father of Time, which yielded abilities.

Late in the afternoon, after he lost concentration yet again, Temujin went back up to the main floor. Reyhan was still at the table, furiously scribbling down something from an ancient book that looked moth-eaten. The spine was damaged, some of the pages had fallen out and others had rotted away. When he was done, Reyhan slid the paper across the table.

"I found an old chest buried in the crypt."

"The crypt?"

"When librarians die, their personal items are interred within the building. Normally, books would never leave these four walls." He was still smarting about the books that had been removed by Nasir. "Amongst the belongings of an old librarian, I found this book. It's a three times translation of another ancient book from a Muslim poet. Read," he said, gesturing at the paper in Temujin's hands.

"'With eyes that are marked, the Kozan stand apart from mankind,'" said Temujin, reading aloud. "'Their connection to the All Father bestows upon them great power and, if used for selfish gains, they could become rulers of the world. Terrible Kings and Queens, unstoppable beings of might. God is good and merciful, because the Kozan are rare.'"

Power. That was something his father would appreciate. However, they were a long way from that. So far he had not been able to summon the Eternal Fire. He could empty his mind and see the candle, but that was all.

"I found something else that might interest you," said Reyhan, pulling out another scrap of paper from the pile. "It talks about connecting with the Eternal Fire. Once you have achieved inner calm, you must surrender yourself to it."

"Surrender?"

Reyhan scrunched up his eyes. "My assumption is you do not summon the Eternal Fire. You connect to it, by leaving yourself open to it. Do not reach for it. Let it come to you. I know what you're going to say," said Reyhan with a wry smile.

"And what's that?" said Temujin, quirking one eyebrow.

"That's impossible. I have no idea what I'm doing," said the librarian, doing a fair impression.

"Well, it is," said Temujin, trying and failing not to sound like a surly child.

"Temujin. I want you to forgive yourself for not being perfect and mastering this immediately. No matter what your father or anyone else says, you are special. They will never be able to do this. You have the potential."

"You really believe that?"

"I don't need to believe. You have the fire inside you. I know it." Reyhan's smile faded a little. "I suspect what you're attempting would normally take years to achieve. But I do not have years, or even months. Will you keep trying?"

"Of course. Nothing is going to happen to you," said Temujin, trying to reassure him. Doubt lingered in his mind, but Temujin knew he had to try. He couldn't give up, because it would mean condemning the librarian to death. Reyhan was an old man by any standard, but he shouldn't have to die for Temujin's failure.

On the morning of the tenth day, Temujin went outside to stretch his legs. The air still reeked of smoke but he noticed a distinct change on the streets. His father was re-establishing order and reconstruction had begun, including the breached outer wall. Once that was done, and it could be held against other invaders, rebuilding would move on to the streets. He noticed many of the dead bodies had already been taken away, although the smell of decay lingered.

Temujin passed several units of warriors patrolling the streets. Only a few days ago the same men had been responsible for widespread destruction, rape, pillaging and murder. The irony of the situation was not lost on the local people as they shied away from any Mongol warrior. A few people had reopened their businesses, and small groups moved through the streets, but the Iraqis never travelled alone and immediately gave way to any Mongol. Despite that, the city felt more normal, and the worry in the pit of Temujin's stomach sprouted new limbs. Cutting his walk shorter than he had intended, Temujin retraced his steps to the library. Reyhan was about to ask a question when he saw the look on Temujin's face.

I'm sorry. I don't think we have long. A few days at most," said Temujin, making a guess. The process of rebuilding would be left in someone else's hands. His father and the bulk of his forces would not linger. Winter approached and Temujin knew the plan was to expand the western border into Syria before it was too cold.

Reyhan swallowed and rubbed his neck, perhaps imagining what it would feel like to lose his head. "Then you'd best get to work."

Despite being alone and wrapped in silence, Temujin struggled to find inner calm. Worries of what was to come plagued his mind. Fear for Reyhan, and for himself if he refused to kill the librarian. His father's wrath would be brutal.

With such thoughts swirling around his head, Temujin closed his eyes and tried to focus on the happy childhood memory. He'd watched it play out in his mind hundreds of times, and yet it still brought him joy. It was perfectly preserved, like an insect caught in a block of amber. What came after were the dark times, but those painful memories could not taint the past.

Focusing on the feelings of peace and contentment, Temujin imagined the candle and managed to reach a count of one hundred. The emptiness spread through his head, down his chest and along his arms to the tips of his fingers. Passing down his spine a cool balm washed over his skin, across his hips, down his legs before enveloping his feet.

In the quiet space within, free of fear and regret, the image of a flame emerged. At first he thought nothing of it. The small flickering fire merely represented the candle in the room. A small flame danced on the blackened end of the wick. But as he contemplated the fire, and looked deeper at the image, new thoughts emerged.

Inevitably, thinking of that day made him consider his father and what he had become. In spite of all of his victories, a large family with many children, as well as the wealth he'd accumulated, Hulagu Khan was incomplete. When asked what he wanted, he would talk of his grandfather's vision of a world ruled by Mongols, but achieving the dream was not what drove him. Temujin knew that was a lie his father told himself. A reason to keep moving forward, in the hope that the next victory would fill the hole within. Never satisfied, he would forever be restless and never find peace. Hulagu Khan was a hollow man and someone to be pitied.

Temujin's eyes snapped open in surprise. The new insight had grown in his mind, seemingly from nowhere. His second surprise came when he realised he hadn't lit the candle, and yet he could see a flame in his mind.

It moved gently, as if in a breeze, suggesting it had a life of its own. Without really knowing what he was doing, Temujin reached for the fire.

The left sleeve arm of his robe burst into flames. The image of fire evaporated and his concentration vanished.

Fire leapt up from his wrist then quickly began to run up his arm towards his shoulder. Yelling in surprise he rolled around on the floor, trying to smother the flames. He could feel the fire moving underneath his body, as if it were a living thing. Black oily smoke filled his lungs and he coughed, gasping for clean air. The fire seemed reluctant to be squashed, despite being flattened against the ground. Shrugging out of his robe he stood up and stomped on the material. Tendrils of grey smoke continued to rise for a few heartbeats and then they stopped.

The commotion, or perhaps the smell, had drawn Reyhan's attention and he came hurtling down the stairs. As the librarian stared at the burned robe, Temujin's eyes were drawn to the charred flesh that encircled his left wrist. A narrow ring of skin was smooth and bright red, but apart from a couple of other small burns, the rest of his arm was undamaged. The tight band sent spikes of agony into his head, even before he explored it with careful fingers. It didn't look too severe, and yet it hurt more fiercely than expected.

"What happened?" asked Reyhan.

Temujin shook his head, unable or unwilling to answer. Despite the warning he had reached for the flame. He wasn't sure if the fire in his mind had been the Eternal Fire or something else. Regardless, by reaching for it, somehow he'd brought it into the real world.

Rather than spend another night in the library, he opted to stay in the camp. When Temujin arrived at the tent he shared with other warriors, he found it empty apart from his belongings. A quick glance at neighbouring tents showed many unfamiliar faces. The others had been reassigned and moved elsewhere.

Temujin was glad to be alone. Although the pain had subsided, his burned wrist still throbbed. Nevertheless, it served as a reminder to proceed with caution. He was still fumbling around in the dark. Temujin was reminded of the old parable about three blind men trying to describe an elephant by touching different parts of its body.

After eating, he pulled on clean clothes and was surprised to find his trousers loose around the waist. All of the physical labour he'd done in the trenches must have burned more energy than he'd realised.

Although no less worried than earlier in the day, Temujin felt a shiver of excitement down his spine. Somehow, he had summoned a living flame. And if that was possible, it made him wonder what else he was capable of. He didn't crave power, but if he possessed it, he would be in charge of his own destiny.

Temujin sought the calm of the void again. It was slower in coming this time, perhaps because of his anticipation. Sweat coated his brow. Sounds from the camp intruded many times, and with each interruption he had been forced to start over.

After hours of trying, with aching knees from sitting still for so long, Temujin managed to calm his mind. Focusing only on his breath and the silence within, he pictured the fire and then waited.

For a long time nothing happened. His mindscape was blank. The inner peace from his fond childhood memory wrapped him in a cocoon of emptiness. The pain from his body became a distant thing. His mind, untethered from the mundane, sought a point of focus.

Finally, the fire appeared. Taking long deep breaths he did nothing, just observed the fire. The breeze, whether imagined or coming from somewhere else, animated the flame. It was not sentient, but it was no ordinary fire. As time passed, and he watched the fire, he came to notice small details. The tiny speck of black at the heart of the flame. The crackle as it moved, as if consuming wax, but there was no candle. Despite the threat of injuring himself again, part of Temujin was tempted to reach for the fire.

Instead, he tried to surrender, but then realised he didn't know how.

All of his life he had fought. For life, when he was born. Against his siblings to earn his place. For the attention of his father. Against his urges and hunger. Against the emotions that sought to overwhelm him. Against the fear of becoming a man like his father, or someone even worse. Every time he was knocked down, he always got back up again. He never stopped trying.

The weight of it all was immense and exhausting. Letting all of it go, even for a moment, felt liberating. Temujin felt a surge of relief like no other. He breathed easier and the surge of emotions threatened to overwhelm him. Instead of trying to suppress them he let go, letting them pass through his body like smoke. Tears of sorrow and joy ran down his cheeks as his body expunged all of the pain that had built up within.

Something shifted in the air and, slowly opening his eyes, Temujin stared around the interior of the tent. He was alone, but looking down at his hands, he saw a small flame hanging in the air above his open palms.

The Eternal Fire was real. He was a Kozan.

CHAPTER 24
Kokochin

Kokochin stared in horror at the pool of blood growing under Layla's body.

She was about to scream when Layla opened her eyes. Kokochin stuffed her fist into her mouth to stifle her agony.

"I thought you were dead," she said, kneeling at Layla's side. "Tell me what to do. How can I help?"

"Towel, there," said Layla, gesturing to one side. Kokochin yanked open the cupboard so hard she pulled the door off its hinges, spilling the contents. Grabbing a handful of towels, she thrust them at Layla.

With blood-soaked hands, Layla pressed one of the towels against the wound on her right side. Her pale face blanched further, and her eyes rolled around as she struggled with the pain and staying conscious.

"Don't faint, please don't faint," said Kokochin. She had no idea how to help and was afraid what would happen if Layla passed out. "Talk to me. Tell me what to do."

"Press on the wound, slow bleeding," said Layla.

Kokochin did as she was instructed, which made Layla groan in pain. There was more blood on her face and arms. Wetting a towel with water from a pitcher, Kokochin cleaned it away, trying to find other wounds. Layla had a few minor cuts on her arms, and a nasty wound in her shoulder, but the one above her waist was the worst. It was bleeding faster than the rest.

"What do I do next?" asked Kokochin. Layla closed her eyes and Kokochin shook her by the shoulder until she woke up. "Tell me what to do."

"I need a healer." Layla muttered an address and Kokochin had to lean forward to hear every word. If she ran it would only take a few minutes to get there. This late at night the streets would be quiet. Hopefully she wouldn't draw too much attention. "Ask for Ariana. Tell her what's happened."

"What if she won't come?"

Layla grunted. "Tell her I was injured serving the House of Grace. She will come."

Kokochin guided Layla's hand until it was pressing down on the bloody towel. She desperately wanted to stay, but she had no idea how to heal Layla. She was also terrified that Layla would die, alone, while she was begging a stranger for help.

"Wait for me," said Kokochin. It was a stupid thing to say. Layla wasn't going anywhere, but she understood.

"I'll be here," she promised.

Kokochin raced down the stairs to the alley and then onto the street. Her feet pounded on the stones, and the wind swept tears from her eyes. There was a painful ball in the pit of her stomach as she thought about Layla. She couldn't die. Not now. She was too young. Kokochin tried to convince herself that Layla was fit and healthy. That she would easily recover from her wounds, but then Kokochin thought about the amount of blood on the floor. She had no idea how much a person could lose before they died.

Skidding around a corner, her shoulder collided with the wall. Hissing in pain she used it to drive her on. A few people stared, but she was moving too fast for them to get a good look at her face. Besides, right now she really didn't care about anything but saving Layla's life.

The street finally came into view and she slowed down, counting the houses until she found the right one. Gasping for breath she rapped on the door three times and then again, not giving them any chance to respond. Kokochin was about to knock again when she heard someone moving around inside. Bolts scraped back and the door opened a fraction.

"What do you want?" said a woman. Her face was in shadow, so Kokochin couldn't see her clearly.

"Are you Ariana?"

"Who are you?" said the woman, dodging the question.

"I'm a friend of Layla. She sent me to find Ariana."

The door opened and a woman stepped into the light. She was a local woman, a few years older than Kokochin, with rich black hair cut into a short bob and green eyes.

"I am Ariana."

Kokochin leaned forward to whisper. "Layla has been injured. She was doing a job for the House of Grace."

Ariana's suspicion evaporated, but it was quickly replaced with anger. "Wait here," she said, closing the door in Kokochin's face. She heard Ariana shouting in Farsi at someone inside the house. A brief but terse conversation followed and then Ariana remerged, slinging a bulky satchel over her shoulder.

"Show me," she said. Kokochin was about to start running again, when Ariana's hand caught her by the wrist. "Slowly. We don't want to attract unwanted attention."

"She's dying. We have to hurry."

Ariana chewed her lip. "Follow me," she said.

Taking side streets and narrow alleyways that avoided the crowds, they raced back to the shop. With every step, Kokochin was convinced they would arrive too late. They would burst into the room to find Layla staring at nothing, her eyes wide and unblinking. Kokochin was so distracted she tripped and started to fall. Before she hit the road, Ariana caught her by the arm and pulled her upright. Whatever her connection to Layla, she didn't seem outwardly distressed.

Kokochin tried to imitate Ariana's calm demeanour but failed. Her heart was pounding and her stomach clenched with grief.

Finally, the back of the shop came into view. When they burst through the door into Layla's apartment, Kokochin held her breath. Layla was exactly where Kokochin had left her and her eyes were open. When she blinked, Kokochin felt all of the strength drain from her legs and she collapsed onto the floor.

Ariana crouched down beside Layla, inspected her eyes and then slowly eased the bloody towel away from the wound.

"Get up," she said glancing at Kokochin. "Fetch me a bowl of water and some clean towels," she ordered. Desperate to do something to help, Kokochin forced herself to move. She couldn't stop crying and swallowed her bitter tears. After a quick search, she found a bowl and filled it with cold water.

"I need a pot of water for tea," said Ariana as Kokochin passed her the towels.

She filled the kettle while Ariana cleaned the wound in Layla's side with a towel. Almost immediately fresh blood welled from the wound, but Kokochin thought it was slower than before. She didn't know if that was a good sign or not. Perhaps Layla's heart had slowed because she was dying.

Ariana muttered to herself as she worked. "Arrow wound," she said, glancing at the injury in Layla's shoulder.

When the water had boiled, the healer added some herbs which filled the room with their scent. The smell was so bad it made Kokochin gag, but Ariana made Layla drink two cups of the stuff before she relented. Almost immediately Layla's head began to loll to one side and her eyes drifted closed.

"She's dying!" sobbed Kokochin.

"No, she's not," said Ariana. "It's just the effects of the tea."

Layla's body had become limp and when Ariana checked the injury she didn't respond or make any sounds of discomfort. Sticking three fingers inside, Ariana felt around for something.

Taking a set of metal tools from her satchel, she probed the wound and then took out a curved needle and black thread.

"Don't faint on me. Make yourself useful. Talk to her," said Ariana.

Sitting with Layla's head in her lap, Kokochin talked to her about whatever came into her mind. Her fears. Her hopes for the future. How much she enjoyed their time together. She had no idea how much Layla heard, or if she was even still conscious. Kokochin did her best not to think about what Ariana was doing, although she could see movement from the corner of her eyes.

"There, done," said Ariana, wiping her bloody hands on a towel. "You can stop distracting her."

Kokochin glanced up and saw the vicious wound had been sealed with a neat row of black stitches. After drying her hands, Ariana smeared a greasy unguent onto the wound and then wrapped Layla's torso with a bandage. The other wounds had also been sewn up or cleaned of any dirt.

"Let her rest," said Ariana, gesturing for Kokochin to follow her outside.

"Will she be all right?"

"With plenty of rest and fluids, I'm hopeful she will recover."

"If you need money for supplies, I can pay you," said Kokochin but Ariana frowned. Her resting expression was one of permanent annoyance.

"More money won't make any difference. Come with me."

They went downstairs into the back room of the shop. Moving with familiarity in the dark, Kokochin lit a couple of lanterns. When she turned around Ariana was staring at her from across the room with a furrowed brow.

"I'm sorry if I offended you."

"It's not that, Princess," said the healer.

"You know who I am?"

"Of course."

"Is that why you're angry with me?"

Ariana rolled her eyes, and started to pace back and forth across the room. "No. I'm annoyed because you shouldn't be here. You have no right."

"Layla is my friend."

"You shouldn't know anything about the House of Grace. It's supposed to be secret. To make matters even worse, you're an outsider."

"I won't tell anyone. I swear," said Kokochin, but Ariana continued as if she hadn't spoken.

"We have remained hidden for centuries because we have no priests or ceremonies, and nothing is ever written down."

Kokochin crossed her arms and waited for the other woman to stop talking. Ariana finished her pacing and then observed her with one hand on her hip.

"What now?" asked Kokochin.

"Come here," said Ariana. "Please," she added.

As soon as Kokochin was within arm's reach, Ariana's fist shot out towards Kokochin's face. She instinctively dodged to one side, grabbed her by the wrist and pulled her forward off balance. Instead of stumbling into a hip toss, Kokochin found Ariana had barely moved. Her left leg darted forward, hooked behind Kokochin's left knee and, with a twist, the healer tried to throw her to the ground. As she had been taught, Kokochin turned her hips and landed on her hands and feet. She was about to launch herself forward when Ariana stepped back with her hands raised in surrender.

"Enough," she said, sounding even more annoyed than before. "I should kill you now. Get it over with."

"You are welcome to try," said Kokochin, preparing herself for a fight to the death. Ariana considered it but then changed her mind, relaxing her posture.

"It's bad enough that you know about us, but it's even worse that she's been teaching you. What is wrong with her?" Ariana shook her head in disappointment.

"We're friends," said Kokochin, "and I can keep a secret."

Ariana wasn't convinced. "You'll be the death of us all."

"Will you stay here with Layla?" It had been very late when she'd left the palace, and now the sky was starting to lighten as morning approached. She had to get back as soon as possible. The risk of being discovered was increasing by the minute. If a servant knocked on her door and she didn't respond, they might enter to investigate in case she was ill. Once they saw the unmade bed, an alarm would be raised across the palace and then, perhaps, the city.

"Don't worry about her, Princess."

"But I do worry," said Kokochin, striding forward until they were standing almost nose to nose. She was tired of Ariana's bullish attitude and constant state of annoyance. "Will you look after her, or do I need to find someone else to do the job?"

Ariana finally relented. "I will take care of her."

Kokochin moved around the healer and headed for the back door. Despite her attitude, Ariana knew her business. Although Kokochin was still worried about Layla, at least the healer had given her a fighting chance.

"I will be back as soon as I can," she said.

Kokochin ran, racing against the rising sun to try and get back to the palace before the servants arrived. She was also aware that the guards would soon be finishing their shift and changing over. Kokochin had never been out this late before. A new kind of fear gripped her stomach.

It was only when she was most of the way back that she noticed the bloodstains on her clothing. She had been kneeling in blood and it had soaked into the knees of her trousers and the edge of her robe. There was more on her sleeves and dried blood on her hands. There was too much to casually brush aside enquiries. It looked as if she had killed someone and then bathed in their blood.

After stripping out of the robe, she scrubbed the blood from her hands and dumped the garment in an alley. Her thin shirt underneath had a number of dark spots, but there was nothing she could do about them. Shivering from the cold, she slowed to a walk as the palace finally came into view.

From across the street, she watched the servants' gate for signs of activity. It wasn't yet dawn, but from looking at the sky she guessed it was two hours away, maybe less. Several people were leaving the palace, yawning and chatting after a long night, but there was no sign of anyone waiting to enter. It wasn't a relief, because Kokochin knew the next shift could arrive at any moment. On the walls she could see palace guards moving about, bored and tired on their rounds. There were several close by, but she didn't have time to study their movements. There was no more time to waste.

When the departing servants had turned the corner and disappeared from sight, Kokochin sprinted across the street towards the gate. In her panic she almost dropped the key, but managed to catch it a second before she slammed into the wall. She banged her chest and elbows, but managed to keep her face away from the stone. Holding her breath she listened for any sounds of alarm.

Silence. The guards continued to shuffle about on the wall, and through the door she couldn't hear anyone moving. With hands that were shaking she unlocked the door, slipped inside and locked it behind her. Turning around Kokochin expected to see startled faces at her sudden appearance and bloody clothes. Mercifully, the corridor was empty.

Taking slow deep breaths to try and calm her frantic heart, she took off her shoes and crept up the hallway. As she passed a huge wicker basket full of clothing she paused. After rifling through them, she pulled out a simple grey robe which she slipped over the top of her outfit. It only came down to her knees and was too wide around the waist but, once she'd tied the sash, it covered the worst of the bloodstains.

On bare feet she moved silently, pausing at the slightest sound and ducking into doorways whenever she heard someone approaching. Several times she had to rush into a room and hide behind an open door. Each time, she was convinced someone noticed her peering out through the narrow gap and would come into the room.

Eventually she made it out of the servants' quarters and into the main part of the palace. Wiping sweat from her brow she pressed on. Kokochin was almost back to her rooms when she heard another pair of guards approaching. She tried the door on her left, and to her dismay, found that it was locked. The next two doors were also locked. The heavy thump of their boots drew closer.

She tried a door on her right and almost fell into the room when it immediately opened. In a rush she dropped her shoes, quietly swung the door closed and snatched them inside before the guards noticed. Holding her breath she listened as the footsteps approached, came abreast of her hiding place and then went past without interruption. Only then did she dare to breathe out. Standing up, Kokochin looked behind her into the room for the first time.

A Kheshig warrior stared back at her from his chair. She'd barged into a storage room where sets of armour were stacked up on the walls. The warrior had been in the middle of repairing a mask that they all wore.

"Wait," she said, but he'd thrown down his tools and started to draw his sword. "I'm Princess Kokochin."

The Kheshig paused with his sword half drawn, confusion passing over his face as he took in her dishevelled appearance.

"I think you'd better come with me," he said, grabbing her firmly by the upper arm. She thought about knocking him out and running back to her rooms, but discarded the idea. Once he woke up, it wouldn't change anything. She'd been caught and would have to face the consequences.

The warrior escorted her down the hallway where he met up with two more Kheshig on patrol. Once they'd confirmed her identity, despite her attire, Kokochin was guided back to her rooms and strongly encouraged not to leave. To reinforce the suggestion, one warrior was stationed outside her door.

Wild, stray thoughts ran through her head. About climbing out the window and running away. About killing the guard and fleeing the city. Physically tired, emotionally drained and ravenous, Kokochin washed her hands and scrubbed her fingernails until the dried blood had been removed. After stripping out of her bloody clothes, she washed her body and collapsed into bed.

As she lay there, eyes roaming around the ceiling, sleep felt impossible. Thoughts of Layla and Ariana dominated. She didn't want to think about what would happen if Layla didn't recover. It was a dark alleyway in her mind that she refused to explore.

There hadn't been any time to ask how Layla had been injured, and who was responsible. Kokochin didn't even know if they were still alive. What if Layla had attacked someone in the palace again? She'd said it had been in the service of the House of Grace, which meant it wasn't random. The Empress was an intelligent woman. It wouldn't be difficult for her to find a connection, especially if she knew the intended victim.

At some point while she waited for an inevitable summons by Guyuk, Kokochin passed out. She awoke several hours later, sandy-eyed and stiff from lying in one position for too long. After washing and dressing, she opened her door to find the Kheshig still on duty. A short time later a servant brought her some breakfast, but then she was left alone for hours.

As expected, with nothing to do her thoughts turned inward. With anyone else she would have said it had not been done intentionally, but the Empress did nothing by accident. Kokochin considered what her punishment might be while running through potential conversations in her mind. Torture was probably not something she would have to endure, but then again, maybe she would. If someone had been murdered, and she was part of a group intent on sedition, it might be possible. Besides, she was only one of several wives and not critical to the Empire. She didn't think the Khan would notice if she died.

Hours later, when her stomach began to rumble again, there was a knock on the door. The note was a request for a private lunch with the Empress. Escorted by a pair of guards, Kokochin tried to maintain her composure as she braced herself for what was about to happen.

As before, the Empress was dining alone in the eastern wing of the palace in the sun room. Today she was dressed in a black and gold silk robe, decorated with colourful birds and flowers. Despite the touches of colour, it was quite severe which she took as an indication of Guyuk's mood. The doors to the garden were closed, and the air inside was warm and still. The smell of flowers was slightly overpowering.

As Kokochin sat down, a flurry of servants appeared with plates of food which they quickly deposited. They all had terse faces and couldn't wait to get out of the room as fast as possible. They didn't know what was going on, but even they could feel the tension in the air.

"Eat," said Guyuk, and it was not a suggestion.

Given that she was hungry, and she thought better on a full stomach, Kokochin helped herself to some chicken stew and rice. Once she'd started eating she couldn't stop and filled another plate with lamb kebab and salad. Finally replete, she sat back, waiting for the inevitable onslaught.

"Do you think you're the first to sneak out at night?" asked the Empress.

"I was–"

"Be silent," said Guyuk, slamming her fist on the table. The plates jumped and Kokochin felt the heat of the Empress's glare. The muscles in her jaw flexed as she ground her teeth. Guyuk waited, balanced on the front of her seat for another interruption and, when it didn't happen, she sat back and appeared to relax.

"I thought you had more sense, or at least some notion of discretion." Kokochin wanted to reply, but she said nothing. At some point she would be allowed to speak. "I gave you too much free rein. Letting you roam around, searching for something to do. The city is a dangerous place."

"Dangerous?" said Kokochin, unable to hold her tongue.

To her surprise Guyuk didn't scold her for speaking. "Yes. Did you know Davood, one of the sub-ministers for trade, was viciously attacked last night?"

"Is he dead?"

"No," said Guyuk and Kokochin's heart began to race. "Although it doesn't look as if he will survive. The healers have done all that they can, but his wounds are severe. None of them were hopeful he will wake up."

"Do you know who attacked him, or why?"

"No, and it doesn't matter. Whoever is responsible will be found and punished. They are an enemy of the Mongol Empire and an example will be made of them. Every friend, every family member, every wagging tongue will be ripped out."

Kokochin felt a chill down her spine. She was afraid for Layla but it also reminded her of what had happened to her family. Kublai and his warriors had butchered her parents, her siblings and every other member of her tribe. She felt her hands curling up into fists and struggled to stay calm.

"Tell me, what are your plans for the next few days?" asked Guyuk.

The question caught Kokochin by surprise. Her thoughts were about Layla, but she made sure those emotions didn't show.

"I have no plans. The jeweller is busy working on a special piece. She has no time to teach me for at least a week."

"Perfect," said Guyuk. Her smile appeared genuine, but Kokochin didn't believe her. "I was going to confine you to your rooms as punishment. Instead you will accompany me for the next few days, and learn about some of my duties."

"Thank you, Empress," said Kokochin, despite being treated like an errant child.

"Don't thank me yet. If you genuinely want to manage part of the Empire in the future, then you will have to impress me." Guyuk wiped at her mouth and took a sip of tea. "While they are away, most of the men think everything at home takes care of itself. They have no idea of how much work is done on their behalf. There would be no war without my work. So I will ask you again, are you sure you want to do this?"

"I do," said Kokochin, starting to genuinely hate the Empress.

"You may regret saying that."

"I'm ready."

"We will see," said Guyuk with a chilling smile.

For the next seven days Kokochin barely left Guyuk's side. She had already been quite scared of her, but at the end of the week she was terrified. Guyuk was far more ruthless than she had realised.

The first day flew by in a flurry of activity. Shadowing the Empress, she attended countless meetings with aristocrats from Europe, Asia, and neighbouring territories. The amount of goods passing through Tabriz was astonishing. This was her first real glimpse of what went on to make it a smooth process for all involved. There were a number of areas that supported trade in the city, which she had not considered. They ranged from large issues such as storage space, to small details such as keeping certain produce far apart in warehouses to avoid contamination. No one wanted to buy fresh bolts of silk that stank of fish from being stacked next to the catch of the day.

When Guyuk discovered anyone involved with cheating, stealing or trying to disrupt trade in the Ilkhanate, she didn't hesitate in having them tortured for information and then killed. She would not tolerate disloyalty and when one servant, who had been faithful for ten years, had been overheard making a joke about the Khan, she ordered the man executed on the spot. Thankfully in her business dealings Guyuk was not quite as mercenary, but she was still ruthless in her style of negotiation.

Kokochin collapsed into bed that night and slept without dreams. She barely had any time to think about Layla before being dragged out to another series of meetings the next day. And wherever the Empress went an army of people supported her. Kokochin was familiar with some of them, such as Rashid the Khan's vizier, but most were new to her. Knowing that the Empress was likely to quiz her on what she had witnessed, Kokochin did her best to remember everyone's name and role.

It was only on the third day that Guyuk started to ask for her opinion. Up to that point, Kokochin had been a silent companion, observing and following the Empress around like a servant. But when Guyuk was forced to deal with the head of a mining clan who refused to pay his taxes, she turned to Kokochin.

"What do you think we should do with him?"

The miner was a simple man whose clothes were worn and his fingers gnarled from long years of hard work. "Given the yield from his mines, the rate of tax is too high." Kokochin spoke with confidence she barely felt. The more time she spent with the Empress, the more she loathed the sound of her voice. "I would recommend a tax reduction for the next five years, on the understanding that if yield improves during that time, he will be expected to match what others pay."

Guyuk stared at her for a long time. Kokochin met her gaze and refused to look away first. She would not let herself be intimidated by the ruthless hag. She could bully and threaten people all day, but Kokochin was not one of them.

Slowly, a tiny smile pulled at the corners of Guyuk's mouth. "Master Hafez, do you agree to those terms?" said the Empress.

"Yes. Thank you, Empress. You are most kind," said the miner, bowing so low his forehead nearly touched the floor. "May God bless you and keep you safe," he said, sketching the sign of the Christian cross on his chest.

Once he was gone, Guyuk turned to her and her smile widened. "That was well done."

"Thank you, Empress." Kokochin forced a smile.

And so it went. For the next few days, Guyuk would turn to Kokochin from time to time for a second opinion. Often they spoke privately before announcing a decision to the plaintiff and, while she didn't always agree, Guyuk listened to her ideas.

By the end of the week, Kokochin's head was spinning with names, numbers and information. Even though she had people helping her, she didn't know how Guyuk dealt with it day after day. There was so much to do. When she had the energy, Kokochin practised her stretches before bed, trying to hold on to the agility she'd gained.

As part of their ritual, Kokochin joined Guyuk for an early breakfast before another day of meetings. Kokochin made sure she filled her plate and ate every mouthful. Sometimes there wasn't time to eat during the day and she didn't eat again until late at night. She needed every bite to keep her awake and focused during difficult negotiations.

"Good morning, Empress," she said, before sitting down.

"Hello, Kokochin," said Guyuk.

Kokochin glanced up in surprise. It was the first time since they'd been working together that Guyuk had used her name. It immediately put her on edge.

"What is first on today's agenda?" asked Kokochin, loading her plate with fresh fruit and slices of cheese.

"I have appointments with ambassadors from some of the vassal states," said the Empress. So far Kokochin had not been excluded from any of the Guyuk's meetings, but she noticed the subtle change in language.

"Am I not going to attend those?"

Guyuk sat back in her chair, watching Kokochin over a cup of steaming tea. She inhaled the aroma and took a tentative sip, testing the temperature. Finding it to her satisfaction, she took a bigger drink.

"No. I no longer think it's necessary. You've impressed me," said Guyuk.

When Kokochin was a child a magician had told her the secret to his success was misdirection. In response to such praise from the Empress she said nothing, waiting for the other hand to slap her across the face.

"I think, in time, you will be able to handle some of the reins. You have an agile mind and don't accept everything at face value."

"Thank you, Empress," she said, keeping her expression neutral. The blow was still on its way.

"Learn all you can from your jeweller, but do it quickly. There is much you could manage related to the gold and gemstones that come into Tabriz. You are free to return to your old life," added Guyuk.

"But?" said Kokochin, forcing the issue. Her forthright attitude made Guyuk smile. Kokochin knew they were not equals, but sometimes the Empress wanted to be challenged. The difficulty was knowing when.

"But in the future, I want you to be more careful." Despite the fact that they were alone she lowered her voice. "I have had several dalliances, but I was cautious. If our husband found out he wouldn't care, but others might seek to use such information against him. So, whatever you are doing, be discreet."

"Thank you," said Kokochin, smiling for the first time with genuine pleasure. During their week together, there had been no news about finding those responsible for the attack on the minister. Another stroke of luck was that he'd died of his wounds without waking up. For now, Layla was in the clear.

"With your permission I shall return to my duties," said Kokochin, waiting for the Empress to incline her head before getting up from the table. She had barely cleared half of her plate, but she was already bursting with nervous energy at the prospect of seeing Layla. Her whole body was tingling and she felt light on her feet.

Which made the unseen hand, and the shock that came with, that much more devastating when it landed.

"The siege of Baghdad is over," said Guyuk as Kokochin was nearing the door. "The city is secure and the Khan is currently appointing a governor. Once that is done, he will push west into Syria, but winter is approaching."

"Meaning?" asked Kokochin, turning back.

"In a few short months, our husband will be coming home."

With great effort Kokochin forced a smile. "That is wonderful news."

"I thought so," said Guyuk, dismissing her with a wave.

As soon as she turned away the smile fell off Kokochin's face.

She tried to tell herself that she was only one of many wives and that he would have little time for her but, by impressing Guyuk, Kokochin might have drawn more attention to herself than she wanted. Even if Hulagu had little use for her, she had no doubt that the Empress would mention her potential to the Khan. Everyone was expected to serve the Mongol Empire, and now that she had proven herself competent, it would be no different for her. By demonstrating her intelligence she may have made her future worse.

CHAPTER 25
Kaivon

At the victory banquet the previous night, Kaivon had smiled and tried his hardest to appear at peace. Esme had impressed upon him to make it a convincing performance, and it had worked.

In the morning, his Kheshig bodyguards were gone. He had finally reached a place where Hulagu Khan trusted him, or at least, trusted him enough not to have him constantly followed.

Last night he'd casually gathered information from a dozen senior figures. He'd listened, and occasionally asked open-ended questions, but never led the conversation. It had been slow and laborious, but eventually he'd found the right person. There was little that General Kitbuqa didn't know and, as Kaivon was now a fellow general, he'd been happy to share information.

As he got dressed, Kaivon tried not to wake Esme who was still dozing in bed, but she came awake, rubbing sleep from her eyes.

"I was just about to leave."

"I need to tell you something first," said Esme. "I tried to stay up, but you were late back."

"I need to go soon."

"Something happened," said Esme.

Her tone of voice made Kaivon sit down. "Are you all right?" he asked.

"There's something I need to tell you," she said with a smile. "Before the invasion, I was part of a group called the House of Grace."

"You were a rebel."

"No, you don't understand. This is different," said Esme, shaking her head. "It's an ancient order and it's widespread. The network is massive, and it covers all of Persia and beyond."

"What are you saying?"

"I'm saying we're not alone anymore. Someone made contact with me last night. They're here, in the army, watching and reporting on the Khan."

"Did you tell them about the plan?" asked Kaivon.

"No, but they carried a message from my sister, so I would know they were genuine. They've offered to help us with whatever we need; resources, money, information. I have a couple of contacts that I can call on."

"That's good news. We'll have to talk about this more when I get back," said Kaivon, pulling on his belt. "If I get back," he added.

"You'll be fine."

"If I don't return, you should see if your new contacts can get you out."

"Please don't talk like that."

"I'm sorry," he said, wrapping his arms around her. "I'm just worried."

"Be safe," said Esme, holding him tightly. Kaivon enjoyed a moment of peace before stepping back.

"I'll see you soon," he said, hoping that it was true.

Outside the sky was grey, clogged with smoke and ash from burning the dead, but in a few places beams of sunlight had broken through. Everyone else from the banquet would also be suffering, which gave him time to use what he'd learned.

After a quick breakfast, he marched to the stockade. This

close to the gates, the streets had been cleared of rubble, creating a semblance of normality. Further in, the city was still a charnel house, but here a veneer of civilisation had been painted over the destruction. Looking to his left, Kaivon saw two stray dogs fighting over something, worrying it between them, until the thing came apart. Each dog claimed half of a child's severed leg and then disappeared into the shadows to enjoy their feast. Most of the bodies had been cleared away, but a few remnants remained. The smell of death and rot lingered.

Close to the gate, one of the larger buildings was still intact and had been converted into a temporary prison. The two guards outside were dozing at their posts, but they came awake when they saw Kaivon approaching. He was the only Persian general in the Khan's army and, despite his wishes, he'd become known for his heroism in battle.

"General," one of them said around a yawn. "What do you need?"

"I need to speak with one of the spies."

Since they'd been discovered in the city, the Mamluk spies had been tortured and questioned. Twenty had been caught and only nine were still alive. The inquisition had been brutal, and the others were often made to watch or listen to what their friends had to endure. So far, little useful information had been extracted, but there was a growing collection of spare teeth and fingernails.

"Follow me," said the guard, leading Kaivon through the front door. The building used to be a bank. From the remnants of the intricate mosaics on the floor, to the few surviving marble statues, it must have been magnificent. Now the upper two floors had been utterly destroyed, leaving only the ground floor and an extensive basement intact. The warren-like rooms underground were extremely cold, dry and protected by heavy iron grates with sturdy locks, making them ideal to hold prisoners.

In addition to the two guards at the front door, Kaivon

passed two more inside the building at the top of the stairs, and another guard inside the thick iron gate. The bars were as thick as his leg, but so close together that he would barely be able to squeeze his hand between the gaps.

This far below ground the cold was biting. Kaivon's breath frosted in front of his face and the tips of his fingers began to tingle. With no movement, the air smelled of unwashed bodies, blood, fear sweat, piss and human waste.

The guard had a lantern at his side and another had been placed on the wall at the far end of the short corridor. It kept the shadows back from the middle but little else.

"Which one are you here to see?" asked the guard. He was wearing a pair of thick gloves and a fur-lined helmet that covered his ears.

"Masuud."

The guard grunted. "He's popular. Last cell on the left."

One or two gaunt faces peered out at Kaivon from behind the bars, but most of the prisoners stayed in the shadows. One man was wheezing so badly that the time between each breath was longer than the last. Death roamed the cells, waiting to claim its next victim.

In the last cell was Masuud, sitting on the stone floor with his head dangling between his knees. In the dim light, Kaivon could see dried blood on his scalp and the end of each finger was raw. There would be other less visible injuries, but when Masuud realised he wasn't alone, he raised his head in defiance.

"I'm here to get you out," said Kaivon, keeping his voice low so that it didn't carry to the guard at the end of the hallway.

Masuud grinned, showing gaps in his teeth and bloody gums. "Funny."

"This is not a game."

"You've tried the stick, so here is the carrot," said Masuud. "And what do you need from me for this generous gift?"

Kaivon moved closer to the bars, squatting down until their eyes were level. "Nothing. I just need you to be ready." Masuud still didn't believe him, but it didn't really matter. Even so, he had to give the Mamluk something to stop him from talking to the wrong person. "I am also a prisoner of the Khan. My homeland has been overrun and my people butchered, until they had no choice but to surrender. Now he has done the same thing here, and the Mongols will do it again and again, until all countries are under their boot."

Masuud didn't reply, but Kaivon could see that he was listening. If he stayed too long the guard would become suspicious. He had to get to the point and hope that it would be enough.

"If I get you out of here, I want a promise."

Masuud raised an eyebrow. "What sort of promise?"

"Fight. Make whatever deals you have to. Form alliances with hated enemies, but fight and keep fighting, so that this," said Kaivon, gesturing at the city around him, "doesn't happen to anyone else."

"I can do little from inside my cell," said the Mamluk.

"I know, which is why I'm going to free you tonight. All you have to do is stay alive until then."

Masuud stared at him for a long time before speaking. "Where are you from?"

"Persia."

"And what do you want?"

"I want to free my people from Mongol rule," spat Kaivon, letting his real feelings show for a moment. "And the first step to doing that is to help you."

"What about the others?" asked Masuud.

Kaivon shook his head. "Smuggling you out is risky enough. More than that would be impossible."

"When?" was all he asked. Masuud understood that Kaivon was condemning his fellow spies to death, but he didn't flinch.

"As soon as it's dark. Be ready."

Kaivon waited until Masuud nodded before walking out of the prison. He had taken the first step. Now he had to try and build on it. What came next was infinitely more dangerous, and likely to get him killed. He didn't want to die, but if his plan should fail, then at least it would have been in the service of liberating his country. For the first time in months, Kaivon felt alive.

When he approached the prison late that night, the guards on duty at the door had changed. However, word of his visit must have spread as the newcomers were not surprised to see him. One of the warriors held open the front door, but raised an eyebrow when he didn't immediately go inside.

"Is there something you need?"

"Yes. You're going to help me break out a prisoner."

The guards exchanged a worried look. "General?" asked the taller one, on the left.

"Torture isn't working, so I've been given a plan from the Khan and I need your help."

At the mention of the Khan their attitude shifted immediately. "Of course, whatever you need, General."

"You will pretend to be drunk on duty," said Kaivon, handing one of them a pouch of airag. "Then I will sneak out with the prisoner. Once we're away from the city, he will trust me and tell me everything. Splash some around on your clothes," he suggested.

"Don't waste it," said the other guard, snatching it off his friend. He took a healthy pull from the pouch and smacked his lips. The other guard took it back and had a long drink.

"I'll be coming out with him soon. Pretend to be asleep," said Kaivon.

Inside he repeated the story with the other guards, passing them another skin of airag which they all shared. The sounds of merriment attracted the guard at the bottom of the stairs, who came up to see what was going on. He had two long pulls before going back down into the cold. The guard let him inside the cell block, passed over the keys, and then resumed his post by the open gate.

Masuud was waiting at the front of his cell. His eyes never strayed from the guard lounging nearby. "How are we to get past them without being seen?"

"Wait," said Kaivon. He had not been idle during the day. He'd used some of his own money to buy the ingredients from different shops across the city. In all three cases, it had taken him a while to persuade the owners to let him inside. They needed the money, but most Iraqis were still barricading themselves away, only venturing out when they needed food. The river and roads had been reopened, but trade was slow in returning to the city.

The guard at the gate nodded, his head moving down towards his chest, before he suddenly jerked himself awake. Slurring his words he took two steps towards Kaivon and then dropped to his knees. The blood drained from his face and then he fell forward. If any of the other prisoners had noticed, they gave no sign. If even one of them said anything Kaivon was dead but, given their hatred of the Mongols, he believed they would feign ignorance.

Kaivon let Masuud out of his cell and together they dragged the guard out of sight. Taking the guard's dagger from his belt, Kaivon offered it to the Mamluk.

"If you still think this is a ploy, use this now. I do not want you stabbing me in the back."

Masuud looked at the heavy dagger for a moment before finally accepting it. "I believe you."

"Good. It will make this much easier." Kaivon drew his own dagger and then slit the guard's throat. He would eventually have died from the poison he'd ingested, but there had still been a small risk he could raise an alarm. As the blade opened his flesh, the guard came awake, choking and gasping for air. His fingers flapped about and in a few heartbeats he was dead.

"They've seen my face," said Kaivon as way of explanation but Masuud just shrugged. One more dead Mongol made no difference to him.

Upstairs the other guards were all face down at the table. One had fallen off his chair to the floor. Somehow he was still awake, and one of his legs twitched as Kaivon knelt on his chest holding a bloody knife.

"Why?" he wheezed before the blade went into his chest.

Leaving the bodies where they had fallen they moved to the front door. Kaivon paused, listening for any sign that the guards outside were still awake. Hearing nothing, he eased the door open, then quickly stepped back as one of the guards fell into the room. He landed without a sound, but his eyes were open.

Together they dragged the bodies inside, laying them down beside the others. Only then did Kaivon kill them, stabbing them in the back, to help with the story of the prisoner's daring escape. Masuud dressed in one of the guard's uniforms and showed no signs of discomfort at the blood. If someone stared at him too closely, it would be easy to tell he wasn't a Mongol.

It would be dawn before the guards changed over and, hopefully by then, they would be far away from the camp.

"Keep your eyes down and don't talk to anyone. I'm a general, so follow me and do as I say. Is that clear?"

"Lead the way," said Masuud.

Kaivon still felt a prickle of fear as he turned his back on the Mamluk, but he had to trust that the spy wouldn't betray him. It was possible he might disappear into Baghdad, reconnect with contacts and try to escape, but Kaivon didn't think it likely. The best thing the spy could do was return to his people, to tell them what he had seen.

Sweat formed in Kaivon's hairline as he led Masuud through the dark streets towards the main gates. There were a few people about at such a late hour but none of them stopped to ask what he was doing or where he was going. Only a few days ago, this plan would have been impossible. It was still a huge risk, but it was better than doing nothing.

Despite the potential gains, he thought about killing the spy and going back to his tent. He worried about what would happen to Esme if this went wrong, but he pushed the thought aside. She would be furious if she found out he'd given up, or sabotaged the plan on her account. Besides, she had contacts that could help if she got into trouble.

At the edge of the camp he headed west towards the paddocks, trying hard not to appear in a hurry. There were more Mongol warriors about and one or two recognised him. Kaivon greeted them, but otherwise he kept walking, trying to swallow the lump in his throat. Sweat trickled down the inside of his clothing, gathering at his waist. His heart was pounding so loudly it felt as if it would burst out of his chest.

Moving slowly so that he didn't drop anything or appear panicked, they saddled two horses and then led them out of the camp. When they were beyond the final line of tents, Kaivon gestured for Masuud to mount up. At any moment, he expected someone to raise the alarm, call him a traitor and drag him from the saddle. Unable to speak, he nudged his horse into a gentle trot.

They rode west for an hour, wrapped up in their own thoughts and fears. Kaivon was unable to relax until he had put some distance between them and the Mongol horde. Looking behind him into the darkness, and cocking his head to one side, Kaivon listened for sounds of pursuit. If there was anyone back there, they were far enough away that he could speak freely without the risk of being overheard.

"I feel as if I can breathe for first time in weeks," said Kaivon, getting down from the saddle to stretch his legs. Masuud left the Mongol helmet on the pommel and also dismounted. "What will you do now?"

Masuud rubbed a tired hand over his face. Kaivon noticed all of the fingernails on both of his hands had been pulled out.

"I didn't think we were going to make it," he said. The spy's hands shook with adrenaline before he laughed with relief.

Kaivon smiled and the tension in his chest eased. "I know. I felt the same."

"I'll report back to my superiors. Tell them about what I've seen in Baghdad. Numbers, siege engines, tactics and the number of men and horses."

"Do you have enough warriors to stop them?" asked Kaivon.

Masuud shook his head. "I don't know. Perhaps not in a direct fight on a battlefield, but there are many cities between here and Cairo."

"And the Khan will stop to claim each as a new prize," said Kaivon, finishing his thought.

"Exactly. It will give us time to prepare and, as you said, make alliances."

"Who with?"

"Perhaps the Syrians and Palestinians," said Masuud and then he grimaced. "We may even need to make peace with the Baybars."

Egypt was rife with its own factions and struggles for power. The Baybars were the main rivals of the Mamluks.

"It may be the only way to stop his expansion into the west."

"Come with me," said Masuud, catching him by surprise.

"What? Where?"

"To Cairo. You know far more about Hulagu Khan's army and his tactics than me. You could be a valuable asset in the fight against him. Why else would you stay at his side?"

It was not something Kaivon had considered, but he took a moment to think it through. Aligning himself with the Mamluks, and their allies, put him in no better a position. He would be an outsider, and directly in the jaws of the Mongol horde. Besides, it would also mean abandoning Esme.

"I cannot abandon my people," said Kaivon. "There are those back home, but also other Persians in the Mongol army. I must free them."

"I understand," said Masuud. "I will tell the Sultan what you have done for us."

"You know the Sultan?" said Kaivon, unable to hide his surprise.

"Of course, we're cousins. Qutuz is also a good friend."

"Then there is something else you must tell him. The Khan is going to send letters to the King of France, and also the Pope in Rome, for support. With the loss of warriors from the Golden Horde, he will need their numbers."

"It is something we feared might happen," admitted Masuud. "That is why we have been speaking to the church for months."

Kaivon was taken aback. The church had sent many crusaders against the Egyptians, for their beliefs, but also for seizing the Christian Holy land. "An alliance with the Pope?"

Masuud shrugged. "He will have to choose between the lesser of two evils." Mamluk offered his hand and Kaivon shook it. "Thank you, for all that you've done for me."

"You should take that off," said Kaivon gesturing at the Mongol armour. "You don't want to be killed by your people by accident."

As the Mamluk reached behind his back to unfasten his belt, Kaivon stabbed him in the throat. Ripping the blade away he stepped back out of arm's reach.

Masuud's eyes bulged in surprise and he feebly grasped at the wound, trying to hold back the flood that was pouring down his neck. Kaivon kept his distance, watching impassively as the man gasped his final breaths. The spy had given him a lot to think about and much information that, assuming he lived long enough, he could use to his advantage. When he was dead, Kaivon used the guard's sword to cut off Masuud's head. He wrapped it in the dead man's shirt and fastened it to his saddle. The horses were well-trained, but even they didn't like the smell of so much blood.

Checking the stars overhead Kaivon turned his horse around and headed west to complete the last part of his plan.

The caravansary was busy with a constant flow of merchants, pilgrims and one or two solo travellers. Even so, Kaivon knew it would be impossible for him to go unnoticed. They were no longer within the Mongol Empire but a Persian warrior, dressed in Mongol attire, would draw a lot of unwanted attention.

After sleeping outdoors under a blanket he was sore, tired and eager for a hot meal, but a fire would also attract unwanted attention. He ate a cold breakfast and resumed his study of the road, watching as merchants loaded up their wagons headed both west, into Mongol territory and east, into Turkey and Europe. Some turned north towards the Caucasus and beyond, into the territory of Berke Khan and the Golden Horde. His withdrawal from Baghdad had been the first piece of the puzzle.

Every time a lone rider appeared on the road, coming from the east, Kaivon prepared to break camp and pursue them. And every time, when it turned out not to be someone he needed, he slumped back in disappointment. After straining his eyes for most of the day, Kaivon was exhausted, stiff and agitated.

An hour later, when another rider came into view, it took Kaivon a while to notice that it was a Mongol. Although this was not a Mongol waystation, the rider did pause to rest his horse. Within the Empire, such messengers were able to swap one mount for another and immediately continue with their journey, enabling them to cover huge distances in a short amount of time.

Anyone interfering with such a person would face severe consequences. The messenger was carrying the written word of the Khan. Here, they were not as revered, but were still highly regarded, and messengers wore an almost invisible cloak that protected them from harm.

The messenger dismounted, left his horse to be attended by the stables and went indoors. As soon as the door was closed, Kaivon gathered up his belongings and walked his horse west to a sheltered spot on the road. After an hour, with no sign of the rider, he began to worry the messenger had decided to spend the night at the caravansary. Even worse, he could have decided to ride across country. Kaivon's chest swelled with relief when he finally spotted the rider approaching at a steady trot.

He nudged his horse forward until it rested half on the road, not blocking it, but making his presence known. At first the messenger looked apprehensive, but then he relaxed when he recognised the Mongol uniform Kaivon wore.

"Are you here for me?" asked the messenger. He was a young man, barely out of his teenage years, with a downy moustache and a few hairs on his chin. His skin was clear of any blemishes, his forehead smooth without lines from worry. Even his black hair was perfect, with no hint of grey or white. His face was one that Kaivon would never forget.

The messenger's eyes widened in surprise and then horror as Kaivon's sword punched him in the chest. The force of the blow drove him off his horse. The animal whickered and took a few steps away, but mercifully didn't run. Kaivon sat with the young man, holding his hand, as he coughed and tried to breathe through the blood filling his lungs. It didn't take long. He managed a few ragged, phlegmy breaths and then his eyes glazed over.

Kaivon stripped the body, leaving it for the scavengers, but he buried the messenger's clothing. Leading the other horse by the reins he headed south-east, away from the road into the rugged landscape, retracing his steps towards Baghdad.

At night he went through the messenger's saddlebags and found a few personal belongings, all of which he burned. Nestled at the bottom, in a leather pouch, were the letters. There were three to King Louis of France, which he didn't need to read. They went into the flames, quickly caught fire and were reduced to ash in seconds. There would be no support from France.

He opened the package of letters to the Pope and scanned them for useful information. It had been too late to stop the return of the prisoners and artefacts. However, the letters detailed what the Khan required of the Pope, and his plans for the Christian Holy Land next year. A few Italian soldiers or Holy Crusaders might still make the journey, but without specific dates, few would take such a risk. It was a good step in slowing the expansion of the Ilkhanate.

Tomorrow, if he survived what came next when he returned to the Mongol camp, Kaivon would take another step and then another. And if what Esme said turned out to be true, then they were no longer alone in the fight. They would build momentum and, piece by piece, they would destroy Hulagu Khan and all that he had built.

CHAPTER 26
The Twelve

The meeting had been called in haste, and all but three of their number could attend. The others would be told what had transpired, but with such important news the gathering couldn't wait.

Kimya was desperate for word about her sister and had arrived early. The large storage room, in the back of a spice merchant's shop, was still being swept by a teenage boy. The owner ushered him out, muttering an apology while the boy stared at her expensive clothing and jewellery. The family had been carefully vetted, so she knew they could be trusted. However, as a rule, she didn't like too many people to see her face before the meetings.

Eventually the others started to arrive, by which time One was tapping her foot and trying not to bite her nails. She waited until everyone was settled before turning towards Seven for an update.

"Your sister is alive and well," said Seven.

One heaved a huge sigh of relief and had to stop herself from laughing. There was a deep ache in her shoulders from hunching them. Some of the tension drained away from her body.

"Thank you. Please continue," she said.

"We've made contact and it's as you thought," said Seven. "Both she and the Persian General are working together against the Khan. They intend to disrupt Hulagu's plan to form alliances with France and Rome."

One's heart swelled with pride. Even after all this time, and with everything she must have endured, her sister was still fighting.

"Hulagu has sent many Christian prisoners and artefacts to Rome," said Four. Her hand inadvertently strayed to the gold crucifix around her neck. "Even with this gesture, it will take little effort to keep the Pope set against him. The prisoners and their first-hand stories will do the work for us."

"There's more good news," said Five, tucking a loose strand of hair behind an ear. One noticed the seven silver piercings and wondered at their significance. "Berke Khan and his men are returning home to Sarai. He had a disagreement with Hulagu Khan about the treatment of Muslims in Baghdad. He's also furious that they burned down the Grand Mosque."

"That's good for us," said One.

"I have multiple contacts spreading stories across the north about the desecration, as well the murder of men, women and children." Five was utterly calm, but Eleven snarled and looked ready to spit. "The Mongols also executed the Caliph, in front of everyone. This was after they had paraded him through the streets."

"His murder will not be forgotten," said Ten. "It has angered many Muslims. Hulagu may come to regret what he's done."

"Let us hope that he does," said One.

They discussed other matters for a while, contacts who needed further guidance and plans for the future. Two normally contributed to their discussion, but since arriving she had not spoken. One thought she looked troubled, but didn't want to draw attention in front of the others.

An hour later they were almost done. "Any other news?" asked One, looking around the table.

"I have news," said Two, breaking her silence. "One person in the Trade Ministry could not be persuaded, blackmailed or bought. He was scheduled to be removed, but something went wrong. He injured one of my people."

"Is she still alive?" asked One.

"Yes, and I hope that she will make a full recovery. The sub-minister will not."

"Then what is the problem?"

Two cleared her throat before speaking. "Layla was discovered by a friend who called for a healer. It turns out Layla had been training this friend in the ways of the House."

The silence in the room was heavy and absolute, like the moment before a lightning strike. One realised she was holding her breath.

Two broke the silence. "The friend is Kokochin, the Blue Princess. She is the newest wife of Hulagu Khan."

The room erupted as everyone started to shout or swear. A couple of women were stunned into silence, but the rest were animated, on their feet, waving their arms, appalled that such a thing had happened.

"*Calm down,*" signed Twelve, but no one paid her any attention.

"She must be put to death. Immediately!" yelled Eleven. For once she was not an outlier as others agreed.

"How could this happen? What was she thinking?" asked Seven, her words running together. "She could know all of our secrets. The Khan could know everything!"

"Calm yourselves," bellowed Ten, her powerful voice echoing off the walls. The noise faded and everyone regained their composure. "We must proceed with care."

"Thank you," said One, before turning towards Two. "How much does she know?"

"Very little," said Two. "So far she's only met two members of my network. Apart from the basics, she knows nothing about how we operate. But she does know that the Inner Circle exists."

"How did this happen?" said Ten, drawing all eyes to her. "Why did Kokochin want to be trained?"

"She was robbed one night and wanted to learn how to defend herself. It wasn't premeditated," said Two.

"That's it?" Ten laughed with relief. "There's no danger to us. Just a scared girl wanting to feel safe."

"I think it's an opportunity," said Two, speaking over the grumbles. "She is young, naïve and was discarded by her husband the moment she arrived in Persia. She's intelligent, ambitious and could be a valuable resource."

"One of the Khan's own wives?" said Seven. "Ridiculous."

"Kublai killed her entire tribe," said Two. "Her hatred for the Empire can be kindled and put to good use."

"*Hate is a powerful motivator, but it will burn out,*" said Twelve, and One agreed. In the long term, Kokochin would need more.

"We should kill her," said Eleven. "It doesn't matter if she could be useful. The risk is too great."

"I agree," said Six. "We have enough people here in Tabriz. There are several in the Ministries, and we are slowly seeding others elsewhere, close to the Khan. What more could she give us?"

"How long do we wait for information to trickle through?" said Two. "We would know of every decision in court on the same day. Even better, she might be privy to what is being planned. There are many ways to skim money, and adjust our plans, as the Khan's strategy is being drawn up. Once the ink is dry, it's more difficult."

"I remain unconvinced," said Six.

"She risked everything to save a friend," said Two.

One was surprised when Eleven spoke up. "I think we should give her a test. Something difficult. If she dies in the process, then we lose nothing."

"But if she survives, then at least we'll know she's dedicated," said Two.

A few heads around the table were looking in One's

direction, waiting for her to pass judgement. She glanced at Twelve for guidance, but she just shrugged.

"For something this important, we need to vote. Who wants her dead?" asked One and four hands went up. "Who wants to give her a test?"

Eleven was the first to raise her hand and One was the last. By the narrowest margin, Kokochin would have a chance to keep her life. She would be watched, to make sure this was not part of some elaborate trap, but One didn't think so. The Princess was just a young woman trying to find her way.

There was little risk to the House. Even so, One found herself hoping that Kokochin succeeded, because they needed every advantage in the fight ahead to free Persia.

CHAPTER 27
Hulagu

As he watched the sun rise over Baghdad, Hulagu felt as if he'd been living outside the city for months. It had been ten days since he'd told Abaqa he would become ruler of the city. It had been five days since General Kaivon had returned with the head of the spy tied to his saddle. And it had been two days since he'd been able to sleep.

On the first night, Doquz had tried to soothe him to sleep with a firm massage and oils to loosen his tired muscles. When that failed she'd exhausted herself, and him, with energetic fucking for most of the night. Afterwards, he'd lain there, spent but wide awake.

He'd not taken a drink since the banquet, and Doquz thought his insomnia could be blamed on that, but he didn't think so. He'd been clear-headed and more focused, alert in the mornings and his joints had ached less. Even his gout had been better. Everything had been going well, until the spy had escaped, and then his sleeplessness had begun.

Unable to help, and at the end of her patience, Doquz said he had too much to do. When the day came that he didn't have a lot on his mind, Hulagu knew he would be dead. As the Khan, there were always a hundred things that needed his attention.

Something else was gnawing at the back of his mind, but after two days of thinking on it, he was no closer to the answer. The next morning Abaqa approached his tent with apprehension.

"Sit, eat," said Hulagu, gesturing at the other side of the fire. Doquz was still asleep, so he kept his voice low. Somewhere in the night he'd managed a short nap, but no more than that. His eyes were still raw and his mind sluggish, but his senses were unusually sharp. Maybe it came with being up before dawn.

Hulagu passed his son a cup and then gestured towards the tea beside the fire. Abaqa held out his cup and Hulagu filled his son's bowl with tea.

"You're not being punished," said Hulagu, before Abaqa could share what was on his mind. "It's a test. One that will require all of your skills, not just those on the battlefield. You will need to master negotiation and compromise."

Abaqa sipped his tea but said nothing. He rubbed his chin, something he'd done since he was a boy whenever deep in thought.

"We both know your brother Jumghur will never be Khan. He's a good warrior, but I did not build the Ilkhanate on bravery alone. If something gets in his way, he knocks it down. You must be able to look beyond the first obstacle and see the whole battlefield."

"I understand," said Abaqa. He sounded resigned, but was still not happy.

"Before winter comes, I will be marching into Syria, but I expect you to accomplish great things. There is much work to be done."

"I have already spoken to several locals who will become spokesmen for the merchants." Abaqa's mouth had a sour twist at the last word.

Hulagu frowned. Maybe this was what was keeping him awake. He expected too much of his son. "My son, the only reason we are here, waging this war, is because of your mother and those like her."

"I remember this lecture," said Abaqa.

"Clearly I must give it again, otherwise you would've learned the lesson." Hulagu waited for his son to interrupt, but he wisely kept his mouth shut. "We cannot fight and move so quickly without our horses, and they cannot survive without sufficient space for grazing. As it stands, we will soon have to move from this place, or else they will starve. Then there is food for all of the men, supplies, equipment for the engineers. The list is long."

"'War is more than a sword and a saddle,'" said Abaqa, quoting something Rashid, his vizier, often said. "I will do all that I can."

"That is all I ask," said Hulagu, gripping his son by the shoulder. "And in the spring, we will expand the borders of the Ilkhanate together, riding side by side into battle."

"I would like that very much."

"I have one final piece of advice," he said, waiting until his son nodded. "Listen to Kitbuqa. He's seen much of the world. Don't be afraid to ask for opinions, but the final decision must be yours."

"I will remember," promised Abaqa.

Hulagu stood and embraced his son. "I know you will make me proud," he said, struggling to keep the tears from his voice. He was overtired and emotionally raw.

"My Khan," said a familiar voice.

General Kaivon waited a short distance away, so he didn't intrude. He bowed to both of them before stepping forward.

"We were talking about the future," said Hulagu.

"I was wrong about you, General," said Abaqa, holding out his hand to the Persian. "Time and again you have proven your loyalty. Saving my father's life, and then hunting down the spy. I'm sorry for what I said."

"There is nothing to forgive, my Prince," said Kaivon, shaking Abaqa's hand. "You were only trying to protect your father."

"Enough of this," said Hulagu, "or we will all start weeping like little girls."

Abaqa smiled and went on his way, leaving his seat free for Kaivon. "He will do well," said the Persian.

"I think so, but he still has a lot to learn. Now, we should talk about you."

"What do you need, my Khan?"

"After what you did with the spy, you should be rewarded."

"It was my fault. I thought I could scare him into telling me his secrets. He must have panicked," said Kaivon shaking his head. "When he escaped, I knew it was because of me. I had to go after him myself."

"There's no way to know. He could have been planning it for days," said Hulagu, dismissing his guilt. "The important thing is, he didn't report back to his people."

"No. They remain in the dark."

"It's in the past, so leave it there. Come, we have much to do," he said.

Hulagu felt buoyed up by his conversations with Abaqa and Kaivon but with every step towards the central library his good mood drained away. Before going inside, he took a deep breath to try and hold onto his temper.

Deep in the building, surrounded by books on all sides, he found Temujin reading from a dusty old scroll. The paper was so worn and old it had cracks running through it and part of the page had crumbled away. Temujin wore a pair of cotton gloves and held the scroll open with only the tips of his fingers. At the sound of approaching footsteps, he looked up and Hulagu received his first surprise of the day. His son met his gaze and didn't break eye contact. Temujin's face was slightly thinner than he remembered and his clothing, which normally strained around his bulk, was loose at the waist.

Sitting beside him was the ageing librarian who had been

in the process of copying part of the scroll. Hulagu didn't recognise the language, but he read a few words from the librarian's translation and none of it made sense.

"I'll leave you alone to talk," said Reyhan, waiting for Hulagu's permission before withdrawing.

The building was practically empty of people and mostly silent, giving it a religious quality he'd felt inside churches. Some of that spirituality must have rubbed off on Temujin, as there was a strange aura of calm around him. Maybe he had finally found his calling and had always been destined to be a librarian. If he had not been the Khan, then it would have been possible, but a quiet life cataloguing books was not something any child of his would suffer. All of them had to serve a greater purpose.

"You've been here for days. What have you found?"

Instead of excuses, Temujin offered him a seat and then poured some tea. Maybe he should have sent the boy to a monastery. There might still be time. He could tell people Temujin had died in the siege of Baghdad. That would be a definitive end to his headache.

"I've been studying an ancient practise," said Temujin.

"Does that make you one of those, what did the librarian call them, Wise Ones?" scoffed Hulagu. To his surprise Temujin smiled.

"Not yet. Maybe never, but I'm slowly learning about them."

"Knowledge is useful, but only when it serves a purpose," said Hulagu.

Temujin raised an eyebrow. "Who said that?"

"I did. As a warrior in your Khan's army, what can you show me that is useful?"

"Give me a moment," said Temujin, clearing some space on the table. Moving with great care, he stacked books on the floor until his half of the table was clear. "I need time to focus."

Hulagu thought it was nothing more than a delay tactic to spare the old man's life, but he was genuinely curious.

Temujin closed his eyes and set his hands on the table in front of him, as if cupping a bowl. As time passed and nothing happened, it appeared as if Temujin had simply learned how to meditate. Hulagu was about to interrupt when he felt a distinct shift in the air. Looking over his shoulder, he thought someone had opened a door, but there was no one in sight. He was alone with Temujin and yet something had changed.

A strange prickle ran down Hulagu's spine, but he dismissed it as nothing more than a chill. But when Hulagu looked back his jaw fell open.

Dancing above the open palms of his son's hands was a naked flame. It was barely bigger than the flame of a candle. It bobbed and weaved as if in a draft, but the air was perfectly still.

It had to be a trick.

When Temujin opened his eyes the blue one sparkled. His son smiled at seeing the flame, but then it vanished, leaving no hint of smoke in the air.

"A good trick, but I have flint and tinder. What use is that to me?"

A nerve twitched in Temujin's jaw. "Winter is almost here, is it not?"

"Yes."

"Now is the time to conserve your strength. Bolster existing defences, shore up Baghdad to make it impregnable, and plan for the future."

"Why are you telling me what I already know?"

Temujin smiled but there were more teeth than before. "In the spring, I will have learned more. I will be able to do more to serve, my Khan."

"More than light fires?"

"Yes. I will."

Temujin spoke with such confidence Hulagu felt a glimmer of hope. Perhaps his youngest son would finally amount to something. It would be easy to turn down Temujin's request and send him back to the army. And yet he had summoned fire without any oil or wood.

"There's still the librarian to think about."

"I have not forgotten. If nothing comes of my studying, then I will end his life."

Again, there was no hesitation. Hulagu had never heard him talk with such confidence.

"Very well. Take your books and the librarian back to Tabriz."

"Thank you, my Khan," said Temujin, bowing in his seat.

When Hulagu stepped onto the street he felt relieved. He wanted to believe it was nothing more than trickery, but his instincts told him otherwise. It might lead nowhere, but for now, he was willing to let his son indulge his passion. At least that is what he would tell others, if they asked. In truth, he'd been scared.

Although not a deeply religious man, he knew that all faiths spoke of unnatural beings that granted favours and dark powers. It was ridiculous and yet, how else to explain it?

However, if there was a way to benefit from whatever his son was learning, he would find it. If not, there was always the story about Temujin dying on the battlefield.

He'd lied about one thing to his son. Knowledge that served a purpose was useful, but not everything should be known. Some secrets should remain buried, and if this proved to be one of them, then it would be easy for Temujin to suffer an accident.

That evening a messenger arrived with a letter from the east. Hulagu was weary from a lack of sleep, short-tempered and still thinking about what he'd seen in the library. His hand shook when he accepted the letter. He quickly dismissed the rider before anyone noticed his trembling.

Doquz came into their tent a short time later to find him drinking, breaking his dry spell.

"What is it? What's happened?" she asked, noting his distress.

"It's a letter from my brother, Ariq. He has sent identical letters to my cousin Berke, and Buqa-Temur." The ruler of the Chagatai Khanate was a friend of Ariq's and yet, up to now, he had been without bias in his decisions. "He asks that all of us declare that he is the Great Khan, or else in the spring, he will go to war with my brother, Kublai."

The kurultai had been fair. There had been no tampering, and yet Ariq would still not accept the decision. Hulagu had no way to know what Buqa-Temur would do, but he guessed that Berke would side with his younger brother. It was finally happening.

Civil war.

PART TWO
Year of the Iron Bird
(1261)

"THE SUPREME ART OF WAR IS TO SUBDUE
THE ENEMY WITHOUT FIGHTING."
— SUN TZU

CHAPTER 28
Kokochin

As she walked through the hallways of the palace in Tabriz, Kokochin saw numerous servants hurrying past her, all of them avoiding any eye contact.

It had been this way for almost two weeks since the Khan's return from Iraq. He had not been due back for at least another month, but urgent business had prompted his sudden return. As a result, everyone in the palace was on edge, performing their duties with more diligence than ever before. All of the servants were afraid for their lives, in case even the smallest mistake resulted in their sudden and unexpected death. The Khan's temper often flared white hot, but usually it cooled almost as quickly. Since his return, he'd remained in a permanent state of annoyance that sent everyone scurrying for the door when he raised his voice.

The bulk of the army was still in Iraq, gobbling up large chunks of the country while facing little or no resistance. With the fall of Baghdad and the death of the Caliph, the heart of the Muslim faith in the region, local forces had been decimated. Despite such gains, it was not the vast swathes of occupied territory Hulagu had been hoping to claim. Taking towns without a fight did not fire the blood, or inspire fear in the heart of the enemy. As the temperature fell, and fodder for

269

the horses began to dwindle with the approach of winter, all thoughts turned to returning home until the spring.

Momentum in the west had been lost and it would be noticed. The Mamluks had spies inside the Ilkhanate. There would be speculation as to the reason behind the sudden shift in Hulagu's strategy.

Kokochin had learned all of this through gossip around the palace, but also because of the time she'd spent with Guyuk. Although she was no longer shadowing the Empress during the day, they still regularly had breakfast together, where each of them would discuss their affairs. With little progress in her attempt to become a jeweller, and because Guyuk liked to lecture others, the Empress did most of the talking. Kokochin also thought she was in love with the sound of her own voice. Occasionally she would ask Kokochin for an opinion, but not often.

In the end, all of her worry about Hulagu's return had amounted to nothing. Her life had not changed in the slightest. He had been in the city for days, and she had only seen him once, at a distance. Every day he was sealed away in urgent meetings with diplomats, senior military figures and his vizier. All of it was done behind closed doors under heavy guard. Despite being his wife, Kokochin knew even she would be turned away by the guards.

The Ilkhanate and the entire Mongol Empire was under threat. The thought of it gave her a peculiar thrill.

From what Guyuk had told her, their husband was extremely angry at being forced to come home. By now, he should have been deep into northwest Syria, but instead he was stuck here, dealing with the internal squabbles of his siblings. It would have been a laughable situation, if not for the widespread and dangerous repercussions. Open civil war between the four khanates would severely weaken the Empire, show their enemies they were divided, and possibly susceptible to attack. If any of them were to join forces, then the tide could begin to turn the other way, and Mongol-occupied cities could find themselves under attack.

After taking a luxurious bath, Kokochin went in search of some breakfast. Some mornings Guyuk was already there, and other days she had left early for a meeting. When Kokochin arrived in the eastern wing, the slightly relaxed mood of the servants told her she would be dining alone. She had tried reaching out to some of the Khan's other wives, and even one or two of his concubines, but all of them had rebuffed or ignored her.

Turning her mind to more pleasant topics, she thought about the day ahead, spending time with Layla. It had been weeks since she'd been injured and she was slowly recovering her strength and flexibility. Even so, she still moved like an old woman and wasn't well enough for them to train together. Thoughts of her new training partner threatened to spoil her appetite, but Kokochin made sure she ate every mouthful on her plate. She would need the energy.

The mood in Tabriz was unchanged, the people unaware of the rising tension behind the walls of the palace. Life continued as before with goods flowing in and out of the city at a remarkable rate. Pulling her robe tight around her to ward off the chill, Kokochin walked faster to get her blood flowing. Her fingertips tingled from the cold, but she knew that would be the least of her worries. She still had a number of half-healed bruises on her body, and her shoulders and hips were sore from daily exercise.

Layla sat behind the counter in the front of the shop. She couldn't train, but as long as she didn't move around too quickly she could still manage her business. Her face was pale, but she still managed a smile as Kokochin entered the shop. They had barely embraced, with Kokochin taking a deep breath of her hair, when she heard the back door open. When she kissed Layla she felt her smile.

"No matter what she says, you're doing very well."

There was no time to reply as Ariana came into the room, scowling at Kokochin. Whenever they were together, it was her default expression. The healer was still angry that she knew about the House of Grace. Her attitude had not changed since the first time they had met.

"Get changed. I need to check her wounds," said Ariana.

While Kokochin slipped out of her clothes, she noticed Layla was watching from over Ariana's shoulder. She waggled her eyebrows in appreciation, so Kokochin made a show of peeling off her clothes until Ariana noticed, ending their fun. The black clothes were now tight in places where she'd built up her muscles, but they were still comfortable for exercising.

"Have you been stretching?" asked Ariana. She lifted Layla's left arm while she pressed an ear to her chest, listening to her breathing. One of Layla's lungs had been punctured, but thankfully the damage had not been severe. Whatever she thought of Ariana personally, Kokochin appreciated her skills as a healer.

"Every day," said Layla, demonstrating by lifting both arms. She had regained most of her movement in her upper body.

Ariana grunted. Kokochin had come to realise that meant she was satisfied, but would never say it. Only twice had she earned a similar grunt during their daily training sessions. Normally Kokochin only received feedback on how awful she was. Her style was sloppy, her balance was off, or she was as uncoordinated as a three-legged dog.

"Keep doing them."

"I will," said Layla, somehow managing to keep her smile, despite the healer's sour face.

The next two hours passed in a blur as Kokochin fought for her life. Layla taught through demonstration, repetition and practise. Ariana's style was more aggressive. She attempted to punch, kick, throw and suffocate Kokochin to death. Every time she was thrown to the floor, or had to tap out or risk being choked unconscious, Ariana would relent but then tell her what she'd done wrong. Not once did she show her the right way to do it. She expected Kokochin to work it out for herself and do it correctly the next time.

Thankfully she had been training with Layla for a few months, during which time she'd built up her strength, flexibility and hand-eye coordination. Her technique was still crude, but she was proficient and quite often knew the countermove and the finishing strike. The problem was, Ariana also knew those moves and how to avoid them. And so a peculiar dance developed, where an attack was met with *Hare's Sprint,* but before Kokochin could deliver *Owl Hunts,* Ariana had moved out of range, leaving her off balance and vulnerable to attack.

"You're thinking in straight lines," said Ariana.

Kokochin had been trying to remember Layla's teachings about remaining calm while everything around her was chaotic, but after days of Ariana's attitude, her calm finally evaporated.

"What does that mean?" she snapped.

The healer raised an eyebrow and stepped back, lowering her guard. "It means training here, in a House of Grace, is not always ideal. It's quiet and the space is empty. In some ways, it would be better if the floor was littered with objects, or we practised in the street, surrounded by people. Whenever you are out there," she said waving a hand at the world beyond the shop, "there is noise, people and things in the way. Think about your walk to here from the palace. How many carts do you have to dodge? How many pedestrians? The space will never be this empty."

"Then why train this way?"

"Because you need to master the technique until it is instinctive. You need to build up your muscle memory. Then you can learn how to adapt to any situation, any environment. We always train with one opponent, but what if there's two or three?"

This was not something Kokochin had considered. She

remembered Layla had disabled a number of Kheshig in the palace. She knew that they always patrolled in pairs.

"Adapt and survive. That is why you must remain calm, while everything else around you falls apart."

Kokochin was still distracted, but she noticed when Ariana raised her fists and came towards her. She threw a high punch and Kokochin dodged to one side with *Nightingale Sings,* but instead of moving into *Falcon Hunts,* she adopted a wide stance and lashed out with both fists at waist height, modifying *Serpent's Bite.* Ariana had been rushing forward and the blow caught her in the pit of her stomach, knocking her backwards. If Kokochin had delivered it while standing fully upright, it would have caught Ariana in the middle of her chest and could have stopped her heart.

The healer fell back onto her arse and sat there for a couple of minutes, wheezing as she caught her breath. Kokochin made no attempt to help her up. None had been given to her in the countless times she had been knocked down. Part of her still wanted to help, but she squashed the compassionate voice within.

When she could stand up, Ariana gathered her belongings and changed back into her normal clothes, indicating that their training was done for the day.

"I'll see you tomorrow," she said in a raspy voice.

When she was gone Kokochin pulled the workbenches into the middle of the room again and then slipped back into her palace clothing. When she turned around, she saw Layla was leaning on the doorframe.

"How long have you been there?"

"Long enough," said Layla with a smile. "She's impressed."

"Ariana?" said Kokochin, laughing because she knew it had to be a joke.

"You caught her by surprise."

"You saw?"

"I did."

"What was it she said, 'adapt or survive.' I adapted." Kokochin shrugged, doing her best to pretend it hadn't been extremely satisfying to knock Ariana down.

"She likes you," argued Layla.

"No, she doesn't. She hates me because I'm an outsider, and she thinks I can't be trusted."

"Give her time."

"I've kept your secrets so far. I'm not as naïve as I once was," said Kokochin. She had no illusions about herself. Every day in Guyuk's company showed her there was still a lot about the city, the Mongol Empire and the world beyond about which she was completely ignorant.

"I know that you killed Davood, the sub-minister for trade. And I know that he was replaced by a local woman. Is she a friend of yours?"

Layla shook her head. "She doesn't know about the House of Grace, if that's what you're asking, but she is a patriot. In her own way, she will do her utmost to impress them, while also serving her country."

"The night we met, you killed a man at the palace. What about his replacement?"

"They are also loyal to Persia. What I'm about to say, know that I don't blame you," said Layla, gripping Kokochin's hand before continuing. "Hulagu Khan and his Mongol army slaughtered thousands of my people, and now they want us to pretend that it didn't happen. That living this way, with them occupying our country, is normal. The war against them is not over. It will never be over, until they have been driven from Persia, but this time it will not be fought with swords and fire. My country needs time to recover. The people need a chance to heal, but in the meantime, we will creep into every corner. Infiltrate every industry, bank, embassy and place of power. And then, slowly, ever so slowly, we will begin to squeeze," said Layla, wringing her hands together. "That is how we will reclaim our nation, from the inside."

Kokochin held onto her hand tightly. "I have no family, and no home but a borrowed room in a stolen palace. I have nothing, but, when I am with you, I feel at peace. I feel as if I have come home for the first time in my life."

Layla pulled her close, holding Kokochin in her arms until the tide of emotion sweeping through her started to ebb away. Worry about Layla's recovery had been on her mind for weeks, making her feel fragile and often close to tears. In addition, Hulagu's return had been plaguing her dreams and thoughts about the future as his wife were bleak. Layla stroked her hair and whispered soothing words. Slowly Kokochin found her centre and a new, deeper form of calm returned.

"This is all I want," said Kokochin. "The two of us, together. And there is nothing I wouldn't do to protect that. I would never betray you. Ever."

"I know," said Layla, touching her cheek.

Sitting side by side at a workbench, often finding excuses to touch one another, Kokochin spent the afternoon practising her other new skill. Sadly, she had not reached the point where she could make any jewellery that someone would actually be willing to buy. Nevertheless, it was a pleasant way to spend a few hours in Layla's company, watching as the jeweller deftly turned ugly lumps of metal into a delicate necklace and matching pair of earrings.

When the front door of the shop opened Kokochin went to investigate, so that Layla didn't have to struggle to her feet. As she entered the front portion of the shop, her mouth fell open in surprise. Guyuk, Empress of the Ilkhanate, stood inside the shop inspecting a necklace. Thankfully her back was to Kokochin, so she hadn't noticed how much her appearance had come as a shock. Standing outside the window were four Kheshig, scanning the street for trouble, but every pedestrian gave them a wide berth, crossing to the far side of the street.

"Can I help you with something?" asked Kokochin.

Guyuk turned her head and smiled expectantly. "There you are. Since I missed breakfast this morning, I thought I would visit and see where you spend all of your time."

"It's always a pleasure to see you," said Kokochin, coming out from behind the counter. "Can I show you an interesting piece?" she said, gesturing at an intricate necklace made of steel wire coated with silver. A kingfisher, with sapphire eyes, was swooping down to catch a fish.

"It's beautiful, but it looks fragile to me," said Guyuk.

"You might be surprised," insisted Kokochin. "It has steel at its core."

A brief smile tugged at the corners of the Empress's mouth before she turned away. "And where is the artist?"

"She's busy working on a new piece in the workshop."

"Is that where all the magic happens?" asked Guyuk. The question sounded innocent enough, and yet it sent a shiver of fear down Kokochin's spine.

"Would you like to see?" she asked, pretending nothing was wrong.

"Lead the way," said Guyuk.

Layla must have overheard their conversation, but she still had her head bent over her work. She only looked up when Guyuk came into the room. She started to get up, but the Empress waved her back.

"There's no need to stand," said Guyuk with a generous smile that was fake. It reminded Kokochin of porcelain dolls she'd seen in shop windows. Their smiles had also been painted on the surface.

Kokochin sighed with relief. There would have been no way for Layla to conceal her injuries. The Empress was naturally suspicious and good at reading people. The last thing she wanted was for Guyuk to find Layla intriguing and start asking questions.

"What are you working on?" asked the Empress.

Layla leaned to one side, revealing her work in progress. It was a hollow golden pendant in the shape of a teardrop, inlaid with a weave of narrow filaments. Trapped inside, like flies caught in a web, were an array of tiny gemstones.

"That's incredible work," said Guyuk. Kokochin thought she sounded genuine in her praise, although it was becoming increasingly difficult to tell. "And do you have anything to show?" asked the Empress.

"I do, but it's also a work in progress," admitted Kokochin. Hers was also a pendant, but it was made of steel wire. The idea was for her to practise with durable and inexpensive metals before moving on to something more fragile.

"And what is it?" asked Guyuk.

Admittedly, it was difficult to see that it was a running horse. At times, she thought it resembled an oversized dog, but it was better than her previous efforts.

"A horse," said Kokochin, showing her the sketch.

The Empress stared at the pendant, then the design, and then back to the pendant. "That's interesting," was all she said. "I will buy the kingfisher necklace. Have it sent to the palace," said Guyuk, placing a purse on the workbench. The heavy clink of metal indicated a small fortune inside, far more than the necklace was worth.

"Thank you, Empress," said Layla with a seated bow.

"Kokochin, walk me out," said Guyuk, heading for the front door. Kokochin noticed it had not been a suggestion.

Taking a deep breath to steady her nerves, Kokochin dutifully followed the Empress into the shop. Guyuk waited by the front door and the lines between her eyebrows were more deeply etched than usual.

"We will speak in private when you return to the palace."

"Of course, Empress," said Kokochin.

Kokochin watched until the Kheshig had disappeared around the corner before slumping against the wall.

"What did she want?" asked Layla. She was leaning on

the counter and obviously experiencing some discomfort. Kokochin wished she could take away her pain.

"To put me in my place."

"She's arrogant."

"She is," said Kokochin. Moving to Layla's side she supported part of her weight with an arm around her waist. "I'm also worried about why she came here."

"You don't think she was checking up on you?"

Kokochin considered it. "Perhaps, but why now? Why not earlier?"

"I know what you're going to say," said Layla, pulling her close. "She doesn't know. She can't."

"I know you think I'm being paranoid, but you don't know her. She's the most ruthless and dangerous woman in the Ilkhanate."

"Then here's what you should do," said Layla, resting a hand on Kokochin's cheek. Her touch was normally soothing, but she was too agitated to relax. "Nothing."

"Nothing?"

"Don't change your routine. That would look suspicious. See what she wants and deal with it accordingly. Maybe she wants you for a task. Didn't you say she was impressed?"

"That's true."

"If you can't come here for a few days, I won't be worried, but send a note if you can. I'll let Ariana know if you're not here tomorrow. Don't rush back on my account. I'm not doing anything or going anywhere for a while. I'm safe."

"I don't want to be without you," said Kokochin pulling her close. "I can only be myself when I'm with you."

It might be a few days before she could return so Kokochin took a deep breath, trying to fix the smell of Layla in her mind. Layla locked the front door and closed the shop early. The Kheshig had scared away any potential customers and the street was quiet.

Leading Kokochin by the hand, Layla took her upstairs.

They stayed in bed for a long time, their bodies pressed together, sharing warmth, until it was time for her to return to the palace.

The walk back through the streets of Tabriz had never felt so lonely.

Kokochin expected to be summoned the moment she entered the palace. However, she was duly informed upon her arrival that Guyuk was extremely busy and would speak to her during the evening meal. Until that time she was to wait for an invitation. The servant delivered the message without making eye contact, doing his best not to have any opinion. Perhaps Guyuk expected, or even wanted, her to rage and beat the servant. It was not unheard of and, if she did such a thing, nothing would happen as a result.

Remaining calm and at peace in the face of such adversity did not make her passive and without the will to act. The more she learned about the House of Grace, the more she realised it was about choosing the right time and place, not lashing out and feeding wild impulses.

Kokochin dismissed the servant without raising her voice. He practically ran down the hallway in case she changed her mind. With nothing else to do, she bathed and then lounged about her rooms, wishing she had made at least one friend in the palace. The more time she spent with Layla, the more she realised how cut-off she was when away from the shop.

A few hours later she was summoned to a different part of the palace. As expected, this meal was being conducted in a more formal setting. Kokochin had dressed accordingly in a turquoise silk dress and matching slippers. It accentuated her slim figure and left her arms bare, which previously would have upset her as she'd thought them too skinny. Now her muscles had definition, and every flex reminded her of time spent with Layla which made her want to smile. Instead she lifted her chin, remembering her position and what Guyuk had told her.

She was the Khan's wife and she had power and authority. She let the words fill her chest with air and focus her mind.

Guyuk sat alone at the head of a polished wooden table that could easily accommodate twelve guests. The room had plain wooden panelling on the walls, but the ceiling was majestic with a mosaic made of thousands of tiny colourful squares. It depicted what she thought was a Persian folk hero wrestling with a horned monster. It must have taken years to complete, but like so much of the history and culture in the city, Guyuk took all of it for granted. The only things relevant to her were that which she could control, or exploit, to further her plans.

From the two place settings it would just be the two of them. Kokochin was expected to sit beside her and act subservient. Instead she sat down at the opposite end of the table. Guyuk said nothing and they stared at one another for some time.

The moment ended when half a dozen servants entered the room bearing trays laden with food. The first servant paused at seeing where Kokochin was sitting until Guyuk gestured for him to proceed. Once all of the plates of steaming rice, meat, vegetables and three kinds of stew had been laid out, and her cutlery moved up the table, the servants retreated.

"Eat," said Guyuk, reaching for some rice.

It was another mind game. The Empress thought stretching out the moment and building anticipation would make her feel more uncomfortable. It was working, but Kokochin did her best to hide it, eating with her usual vigour.

"Your work is crude," said Guyuk, after they had been eating for a while. "I think it would take twenty years before you approached the same level as your teacher."

"I agree," said Kokochin, sitting back in her chair. She had almost finished her meal and decided to leave the rest, giving the Empress her full attention. "She is extremely talented, and I don't have the skill or the time."

"I'm glad to hear you say that. The Khan's plans have been forced to change and so we too must adapt," said Guyuk, with a sour twist of her mouth. Her own affairs must have been interrupted by his early return. Kokochin suspected she also had a life that was mostly separate from Hulagu. The Empress didn't strike her as someone who was comfortable with sudden change.

"And what, exactly, did you have in mind?" said Kokochin, fighting to keep her voice level.

"In the spring you will begin shadowing me again. I will then introduce you to all of the relevant people related to the precious metal and gemstone trades. Thereafter, you will spend the next year learning everything that you can about how it works within the Ilkhanate. After that, if I believe you have absorbed enough knowledge and are competent, you will take over and manage it on the Khan's behalf."

Guyuk spoke with absolute confidence and authority, as if everything that she had said had already happened and would come to pass as described. In her mind, the only thing in question was Kokochin's level of intelligence.

"And do I have any say in this decision?" said Kokochin.

"No, of course not."

"Despite my position as the Khan's wife."

Guyuk laughed, but it was a cold and empty sound. "Girl, you are nothing more than a trinket that was gifted to Hulagu because no one else wanted you. The last of a rebellious clan of idiots. You are his wife in name only. I told you those things so that you would stop acting like a simpering and insipid girl. The Khan prefers women with a backbone, but make no mistake, you are nothing more than a toy to him. Something to be picked up and played with until he gets bored."

Kokochin knew there was some truth to what Guyuk said, but hearing it aloud still hurt when it was said with such venom. All of it had been nothing more than an act, to manipulate her into being a thing that would please her husband. If Guyuk was to be believed, that was Kokochin's only purpose in life.

"You have no family, no power and no children with our husband. You could disappear tomorrow and no one would mourn you. I doubt many would even notice you were gone." Guyuk was using her lecturing tone of voice again as if talking to a child. "Tell me, has Hulagu been to visit you since his return?"

"No," said Kokochin, for which she was extremely grateful.

"Perhaps I should make him more aware of you." Guyuk tapped her chin thoughtfully, as if the thought had just occurred to her. "I could tell him about your night time adventures in the city. I could tell him you are too wild. That your behaviour is a bad example, and that it might give others ideas. It would be much safer for all if you were to be kept at the palace, like a good little pet."

Kokochin said nothing and demurely lowered her gaze so that the Empress didn't see the rage behind her eyes. Her hands curled into fists in her lap and she focused on her breathing. She tried to find a moment of calm, but the struggle was immense. Every single part of her wanted to leap across the table and strangle Guyuk with her bare hands. All of her training with Layla was forgotten, blown away with a single breath. The only thing that stopped Kokochin from doing something she would later come to regret, was what would happen to Layla if she killed the Empress.

"So, will you do as you are told, or should I speak to the Khan?" asked Guyuk.

"I will comply, Empress," she said.

"Good girl. Now finish your meal."

Finally alone in her rooms, once she had been dismissed and the charade of civility was over, Kokochin let herself feel everything. The despair, the furious rage, the pain of potential loss and the bitterness of her position. She screamed into her pillow to muffle the sound until her throat was raw.

Emotionally drained she lay on her bed, staring at the ceiling, her mind turning in circles as she contemplated the rest of her life. There would be no real future for her, or Layla, or anyone in Persia, while the country was occupied by Mongols. Despite being born in Mongolia, in her heart Kokochin knew that she was not one of them.

She had no home, but wanted to build one here and the only way to do that would be to rid the country of interlopers. In a way, she was glad that Guyuk had spoken to her in such a fashion. It made her decision easier. For a long time, she had been thinking about how to get revenge on those who had murdered her family. Kublai was beyond her reach, but any damage to the Empire would, in turn, hurt him. She despised Guyuk and had come to loathe her husband. Killing them would be satisfying, but ultimately pointless, as it would only leave her in a worse position.

Guyuk was wrong about one thing. Her position gave her power and, thanks to Layla, she had strength. She wasn't afraid anymore.

Kokochin swore that the rest of her life would be dedicated to one cause. Destroying the Ilkhanate from within.

CHAPTER 29
Temujin

Since returning to Tabriz, life for Temujin had remained much the same. While the Khan tried to smooth over the cracks appearing between the khanates, Temujin mostly remained in isolation, with only Reyhan for company.

The central library in Tabriz was not as vast as the one in Baghdad, but they had done their best to bring as many relevant books with them as possible. As before, the two of them spent most of their time in a quiet room. There were other academics engaged in studies of their own, but everyone left each other alone.

Despite his father's efforts, Temujin knew that civil war was inevitable. Attempts to convince Berke Khan of the Golden Horde to accept the previous vote had been ignored. His uncle, Ariq, still claimed that he should have been chosen as the next Great Khan instead of Kublai.

On some level, none of it mattered. When spring arrived, and it was rapidly approaching, his father would again look to the west. Baghdad had been a great victory and a severe blow against their enemies, but it was only the first city of many that would fall to the Mongol Horde. How fast that happened depended on a number of factors that could not be controlled or predicted. However, if Temujin couldn't prove that what he was doing was of value to his father, then his meditative respite would come to an abrupt end.

If nothing else, the weeks spent in quiet contemplation had changed him. Sitting and doing nothing for long periods of time was anathema to his father. Even as a boy, play for Temujin involved running, riding a horse, archery and learning how to fight with weapons. While reading and writing were useful skills to master, his father regarded them as pursuits for those who would become scribes and money lenders. Such a role would never be the fate for one of his sons. They were expected to be great warriors. His daughters, on the other hand, could become masters of trade and industry, but never war leaders.

If the sole outcome of his time researching the Kozan was a calmer and more thoughtful mind, then Temujin would have said it had been worthwhile. However, Reyhan's life hung in the balance, together with his own fate. He would be thrown back into the army and Temujin did not want to die with a sword through his gut.

Physically he continued to lose weight at an astonishing rate, and several times he'd been forced to buy new clothes. Reyhan had said nothing at first, but Temujin knew his friend was worried about his health. If Temujin were to die suddenly, then Reyhan would end up in a shallow grave. He needed to make sure that didn't happen.

While dramatic weight loss might be symptomatic of some illnesses, Temujin had never felt healthier. His joints didn't ache anymore when he moved around. Getting out of bed was easier, and he had more energy. Temujin still ate with gusto, as his appetite had not diminished, so they were both at a loss to explain it.

Taking a deep breath, he pushed all worries to one side, let them pass through him and focused only on the moment. As before, he fed all of his worries and doubts into the imaginary fire in his mind. This time, without opening his eyes, Temujin knew the mysterious Eternal Flame was there. It floated above his hands, moving in time to some hidden breeze, despite being in a room without any wind. It had no heat or smell, but there was a distinct weight pushing down on his hands.

Focusing on the centre of Eternal Fire, Temujin felt a glorious wave of calm pass over him from head to toe. It was as if he'd been dipped in cool water on a scorching hot day. Temujin's heartbeat began to slow, the tension in his muscles eased, the worries in his mind melted away and, for a while, he simply existed.

An immeasurable amount of time passed. Alone in a room, he had no idea if an hour or a day had passed. Part of him was afraid that if he turned his head away, his concentration would be broken and the Fire would be extinguished. A quiet low tone, as if someone were humming one single note, caught his attention. The sound was faint but nearby, and he was desperate to find the source. Turning his head and hands slowly, keeping the flame in sight, he searched for what was creating the noise.

Hovering in the air was a fly in mid-flight. It was barely moving and Temujin counted to ten in his head between one beat of its wings and the next. Moving slowly and with caution, he lifted one palm until the flame was at eye level. He walked into the main room of the library and paused in shock.

The flame flickered, as if about to go out, but then resettled. It wasn't just the fly. The entire world around him was moving at a fraction of its normal speed.

A young woman conducting research had knocked over her ink well. It travelled across the surface of the table, as if it were made of molasses. Other people were walking so slowly, Temujin could step around them and he knew they were not aware of his presence. Even when he stared straight into their eyes, they couldn't see him.

As he moved from room to room in the library, encountering more people, a worrying thought occurred. What if he was stuck like this, forever, caught in a place in-between heartbeats?

Fear of being alone forever snuffed out the Eternal Fire. The world lurched back to normal speed so quickly that Temujin stumbled. His hip collided with a table and someone reading on the other side looked up in surprise.

Wiping the sweat from his brow Temujin retreated to his room and realised that he was famished. A short time later Reyhan came into the room carrying another new book. He found Temujin picking at crumbs of what had been their lunch and evening meal.

"What's happened?" asked the librarian.

Once Temujin had told him everything, Reyhan sat back in his chair with a troubled expression.

"What? What is it?"

"If your father were to learn about this, the results would be appalling. You could kill anyone and no one would know you'd been there. There would also be no way to stop you. No wall or lock would make the slightest difference."

"It's more likely he'd ask me to kill a thousand men rather than one," said Temujin, knowing how his father's mind worked. "Why would he waste the lives of his warriors when he can send me instead?"

Temujin didn't know if he would be able to repeat what had happened, but he was absolutely against the idea of telling his father about it. His stomach growled again and he bit into a peach, gobbling it down in three mouthfuls. Today, for some reason, he couldn't stop eating.

"I have a theory," said Reyhan. "It's connected to your weight loss and summoning the Eternal Fire."

"I told you, I'm fine. I'm not sick," said Temujin.

"I know. I think you're still reaching for it."

Temujin shook his head. "I was at first, but I've learned my lesson," he said, gesturing at the burned skin on his wrist. "I've found a way to channel it."

"That's the problem. You're supposed to let it come to you by being an empty vessel. You're feeding it with emotion and memory. In return, it's been using your body for fuel. Haven't you noticed that you're always famished after meditating with the Fire?"

"I thought being hungry was a result of practising more often."

Reyhan leaned across the table. His grip was surprisingly strong, but Temujin noticed the liver spots on the back of the librarian's hands. It wasn't fair that he'd been put in this situation.

"Temujin, I've been gone for less than an hour and you've eaten a meal for four people. If you keep doing the same thing with the Eternal Fire, it will kill you. And then I will be murdered," he said bitterly.

"I won't let that happen. No one is going to hurt you," said Temujin.

Reyhan released his hand and nodded, but Temujin knew he wasn't convinced.

"What should I do?"

"Try to go back to the beginning," said the librarian. "Let it come to you. Clear your mind, don't try to summon or feed it."

"That's a lot easier said than done."

"I know," said Reyhan, with a sad smile, "but what other choice is there?"

And that was the problem. Both of them had to do what the Khan wanted, or face the consequences.

The following day Temujin was summoned to the palace to speak with the Khan. Since their return, he'd not seen his father and had managed to dodge his siblings. The truth was, he'd been doing his best to avoid everyone, leaving the palace early in the morning and returning late. He'd become a ghost in his own life and it suited him.

As he marched down the hallway towards the throne room, Temujin did his best to embrace the calm within that filled his being when he meditated. His heartbeat slowed and his jaw loosened. He'd been clenching it in anticipation of another argument. He already knew what was going to happen. The Khan would make an unrealistic demand, putting a time limit on that which was profound, and Temujin would have to comply. When his father gave an order, no one had the power to disagree.

As he approached the double doors, Temujin expected a confrontation with the Kheshig. Despite being the son of the Khan, many were disrespectful, when no one else was around. They asked who he was and did their best to obstruct him at every opportunity. It had grown worse since the death of their colleague, Mahmud, for which they all blamed him.

Much to his surprise the Kheshig on duty said nothing. They opened the doors and stepped back, treating him with respect. Temujin paused, and peering at the guard on his left, he saw wide, nervous eyes. Perhaps someone had noticed their lack of respect and had spoken to them on his behalf. He would have to thank his adopted mother, Empress Guyuk, for her intervention.

His second surprise was finding the throne room busy with a dozen senior figures including Rashid, his father's vizier, Kaivon, the Persian General, and several other officers. A few were surprised to see him at such a gathering, but they said nothing. Temujin had barely been in the room a minute before the Khan came striding in through a side door. These days he was permanently in a hurry and a bad mood.

All conversation came to an abrupt end as the Khan sat down on the throne. At first, he said nothing. His eyes roamed over the crowd, taking in the faces of those in attendance. Temujin briefly made eye contact with his father. He expected surprise and annoyance. This was not the sort of gathering to which he was ever invited. Instead the Khan grunted and moved on.

"The plan has not changed," said Hulagu, breaking the unusual silence. Temujin noticed there were no servants in attendance, and no refreshments. This was not a casual meeting. The mood was uncomfortable despite everyone being allies. He also had the impression it had been called in haste.

"In the spring, we will ride towards Baghdad and then join up with my son, Abaqa. He will bring the majority of his men north and then we will head west, into Syria. We will march on Aleppo. As before, I will give them the chance of mercy, if they surrender."

After the horrendous bloodshed and long days of violence against the people of Baghdad, they would be fools to ignore such an offer.

"After that, we will head south to Damascus. With luck, we will join up with our Christian allies and go south towards Jerusalem. Then we will reclaim the birthplace of Christ from the Mamluks."

The vassal states would supply warriors, but Temujin noticed there had been no mention of support from the other khanates. The division between them was wider than he'd thought.

One or two of the Generals asked very perfunctory questions, but nothing in depth. This sort of meeting was not typically held in the throne room. Normally, his father spent hours in lengthy discussion with his officers, going over tactics while studying the terrain. Something was wrong.

Contemplation brought clarity, and with it, insight. Temujin remembered the way the Kheshig on the door had stared at him. It was the same expression his father had worn when he'd summoned the Eternal Fire in the library of Baghdad. Normally, the Khan was better at concealing his emotions than most. Temujin hadn't realised what he'd seen on his father's face until now.

His father was afraid of him.

With nothing more to be said, the Khan left the throne room and everyone began to disperse. Temujin was about to leave with the others when he was politely directed towards the side door by one of the Kheshig. With no one else in attendance,

Temujin found he was alone in the next room with his father.

There were deep shadows under the Khan's eyes from lack of sleep, and his shoulders were hunched as if carrying a great weight. His father was trying to hold the Mongol Empire together by himself with the force of his will. In the past Temujin would have felt something. Compassion, despite everything that he had endured during his childhood and of late. Maybe even hate, because his father could commit himself to something so completely, and yet Hulagu had never shown his youngest son the same level of dedication. Instead, Temujin realised he felt nothing. Not even pity.

"In the spring you will come west with me," said the Khan, without looking up from the map table. "When we join up with your brother, you need to be ready."

"I will do my best," said Temujin, unwilling to make a promise he couldn't keep.

Instead of expressing rage or surprise, the Khan merely nodded, his eyes still on the maps. "Can it be made into a weapon?"

"I don't know," he answered honestly. "We're doing the best we can, but we're piecing together a thousand year-old mystery." He thought about mentioning the accident, but said nothing. The Khan wanted solutions, not more problems. "I need more time."

Once more the Khan remained cold and distant. "You have your orders," he said, dismissing Temujin.

For the next five days Temujin redoubled his efforts. When he was not scouring the library and booksellers across the city, Temujin spent countless hours meditating.

On the fourth day he achieved inner balance and summoned the Eternal Fire without feeding it. Sinking into a pool of calm he waited, focusing on the image of the flame in his mind and nothing else. Thoughts of the future tried to impose, but he ruthlessly dismissed them. Listening only to the drum of his heart, he breathed, suspended between the waking world and sleep.

With the flame cradled in his hands, it was a struggle not to turn his mind to how it could be used as a weapon. Time and again, Reyhan had stressed that it was merely a channel to other mystical abilities the mysterious Kozan had been able to perform. In the wake of everything happening around him, maintaining inner peace was the most difficult thing he had attempted.

At one point, with the Fire in front of him, Temujin closed his eyes and drifted, trying to think of nothing. In spite of his efforts, he fell asleep.

In his dream, he was flying across the city of Tabriz like a falcon. It had been many years since he'd had such dreams, and he had always found them exhilarating. It brought to mind the happy memory from his childhood, when he had gone hunting with his father. He'd often wondered what it would be like to soar through the air, being held aloft by nothing more than the wind. Instead of wings, Temujin noticed he was still himself, but it didn't stop him from spreading his arms like wings.

He soared and swooped through the sky, passing along streets, skimming over the top of people and carts. None of them noticed him. He was an invisible ghost, able to pass through any wall or person like smoke. Laughing at the freedom, he spiralled up and up until the city began to recede below him. The streets became narrower, until they were nothing more than ribbons, and the people ants crawling along. Drifting through the clouds at such a height, it should have been freezing, but he couldn't feel anything.

In most of his dreams, Temujin was an unwilling passenger, dragged along through a series of events, both mundane and impossible. It was rare that he experienced absolute control. Determined to make the most of this experience, he drifted back down to street level and began to explore. As he moved along streets and entered buildings he'd never seen before, he was amazed at the power of his imagination. The conscious part of his mind knew all of it was merely borrowed from what he'd seen elsewhere, but it didn't stop him from enjoying it. He only wished he could touch, taste and feel, but he was without substance and weight.

Something began to tug at him, gently at first and then with more insistence. Reyhan had probably returned with another book and had found him asleep on the floor. The librarian was probably shaking him, trying to get him to wake up. Temujin did his best to ignore it as he was having too much fun. Eventually the pulling sensation faded and he was able to float free again.

As he flew through the streets as a silent observer, he often paused to listen to snatches of conversation. He listened to a man moan about his wife, a couple bickering about their family, and an old woman berating a young boy for his behaviour.

Somewhere in the distance, he heard the thrum of a harp and the beat of a drum. Drawn by the sound, he came across a couple of street performers. A small crowd had gathered where a beautiful young woman sat with a harp on the ground. Beside her was a handsome young man, keeping a steady and insistent beat on a pair of small drums. The music was ethereal and haunting. It spoke of sorrow and loss, old wounds and dark times.

Staring at the crowd, he saw all of them had been touched by the music. Their faces were sombre and all of them were utterly engrossed. Even if he had been standing beside them on the street, Temujin doubted they would have noticed him.

One person in the crowd caught his attention, but at first he couldn't say why. She was not a local woman. Although her hair was black as midnight, her skin was far too pale and she was tall with sharp angular features. Like those around her, she was rapt by the performance. Her eyes were closed and she was swaying gently to the music. Some instinct made him drift closer until Temujin was standing beside her. Like everyone else she remained oblivious to his presence. When the song came to an end the crowd burst into rapturous applause. The drummer moved around the crowd with a cap in his hand. People congratulated them both, with words and some coins.

The woman opened her eyes, smiled at the drummer and dropped a coin into his hat. Only then did Temujin notice that, like him, she had different coloured eyes. One was pale green and the other bright blue.

"Hello. Who are you?" she said, turning her head towards him.

Temujin glanced behind him, but there was no one there. When he turned back the woman was still staring.

She could see him.

With a start Temujin came awake in the library, gasping for air.

He was still cradling the Eternal Fire in his hands. In his haste, he pressed it against the metal base of the table.

The table collapsed, scattering its contents, as the metal dissolved into a pool of liquid. The room began to fill with a cloud of acrid black smoke.

The Fire was extinguished and Temujin could only stare in surprise at the destruction.

CHAPTER 30
Kaivon

Kaivon, together with the other generals, left the throne room after being summarily dismissed by the Khan. It was the shortest meeting he'd ever attended and the most peculiar. No one had known why they had met in the throne room, and why the Khan's youngest son had been invited.

Even now, as they milled around in the corridor, no one knew what purpose it had served. Temujin had been asked to stay behind, but no one else. It was well known that Temujin was a huge disappointment to his father. No one wanted to listen to Hulagu shout at his son. At first, Kaivon had struggled to recognise Temujin. He'd lost so much weight, but also carried himself in a way that was difficult to describe.

Some warriors were arrogant and swaggered about, certain of their immortality. Priests were often detached from reality, arrogant in their own way that everything that happened was a part of their god's unknowable plan. Temujin had carried himself with a surety and grace that was both priest and warrior. Something had changed, but no one knew the cause.

"Time to be elsewhere," said Rashid. Kaivon had been so caught up in reverie that he hadn't realised he was one of the few still lurking in the corridor.

"The Khan would speak with you," said a Kheshig, as Kaivon was about to leave.

Rashid gave him a sympathetic smile and hurried away before he was corralled. Only a few minutes later Temujin emerged from the throne room. He offered Kaivon a faint smile and walked away, wrapped in a shroud of mystery.

"My Khan," said Kaivon.

Hulagu was pouring himself a measure of a potent European spirit called whiskey. Kaivon noticed the bottle rattled against the rim of the glass. The Khan didn't normally drink during the day and never this early. As he thought about the potential cause, Kaivon struggled to keep a smile off his face. Bad news for the Mongol Empire meant good news for his people.

"Drink?"

"No, thank you."

Hulagu took a sip of his whiskey, grimaced at the taste and put it down. "I need you to go on an important mission."

"Of course. When do we leave?"

"I won't be coming. Follow me," he said, leading Kaivon through the hallways to an area he'd not visited before. The decorations on the walls were not as plush and there were no guards. Without knocking, Hulagu pushed open a sturdy door and went inside a room filled with books and papers, all carefully arranged around a large desk. Rashid, his vizier, stood up as they entered the room, bowing carefully.

"My Khan."

"Sit down. Both of you," said Hulagu, dropping into one of the two plush seats in front of Rashid's desk. The vizier waited until the Khan was seated before lowering himself.

"I'm going to send the General."

"Of course," said Rashid, pulling a huge leather-bound book off the shelves.

Kaivon looked between them. "Where?"

"North," said Rashid. "To Sarai, capital of the Golden Horde. You will meet with Berke Khan."

"You saw what happened when we executed the Caliph in Baghdad," said Hulagu, picking up the story. "He begged me not to kill him, but it had to be done. My cousin left the city before claiming his spoils. And now there is this feud with my brother."

Hulagu needed support from Berke Khan and the Golden Horde to continue his expansion of the Ilkhanate. He also needed to stop the threat of civil war before it began. That meant getting Berke to agree that Kublai had rightfully been elected as the Great Khan.

"What do you need me to do?" asked Kaivon.

"The roads are hazardous, but you will take Berke his spoils. You will also be accompanying my son, Taraghai."

Kaivon knew little about Taraghai other than he was one of the youngest and his mother was one of Hulagu's concubines.

"Mongols do not kill Mongols," said Rashid, quoting an old refrain that Kaivon had heard several times since entering Hulagu's service. It wasn't strictly true, but everyone in the Mongol Empire did their best to adhere to it. "As a demonstration of brotherhood, Prince Taraghai will enter into the service of Berke Khan, to learn how to become a great warrior. I will provide you with all of the appropriate letters."

"You will protect the bounty, and my son, with your life," said Hulagu.

"Of course," said Kaivon.

"Berke is stubborn, but he has an ego. Flatter him. Tell him I am sending my son so that he can learn from the best. Taraghai is a good talker. He will convince my cousin. Even so, keep your ears and your eyes open."

"What should I be looking for?"

Rashid and Hulagu exchanged an unreadable look. "There are rumours," said Rashid, speaking tentatively, "that some in the Golden Horde prefer their Muslim brothers over their Mongol family."

"Speak plainly," snapped Hulagu. "The General has earned my trust."

Rashid nervously licked his lips. "Watch for signs of sedition against the Great Khan and reluctance to expand into Muslim-held countries. It's unlikely they will say anything while you're there, but just in case."

"Prince Taraghai is to be a spy in Berke's court," said Kaivon.

"He is young and brash," said the vizier, "so people think he's dim-witted. He's far more cunning than they realise."

"The money doesn't really matter. Just make sure my son gets there safely," said Hulagu.

The cracks between the khanates went much deeper than Kaivon had realised if Hulagu was putting a spy in Berke's court.

"You will leave for Sarai tomorrow," said Rashid. "I will have the gold and other items loaded onto donkeys for the journey."

"Make sure you're back before the start of spring," said Hulagu. "I need you at my side when we head into Syria. And then, we'll be going after the Mamluks."

"As you command, my Khan," said Kaivon.

As Kaivon walked through the streets of Tabriz, he studied the local people. They appeared at ease, but when there were no Mongols on the street he saw the furtive looks. They were not free, but that could change. For the first time since he'd entered Hulagu Khan's service, he had a significant opportunity to create more division between the khanates. If civil war blossomed, their plans for expansion would waver. Allies would question their loyalty, and vassal states might wonder if they had to stay under the boot of a broken empire.

The tug on his waist was so light, Kaivon almost didn't feel it. It was only when he turned his head that Kaivon saw the teenage boy was holding his coin purse.

"Thief!" he shouted, making a grab for the boy.

Slick as an eel, the boy dodged and ran. Kaivon set off in pursuit and although the boy was fast, he had longer legs. As the boy skidded around a corner, Kaivon realised he was gaining on the thief. Looking ahead, he was pleased to see the narrow road was a dead end.

Kaivon was about to follow the boy when someone shoved a sack over his head. At the same time, something heavy slammed into his kidneys. He stumbled forward and tripped over an obstacle, smashing his nose into the ground. A heavy weight settled on his back and someone tried to tie his hands together.

Flailing backwards with his arms, Kaivon caught someone with his elbow and his attacker fell away. He managed to flip over onto his back when a boot slammed into his midriff, driving the air from his lungs. Several people began to kick him, forcing Kaivon to cover his head with his arms. His armour provided some protection, but he knew there would be bruises.

"That's enough," said a voice and the beating stopped. Something cold and sharp pressed against the side of his neck and Kaivon knew it was the point of a sword. "Tie him up," said a man. This time Kaivon didn't resist. He was turned over and his hands tied together behind his back.

Rough hands pulled him upright. He was relieved of his sword and dagger, then dragged through the alleyways. The sack over his head was so thick that it was impossible to see where he was going. Nevertheless, he tried to keep track of the general direction. Several times they passed through doorways, into the back of buildings and then out a different door. They were taking him on a twisting path to muddle his senses.

Eventually the light changed enough that Kaivon realised they had moved into a dark space. He was thrown forward and braced himself for a hard landing. Instead of slamming into the ground, he fell against something soft, bounced off and then landed on the ground. The smell of straw and horses surrounded him. At least they hadn't dropped him onto his face.

Someone grabbed him by the elbows and he was pulled up and then shoved onto a seat. His restraints were briefly loosened, but a blade was tucked under his chin so he didn't try to escape. When his hands had been secured to the chair, the steel was withdrawn and silence filled the stables.

At first the only sound Kaivon could hear was his own breathing, but as his panic began to fade he realised he was sitting in the middle of a circle of people. He could see flickers of movement and hear people shuffling and breathing all around him. One person had eaten a lot of garlic, and another on his left smelled of fish.

"We should cut his throat," said a woman on his right. Her accent was familiar as it reminded him of home in the south.

"He's a traitor," said another woman, a northerner.

"I'm not a traitor," said Kaivon, assuming they were all Persian.

"I never thought he would serve Hulagu Khan," said a familiar voice. It was a voice Kaivon had heard a thousand times. Even so it took him a moment to recognise. Disbelief warred with fear that this was some kind of elaborate trap.

"Karveh?" he whispered.

The sack was yanked off his head and it took Kaivon's eyes some time to adjust to the light. Slowly, his surroundings came into view. As he suspected, Kaivon was in the middle of a stables, surrounded by a group of twenty locals. Standing directly in front was his younger brother, Karveh.

"The last time we met, you were coming north to kill him," said Karveh. "What did he offer you?"

"Nothing. He gave me nothing." Kaivon took a deep breath. "I was going to kill him, but then I remembered what you told me."

Karveh squatted down until they were eye to eye. "What are you talking about?"

"I could have killed Hulagu Khan, but nothing would've changed and I would be dead. They would have just replaced him with another despot. Our people would still be under Mongol rule. The only way is to rip them apart is from the inside."

"He's lying," said the local woman. "Look at how he's dressed. They've bought him with money and women."

"Brother," said Kaivon, focusing on Karveh's face. "I swear to you, on the memory of our mother, I'm not a traitor."

Karveh sat back on his haunches, holding his head in his hands. "When you left, I thought I'd never see you again. You were right, but I was tired. I needed some time to rest. But then when I came north, I couldn't believe the stories." Karveh stared at him, still unsure. "Tales of a Persian General who'd saved the life of the Khan. A hero, who stormed the walls of Baghdad. Explain how that is helping our people. Convince me, brother."

"I had to do all of those things to earn their trust. Before that I was watched, day and night. Now, I can go wherever I want. I have already taken some steps to destroy the Ilkhanate from within. Even better, the Empire is on the brink of civil war."

"Tell me," said Karveh, hungry for news.

It came as a huge relief to tell them everything that he'd learned over the last year. He told them about the fractures between the four khanates, and Ariq's declaration that Kublai Khan had stolen the kurultai. He told them about murdering the messenger to delay aid from France and Rome in the spring. He told them about Berke Khan's anger at Hulagu for the murder of the Caliph. And finally he told them about his latest mission.

"They are already at each other's throats," said Kaivon. "All we have to do is keep sowing dissent between the khanates. If civil war breaks out in the east, it will have an impact here. Hulagu will not receive any aid."

The rebels were all listening and many of their expressions

had softened. There were still a few that remained unconvinced. They were more like the person he used to be. They wanted to fight and kill and get things done, today. This slow and subtle approach was difficult to appreciate, and he understood it could feel like nothing was being done.

"I have an idea, if you're willing to listen," said Kaivon.

His brother glanced around the circle and all but a few gave their agreement. Kaivon's bonds were cut, but he stayed in the centre with everyone still focused on him.

"Even with this slow way of doing things, direct action is necessary from time to time. Sometimes people need to be bought or silenced." That caught the attention of the few who were undecided about his loyalty. "And to do that we need money."

"We don't have much," said his brother.

"I know how we can steal a large amount and makes things worse for Hulagu Khan," he said with a fierce grin.

The others listened in rapt silence as Kaivon outlined his plan. When he was done, even those who had been uncertain were smiling.

"That is daring and risky for you," said Karveh.

"It's worth it," insisted Kaivon. "What choice do we have?"

With a plan in mind, and a way forward, the group dispersed leaving Kaivon alone with his brother.

"I'm sorry. There was no way to know," said Karveh.

"If I'd been in your position I would have done the same thing."

"I can't imagine what you've had to endure this past year," said Karveh. "Know that I am with you now, until the very end. You are not alone anymore."

Hearing those words eased the ache in Kaivon's chest. He took a deep breath and felt a glimmer of hope kindle inside his heart.

"We will take back our country from these dogs, together," promised Kaivon, embracing his brother.

* * *

The following morning Kaivon met Rashid, the Khan's vizier,
at the royal stables. Twenty sturdy mules had been laden with
a huge amount of wealth from the siege of Baghdad. Kaivon
checked the animals carefully, knowing that they had a difficult
journey ahead. The stable master knew his job, as each beast
was fit and healthy. When he was satisfied, he made sure all of
the bags were secure.

The stable master, together with several other grooms, were
lurking nearby. They probably knew little about the mission,
but it was rare that both the Khan's vizier and a general came to
the stables. Just as he was checking over the last beast, Kaivon
made eye contact with one of the grooms. The man nodded
slowly just once, letting him know that it was done. Kaivon
returned to the front of the line where Rashid was waiting.

"You've done a good job," said Kaivon, addressing the stable
master.

"Thank you, General," he said.

Rashid dismissed them, but still spoke in a quiet voice,
just in case anyone was lurking within earshot. "This will
help smooth things over with Berke Khan," said the vizier.
"Everything will work out." He sounded like a desperate man
praying for a change in the weather.

"I'm sure it will," said Kaivon, smiling at the vizier.

Despite being a difficult journey, the roads littered with frozen
men and horses that had died in the extreme cold, it passed
without incident. As befitting his station, and the enormous
amount of wealth they were carrying, Prince Taraghai was
escorted by thirty armed warriors. All of them were veterans,
used to the hardship of travelling in winter.

By the time they arrived in Sarai, capital city of the Golden
Horde, Kaivon knew everything about the Khan's son. At

first glance he was much like his brothers, brash and more interested in fighting than politics. But behind the bravado was a cunning mind. People expected him to be arrogant and he used that against them.

From what Kaivon had been told, the city was usually a warm and welcoming place, but in the depths of winter it was gloomy and grim. Howling gales and ice flew at them down wide streets, and the stone buildings created long and heavy shadows. By the time they arrived at the palace, everyone was cold and in desperate need of a wash.

They were welcomed by Gurban, the Khan's vizier, and quickly escorted inside. Food and drink were being prepared, but first Prince Taraghai and then Kaivon were escorted to their rooms. Whatever disagreement Berke had with the boy's father, it was incumbent upon him to act as a good host.

An hour later, they were summoned to the feasting hall where Berke Khan waited with his senior officers.

"It's good to see you again, nephew," he said, embracing Taraghai. "The last time you were only a boy."

"It's been far too long, Uncle," said Taraghai. "My father has always spoken about you with great respect, as a warrior and a leader. There is much I can learn, if you would allow it."

The Prince bowed to the Khan and then held out the letters of introduction he'd been given. In truth, this was merely a formality. Letters had been sent ahead of their arrival.

"It would be my honour to teach you," said Berke. "Tell me, who are your companions?"

Once the introductions were out of the way, they sat down to eat. Tired of the same food on the road, Kaivon was pleased to see a lot of rice, vegetables and thick stews. He ate his fill and, for the first time in weeks, didn't have a chill. Wiggling his feet inside his boots, Kaivon was pleased to feel all ten toes.

He'd been relaxed throughout the journey, but now had to force himself not to doze off, despite the fires and warm food. Hours later, when everyone had drunk far too much, he was allowed to seek out his bed. Like his father, Taraghai gave the impression of great indulgence, but he'd drunk sparingly and his behaviour had been an exaggeration. Tomorrow, when everyone had fuzzy heads and loose tongues, he would be alert.

Kaivon woke early so, while the others slept, he went to the nearest bath house. On the way there, the call to morning prayers echoed around the city. Several men with loud voices shouted from the top of tall towers. Even on his short walk, Kaivon noticed several large mosques as grand as the palace. The huge stone buildings rivalled the majesty of the Khan's home, but were also far more numerous. Never before, in a Mongol controlled city, had Kaivon seen such devotion to a single religion.

After washing the grime from his body, and taking a long soak, he felt clean for the first time in weeks. As he headed back to the palace the previously abandoned streets quickly filled with men, women and children, pouring out of the mosques.

When Kaivon returned to his rooms, he found Gurban waiting for him.

"Minister, I thought you would be at morning prayer," said Kaivon.

"I'm a Christian," said Gurban, sketching the cross on his chest. "My Khan has asked to speak with you about an urgent matter."

"Lead the way."

He followed the vizier through the wide corridors of the palace, away from the throne room to the large office. The walls were lined with books and there were several sets of weights and measures on the desks. On the floor were several strongboxes and bags which Kaivon recognised. Berke Khan was angrily pacing back and forth, muttering to himself.

"What is the meaning of this?" he roared as they came into

the room. Reaching into one of the bags, he pulled out a thick bolt of luxurious silk cloth. Before Kaivon had a chance to reply Berke ripped open another bag and pulled out a small marble statue of a woman. Berke hurled the statue at the wall where it shattered into three pieces.

"Lord Khan, please tell me how I have offended you?" said Kaivon, making sure he bowed low. Beside him Gurban was practically bent double with his hands on his knees, eyes on the ground.

"Gurban, you talk to him," snarled the Khan.

The vizier stood upright and gestured for Kaivon to get up. "This is about what my Khan was due for helping to conquer Baghdad."

"I assure you, everything that Hulagu Khan gave me was delivered," said Kaivon. "Twenty mules were loaded with wealth."

"Wealth!" shouted Berke, yanking out more trinkets from some of the bags. It was an effort not to laugh, but Kaivon had known this was coming. He'd had weeks to practise his shocked expression. One of his brother's friends was a groom in the palace stables. Half of the wealth from Baghdad had been replaced with items of less value. The money would be used to fund the rebellion. To silence people. To buy weapons. To slowly grow their network for the future.

"General, we know you are an honourable man," said Gurban. "We do not doubt your word."

"No, of course not," said Berke, getting control of his temper. "I saw you on the walls that day."

"Thank you, Lord Khan."

"We would appreciate your discretion in this matter," said Gurban.

"Of course," said Kaivon.

"Leave us," said Berke Khan.

Kaivon bowed again and then firmly closed the door behind him. The corridor was empty, so he lurked by the door.

"My cousin thinks I'm a fucking idiot," said Berke. "First, he sends his son to spy on me, and now this. This is barely a fraction of what he took from Baghdad. Half of the bags are full of trinkets and spices. Where is the gold?"

Kaivon grinned. It was working far better than he'd hoped. The letters Kaivon had delivered from Hulagu Khan spoke of friendship and family, in the hope that Berke would side with Kublai.

Berke was ranting. "Because of his wife, all the Christians were spared, but he refused to save the Caliph. He says we are family, and then treats me like this."

"May I offer a suggestion?" asked Gurban.

"Speak your mind."

"Pretend that no insult has been given. If Hulagu wants his son to be trained, then so be it. Let him learn, but he should be kept away from your interests in Egypt."

Kaivon double-checked he was still alone then leaned closer to the door.

"I received another letter from my counterpart in Cairo. He wanted to thank you for the slaves we sent in the summer. They will be extremely useful in the spring when your cousin goes to war again."

If Hulagu Khan were to find out that his cousin was communicating with the Mamluks in Egypt, it would create an even greater wedge between the Golden Horde and the Ilkhanate. It could even lead to an all-out war between the khanates.

Doing his best not to laugh Kaivon hurried back to his room. The future had never been so exciting.

CHAPTER 31
Kokochin

After another long and tiring day of training in the House of Grace, Kokochin was relaxing with Layla in bed. Lying face down, stripped to the waist, Layla was working the knots out of Kokochin's shoulders.

Throughout winter, Kokochin had continued to train with Ariana at the jewellery shop. Every day, she was thrown around the back room by the healer. But every day she improved and, sometimes, she was not the one who she ended up on the floor. Thankfully, before the resentment between the two of them came to a head, Layla was declared fit enough to resume teaching Kokochin. Ariana was many things, but she didn't take any risks with those under her care, and by that time Layla was almost back to full health.

Kokochin was glad to see the back of the healer. It made her daily visits much more relaxed and enjoyable. Even when she was being tripped or spun upside down by Layla, it was never done with relish.

"Aaargh," said Kokochin as Layla's thumbs dug into a knot beside her left shoulder.

"Sorry," said Layla, adding more lavender oil to her hands. Her finger glided across Kokochin's skin with ease. She inhaled the floral scent and tried to relax.

"What were you saying about Guyuk?"

"I hate her. She's nothing but a vicious old hag. She's cold and cruel. I had no idea."

"You're tensing up," said Layla, tapping her on the back with her fingers.

Kokochin took a long deep breath and tried to stay calm. "To her, I'm nothing but a thing. A tool to be used to help the Mongol Empire."

"What do you want?" Layla's hands warmed the oil against her skin, stretching out Kokochin's spine.

"To be free, and live my own life."

"And how would you get there?"

"By helping you free Persia of Mongol rule."

Layla's hands stopped moving and then withdrew from her back. "You shouldn't say such things."

Kokochin sat up and pulled on her shirt. "I mean it," she said, but Layla remained unconvinced. "I've been thinking about it for a long time. Revenge against Kublai, for the death of my family, wouldn't change anything. Here, I can actually make a difference."

"I don't think you've thought it through, Kokochin."

"Then why are you training me? What is all of this for?" she asked.

"You're talking about destroying your own people."

"My people are gone, Layla. I'm the last left of my clan. Join or die. That was the only choice we were given. Like your people we fought and lost. I am a Mongol by birth, but I owe them nothing." Kokochin felt a chill and pulled on her robe. "I want a home, here in Persia."

"And am I part of this future?" asked Layla.

Kokochin grabbed her hand and squeezed it tight. "I didn't want to presume. I want you with my whole heart, but this isn't just about you, or revenge. It can't be."

"Good," said Layla, kissing the back of her hand.

"You were testing me?"

"I needed to make sure you were not saying all of that for my benefit."

"I understand," said Kokochin, rotating her shoulders. The massage had definitely eased some of the aches. "I'm committed to my decision. So, what's the next step?"

"I will speak to my superior in the House of Grace, and see if she will agree to meet with you. The final decision will be up to the Inner Circle. I warn you though," said Layla. "It will not be easy to convince them about your sincerity."

"I managed to persuade Ariana."

"You did," said Layla with a wry smile, "but she's not a member of the Inner Circle."

"Oh," said Kokochin, feeling her heart sink.

"One step at a time, love," said Layla, kissing her on the cheek. "One step at a time."

It took a few days to arrange, but eventually Layla's superior agreed to meet with Kokochin. On quiet afternoons in the jewellery shop, they sometimes frequented a nearby tea room. Layla and Kokochin sat at their usual table awaiting their visitor while the owner, Shirin, bustled around serving customers. Only a few tables were occupied, which meant Shirin had plenty of time to stand and chat. She loved to gossip and often could be heard discussing the latest rumours about businesses in the area. Shirin always knew what was going on in everyone else's life.

She was a matronly local woman with a big smile and a generous bosom. Her long black hair was still luscious, but there were streaks of grey at her temples giving her a distinguished appearance. She had four grown children but could still turn heads when she walked down the street, although these days she limped after a cart fell on her leg. Two of her daughters often helped out in the shop, but today she was working by herself.

Almost an hour later, in a lull between waves of customers, theirs was the only table that was occupied. Without asking for an invitation, Shirin sat down opposite. Kokochin was about to say something, when she noticed the shift in Layla's posture.

"Hello Kokochin," said Shirin. She was still smiling, but there was a speculative look in her eyes. Kokochin felt as if she were being weighed and assessed.

Layla waited in silence, her hands clasped together in her lap, so Kokochin chose to say nothing as well.

"Is she ready?" said Shirin, directing the question at Layla.

"We've been training for a year now. She's ready," said Layla, beaming with pride.

Shirin grunted. "We'll see."

"Does that mean I'm a member of the House?"

"No, girl," said Shirin with a laugh. "It means I'm willing to let you prove your loyalty. So, I'm going to give you a task and if you die in the process, then it has nothing to do with me. I'm just the owner of a tea shop, and you're a Princess who lives in the palace. But if you succeed, then I will ask my superior to speak to the Inner Circle on your behalf. The House has no reason to trust you yet."

In some ways she reminded Kokochin of Guyuk, but at least Shirin had the decency to tell her the truth up front. Kokochin was under no illusions. There would be much that was being kept from her. But, if she passed the test, she was one step closer to making her ideal future a reality.

"What do you need me to do?" asked Kokochin.

Shirin smiled. "I like you, girl. You cut straight to the bone. So, let me speak plainly. I need you to kill Boabak, he's a sub-minister for agriculture in the city."

"Why him?"

"Does it matter?" asked Shirin.

"Of course. It depends on the desired outcome," said Kokochin. "If you want to control all agriculture flowing through the city, then you'd take out the Minister and replace her with someone loyal. Unless you want her kept in the position for some reason."

"The Minister has a number of bad habits, so we're putting pressure on her to ignore certain facts," said Shirin. "She can't be seen making sweeping changes. The Empress and the Khan's vizier know roughly what to expect, but they pay less attention to the sub-ministers. They are the ones who actually inspect the weekly shipments. We need someone who can adjust the numbers without it being too obvious. The Minister will then do as she is told, reporting the figures we give her. Does that satisfy you?"

"It does. When and where is the job?"

"How do you feel about a trip to the theatre?" asked Shirin.

Three nights later, dressed in an elegant red silk dress and matching slippers, with Layla on her arm as her companion, Kokochin went to the theatre. Layla wore a loose-fitting gown that dragged along the floor, sweeping along the dust.

The theatre was hosting a local production about Persian folk heroes with poetry readings, songs and even some comedy. Kokochin had chosen this theatre because the show went on for nearly two hours. In theory, that would give her more than enough time.

Despite Guyuk's claim that she was nobody, Kokochin's presence outside the theatre was noted by many people. Before she set foot inside, she was approached by the owner and told that she could sit anywhere she liked. Her patronage would mean that others would attend the show, for no other reason than she had been there.

Although she was not someone who used her position to her advantage, Kokochin did on this occasion. The tiered seats were arranged in a semi-circle around the stage. Those on the far left and right, closest to the performers, were sectioned off with privacy screens. Once Kokochin and Layla were settled in a private section, and had been plied with free drinks, they were left alone until the performance began.

As soon as the door was closed, Kokochin slipped out of her dress and slippers. Underneath she wore her tight black clothing that she used for training. Beneath Layla's long gown she wore a pair of rubber-soled shoes that were slightly too big for her.

"You really do have big feet for someone so slight," said Layla as Kokochin slipped on the shoes.

Kokochin grinned, feeling a thrill at what lay ahead as she tightened the fastenings. On stage one of the performers emerged and a hush fell over the crowd. There were a number of lanterns dotted around the seats, but they were muted with hazy glass panels compared to those on stage. Layla extinguished the lantern in front of their seats as a precaution, shrouding them in shadow. All eyes were drawn to a barrel-chested man who began to sing in a voice that carried to the rear seats.

"Good luck and be careful," whispered Layla.

"One night, we should come here and do this properly," said Kokochin gesturing at the stage.

With all eyes on the singer, Kokochin slipped away. It took longer than she liked to get out of the theatre, as there were a number of people serving drinks, but eventually she made it to a side door. She'd spent the last three days practising how to sneak out of the theatre, get across the city and into the sub-minister's house. Assuming nothing went wrong, she would be able to make the whole trip in less than an hour.

Once she was finally on the streets, she darted away from the theatre, moving along alleyways and narrow side roads. At this early hour of the night there were plenty of people abroad, which meant it took her a while to reach her destination. She was often forced to duck into doorways or hide behind walls to avoid being seen. Eventually the right street came into view, but Kokochin went past it to the end of the road and cut back down the street behind.

The buildings here were sturdy and well-made, built on two levels with stairs going up and down to separate homes. Skipping up the stairs of the nearest home, she pulled out the rope she had stashed there the previous evening. The person who lived upstairs worked late into the evening, so there was no risk of being discovered. After securing the rope to the front door, she lowered herself into the house behind.

Sub-minister Boabak lived alone, in a three-storey home. In the grand scale of the city, he was nowhere near the top, but in his little corner he was an important man.

At the rear of the building was a small garden with a pond and paved area. Every flower, shrub and bush had been trimmed and shaped until it felt unnatural, as if they were made of silk. The only point of chaos was the fish in the pond. They swam in lazy circles of their own making, refusing to do anything in unison.

The house was mostly in darkness, but there was a single light in a window on the top floor. Access to the rear of the building was impossible from the front as it was built tight against its neighbours. The front door of the property had two locks. She had neither the skill nor the time to pick them, but the back door was less secure. With no onlookers, Kokochin was able to take her time. She had been practising for three days until her fingers were sore. Closing her eyes, she put one ear to the lock and carefully worked the picks, listening as each pin shifted about. With a satisfying click the lock opened.

Before the door had a chance to move, she grabbed the handle and then slowly eased it open. The hinges creaked, but there was no chance that Boabak would be able to hear from the third floor.

Just as they had practised many times in the House of Grace, she took a deep breath and tried to find her focus. Inside there would be many unknowns. She had a vague idea of the layout, but that wouldn't stop her from walking into unseen obstacles. Although she hated to admit it, Ariana had been right about one thing. Outside the House everything was in a constant state of chaos. It was people who tried to impose a sense of order on that which had no rhyme or reason.

Once her eyes had adjusted to the gloom, Kokochin went inside, carefully placing her feet. Thankfully the inside of the house was as tidy as the garden, with every pan, glass and book carefully in its place on a shelf. There was nothing on the floor to step on by accident. Even so, she nearly nudged a vase off a pedestal with her hip and quickly made a grab for it as it wobbled. Righting the vase, she waited a moment for her heart to settle and then ascended the stairs.

Many times over the last few days, she had considered what she was being asked to do. Kokochin had thought it would be more difficult to come to terms with it, but she was at peace with what needed to be done. Perhaps it was because she understood that some people could not be bought, bargained with or blackmailed and removing them was the only way forward. Or perhaps, and she hoped it wasn't this, she was looking forward to finding out what it was like to kill.

One of the stairs creaked and she paused, letting her weight settle, silently cursing herself for becoming distracted. For a while Kokochin stayed perfectly still, just listening to the house groan and tick. When Boabak didn't come to investigate, she moved up to the next step, trying to keep her mind in the present.

On the top floor was the sub-minister's bedroom and office. Looking to her left she could see the edge of his bed. The room was in darkness and on her right, down a short hallway, was his office. Boabak was hunched over his desk. A cup of tea and a plate of dates sat beside one elbow and the lantern beside the other.

The plan was simple. He was quite a large man, so her best chance was to stop his heart. The problem was, that meant facing him head-on. Strangling him from behind would be simpler, but it would be difficult to make that look like an accident.

Kokochin felt her heart flutter and then settle. Moving onto the landing she found her centre, took a deep breath and then loudly cleared her throat. At first Boabak didn't notice. He continued writing while muttering to himself under his breath. It was only when she tapped her foot on the floor that he realised she was there.

She had thought to cover her face but ultimately, it didn't matter. Even if he recognised her, only one of them was leaving the house alive.

"What? Who are you?" said Boabak looking over his shoulder. When she didn't respond he got up from the desk. She'd been told he was big but the top of his head scraped the doorframe. Most of his bulk was fat, but he still outweighed her by three or four times.

"Get out of my house!" he shouted. "Get out!"

When he reached out with one hand, trying to grab her by the neck, muscle memory took over. She tried to use *Salmon Leaps* to pull him forward off-balance, but he was too heavy. Boabak grunted in discomfort as she pulled on his arm, but otherwise his body didn't move. When his fingers closed painfully around her shoulder, Kokochin's instincts kicked in.

Slipping free of his hand, she moved towards him, under his arm and then behind him. Before he had a chance to respond, she used *Fox's Bark*, slamming a fist into his lower back.

The blow was perfectly placed as his legs gave way and he dropped to his knees, crying out in pain. Wrapping both arms around his neck she began to squeeze. With a squeak of surprise, she was lifted off the floor as he stood up with her clinging to his back.

Despite squeezing his neck as tight as she could, Boabak moved around as if perfectly comfortable. He tried to shake her off but she clung on, wrapping her legs around his broad back for additional purchase. When he slammed her into the wall, it drove most of the breath from her body. Black spots danced in front of her eyes. Before he did it again, she dropped to the floor and rolled to one side. Boabak's head rapped against the wall and one of his feet slipped. With a heavy thump, he dropped to the floor on his arse and hissed in pain.

"You're dead meat, girl," he said, slowly climbing to his feet.

Kokochin took a moment to catch her breath. Thankfully her vision had cleared, so she saw his hands coming towards her. Despite the narrow hallway, she was able to duck under and around him, bending her body to avoid his limbs. All those countless hours with Layla telling her to be more like a willow finally paid off. He tried to grab her twice more and each time she managed to avoid him.

"Stand still!" he roared, swinging a fist instead. This time he was in motion, balanced on his left foot, coming towards her on the right. Using *Nightingale Sings* she dodged to one side and then countered with *Lion Roars*, striking upward with a fist, catching him in the throat.

His momentum carried him forward into her hand. Boabak's face turned red and then purple as his throat swelled up. He struggled to breathe, stumbled backwards and landed heavily on the floor. The bruising wasn't too bad, but his own weight had worked against him. While he wheezed and massaged his throat she watched and waited to see if a killing blow was required. Some pink returned to his face as the initial shock wore off and slowly he managed to breathe, air whistling in and out of his restricted throat.

With a knee against his back, Kokochin wrapped the silk cord around his neck and pulled backwards with her full body weight. Boabak was already short of air and much of his strength had already been leached away. His fingers scrabbled at the material and his legs thrashed about, but even light pressure was closing off his damaged airway. He gasped and choked but she grimly held on as he fought for his life.

Eventually his arms dropped to his sides and he became a dead weight. Keeping an even pressure for another couple of minutes, in case he was faking, Kokochin waited but nothing changed.

When she finally let go, Boabak slumped over to one side. His vacant eyes stared at the ceiling. As she looked at his cooling body, Kokochin was surprised that she didn't feel any different. Surely she should feel something?

There was still work to do. Studying his neck, she realised that despite her best efforts there was still some bruising. She tried to lift him up and found that he was so heavy she could barely move him. Searching the bedroom she found a small prayer carpet in the corner.

After rolling the body onto it, she dragged him along the corridor back towards his study. By the time she had lifted him onto his seat, the muscles in her arms and back were screaming. Sweat coated her face and her lungs were burning.

While his head lolled backwards she grabbed a couple of dates and shoved them down his throat. Using a rolled-up bit of paper, she pressed them down until they were firmly wedged. It wasn't perfect, but it would have to do.

Imagining what would have happened if he'd been choking, she scattered the objects on his desk, knocking over the ink pot, flipping one book onto the floor, scrunching up the papers with her fingers. With a final nudge, he slumped forward on the desk, his face resting in a pool of black ink.

Making sure that nothing else was out of place, she double-checked the room and then slipped out of the house, locking the door before she left through the garden. By the time she had climbed up the rope, unhooked it and taken it with her, Kokochin's hands were shaking. At first she thought it was because the adrenaline had worn off, but as she moved through the shadows she realised it was something else.

Finding a dark corner between two shops she hunkered down and waited for the shock to pass. Her hands trembled, her teeth chattered and her whole body thrummed with a foreign pulse. Whatever her reasons, however necessary it had been for the greater good, she had still killed another person. As far as she knew, Boabak hadn't been particularly evil. According to Shirin, he'd been greedy and corrupt, which made bribing him impossible. It was likely he would have taken money from the House of Grace and then broken his word. It had to be this way. That thought didn't make it any easier as she sobbed and tried to dispel the image of his dead eyes staring at her.

Even though she knew there wasn't time for this, her body refused to obey. Any minute the play would end and the theatre owner, delighted by her patronage, would seek her out to see if she'd enjoyed the show. Her absence, as much as her presence, would be noted and that was something she desperately wanted to avoid.

Later there would be time for more tears and probably nightmares. It had to be later. Gritting her teeth Kokochin stood up and started back towards the theatre, wiping her face as she went.

Sneaking into the theatre was a lot more difficult than when she left. There were more people in the surrounding streets, and several times she was nearly discovered. By the time Kokochin made it inside the building, her nerves were stretched to breaking point and she jumped at the smallest noise.

A faint scuffing of someone's shoes sent her scrambling backwards, trying every door for a place to hide. The fourth door opened and she rushed inside, quickly closing it behind her. Thankfully the room was empty and used to store props. Part of her wanted to stay hidden until everyone had left. When the footsteps had gone past she peered outside, saw the hallway was empty and hurried towards her seat.

After everything that had happened, there was little strength in her arms and it took an age for her to climb up. By the time she slumped down in her seat Kokochin was exhausted and had little energy to move. On the stage, four singers were building towards the finale.

"It's done," said Kokochin. "I can barely move."

With some help from Layla, she changed her clothing and they swapped shoes again.

"Sit still a moment," said Layla, studying her face. "Your face-paint is a mess."

Layla knelt in front of her and reapplied her make-up, covering the redness of her eyes and the fresh scrapes. Behind her the final song finished to huge applause from everyone in the audience. They stomped their feet and the whole cast came out to take a bow.

"Eat something for energy," said Layla, directing her towards the pastries. Kokochin stuffed a piece of baklava in her mouth, savouring the syrupy taste. As soon as she began chewing, she realised she was famished and ate three more pieces. Finally the applause began to wind down and people started to get ready to leave. Layla resumed her seat and less than a minute later there was a knock at the door.

"Come," said Kokochin.

As expected it was the theatre owner. "Did you enjoy the performance?"

"It was wonderful, very emotional," said Kokochin. "I will tell other ladies in the court about tonight."

"Thank you, Princess, thank you," said the owner, backing away.

"You look pale," said Layla, loud enough for the owner to overhear. "Let's get some fresh air."

With Layla supporting her heavily on one side, they left the theatre, mixing in with the rest of the crowd. When people saw her coming, they immediately gave way, creating a pool of space. Kokochin felt her legs trembling with every step, but she kept her back straight and her head high, adopting a posture people expected to see.

Once they were a few streets away, Kokochin slumped against a wall to rest and told Layla what had happened.

"Hopefully it will be enough to convince people he choked to death," she said.

"I'm sure it will be fine," said Layla. "You need to rest."

An hour later the shock had worn off and, after eating some more sugary food, Kokochin felt well enough to return to the palace. From the way her body ached, she knew there would be a few bruises to conceal tomorrow but, no one other than Layla would know they were there. It felt strange to enter the palace at night via the main gate. She fought the familiar urge to sneak in through the servant's entrance.

It had been a long night, and by the time she reached her rooms, she wanted to collapse onto her bed and sleep. As soon as she pushed open the door Kokochin froze. Someone had lit the lanterns and also a few of her favourite candles, filling the air with the scent of sandalwood. At first she thought it must have been an overzealous servant, but then she detected something in the air. Closing her eyes she tried to brush aside her exhaustion and listen to the room.

Kokochin instincts told her she was not alone.

There had been Kheshig at the front gates and she'd seen them moving along the hallways, but they'd ignored her. Had someone already discovered Boabak's body? Maybe someone seen her leaving his house?

"Are you going to stand out there all night?" said Guyuk.

Kokochin's heart skipped a beat, but she stepped forward, moving around a pillar until she could see the Empress. She was sitting in one of Kokochin's comfy seats with a book in her lap.

"You startled me, Empress," she said. Guyuk had never been to her rooms. It was uncommon for anyone to turn up without an invitation. Then again, as the Empress had reminded her during their last meeting, Kokochin was nothing more than a pretty ornament and she was the Khan's real wife. She could do whatever she wanted at any time. "Do you need something?" asked Kokochin.

Instead of answering the Empress closed her book and briefly glanced around the rooms. Even if she had thoroughly searched every room, Kokochin knew there was nothing incriminating to find. Layla had forbidden for her from writing down anything she had learned in the House of Grace. She had no notes of any kind, and nothing that pointed at what she was really doing.

Without being given permission, Kokochin sat down opposite Guyuk who frowned in annoyance. It was a minor breach of decorum but Guyuk let it go, probably because she was in Kokochin's rooms.

"I know what you've been doing," said Guyuk, leaning back with a smug grin. "What you've really been doing."

"I don't know what you're talking about," said Kokochin.

"You may genuinely have an interest in jewellery, but I know why you've been spending so much time at that particular shop."

Kokochin said nothing, waiting to see how much Guyuk knew. Her worst fear was coming true. She was going to lose everything. She'd told Layla this would happen. Not for the first time, she considered what would happen if she killed the Empress. There would be nowhere she could hide that the Khan's men wouldn't find her. And no matter how strong she thought she was, eventually she would tell her torturer everything. The only way to protect Layla and the House of Grace would be to take her own life.

Guyuk sighed and rolled her eyes. "Do you think you're the first of the Khan's wives to fall in love with a woman?"

It took a couple of seconds for the question to register. "What?" said Kokochin. It felt as if she had fallen from a great height and yet was perfectly still.

"Don't lie, you're not very good at it," said the Empress. "Before she met Hulagu, Doquz Khatun loved a woman for many years. A couple of his concubines are together, but at least they're discreet."

"Discreet," said Kokochin, struggling to focus. She'd been so certain which direction the conversation had been going that now she felt totally off balance.

"You need to remember that no matter how you really feel, our husband always comes first. If he pays you a visit and you're not enjoying it, fake it. Wriggle about. He also likes a lot of noise." Guyuk was obviously speaking from experience, which made Kokochin wonder if the Empress had a lover. "Will you remember that?"

"Yes, Empress," she managed to stammer.

"Good. Now get some sleep, you look very pale." Guyuk moved towards the door and Kokochin was so stunned that she didn't move. "You need to be more careful, because if I've noticed, others will have too and someone might go after your friend to get to you."

Before Kokochin had a chance to reply, the door closed behind Guyuk. The words of the Empress rang in her ears. On the surface, it sounded like good advice, but the more Kokochin thought about it, the more it sounded like a threat.

CHAPTER 32
The Twelve

With a couple of hours to spare before the meeting, Kimya wandered through the streets, making a note of what had changed under Mongol occupation and what had remained the same. There was still a broad mix of people from the four corners of the globe, light and dark skinned, tall and short, but many were on edge. When a Mongol patrol went by several people froze, muttered prayers or averted their eyes. She saw no violence, which gave the illusion of safety, but Tabriz was much like the rest of the nation; being held hostage by bloodthirsty invaders. The warriors who had brutally slaughtered thousands of her people now maintained the peace.

As she passed through a bazaar, tantalising aromas assaulted her senses from the spice merchants and cooking stalls. Rich smells from sizzling meat on skewers tempted her. The lean pieces of lamb were wedged between chunks of peppers and onions, all of it wrapped in fresh bread and then drizzled with yoghurt and spices. Her stomach growled but she didn't stop to indulge.

Kimya criss-crossed the city, taking in the sights, as she slowly made her way towards a particular tea room. Along the way she paused outside a jewellery shop to peer at the items in the window. She could see the owner behind the counter, but didn't go inside. A short walk brought her to a busy tea room, where the owner and three young women bustled around the tables, serving food and drinks. Shirin gave her a cool nod, gestured at an empty table, but didn't stop to talk.

Kimya ordered something to drink from one of the girls, then bided her time watching the crowd. While she waited for the lunch rush to end, Kimya noticed how different Shirin behaved in familiar surroundings. She talked more, laughed often and flirted with several men who were eyeing her up.

An hour later, the crowd thinned until only a third of the tables were occupied. Shirin limped over and sat down with a fresh pot of tea and a plate of baklava. They talked about the price of tea and fresh dates, the weather and the welfare of their families. They were just two old friends, catching up on each other's news.

When she'd finished her tea, Kimya paid for her food and then walked alone to the abandoned shop. Until recently, it had been occupied by a European fortune teller and her two brothers. They'd left the city under a cloud, with large debts to pay, under suspicion for at least two murders.

As she pushed open the front door, One wrinkled her nose at the smell. There was a faint aroma of old incense, but it was overladen with the stink of blood. A worn old rug sat askew in the middle of the shop. Lifting one corner, she saw a dark stain on the ground. Perhaps it was more than two murders.

Two was the first to arrive, but neither of them said anything about their previous conversation. Working together, they cleared some space in the room and gathered enough chairs and tables for everyone to sit or perch. In lieu of a large table, One spaced them around the worn rug.

A short time later the others began to arrive, via the front and back door. One or two of the women glanced at the rug but said nothing. All of them understood that freedom required sacrifice.

Once everyone was assembled, One cleared her throat and the whispered conversations faded.

"Do you have any news on the Blue Princess?" she said, turning towards Two.

"Kokochin's mission was a success. Boabak, the sub-minister for agriculture, is dead. He was very fond of dates, and it appears he choked to death in his home. There were no signs of an intruder, and she is not under suspicion."

He had been a stubborn, short-tempered and difficult man with no friends and no living relatives. One suspected he would not be missed by his colleagues. "We need to proceed with caution."

Ten nodded. "Slow and steady."

"*His replacement must be beyond reproach*," said Twelve with a flick of her hands.

"She is," said Two.

"Is she one of ours?" asked One.

"Yes, and she's a patriot," said Two. "She will do as we ask."

"So, what do we do with Kokochin?" asked Eight.

"She passed the test," said Eleven.

"That doesn't prove she's loyal," said Six.

"Kokochin is loyal to her friend," said Two. "She loves her and would die for her."

"How do you know?" asked Three. "Did you meet with her in person?"

"I did, but she doesn't know who I am," added Two, before anyone complained.

"Why take the risk?" asked Four.

"I needed to know what kind of a person she was."

"Then we vote," said Seven, twisting a strand of her hair between her fingers.

"You want to let an outsider into the House? A Mongol?" scoffed Nine. In the pleasure houses she saw them at their worst. To them, lust was just another thirst to be quenched in whatever way they deemed fit, regardless of the damage. If a whore died, what did it matter? They could just get another one. "This goes against centuries of tradition," said Nine.

"These are unusual times," said One, drawing a few puzzled looks. "Make no mistake. The unrest brewing between the khanates is only the beginning. Eventually, it might be the death of the Empire, but before then, we will need help from all corners to drive the Mongols from Persia. If she can help us achieve our goal, then we will use her, like every other member in our network."

The vote was close, but by a margin of three votes Kokochin, Blue Princess and youngest wife of their most hated enemy, was accepted into the House of Grace.

Once the meeting had broken up, One lingered behind to check the room for any signs of their presence, but the women knew their business. Nevertheless, experience had taught her caution. Familiarity bred laziness and bad habits, which were dangerous for the House. Other than footprints in the dust, nothing about their identities could be gleaned from so little. One was stalling. Eventually, she left the building and headed east.

On the edge of a small bazaar, where many of the stalls were selling spices, fresh fish and sacks of rice, she entered a quiet tea room. The woman behind the counter glanced up, took note of Kimya's expensive clothing, and was suddenly very welcoming.

"How can I help you, madam?"

Kimya put several coins down. "I would like to hire a private room for an hour."

"Of course. This way, madam," said the owner, sweeping the coins into her apron.

At the end of a short corridor was a small room with a table and six chairs. It had been decorated tastefully with colourful cushions. The air smelled of jasmine and sweet wine. Kimya sat down at the low table while the shopkeeper lurked by the door.

"Would you like some tea and refreshments?"

"Yes, for two people. My guest will be arriving shortly."

"Of course," said the woman hurrying away.

Kimya's heart raced and her hands were sweaty. When the tea arrived she drank it too quickly and scalded the roof of her mouth. She left the rest to cool and was contemplating the pastries when she heard the sound of someone approaching.

The woman in the doorway was familiar and yet there were things Kimya didn't recognise. There was a bitter twist to the corners of her mouth and a darkness behind her eyes that spoke of grave deeds. Sadness and suffering hung about her like an invisible shroud. Although she wasn't branded, it was clear that she was a slave.

Kimya embraced her sister while doing her best, and failing, not to cry. Esme's once luscious hair was coarse against Kimya's cheek, and although she wasn't forty, there was a wide streak of grey amidst the black. When their tears of grief had subsided and become tears of joy, they sat and drank tea.

"I never thought I'd see you again," said Kimya, gripping her sister's hand, to make sure it was real. Many times she'd dreamt about Esme coming home only to wake up alone, filled with bitter heartache.

"It's been a long time," said Esme. "You look well. How are your husband and children? Do they still remember me?"

"Of course," said Kimya, wiping away fresh tears. "I've never stopped telling them stories from our childhood. Playing in the lagoon, swimming in the Caspian Sea and fishing with father in the rowboat."

"Those memories feel like they belong to someone else." Esme's expression hardened and, for a moment, Kimya faced a stranger. Kimya wondered how long it had been since her sister had laughed.

"What about you? Do you have someone?" she asked.

A smile crept onto Esme's face. "We found each other in the dark, when it seemed as if all was lost."

"The General."

"His name is Kaivon," said Esme, somewhat defensively.

"That was not an accusation. I don't know what you've endured."

Esme's expression softened. "His position has served us well. We are still slaves, but we have more freedom than most. The Khan relies on him and believes that Kaivon is his man, down to the marrow."

"What can you tell me of the Khan? What is he like?"

"'Know thy enemy, and know thy self, and you will win a hundred battles,'" quoted Esme. The ancient book was one their father had read to them as children. "Hulagu Khan is arrogant and prone to fits of rage, but his temper cools quickly. He claims to bring peace and prosperity, but I don't believe that. He relishes violence. Kaivon said that Hulagu is never more alive than in the midst of battle. He is ruthless, fearless and has dreams of uniting the world."

"Under Mongol rule," said Kimya and her sister nodded.

"Of the four brothers, he was always the peacemaker. He made several attempts to stop the feud but failed. Ariq believes he was cheated and should be the next Great Khan."

"We have been fanning the flames, although little effort was needed. Many senior Mongols agree that it should not be Kublai," said Kimya, choosing a honey dipped pastry.

"War between them is inevitable," said Esme, flashing her teeth. A shred of her humour remained, but it had become something more savage.

"Esme," said Kimya, gripping her sister's hands across the table. "We can talk of politics and make plans another day. Come home. Leave with me right now, and I swear you will never again be a slave. You can rejoin the Inner Circle and, together, we can tear them down."

Esme heaved a long sigh. "I've dreamed of this moment, many times. Seeing you again, and talking as if nothing had changed, but there's no going back."

"Come home," said Kimya.

"I can't." Esme stubbornly shook her head. "I can do more where I am. Besides, if I were to suddenly disappear, it could put Kaivon at risk."

A heavy silence filled the room.

"I understand," said Kimya, swallowing the lump in her throat. She knew Esme was right, but as the eldest it was her duty to protect her sister. Letting her go felt like failure. "Do you have everything you need?"

"There are several contacts from the House in the Khan's army. I will pass any useful information on to them."

"One day, our country will be free," promised Kimya, "and on that day, we will drink tea and talk of meaningless things for hours."

Esme's smile lit up her whole face and, for a moment, they were sisters again.

CHAPTER 33
Hulagu

When the spring thaw arrived, making the roads safe for travel, Hulagu was ready to leave. Spending too much time in Tabriz left him entrenched in the city's governance and trade, neither of which interested him. Both his first wife, Guyuk, and his vizier, Rashid, were better suited to such work and far more capable. He'd spent most of winter caught in an endless cycle of sending messages to the other khanates, and then waiting for a reply, in an attempt to head off the possibility of war. The matter was still not resolved, as neither Berke Khan nor Buqa-Temur had given him a definitive answer about who they would favour.

There was also the additional annoyance of receiving no word from either the Pope or the King of France. Despite the gift of Christian prisoners and relics from Baghdad, neither had answered his letters. He thought reclaiming the Christian Holy Land would tempt them to form a temporary alliance. Without their support, or any from the Golden Horde, it would be difficult to expand the Ilkhanate.

Only those closest to him realised how many men he had under his command. The horde mustered against Baghdad had been vast, but it would be hard to replicate. Hundreds had died in the previous year, and it would take time before they could be replaced. He'd received word that allies in the Caucasus region had already committed their forces and would soon be ready for battle. He could not appear weak in front of them, or else they might realise how much he needed them. If Kaivon's journey did not mend his rift with Berke, then he didn't know what would happen.

Soon he would be on a horse again, riding west with the wind in his hair. It was where he belonged and felt at home.

At least when he left the city his faithful wife, Doquz Khatun, would accompany him again. As if she knew Hulagu was thinking of her, she swept into the room, dressed in a jade silk dress and matching shawl, edged with gold thread. Her long dark hair was tied up in a complicated plait and swept over one shoulder. The time in Tabriz had done her good. With more rest, the dark smudges under her eyes had gone.

"A messenger brought this," she said, holding up a letter. "It's from General Kaivon."

He should have returned from Sarai weeks ago. Hulagu scanned the contents and then passed it across to his wife. The delay had not been caused by hazards on the road, but something more complicated.

"It sounds as if his trip has gone well," said Doquz, pouring herself a cup of tea. "Ten thousand warriors shows your cousin is still committed."

Hulagu grunted. "It's a third of what he committed last year. And now he's sending me three of his sons to spy on me."

"To learn from you," said Doquz.

"What am I going to do with three of them?"

"Exactly what he would expect you to do. Take them to war."

"We cannot wait for them to arrive. They will have to catch up on the road," said Hulagu.

"Have you heard anything from Aleppo?" asked Doquz.

Letters had been sent to the rulers asking them to surrender and declare their loyalty, or else face his wrath. They had seen what he had done to Baghdad. They knew what he would visit upon them if they refused.

"No. There's been no word," he said.

"Is that what's playing on your mind?"

"No, it's not that." Despite intelligence from his spies, the number of Mamluk warriors was shrouded in mystery. The Egyptians had not aided their allies when he'd laid siege to Baghdad, but as he drew closer to their border a conflict with them was inevitable.

"Then what's wrong?" asked Doquz, raising an eyebrow.

"I sent a letter to Ariq, asking him to call off the feud with Kublai."

"He refused."

"He sent back the messenger's head."

Doquz set her cup aside and embraced him tightly. "Can nothing be done?"

"I don't think so. I have thrown my full support behind Kublai. He is the rightful Great Khan. We will see who Berke and Buqa-Temur choose, but I have little faith in either. One seems more committed to his god than the Empire, and the latter is weak-willed."

They should have put someone else in place to rule the Chagatai Khanate, instead of Buqa-Temur. There would be changes if he voted against Kublai.

"You've done all that you can. Today you should focus on what is within your power to control," said Doquz.

"That sounds like a quote or scripture. Is it something from your Bible?" he asked.

"Something like that," said Doquz with a wry smile.

Hulagu pulled her into his embrace and, despite his many worries, he felt his passion stirring. He kissed her neck and ran his hands over her body, savouring the taste of her skin.

"Come wife," he said, leading her towards the bedroom. "Let us lie together one more time in a comfy bed before we leave."

"That sounds like a good idea, husband," she said, reaching behind her back to unfasten the buttons of her dress. Hulagu growled in appreciation and started pulling off his boots. A loud knocking at the door made him frown, but he ignored it. He watched in appreciation as Doquz started to ease her dress down her back, revealing her bare shoulders.

The knocking persisted.

"Go away!"

"My Khan, it's your son, Temujin," said the Kheshig. "You asked to see him."

Hulagu felt as if someone had thrown a cold bucket of water over him.

He had requested Temujin's presence, but then promptly forgotten. Every day his son became more peculiar, and every visit left Hulagu unsettled.

There were many whispers floating around the palace. Strange lights and sounds coming from the library. Some thought Temujin possessed. Others that he was cursed. Hulagu had noticed a few Christians made the sign of the cross at Temujin's back. Whatever mysteries Temujin was delving into, his presence was having an effect on those around him. If it turned out to be a weapon, Hulagu would tolerate the superstitious nonsense because, in the battles ahead, he needed an edge.

Doquz noted the change in his mood. "Don't be too long," she said, heading into the bedroom.

Temujin came into the room and, for a moment, Hulagu didn't recognise his son. The physical changes were significant, but it was more than that. Before, he had been embarrassed or ashamed of his miscoloured eyes. Now he boldly made eye contact, as if willing anyone to make a disparaging comment. If someone had shaved his head and dressed him in a robe, Hulagu would have said Temujin was a monk. He had the same calm mastery of self.

"My Khan," said Temujin, giving him a deep bow, fist

pressed to his heart. Even the way he spoke had changed. Gone was the indecision. He spoke with confidence and something bordering on pride.

"The thaw is nearly done. In a few days we will be leaving for Syria. Your brother Abaqa will join us, and together we will march on Aleppo. Be ready."

"As you command, my Khan." His son's expression was unreadable. A long silence stretched out, but instead of fidgeting, Temujin was content to wait. A cold prickle ran down Hulagu's spine and he broke the silence.

"Are you ready?" asked Hulagu.

A flicker of uncertainty passed across Temujin's face. "I will be."

"You may go," said the Khan, watching as his son bowed and left the room.

Hulagu stared at the door for a long time, wondering what had changed. His instincts told him it was more than a façade.

They would conquer several towns and villages before arriving at Aleppo. The city would be the first major challenge, and also Temujin's first test. Part of Hulagu was curious to find out, but another part was afraid.

In northern Syria, with the burning ruins of the city of Manbij at his back, Hulagu watched as warriors from the Golden Horde arrived. At the head of the column rode General Kaivon. Beside him were three well-dressed warriors, who he recognised as sons of Berke Khan.

"My Khan," said Kaivon, getting down off his horse to bow. The three princes remained on horseback, looking down at him from on high.

"Prince Tinibeg," said Kaivon, gesturing at the lankiest of the three with lean features.

"Prince Ahmad." The middle brother with one lazy eye.

"Prince Yotaqan." The youngest and yet the calmest with a

lazy smile. He would be the one to watch. Most people would overlook him, but he was clearly the smartest.

"You missed the battle, such as it was," said Hulagu, gesturing at the city behind him. The locals had put up some resistance, but their numbers had been insufficient. His army had swept over them like the tide, killing and burning until the city surrendered.

"Perhaps we can join you for the next battle, Lord Khan," said Prince Yotaqan.

"I would like that," said Hulagu, turning to Kaivon. "Get the men settled and then find me."

He was pleased to see that the warriors from the Golden Horde looked competent. Berke had not sent him just the old and lame.

An hour later Kaivon was shown into his tent. "My Khan," he said bowing again.

"Sit, sit," said Hulagu, waving him towards a chair. "Tell me about your visit with Berke."

"Everything went as you hoped. I delivered his share of the wealth, and he accepted Prince Taraghai into his service."

"And?" asked Hulagu. "How did he react? Be honest," he said, noticing Kaivon's reticence.

"I do not want to speak ill of your family."

"Tell me," said Hulagu.

"I was called to meet in private with Berke Khan and his vizier. He was angry and said that you'd cheated him. He expected you to send more, given the efforts of his warriors during the siege."

Hulagu snorted. "Mine was the larger force. He should be grateful, especially as he left early. I knew he had an ego, but I didn't think he was greedy. What else?"

"He was under no illusions about why you had sent Taraghai."

"What aren't you telling me?" said Hulagu, sensing something. "You don't think he would hurt my son, do you?"

"No. I'm certain he would never do that," stressed Kaivon, shaking his head. "Regardless of whatever else is going on, you are family. And he has entrusted you with three of his own sons in return."

It was a fair exchange, and now they were spying on each other. He would have to make sure the three princes were kept safe, even in the midst of battle. If something were to happen to them, Berke would not believe it had been an accident, and Taraghai would suffer.

"Make sure the princes are protected at all times," said Hulagu. "Arrange it with the Commander of the Kheshig."

"Yes, my Khan."

"Even though you bring ill news, it's good to have you back," said Hulagu. The Persian always spoke his mind, and his insights had proven useful. Too many of his Generals were used to the old ways. Kaivon would be a valuable asset for the forthcoming sieges.

"Tomorrow we march on Aleppo."

"I'm ready."

"Good. Tonight we will celebrate the destruction of Manbij. Make sure the princes are invited. You will also attend."

"I would be honoured."

"Get some rest, if you can," said Hulagu with a smirk. "I expect Esme will be pleased about your return."

"I look forward to our reunion," said Kaivon, with a grin.

Hulagu dismissed the General, but his smile faded as he thought about what lay ahead.

Stepping outside the tent, Hulagu looked behind him towards the smoking ruins. Standing at the edge of the camp, surveying the remains of the city was a lone figure. With an expression that bordered on serenity, Temujin stared at the ruined city. His lack of emotion was worrying. Every day he became more of a stranger and Hulagu felt uncomfortable in his presence.

He'd seen the looks others gave Temujin behind his back.

They moved a step or two away if he came too close, even the Kheshig. He made stoic men twitch and talkative men fall silent. Thankfully, Temujin spent most of his time alone. The librarian had remained in Tabriz, scouring for more clues about whatever power possessed Temujin. Maybe that was why everyone was so uncomfortable. It was something unnatural that did not belong.

Later that evening, thoughts of Temujin were lost in a haze of smoke, drink and food. In addition to the usual generals, Hulagu was happy to be reunited with his old friend Kitbuqa and his son, Abaqa. Throughout the winter months, the old General had been advising his eldest as they sought to rebuild and rule Baghdad. It was slow and difficult work. The politicking and bureaucracy already showed on Abaqa's face, but he needed to learn for the future.

Although his letters to both the King of France and the Pope had gone unanswered, other allies had sent warriors in support of his cause. King Hethum of Armenia, a hearty man with a big appetite, sat laughing with Jumghur and said something that made his son spray beer from his nose. Hethum laughed again and slapped Jumghur on the back until he stopped choking.

A little further away, at another table, sat Prince Bohemond of Antioch. Wiser than many, he had seen how inevitable it was that the Mongols were destined to rule everything. Bohemond had agreed to serve, sparing the destruction of his cities and the slaughter of his people. His fealty to Hulagu had angered his Latin allies, but now, with the Ilkhanate pushing ever west and south, they understood.

Called the Fair by some, Hulagu didn't think Bohemond was particularly handsome, but perhaps it referred to his style of rule. It didn't matter. The Prince had brought men to fight in Hulagu's army. If Aleppo did not receive support from its allies, then he had enough men to take it.

As a messenger entered the tent, the seed of worry in Hulagu's stomach sprouted tendrils.

"My Khan. I have an urgent message," said the man who stank of horse.

Hulagu took the message and read it once. It had been scribbled in a rush, but the words were still clear. Swallowing the bile rising in his throat, Hulagu gulped down the rest of his airag, but it tasted of betrayal.

Hours later, more drunk than intended, Hulagu stumbled into his tent. The brazier was low, but the air inside was still warm and welcoming. The sight of his sleeping wife, Doquz, was even more appealing, her dark hair fanned out across the bed. She muttered in her sleep as he sat down on the edge of the bed.

"Ugh, you stink of beer," she said, coming awake. "Did you bathe in it?"

He'd spilled some down his front, matting the fur on his armour and staining his shirt beneath. At some point, there had also been some wine. A cache from France had been found in Manbij. Pain was already beginning to blossom in his head, and that wasn't a good sign.

"What's wrong?" asked Doquz, sitting up in bed. "You look…" she trailed off, unwilling to say aloud what he knew was clear. He was afraid.

"There was a messenger. Ariq has declared war on Kublai."

Doquz shook her head sadly. "You knew this was coming. What else did it say?"

Hulagu snarled and spat on the floor. "Berke and Buqa-Temur are siding with Ariq. I am the only Khan to support Kublai." He had known that Berke was unhappy with him, but Hulagu hadn't thought his cousin would go this far. Buqa-Temur was less of a surprise. He was weak-willed. If the wind blew in one direction he would follow. Hulagu worried how civil war between the khanates would look to their enemies. Some might think the Mongol Empire was weak.

"There is nothing you can do for Kublai or Ariq. They must decide this by themselves. I know it pains you, because they are your blood," she said, holding his head between her hands. Her skin was cool and refreshing against the warmth of his cheeks. "But you cannot help them. We are here now, in Syria, and there is much work to be done. The dream must be fulfilled. First Aleppo, then Damascus and then further south, towards Jerusalem."

"Berke's sons will know of this. They may have even known before they left Sarai."

"Let them whisper and gossip. Remain focused on what lies ahead. You made an example of the people of Manbij. Aleppo will suffer the same fate if they don't surrender. They are nothing. You are the Khan."

Hulagu felt the tension ease at her words. "You always know what to say."

"I know you, husband," she said, murmuring in his ear. "Tomorrow, we march for Aleppo and you will show every warrior in the army your strength. That will silence the whispers, and no one will doubt your power."

"Dawn is many hours away, wife," he said, running a hand up her thigh. "And suddenly I find that I am very hungry." She groaned and lay back as he explored her body with his mouth.

In the morning Hulagu had a slight twinge at his temples, but otherwise suffered no ill effects from the previous night. A smile tugged at the corners of Doquz's mouth as she helped him dress. By the time he'd finished eating his breakfast, and had strapped on his sword, Hulagu felt good about what lay ahead. The future of the Mongol Empire was uncertain, but he knew the future of the Ilkhanate was secure.

"Remind them who you are," said Doquz, giving him a fierce kiss.

When Hulagu emerged from his tent, a large portion of the camp had already been packed up. Groups of warriors were readying themselves for the ride to Aleppo. The supply carts would follow and, by the time they arrived, the siege would be well underway.

Under heavy guard, Nasir and his engines of war had gone ahead. Once again it was time for his chief engineer to prove his ingenuity and skill. The walls of Aleppo were not as thick and high as those of Baghdad, but it would still be a challenge to break them.

Surrounded by his generals, with the wind dragging at his hair, Hulagu rode through the camp to cheers.

"To war!" he shouted. "To war!"

The men roared back. Mongol warriors, men from Armenian Cilicia, Georgia, Frankish knights, Persians and Chinese. All of them bound to serve him. Ready for battle, bloodshed and glory. Ready to crush their enemies and drive fear into their hearts. Ready for victory.

When the walls of Aleppo came into view, Hulagu was impressed. It was a magnificent looking city with sturdy walls and huge gates. An ancient place, people had been living on the same site for thousands of years. There were immeasurable layers of history and culture and countless people had been born, lived and died within its limits.

It had been conquered and occupied many times, by different nations, over the centuries. Pillaged and burned only to be rebuilt, time and again. If necessary, he would topple the walls. The people were brave and stubborn. In time, they would rebuild, but all of that was for tomorrow. Today was the beginning of the siege.

Leaving his horse, Hulagu approached where Nasir and over a hundred engineers, Persian and Chinese, had been working on their engines. Four huge catapults had been carried by cart and then carefully assembled. Beside them sat two Chinese mangonels which were still being erected.

"We are ready, my Khan," said Nasir. "We need to fire a couple of test shots, check our calculations and then we can begin the assault."

It would still be several hours before the rest of the men arrived, giving the engineers plenty of time to finish their preparations.

A disturbance passed through the men around him. Turning his head, Hulagu searched for the source. Dressed in loose-fitting clothing that did little to hide his physical transformation, Temujin approached. Fierce warriors and veteran generals alike stepped aside, doing their best to go unnoticed. Once they had called him Round Eye, but those days were gone. Hulagu swallowed the lump in his throat and forced himself not to turn aside as his son approached.

"I am here, my Khan," said Temujin, giving a deep bow.

Everyone was transfixed, unable to tear their eyes away.

"When the rest of the men arrive, we will lay siege to the city. You have a few hours to prepare."

"I will be ready," said Temujin, giving him a peculiar smile.

For the first time in years, fear ran down Hulagu's spine.

CHAPTER 34
Temujin

Temujin could smell their fear.

At first, the changes had been slight. A few double takes as people noticed the physical changes, but then he'd feel their eyes lingering. Somehow they could sense the changes within him.

As Temujin spent more time meditating on the Eternal Fire, the doors within his mind were being thrown open. Some of the changes he could recognise and others he didn't understand. Insight into the people that surrounded him had become much easier. Temujin could glance at a person and know things about them which they kept hidden from the world.

He was under no illusions. He was not wiser or more intelligent than before. It was merely that, until now, he had been walking around with blinkers on without knowing. While insight was easier, the more overt powers of the Kozan still evaded him. His dream of flying over the city had not been repeated, and the woman from the dream had not returned.

Despite all the research, he still couldn't see how it all fit together. The Eternal Fire was merely a conduit but, without a guide, he was fumbling along. So far, he'd been lucky. The physical damage had been minor, but Temujin understood he was walking along the edge of a sword. One wrong step and he could die.

Staring at the city of Aleppo from the edge of camp, Temujin knew the fate of thousands was in his hands. If he did nothing, the siege would continue as before. Nasir's engines would pound the walls until they broke. Fire and destruction would reign down on the people inside, and his father's army would kill many of the defenders. Eventually the city's defences would be overrun, at which point it would be too late to beg for mercy. Days of slaughter would follow, just as it had with the destruction of Manbij and the siege of Baghdad before that. On both occasions, he'd watched and done nothing as thousands were murdered or sold into slavery. If the city could be conquered without bloodshed then, with luck, the transition would cost fewer lives.

If he had the power to save them and did nothing, what did that make him?

It was dangerous, but Temujin didn't have a choice. One life was a small price to pay if it saved thousands.

Warriors shifted uncomfortably and turned away as he walked through the camp. Boisterous warriors laughing with their friends fell silent. Brooding stares and fear followed in his wake. There was also something else simmering underneath. Many wanted him dead. Not for something that he'd done, or who he was, merely the fact that he was different.

Dozens of men were busy working on the catapults under the watchful eye of the chief engineer. Nasir bellowed and kicked a few who weren't moving fast enough. He understood that the wrath of Hulagu would fall on him if he didn't deliver as promised.

Nasir sensed his presence and his tirade tailed off.

"Prince Temujin," he said, sketching a short bow. "Your father said you wanted to see the engines."

"Are they ready?"

"We will fire two test shots, if these lazy idiots do as they're told," said Nasir, watching as they redoubled their efforts.

A few minutes later the catapults were ready. Nasir double-checked the calculations and agreed that their information was sound. With a deep grinding and clicking of metal, the arms of the two catapults were lowered. Two huge wheels were turned by teams of half a dozen men. A large boulder was dropped into each of the waiting slings and the counterweights were raised on high. With a fierce grin Nasir dropped his arms.

The trebuchets creaked, the weights dropped and a sling ran backwards before flinging the boulders towards the city walls. Temujin shaded his eyes, watching as the missiles arced up and forward falling towards the outer wall of Aleppo. Both hit their target, cracking the wall at the point of impact, but, beyond that, there was little obvious damage. Nevertheless, the engineers were delighted with their first attempt. Normally it took them a half dozen strikes before they found their mark.

"Now what happens?" asked Temujin.

"Now?" said Nasir. "Now we hit them in the same spot, again and again, until the wall comes tumbling down. We have plenty of boulders," said the engineer, gesturing at the pile of stones nearby.

"How fast can you reload them?"

"It will only take a few minutes. Why?" asked Nasir. "What are you going to do?"

"Keep your distance and ready the catapults," said Temujin, sinking to his knees. Ignoring the worried glances and the smell of unwashed bodies, he turned his senses within. Around him, everything was in motion, but he remained utterly immobile. A stubborn, unmoving pebble in the rapid flow of a river. The familiar sense of calm washed over his body, enveloping Temujin in its serenity.

On the periphery of his senses, Temujin heard the wheels being turned, the arms lowered and two more boulders were cinched into their slings. One by one the engineers stopped what they were doing, fell silent and became still. Waves of calm rippled outward from Temujin until everyone close to the catapults was holding their breath.

Moving his hands to either side of his body, with his palms up, Temujin waited. The Eternal Fire blossomed in each hand.

"Prepare to fire," he said. A few people scurried away from his position and he heard frantic conversations between the engineers. Temujin slowly rose to his feet and approached the first catapult. The Fire bobbed and weaved, but it never went out. Placing his hand on the boulder he gritted his teeth and tried to tether the flame in place.

Nothing happened.

It was as if the Fire was attached to him, but with some coaxing he urged it to the edge of his fingertips. When it slipped off and landed on the stone a huge weight settled on his shoulders. It drove Temujin to one knee and there was a loud churning in his stomach.

His muscles screamed in protest as he took one unsteady step towards the other catapult, while keeping the image of the Fire in his mind. Going against what he had promised, Temujin fed the fire with resentment at his brothers, rage at his father and grief at the loss of his mother. On shaky legs, with his whole body thrumming, the air came alive with energy. Those around him felt it. A charge lifted the hairs on their arms and heads.

One more step. Just one more. And then one more. The distance between the two catapults was not far, and yet with each step it became increasingly difficult. Slowly he became aware of a rattling sound and eventually realised it was his own teeth chattering together. The skin on the sides of his face grew taut. The muscles down his back went into spasm. Mercifully, when he stumbled, he fell against the second catapult. His hand touched the stone and he fell backwards onto the ground, one arm stretched out towards each flame.

It felt as if a herd of horses was attached to each arm and he were being torn apart.

"Fire!" he gasped. "Fire now!"

There was an impossibly long wait, no more than three

heartbeats, before he heard the click and whoosh of the catapults. The pain running through his body became infinitely worse. If not for the bubble of serenity, Temujin knew it would have killed him.

In the distance, he felt the moment of impact. Wreathed in the Eternal Fire the boulders struck the wall and a second later he blacked out.

He came awake shortly after, as everyone was still staring at the city. His whole body felt as if it were one massive bruise. Even his teeth ached. His clothes were soaked through with sweat which sent a chill down his back. One of the engineers saw he was awake. By leaning heavily on the man, Temujin sat upright. On legs that felt ready to collapse, he moved to the front of the crowd and stared at Aleppo.

The test strikes had cracked the wall, but done little real damage. Over time, the repetition would have been devastating.

This time the boulders had punched clean through the wall. As it had done with the table, the Fire melted the stone like warm butter.

Two huge sections of the battlements collapsed, creating huge breaches in the city's defences. In the distance, Temujin heard the grinding of stone and a moment later, a huge cloud of dust was thrown into the air.

When the smoke cleared, the level of destruction was apparent. He had done in a moment what would normally have taken several days of constant bombardment.

Nasir stared at Temujin with a mix of awe and fear. Some of the engineers dropped to the ground, pressing their faces to the dirt. Others drew symbols on their chests, superstitious wards to protect them from evil.

"Take me back to my tent," said Temujin to the engineer. With someone supporting him on either side, he made it back to his tent before blacking out.

* * *

Time became difficult to judge after that. Temujin woke often, looking up at the ceiling of his tent. At one point his father was there, looking down at him. Later, he felt someone moving his body, but he was so weak he had no energy to fight. Slowly he became aware of being cocooned in warm blankets, however, it took a long time before he felt hot.

"Drink," said a gentle voice. He sipped at something warm and sweet, managing a few mouthfuls before he lay back, letting the darkness envelop him. Several times he awoke to drink more broth. It was warm and filling, full of meat and spices. Gradually it gave him some energy, but not enough to move by himself.

The next time he woke up, Temujin felt more like himself. The weight that had been pressing down on his body was gone. He still felt weak and his limbs shook, but he managed to sit up. His stomach churned and before he could ask a full bowl of stew was put into his hands. Temujin gulped it down and found he was still hungry. The healer, an ancient woman with leathery skin, filled his bowl a second and then a third time. After that, he ate a roasted bird, a chunk of bread, a fat heel of cheese and half a dozen apples. It felt as if he had not eaten for weeks, and that his body was starved of nourishment. Slowly his appetite was sated and he sat back, his belly stretched to its limit.

Dreams came and went. None of them very clear until he saw a vision of a woman. At first he didn't recognise her but then he saw her eyes; one blue and one green. It was the same woman he'd seen when flying through the streets of Tabriz, untethered from his sleeping body.

He was standing on a street of a familiar city, but it wasn't real. It was a composite of many places he'd visited. A Hindu temple comfortably sat next to a tiny cottage, surrounded by trees. In the dream it made sense.

The woman was standing right in front of him. She looked incredibly worried and was talking, but he couldn't make out the words. She tried again, enunciating, but he still didn't understand and shook his head.

When she grabbed his hand Temujin winced in pain. Her skin was burning and the shock ran up his arm.

"Let go!" he said, trying to shake her off, but she stubbornly held on.

"If you do that again, it will kill you," she said. "Do not use the Fire as a weapon."

"How do you know about the Eternal Fire?"

She grimaced and became transparent before snapping back into focus. "I know a great deal, which I will share. Come back to Tabriz and I will find you."

Before he could ask her anything else, she let go of his hand and vanished. The moment she blinked out of view the pain disappeared.

The next morning, after a hearty breakfast, he felt much better. There was a deep weariness in his bones, but Temujin believed it would fade in time.

Partly because he was afraid it was gone forever, but also to calm himself, he meditated. Almost immediately the Eternal Fire appeared, hovering above the palms of his hands.

Temujin realised how close he'd been to death. Even without a mirror, he could feel the bones in his face were more prominent. He had fed emotions into the Fire as fuel and then it had started to strip the fat from his body. When all of that was gone, it had turned to the meat, and would have continued through muscle, bone and organs until he was dead.

When the summons came for a meeting with his father, Temujin wrapped himself in a shroud of calm. Even so, he had to work hard to maintain a neutral expression. As he passed through the camp, he received many looks, but he acknowledged none of them. He knew what they were feeling. This was the cold fear that prey experienced when something dangerous had walked past. They watched and wondered what he was going to do next.

At the entrance to his father's tent the Kheshig bowed and held open the door, something they'd never done before. As Temujin stepped inside he was prepared for a formal audience with the han and his senior officers.

Instead he found Hulagu leaning forward on a stool as his wife, Doquz, drove her elbows into his shoulders. Stripped to the waist, his father's upper body was a map of the many battles he'd fought. Old scars and new criss-crossed his flesh. Fading bruises had turned yellow, while fresh swelling spoke of recent scrapes.

Hulagu grunted as something popped loudly in his back. Doquz stepped back, wiped her oil-covered hands on a towel and offered Temujin a nervous smile. She'd never been particularly warm towards him, but now Temujin could see that he made her anxious.

"Sit," said Hulagu, gesturing at a chair.

"Are you injured?" asked Temujin.

"It's nothing serious," said the Khan, daring his wife to contradict him. Doquz rolled her eyes but said nothing. "I was too enthusiastic during the assault."

"The city of Aleppo has fallen," said Temujin.

"Thanks to you," said Hulagu. "Once the outer wall was breached, we entered the city and have been battling the soldiers within. Some were killed in the crush of stone, but many were still able to fight." He sounded pleased.

"They didn't surrender?"

"No, but we have them on the run. Many were killed in the first few hours, and the rest were hunted through the streets, like dogs," said Hulagu laughing at the memory.

Temujin glanced at Doquz so he did not have to see his father's glee.

"You sent for me?"

"Yes, Son," said Hulagu, pulling on his shirt with help from Doquz.

The Khan had not called him son in a long time.

"Aleppo is ours. The next few days will be spent letting the men have some fun."

Temujin knew what that meant. Slaughter. Women and children being sold into slavery. Destruction, desecration and looting the city of its wealth. After all, the war effort could not continue without a robust treasury. And when the Mongol army and its allies had squeezed every last drop of life from the city, they would move on, leaving a ruined shell in their wake.

Temujin had thought that by breaching the city's walls more quickly, he would be sparing the people such misery. All he had done was bring it about that much sooner.

"And then?"

"We will head south towards Damascus." Hulagu hesitated and looked at Doquz, as if he needed reassurance. "Can you do it again?" he asked.

Temujin had been expecting this. "No. It will take me weeks, even months, to recover." He expected anger and bitter disappointment. Instead, to his surprise, his father looked relieved.

"I see."

"However, there might be another way," said Temujin.

"Such as?"

"What if there were three more like me? Or ten?"

Hulagu wiped the sweat from his brow. "There are others?"

"There must be. I think I can find them."

"Even with three like you, my army would be unstoppable," said Hulagu warming to the idea. He said nothing of the toll it had taken on Temujin. The only thing that mattered was the war.

"I should return to Tabriz and begin my search there."

An uncomfortable silence filled the tent. Temujin could see strong emotions warred within the Khan. Fear of his own son versus the potential damage such a powerful weapon could unleash against his enemies.

"You may return to Persia," said Hulagu. "But come back quickly. There are big challenges ahead, and I will need you."

"Yes, my Khan," said Temujin, staring down at his father.

There had always been a gulf between them, but now it felt like an ocean.

Temujin left the tent without another word. Truths he had known for a long time, but failed to acknowledge, could no longer be ignored. His father was not proud of him because of who he was. He only cared because Temujin had become useful for the war. Hulagu was willing to do anything, and sacrifice anyone, to achieve his dreams.

As he walked towards his tent to pack his belongings, Temujin believed that he would never again see his father. He was at peace with the idea.

CHAPTER 35
Kaivon

On the second day of the sacking of Aleppo, while Mongol warriors and their allies ran rampant through the streets, Kaivon was to meet the three princes from the Golden Horde.

"Why haven't they taken part in the siege?" asked Esme, as she helped him into his armour. It had become part of their daily ritual and Kaivon enjoyed the intimacy.

"Once the wall fell, the Khan didn't think it would be safe for them inside. Not straight away at least." He'd expected the princes to be upset, but there had been no reaction. If anything, Kaivon had thought they were relieved.

"Is anyone still resisting?"

"Very few," said Kaivon, tightening his belt. "Most of the Syrian warriors have been hunted down and killed. Those who remain are in hiding. The Khan is taking no prisoners. The rest are being sold into slavery."

Feeding so many new mouths would be impossible. Every day the army consumed a huge amount of food. It sounded reasonable, but Kaivon had seen the rotting bodies lying in the streets. The living carpets of flies, feasting on dead flesh. It was slaughter, plain and simple.

"This could have been our people. It was our people," said

Esme, spitting out the words. "Homes destroyed. Families shattered."

"I know." Kaivon not only shared her pain, he remembered the exact moment when he realised the Mongols had beaten them.

"Each time I sew up a Mongol warrior, I want to stab him with the needle," admitted Esme.

Kaivon held her gently by the shoulders. "We're not alone anymore, remember?"

"Has there been any word from your brother?"

"Nothing. But he said he'd only make contact if there was bad news."

"I hope that's true," she said, tightening his greaves. "I told my sister I wanted to stay, but every day it becomes more difficult."

"You could still leave. We would find a way."

"And leave you behind?" she scoffed, looking up at him. "No. I wouldn't do that to you. I can endure it awhile longer."

"It will not be forever," said Kaivon, pulling her upright.

"Be careful," said Esme, pressing her face against his chest. "The locals will be hungry for revenge. They won't care that you're not a Mongol."

Kaivon found the three Mongol princes, dressed in their armour, waiting for him outside their tent.

"General," said Ahmad.

"Are you ready to enter the city?" asked Kaivon.

A special unit, comprised of veterans, would accompany the three princes to guarantee their safety.

"In a moment," said Prince Yotaqan. "Please, join us by the fire."

Kaivon accepted their invitation and warmed his hands in front of the blaze. The two oldest brothers were nervous and uncomfortable. Only Yotaqan wore an easy smile and made eye contact.

"Who are we hunting in the city?" asked Yotaqan.

The question was said in a casual tone of voice, but Kaivon could feel weight behind it.

"The Khan has said we can kill any who stand in the way, except for the Christians. They will be rounded up and sent to Rome. Their churches are also not to be desecrated or destroyed."

"Why the Christians?" asked Ahmad.

"The Khan's wife, Doquz Khatun, is a Christian and she asked this favour of him," said Kaivon. Hulagu had agreed because, as they pushed further south, he wanted support from Rome, France and other Christian nations. In the past, many of them had tried to capture their Holy Land. Hulagu hoped they wouldn't be able to ignore this opportunity.

"What of the Muslims?" asked Yotaqan.

"They are shown no mercy."

"Not even the women and children?" asked Ahmad.

"Some will be sold into slavery, others killed for amusement." Kaivon shrugged, as if it were nothing. As if he didn't care, like so many others in the army. "The Khan's fight is ultimately with the Mamluks of Egypt, and they are Muslims."

The three princes said nothing for a long time. Kaivon could see the anger welling up inside them.

"Are you ready?" he asked, breaking the silence.

The brothers exchanged a look and the eldest two shook their heads before Yotaqan cleared his throat. "We will not be taking part in this act of mindless bloodshed."

"I shall inform the Khan," said Kaivon, getting to his feet.

"Please do," said Yotaqan. "And let him know of our displeasure."

As he walked through the bloodstained streets of Aleppo, Kaivon felt bile rising in the back of his throat. He saw a pair of Mongol warriors breaking the windows of a shop before throwing a flaming torch inside.

The stench of death and decay was all around. Glancing up at the rooftops, he saw dozens of vultures, bloated from their feasts. Hundreds of smaller black birds flew overhead, squawking and fighting.

In one alleyway he saw the body of a woman, coated in a squirming blanket of flies. She had been dead for some time as her eyes were gone. Staring at her features, Kaivon could see that once she had been beautiful, before being slaughtered and left to rot.

Something larger moved in the shadows beside the body. Stepping closer, Kaivon saw that it was a small child. Boy or girl, he couldn't be sure, but they were staring at the body of their mother with shock. Unable or unwilling to leave her, they hunkered down beside the remains. Kaivon made sure that he was alone in the street before moving closer. The buzzing of the flies grew louder and angrier, but some moved away from their grisly feast.

The small child stared up at him with a blank expression. Brutalised by what they had witnessed, the child had no fear or alarm at seeing an armoured warrior.

"Get out of here," he hissed. "She's gone."

The child said nothing. He wasn't sure if they had understood. The sound of laughter and idle conversation indicated several warriors were approaching.

"Hide or die. Do it now," he said.

The child finally responded. They patted their mother's hand and then ran, disappearing around a corner.

"What do you have there?" said Hulagu, coming to stand beside him. Together they stared down at the body of the woman.

"I thought I saw something," said Kaivon. "It must have been the flies."

"Ugh, the smell," said the Khan. "Come."

With half a dozen Kheshig at his back, Kaivon walked beside Hulagu towards the heart of the city. While the outer city had been claimed within the first two days, the citadel continued to hold out. The promise of a good fight and great wealth had kept the men motivated. Every morning they tried to batter down the doors and scale the walls. And every day, the number of defenders was halved. Kaivon estimated it would fall into Mongol hands today.

Many buildings had been utterly smashed to rubble, but some structures remained untouched. One of the most impressive buildings, the Grand Mosque of Aleppo, was still pristine, although Kaivon wasn't sure how it had escaped being damaged.

The mosque was a thick stone building with a huge tiled area in the centre. The floor was made from black and sand coloured stone, arranged into repeating geometric patterns. Standing proud over the building was a huge blue dome, topped with a golden star and crescent. Rising even higher than the dome was a square tower made of the same grey-white stone. It must have taken decades to construct. Even though he was not a Muslim, Kaivon could admire the architectural mastery.

"Did you speak with the three princes?" asked Hulagu, intruding on his thoughts.

"Yes, my Khan."

"And?"

"They declined to join in with what they called 'mindless bloodshed.'"

"What?" spat Hulagu.

"They also asked me to express their displeasure at the murder of their Muslim brothers."

"Displeasure?" shouted the Khan before grabbing him by the throat. "They are displeased with me?"

Kaivon's face turned bright red before Hulagu released him. The Khan was breathing hard and the Kheshig did their best to pretend nothing had happened.

"What are your orders, my Khan?" said Kaivon when he could speak again.

Hulagu had calmed down, but his shoulders were still hunched. At first Kaivon thought he was staring towards the horizon, but then he raised a hand and pointed at the Grand Mosque.

Hulagu grabbed one of the Kheshig and dragged him close. "Find Bohemond and tell him to bring a thousand men with fire."

His bodyguards were not used to being messengers, but the warrior wisely decided not to argue. A short time later, the Prince of Antioch appeared at the head of a column of men. Many of them were carrying torches.

Kaivon was aware of bad blood between Bohemond's people and the Muslim world. Once again, Hulagu had found a way to help an ally settle an old score, strengthening the bonds between them.

"I want to see smoke for miles!" shouted Hulagu. "Bar every door and then burn it to the ground."

There were people trapped inside, priests and at least a couple of hundred Muslims. After seeing their friends cut down in the street, many had fled to the relative safety of the mosque.

For an hour Hulagu stood and watched in silence as the doors were blocked with pieces of wood and carts rolled into place. Then flaming torches were thrown inside through broken windows. Some came sailing back out again, but as more were tossed in, plumes of black smoke poured out. Next came the choking and the screaming, as those inside were overwhelmed. When one door was opened from the inside, a few people tried to flee, but they were shoved back into the mosque. Next the trapped began to plead and beg for mercy, for their lives, for the lives of their children. No mercy was given. Biting the inside of his lip until he tasted blood was the only way not to react.

"My Khan, I received news that the citadel still stands," said Kaivon, hoping to distract Hulagu.

"Not for long," said Hulagu. He sounded calm, but his hands were still clenched into fists. Someone else might have apologised, or at least acknowledged nearly choking him to death had been a mistake. Kaivon knew better than to expect such a display of guilt from the Khan. "Come, General," was all he said.

Kaivon followed the Khan away from the smoking mosque towards the stubborn citadel. It was the last bastion and, perhaps, those inside still clung to a glimmer of hope that help would arrive and save them. As he watched women and children being loaded into carts, Kaivon knew the remaining defenders were doomed.

It was time to turn the knife.

"My Khan, will your son be lending us his gifts to breach the citadel?" Kaivon knew he was slightly overstepping, but he didn't care.

"Do you have any children?" said Hulagu, instead of answering.

"No."

"You're lucky. They always find a way to disappoint." He sounded melancholy, but Kaivon wasn't convinced. Hulagu was relieved that his son had returned to Tabriz. "He taxed himself too much. So he's gone to find others like him and create a cadre."

One Mongol with such powers was a serious threat. More than that would make Hulagu Khan unstoppable. His dreams of expanding the Ilkhanate west into Europe, and south towards Egypt, would become a reality. Kaivon would have to send a message back to his brother. For the good of Persia, and many other nations, the murder of Prince Temujin had become their highest priority.

* * *

As Kaivon had predicted, the citadel's defences were breached that afternoon. To his eternal shame, he took part in the attack that followed. Dozens of units had searched the building, room by room, murdering those who fought back and rounding up those who surrendered.

When they had cleared the entire citadel, all survivors were gathered in the central square. A once-beautiful fountain of a woman had been shattered. The water was stained brown with blood. One of the Mongols pissed into it while others laughed. The intricate mosaic on the floor was smeared with mud, scuffed by hundreds of boots and splashed with patches of blood.

The city leaders, seven once-proud men, were lined up and told to kneel. Kaivon had thought the Khan's anger had passed through him as it normally did, but today he proved why Jumghur was his son.

Gripping his sword in both hands, Hulagu went down the line, beheading each man in turn. Not once did his expression change. It was a fierce grimace of concentration and beneath it, anger that had not been sated. The men cheered and laughed as the city leaders died on their knees. The survivors watched and wept, fearing that they would soon share the fate of their leaders.

By the time Kaivon set off for his tent it was early in the evening and he was sick to his soul. After what he had witnessed in Baghdad, he'd believed himself numb to such atrocities. Away from the Khan and others, when he no longer had to wear a mask of indifference, his hands shook with fear, rage and shame.

As Kaivon approached his tent, someone stepped out of the shadows. Moving on instinct he started to draw his sword, until he recognised that it was Prince Yotaqan.

"General."

"Apologies, Prince Yotaqan," said Kaivon. "It has been a long and trying day."

"Do you have a moment to speak?"

"I need to change out of my armour," he said, gesturing at dried blood, "and to rest."

"Please, General, this is important," insisted the Prince.

Kaivon invited him in and, as protocol dictated, he offered the Prince the one chair. Yotaqan declined and they sat on the floor together. Thankfully Esme was not there so he didn't have to introduce her.

"My brothers and I saw smoke rising over the city. Can you tell me the cause?"

"This morning I delivered your message to the Khan. He became quite agitated." Yotaqan raised an eyebrow and then gestured for him to continue. They both knew Hulagu had a volatile temper which had grown more brittle of late. "Soon afterwards, he ordered men to seal the Grand Mosque and burn it to the ground with everyone trapped inside."

"Merciful God," muttered Yotaqan, putting a hand to his chest in grief. "Did anyone escape?"

"No. All of the men, women, children and priests, died inside. All that remains are tumbled stone and charred remains." The image of a small blackened skeleton being clutched by a dead adult would stay with Kaivon for the rest of his life. "It was monstrous."

Yotaqan bowed his head and briefly muttered a prayer for the dead. Kaivon bowed his head in tribute and the Prince noticed.

"Are you a man of faith?" asked Yotaqan.

"I am," he said, which was a lie. He was no more a Muslim than a Jew. "But I am a private man. I never talk to others about my belief. Nor will you ever see or hear a story about me at prayer. I do not want it to colour how people judge me."

"I understand," said the Prince.

Kitbuqa was one of the Khan's oldest friends and a renowned general, but there were some who thought him soft for being a Christian. Apparently they preached mercy and loving your neighbour.

Prince Yotaqan licked his lips. "And what do you think of the Khan's actions today?"

Kaivon was under no illusions. The shield which protected him against the rages of the Khan was tenuous. Both General Kitbuqa and Abaqa trusted him, maybe even liked him, but that would not protect him.

"I have no opinion," said Kaivon. "My goal is to carry out the Khan's wishes."

"Of course," said the Prince, leaning closer. "But what did you feel today?"

"Ashamed." The word just slipped out. It was the truth Kaivon had worked so hard to bury.

"Do not fear, I will not repeat a word you have said. I swear it," Prince Yoqatan said, touching his heart.

"I spoke with the Khan earlier," said Kaivon, seeing an opportunity. "He proudly informed me of his plans to conquer all of Syria. Then he will gift Jerusalem to his Christian allies in Rome and France."

"I was told he has sent more Christian trinkets and prisoners to the Pope, led by John of Hungary."

That was news to Kaivon. John was another of the Khan's peculiar servants. Despite Hulagu having brought John into his service before Kaivon, they had not met. John did not take part in battles and was often travelling outside the Ilkhanate on important missions. His tactic to delay support from the Vatican had succeeded if John had been sent.

"The slaughter of Muslims and Jews will continue apace," said Kaivon. He had seen countless bodies of both piled up on the streets of Aleppo. "Only the Christians will be spared and, once the Khan has claimed Jerusalem, he will march south through Arabia towards Egypt where he will slaughter the Mamluks. Nothing can be done to prevent this."

"Are you certain?"

"His army is unstoppable and he gathers allies from all corners. So I would suggest in the future, if you are unhappy with the Khan's decisions, you keep your displeasure to yourself."

The Prince sat back as if Kaivon had slapped him across the face. "What did you say?"

"In this tent, in this moment, let us pretend you are not a prince of the Golden Horde and I am not a general of the Ilkhanate." Kaivon waited for the younger man to nod before he continued. "As your elder, I would tell you to stop whining like a spoilt child. You and I can do nothing to change what will happen. Accept it and move on. The fate of our lives is in the hands of one man, Hulagu Khan."

The air in the tent between them became heavy, as if Kaivon had been plunged underwater. He held his breath, waiting for Yotaqan to react. Despite his cavalier façade, the Prince was nobody's fool. His father would not have sent him to spy on Hulagu Khan if that were true.

"Thank you for your honesty, General," said the Prince, preparing to leave.

"Prince," said Kaivon, giving him a seated bow.

Once he was alone, Kaivon didn't know if he'd just made things better or worse for his people.

The following morning Kaivon was woken early. At first, as he lay there in his tent, he couldn't work out what had disturbed him. Then he became aware of loud noises in the distance. It was persistent and coming from all sides.

Lying in bed beside him, Esme was still deep asleep. Sliding out of bed carefully, so that he didn't wake her, Kaivon quickly got dressed and stepped outside.

He was surprised to see thousands of Mongol warriors on the move. No one had told him about a sudden change of plans. As Kaivon wandered through the camp, he saw many warriors with puzzled expressions. He was not the only one who had been caught off guard. Making his way to the Khan's tent was the quickest way to get some answers. As it came into sight, he saw several familiar faces marching towards him. All of them looked as if they had been severely chastised, with hunched shoulders and sullen eyes. General Abaqa saw Kaivon approaching and shook his head.

"If you want to keep your skin in one piece, turn around," warned the General.

"What's happened?" asked Kaivon.

"It's the Golden Horde," said Prince Abaqa, steering Kaivon away by the elbow.

"They didn't even bloody their swords," said Jumghur, storming away.

Kaivon looked closely at the warriors passing through the camp. He recognised some of their faces. He'd travelled south with them from Sarai.

"They're leaving?" he said. "All of them?"

"Yes," said Abaqa, shaking his head. "All ten thousand. They will travel back to Tabriz. The princes have not decided if they will travel home from there. Prince Yotaqan had a messenger deliver the news to my father. Apparently, the princes are dissatisfied with the Khan."

Not delivering the message in person was a grave slight.

"What happened?"

"Father beat the messenger to death."

Kaivon noticed fresh spots of blood on Abaqa's armour. "Did he say anything?"

Together they watched as a pair of Mongols rode past them. "My father swore this did not change anything. We march on Damascus in the morning."

The loss of the Golden Horde was significant, but not enough to stall the army's progress. Even so, losing so many men would affect the tactics for the next battle. More powerful than the loss of the men was what it would do to morale. He could already see it on the faces of those around him. There was already talk in the camp about the division between the four khanates, as well as the ongoing squabble between Kublai and Ariq. Talk of open war between them was known, but it was not discussed in public. Not yet at least. And now there would be rumours of a further division between the Ilkhanate and the Golden Horde.

The western expansion of the Ilkhanate had never looked more uncertain. That thought filled Kaivon's heart with hope for the future.

CHAPTER 36
Kokochin

A week after the unfortunate and accidental death of Boabak, the sub-minister for agriculture, Kokochin was accepted into the House of Grace.

She wasn't sure what she had been expecting. A ritual of some kind in a sacred space, or perhaps a reading from a special book. Instead, one day at the shop, Layla simply told her that the Inner Circle had taken a vote, and she'd been accepted. In the end, it was a bit of a letdown. Besides, any sudden changes in routine might be noticed and commented on. Although Kokochin didn't think she was being followed, the House had not remained a secret organisation for so long by taking risks.

Instead, the celebration had been a private affair between her and Layla. The following day, they visited the local tea shop for a long lunch to extend it a little more. Whether it had been planned, or was purely a coincidence, theirs was one of only a handful of tables that were occupied. Before they had finished eating their salads, the other patrons departed, leaving them alone with the owner.

After they were finished with their main course, Shirin sat down at their table with a glass of tea. She also brought a large tray of pastries, sweet treats and succulent fruit.

"A small gift for your efforts," said Shirin. "You did well with Boabak."

"It wasn't easy," admitted Kokochin. Her aches and bruises were still healing, but Layla had been able to distract her from the pain.

"My first test was also a challenge," admitted Layla.

"It has to be that way, to prove your commitment," said Shirin, exchanging a look with Layla she didn't understand. "Your loyalty is no longer in doubt. We know you would never betray us, Kokochin. Especially when it would also put someone you care about in jeopardy."

Layla's hand found Kokochin's under the table and gave it a brief squeeze.

"Will I get to meet anyone from the Inner Circle?" asked Kokochin.

"No. Anonymity is vital to our survival. You can't betray what you don't know." Shirin glanced around the other tables, but they were alone and anyone on the street was out of earshot. "Going forward, the two of you will work as part of my network."

"So what happens now?" asked Kokochin.

"Now? Nothing," said Shirin. She popped a sugared almond into her mouth and slurped her tea around it. "With Boabak dead, the House has another pair of hands in the right place, but bringing about significant change will take time. We move slowly and quietly, making many small changes. In years to come, the people will never know what we did for them."

"So what is being done?"

"The new sub-minister of agriculture will start to adjust the figures. They will increase the supply of food and money to the right people, while weakening the Mongols and their war effort. Information is being sent to their enemies in Arabia, Egypt and even Europe. Our friend in the census office is also making changes. A person who doesn't exist, or has many names, can move much more freely than you or I," said Shirin with a wink. "Away from the capital, it's easier to manipulate people. We might not be able to replace regional governors without Rashid or Guyuk noticing, but we can undermine them so they stand on a house of cards."

"And when the time is right, you will send them toppling," said Kokochin, earning a grin from Shirin.

"Ariana mentioned a rumour about a new group of rebels," said Layla. Although she had recovered from her injuries the healer periodically visited the shop to check on Layla's scars. Kokochin also wondered if the healer was there to check up on her. Whenever Ariana visited the shop, the atmosphere was always tense. They were civil to one another, but they would never be friends. Kokochin suspected the healer was still upset that an amateur had managed to knock her down from time to time, during their practice sessions.

Shirin grunted. "Yes. And it's not a rumour. I've met with one of the rebels."

"Who are they?" asked Kokochin.

"Locals, for the most part. They're organised and well-funded. The man I met with, he made subtle hints that they have someone in a senior position close to the Khan." Shirin raised an eyebrow, but Kokochin could only shrug.

"I don't know anything about that," she said.

"No matter. They are also being careful, which is good."

"There are other smaller groups of rebels, but they lack the will to act," said Layla, speaking without directing blame. To fight against invaders was one thing, but to risk everything against an occupying force was something else entirely.

"What can I do?" asked Kokochin, knowing she would be unable to just do nothing.

"Watch and listen. We don't need a spy in the palace when we already have you," said Shirin with a feral smile. "What can you tell me about the civil war that's brewing?"

Kokochin shared all that she had been told, as well as the rumours that were flying around the palace. War was imminent and unavoidable between Kublai and Ariq, but there was also the rumbling of problems between the other khanates.

Shirin sat back, sucking on another almond as she thought it over. "We should create as much division between the khanates as possible, spreading disharmony and chaos. Open war between the Ilkhanate and one of the others would spell outright disaster for the Mongol Empire."

"Their dream of the world under one banner would end," said Layla with a sneer. Kokochin expected to feel a stab of guilt about the end of the Empire, but there was nothing. Men with power had taken everything that mattered from her. Her home. Her family. She didn't share their dream. Besides, she suspected that most Mongol warriors didn't share the Khan's vision of a unified world.

"If the Ilkhanate appears weak, it could embolden its enemies to unite and attack," said Layla.

"Perhaps, but remember, the Mongols have never been defeated in direct combat on the battlefield," warned Kokochin. "That fact is often proudly mentioned around the palace. It would take something remarkable for that to happen."

Shirin grunted. "I did hear another rumour that could change that."

Kokochin raised an eyebrow. "What is it?"

"This has not been confirmed, so do not repeat it to anyone," stressed Shirin. "I have heard of an alliance between the Mamluks and some of their enemies."

She did not need to say any more. If it was true, and the Mamluks were able to work with their enemies and those that had previously stayed neutral, they might have enough men to defeat Hulagu's army.

"That would be something," admitted Kokochin.

"The start of it, at least," said Shirin.

It would not be the end, not for some time, but it could be the beginning of it.

Until the Empire truly collapsed, Kokochin would do whatever was necessary. She would tolerate the veiled threats and insults from the Empress. She would accept her isolation from the other wives and concubines. She would even endure bedroom visits from her husband, if that what was required. She would bear all of it, because one day they would be gone and she would be free.

By the time Kokochin returned to her rooms, it was late. The streets were still busy, but she stayed away from the crowds. The air was thick with a mix of heady smells. The aromatic grey smoke from hookah pipes. The tantalising smell of roasting meat. Night-blooming jasmine from trailing vines, and cinnamon from a nearby bakery. In the distance, she could hear the tap of a drum, a woman singing in a rich voice and the cheer of crowds.

All of it would normally be appealing, but her meeting with Shirin had left Kokochin in a thoughtful mood as she considered the future. Instead, she'd had a quiet evening with Layla for company, and that had been more than enough. Now all she wanted was the comfort of her bed and a good night's sleep.

By the time Kokochin reached her front door in the palace, she was already yawning. But as soon as she set foot inside her rooms, her instincts screamed that something was wrong.

She wasn't alone.

Last time it had been the Empress waiting for her in the dark, but this felt different. The silence was too perfect. The air too still. Although the pounding of her heart was suddenly loud, Kokochin could hear something else. Somewhere to her left someone was breathing. A flicker of movement confirmed her suspicions, but then she sensed something coming towards her from the right.

Someone rushed out of the shadows bearing a knife. Kokochin's training took over. *Moth Wings* blocked the strike, numbing her attacker's hand and the blade dropped to the floor. *Bat's Scream* hard to the chest sent them flying away, temporarily out of the fight.

The other person attacked her from behind. As she'd done to Layla in the past, Kokochin used *Squirrel Climbs* to turn the tables, spinning her enemy around, until she was pressed against the man's back. This time she didn't hold back with *Fox's Bark*. Her attacker collapsed to the ground, screaming in pain. As he writhed about, begging her for help, she ignored his pleas. She lit a few candles and then went to check on the other man. He was dead. Her first strike to the chest had stopped his heart.

"Your friend is dead," she said calmly, kneeling down on the survivor's chest. She idly noticed his legs weren't moving and that he was already having trouble breathing.

"Why can't I feel my legs?" he asked.

"You're paralysed, maybe crippled for life," she told him. "Who sent you?"

The man glanced to one side, getting ready to lie, until she pressed her knee into his throat. After a couple of seconds she eased off. "I can't tell you," he rasped. Despite the situation, he was more afraid of someone than the immediate threat of death.

A quiet whisper of material was her only warning. Kokochin rolled to one side. A crossbow bolt hammered into the spot where she'd been kneeling. It punched into the man's chest and he screamed as blood pumped from the wound.

There were two more in the doorway. The first was trying to reload his crossbow, and the other couldn't get a clear shot. Shoving his friend aside, he tried to train the weapon on Kokochin, but she zig-zagged about the room. When she picked up a vase and hurled it at his head, he panicked and fired. In spite of that it still nearly hit her, tugging at the material of her robe.

While both crossbows were out of action, she ran forward, pulled the first man off balance and, with a vicious twist to a nerve cluster, using *Serpent Bites*, she dislocated his shoulder. The man stumbled forward, fell to his knees and screamed. He vomited on himself before he blacked out from the pain.

The other man attacked, swinging the crossbow at her like a cudgel. It clipped Kokochin on the shoulder, spun her about and his boot on her arse sent her tumbling forward. She let momentum carry her, turned it into a roll, and came up on her feet.

The man ran forward with both hands outstretched. Using his speed against him, she grabbed the man by the collar, pulled him close and threw him over her hip. He landed on a wooden table with so much force it shattered the legs, while driving the air from his body. As he gasped for breath, she finished him off, slamming an elbow into his throat, crushing his windpipe.

Three were dead and one was unconscious. Before Kokochin had a chance to question him, she heard the sound of approaching footsteps in the corridor. As she reached for one of the daggers, a familiar voice broke the silence.

"Touch it and you die."

Turning around Kokochin saw Empress Guyuk in the door, accompanied by four Kheshig. All of them were fully armoured, two holding swords and two had crossbows trained on her. At first, the Empress said nothing. She just studied the destruction, then wrinkled her nose at the smell coming from the dead. Guyuk didn't look surprised, but the four Kheshig stared at her with open hatred.

The bodyguards rarely took off their masks, so Kokochin had no idea what most of them looked like. From the glares, she guessed the dead men were Kheshig.

"It's just as I thought," said Guyuk. "You're not nearly so innocent and defenceless as you pretended. I wonder, when did it start?"

From the way she asked the question, it was clear Empress didn't really expect her to answer. Kokochin said nothing while she considered ways to escape. As if they knew what she was thinking, the two crossbowmen moved a step closer, the bolts aimed directly at her heart.

"Try it," said the Empress, daring Kokochin to tackle them.

Her training in the House of Grace had taught her to let the enemy attack first and then retaliate. Kokochin lifted her hands in surrender, bringing her wrists together. Guyuk sneered, perhaps disappointed that she hadn't witnessed Kokochin's skills first-hand.

One of the Kheshig tentatively came forward, watching her for any sudden movements. The other two kept their bows trained on her. Kokochin remained perfectly still, not giving them any excuse. If she was dead, the Empress could spin whatever story she liked. By staying alive, Kokochin created more problems. She also knew that, eventually, her absence would be noticed by her friends. That was assuming she lived long enough for them to wonder.

It was only when the manacles were locked tight around her wrists that Guyuk risked coming into the room. She stood in front of Kokochin, looking her up and down as if seeing her for the first time.

"It's late, so I'm going to bed and you're going to spend the night in the cells with the rats. Use the time wisely," she said, grabbing Kokochin by the chin. When she tried to pull away, the Empress tightened her grip. "No one is going to come for you. No one cares if you live or die. Get that through your thick skull," said the Empress, jabbing Kokochin in the forehead with a finger. "Think very carefully about what you've done, because in the morning I'm going to ask you some questions. And if you don't answer them to my satisfaction, I will hand you over to the Khan's inquisitor."

Kokochin had heard rumours about him floating around the palace for months. Elbuz was a former Persian warrior who had delighted too much in the suffering of others. When his nation was conquered by the Mongols, he had willingly joined the Khan's army. Nothing had been amiss until one of his victims had escaped. The Khan's warriors had found the dismembered remains of twenty-seven men and women. Rather than kill Elbuz, the Khan had found another use for his twisted mind.

"Elbuz would love to get his hands on you," said Guyuk. "Your skin is perfect, without any scars or blemishes. He will spend days carving intricate patterns into your flesh, while you scream for mercy."

She knew the Empress was attempting to scare her, and unfortunately it was working. Kokochin did her best to smother the fear welling up inside.

"Take her away," said Guyuk, smiling as the Kheshig dragged Kokochin out of her rooms.

As promised, the black cells beneath the palace were unpleasant. The cell was seven paces wide by seven paces deep. It was constructed of heavy grey stone on three sides. There was a tall and narrow window set in the back wall, but it was barely wide enough for her hand. It gave her a tantalising glimpse of the sky and a hint of the outside world.

The fourth wall was made of thick iron bars with a heavy door set in the middle. In the corridor a single torch burned, providing her with enough light to see the filthy straw on the ground. There were lots of rats, but once she'd snapped the neck of two, the others left her alone.

Sinking to her knees in the straw, she closed her eyes and meditated, trying to calm her mind and sort through her emotions.

Months ago, when Guyuk had first visited the jewellery shop, Kokochin had thought this would be her fate. She had been positive that the Empress knew what she was really doing, but then nothing had happened. Kokochin had put it down to paranoia, but now she began to wonder how long Guyuk had known the truth, or at least had suspicions. Something had tipped her off, but there was no way to know what. The Kheshig in her room had been a trap and she'd fallen straight into it. The moment she'd realised someone was in her room, she should have just walked away.

It didn't matter anymore. The past was gone and she could not change it. The only thing she was really worried about was Layla, especially as Guyuk had made veiled threats. She had no way of contacting Layla, and it would be a couple of days before she began to worry. Oddly, the Empress had not mentioned her, and had only used the threat of direct violence.

Fear of the torturer's blade was lurking at the back of her mind, but nothing could be done to prevent that. For as long as possible, she would hold her tongue. Perhaps a moment would come when she could turn the tables on the torturer, feign weakness and kill him. It was a tiny spark of hope in a sea of darkness, but it was all she had. Although she wasn't without friends, Kokochin would be alone in this. It was up to her to find a way to survive.

She was proud to be a member of the House of Grace. She would not betray them. For the first time in her life, she had something worth fighting for.

Kokochin was ready to face whatever came next.

CHAPTER 37
Hulagu

The events of the last week weighed heavily on Hulagu's mind.

The withdrawal of warriors from the Golden Horde put the expansion of the Ilkhanate in a precarious position. Without further support, he wasn't sure if they could continue. If the Mamluks mounted a counterstrike, his army would be outnumbered.

Then there was the start of open war between his brothers. Kublai had been forced to break off his assault on the Song dynasty and bring warriors north to fight their brother. They should have been putting all of their effort into expanding the Empire, but Ariq would not listen.

In addition, Hulagu had received worrying reports of several raids along the northern border of the Ilkhanate in the Caucasus. Allies in the region could not explain who was responsible, but had promised to investigate. Hulagu might have written it off as a minor incident, if not for the fact that several messengers had delivered stories of slaughter and looting of villages. The danger was bad enough that some people were abandoning their farms and homes for the safety of cities. Hulagu had sent a number of spies to the region, but so far they had not been able to identify the perpetrators.

It was possible the Pope was responsible, thinking Hulagu distracted with conquest in the south. For all of his pleasantries, Hulagu knew the Pope thought him a demon. Despite sparing the lives of many Christians, and returning numerous religious treasures, Rome had yet to lend any support. Even if he had proof, he could not move directly against the Pope. If it turned out to be true, more subtle means would have to be employed.

News about the warriors from the Golden Horde returning to Tabriz had spread. There had been no way to contain it, but he'd made it clear to all that this did not affect his plans. His army would carve a bloody path south through Syria, right up to the Mamluks' front door, and then he would grind the Sultan beneath his boot.

That was what he needed everyone to believe.

As the ancient city of Damascus came into view, Hulagu forced a smile. A simple target and a straight forward battle. His men would bloody their swords. His engines of war would smash the walls, and then they would scour the city of its wealth. It would bring him one step closer to destroying the Mamluk threat.

Riding beside Hulagu was his son, Abaqa, and several senior officers. Jumghur should have been with them, but he was riding in a wagon, sleeping off a heavy night of drinking. The lack of a decent battle had made his son's moods even more volatile than usual. Two nights ago, he had almost killed a man for accidentally bumping into him. Once he was in the thick of battle again, it would exorcise some of Jumghur's demons and his good mood would return.

Hulagu had to admit that, even from a distance, the city was impressive. It looked green and lush, surrounded by countless orchards and gardens. From the mountains came the river Barada, running through the city, which in turn split into several brooks. His spies had reported there were many fountains, and several lush gardens within the walls. It spoke of wealth and prosperity, which was a good sign.

A vast wall encircled the city, but from his elevated position he could see several large structures rising above. To the northwest was the famous Citadel, a stout fort that had originally been constructed during Roman times and then had been rebuilt, time and again. To the east was the Umayyad Mosque, thought to be the largest in the world.

Kitbuqa and Doquz were both excited about capturing the mosque. It was rumoured to include the entombed remains of John the Baptist.

It made no difference to him. The city as a whole, and what it represented, was what mattered. It would make another fine addition to the Ilkhanate and, once its defences were repaired, they would be able to use it as a staging point to launch more attacks southward.

As they rode closer, Hulagu studied the walls and picked out some of the city's gates. They looked stout enough, but once they felt the touch of his war engines they would burst open, like overripe fruit.

He'd been looking forward to this for some time. A battle where he could ignore all the politics. The only thing that would matter was staying alive. It was simple. Honest. Finally, he would be able to vent all the anger and resentment that had built up.

As custom dictated, messengers had been sent ahead days ago, telling the rulers of Damascus to surrender or else face his wrath. As usual, there had been no response. But as they approached the city, Hulagu was surprised to see the main gates swing open. He called a halt, while they waited to see what happened next.

A short time later, four riders emerged from the city. All of them were dressed in white, and one of them carried a banner above his head with the symbol of the Christian cross on it.

"Kitbuqa," said Hulagu. The other riders made space for the General to approach. "Do you know what this is?"

"No, my Khan. But they are Christians. Perhaps I should speak with them?"

Hulagu was tempted to ride forward, but if it was a trap designed to kill him, then he'd be walking right into it.

"I don't think they will harm me," said Kitbuqa.

"Be careful," said Hulagu.

As the General rode forward, Hulagu had several archers take up positions. If they did attack his friend then none of the riders would make it back through the gates.

He watched in tense silence as Kitbuqa conferred with the men from Damascus. After only a couple of minutes, the four men bowed in their saddles. His old friend returned the gesture and then rode back towards the army.

"What did they say?" asked Hulagu.

"They wish to surrender," said Kitbuqa with a big smile.

"What?"

"The leaders of the city are of one mind. They saw the awesome power of your army when it took Aleppo. It has cowed them into submission."

Hulagu tightened his grip on the reins. It had been Temujin's unnatural fire that had toppled the walls of Aleppo, not his army or his siege engines. Several of his senior officers had come to him separately, expressing their concern. They were afraid that Temujin was possessed, or had made a pact with a devil. Despite what he had achieved, no one was upset when he'd gone back to Tabriz.

"What are their terms?" Hulagu knew they would not give up the city without wanting something in return.

"They have none. But they did make one request," said Kitbuqa.

Hulagu grunted. "I knew it. What do they want?"

"They have asked to surrender to a senior Christian figure in your army."

Looking back towards the city, Hulagu noticed the gates were still wide open. It was too easy. A niggling worm of doubt remained in his stomach.

"It would be my honour to do this for you, my Khan," said King Hethum of Armenia.

"And mine," said Prince Bohemond, not wanting to be outdone.

"We will go together, as brothers in Christ," said General Kitbuqa. As ever, he saw what Hulagu was thinking. The two of them alone might not accurately represent his demands. The presence of Kitbuqa would mean that the right message was delivered. Surrender or die. Those were his terms.

"The three of you will lead," agreed Hulagu. "Make it clear what will happen if they attempt any trickery. I am not in a forgiving mood."

"As you command, my Khan," said Kitbuqa, bowing in his saddle.

The three Christians led a procession of five thousand Mongols into Damascus where the city leaders offered their unconditional surrender.

In a rage Hulagu smashed everything in his tent, using his sword until he was surrounded by scraps of wood, glass, misshapen lumps of metal and shredded cloth.

First the leaders of Damascus had surrendered, robbing him of much needed relief, and now this. When nothing remained upon which to vent his anger, he slumped to the floor, staring at nothing. The air in the tent was sickly sweet from the spilled brandy. An hour later the tent flat opened and Doquz stuck her head inside. She wrinkled her nose at the smell, but still came in and sat down beside him. She slowly uncurled his fingers from the letter clutched in his fist and smoothed out the piece of paper.

More towns had been attacked along the northern border of the Ilkhanate. Hundreds of his people had been murdered. Several towns were now empty, their populations were missing and had probably been sold as slaves. The infirm and the old had been killed, their bodies left to rot. One of his spies had seen smoke rising on the horizon, but by the time he'd arrived, it was too late. There had been no witnesses.

"Who would dare?" he finally said, through clenched teeth. Doquz put her hands on either side of his head, gently rubbing his temples until his jaw eased.

"We will find them."

"I am the Khan. It is my responsibility," said Hulagu slapping her hands away. The lack of a battle still chafed but, even worse, they had surrendered because of Temujin and his unnatural powers. It had nothing to do with the might of his army.

Fear of one man had inspired an entire city to surrender, and it wasn't him.

Doquz pursed her lips and let the silence build. She remained perfectly still while Hulagu fidgeted. His mind was like a tangle of overlapping snakes as thoughts fought for dominance.

The civil war between his brothers weighed heavily on his mind. It showed they were not a unified empire. Their enemies must have found out and thought the khanates weak. The raids could be a test to see how he responded.

"Do you know what some of your men call me?" asked Doquz, breaking the silence. Hulagu had been so lost in thought he'd forgotten she was there. "Your War Wife."

"I have heard this before."

"And do you know why?"

"Because you are always at my side."

"Perhaps at the start, but they know you listen to my counsel, and that I have helped you plan more battles than your Generals."

"That is true," he said.

"Do not let pride destroy all that you have built."

"You think this is about my pride?"

"I know you, husband." Doquz used the word like a weapon, in a way he'd never heard before. "I know that you desperately want to push south, towards Jerusalem and claim part of Arabia."

"I want to kill the fucking Sultan, and his damned Mamluks. That's what I want, wife."

"But at what cost?" she asked him. "You cannot do all of it at once. I know we do not have the numbers. You need to hold on to what you have taken in Syria. And you need to protect the northern border."

He knew she was right, but he hated it. He hated that they were barely into spring, and the western expansion would have to stop.

His forces were stretched too thin. He had sent some north to investigate the raids, as well as reinforce towns and cities. There were others spread out across Persia, maintaining the peace and squashing any signs of rebellion. More warriors held Baghdad, Aleppo and now there would be some left in Damascus. The city had been taken without a fight, but that did not mean its defences were perfect.

"I think my cousin is to blame for the raids," said Hulagu.

He expected Doquz to defend Berke because he was family, but instead she stared into the distance with a grim expression.

"I fear you may be right," she said. "But we would need to be certain, before taking action. Mongols do not kill Mongols."

It was one of the few things from his grandfather with which Hulagu did not agree. Genghis Khan had killed many of his own people to create one Mongol nation. He'd eradicated tribes and beaten others into submission. Killing their own was not something relegated to ancient history. Kublai had been forced to crush uprisings from those who thought the descendants of Tolui should not continue to rule. After all, that was how Kublai had ended up with Kokochin.

And now his brothers were at war. If he was to go to war with the Golden Horde, Hulagu would need more than rumours and hearsay.

"If Berke is responsible, then the old saying will not matter," promised Hulagu. "I will kill him myself."

"Let us hope it doesn't come to that," said Doquz, gripping

his hand. "But if it does, you will have to kill all of his children as well. You don't want one of them coming after you in years to come." Hulagu grinned, delighted at her fierceness and desire to protect him. Whatever lay ahead for him, at least he wouldn't be alone.

Later that day, before Hulagu called his senior officers to a meeting, Kaivon arrived at his tent looking flustered. Hulagu had spent a couple of hours making up with Doquz. Although he still wasn't happy, he was more relaxed. She was currently elsewhere, but the smell of her body lingered in the tent, distracting him.

"My Khan."

"General, are you well?"

"I bring grave news." Kaivon held out a note from a messenger. Hulagu noticed it had already been opened. "It was delivered to me by one of your men."

"Why was it not brought to me directly?" asked Hulagu and then he remembered. The last time he'd received bad news he'd beaten the messenger to death. Hulagu took a deep breath, trying to get a grip on his temper. Every day it became more difficult. He often said Jumghur would never rule because of his rages and yet, right now, he was no better than his son.

The Persian was a brave man to bring him the news.

"Tell me what it says," says the Khan.

"One of your spies from the north has reported back. Berke Khan is selling slaves to the Mamluks. Warriors from the Golden Horde were seen transporting people captured in the north of the Persia, as well as Georgians, Kipchaks and people from the Caucasus. A second messenger has just confirmed it."

His suspicions were true. Berke Khan was a traitor to the Mongol Empire. Not only had Berke's sons suddenly withdrawn their warriors at a critical time, now his cousin was reinforcing the Mamluk army.

"There's something else," said Kaivon. "Although I am loathe to mention it, because of how it was discovered."

Hulagu raised an eyebrow. "This sounds personal."

"I was listening at a doorway in Sarai. This is not a habit, I swear." He was so eager to please, Hulagu didn't question if he was telling the truth. Time and again, Kaivon had proven his loyalty.

"Tell me what you heard."

"It was as I left a meeting with Berke Khan and his vizier, Gurban. They had been angry about the tribute I delivered from Baghdad. It left me unsettled, so I paused outside in the corridor. I heard Gurban say he'd been in contact with his counterpart in Cairo. He even called him a 'brother in Islam.'"

"And you're only telling me this now?" Despite trying to hold on to his temper, Hulagu's hands tightened into fists.

"The next day, Berke Khan committed ten thousand men and three of his sons to the Ilkhanate. I was certain that I had misheard."

The anger drained away, leaving Hulagu feeling despondent. Betrayed by his own family. News of this would have to be contained until the time was right. If Berke had truly formed an alliance with the Mamluks, he would have spies in the Ilkhanate, and perhaps within Hulagu's army. It was what he would have done if their positions were reversed. The three princes and the bulk of their men had gone north to Tabriz, but who would notice if one or two stayed behind?

"Tell no one about this," said Hulagu. "We will strike back against the Golden Horde when the time is right. But they must not see it coming."

"As you command, my Khan."

"Come, we must meet with the others." Hulagu led the way across the camp towards the command tent. As he stepped inside, those gathered must have noticed his mood as few made eye contact.

"We have come far, since the beginning of spring," said Hulagu, moving towards the table. Spread out across its surface was a map of the region. To the southwest were towns and cities within his reach, and beyond them, Arabia and then Egypt. "But now my plan must change. War has broken out between my brother Ariq, and Kublai, the Great Khan," he declared, studying every face for a hint of betrayal. It was possible one of them was secretly loyal to his cousin, Berke.

"I must travel back to Tabriz. The bulk of the army will travel with me. Abaqa," said Hulagu and his eldest son stepped forward.

"Yes, Father."

"You will keep ten thousand men to secure Baghdad and the surrounding areas. Our enemies may see this as a withdrawal, and rebellion will fester. Crush any rumours and make a spectacle of any who speak out against the Great Khan. Destroy any traitors before their rot can spread."

Mongols did not kill Mongols. It was becoming less true every day.

"As you command, Father," said Abaqa, stepping back.

"General Kitbuqa."

His old friend came forward. "You will stay in the area. Our enemies are watching. You will make them believe the rest of the army is still here." Hulagu pointed at several targets in the kingdom of Jerusalem. "You will lead ten thousand men west, to Sidon and Tyre. I will send an envoy southwest to the Sultan in Cairo, asking for his surrender."

It was a bluff, but it was in keeping with what he had done in the past. He always gave his enemy a chance to surrender. Any deviation would be noticed. He had to maintain the appearance that nothing had changed. With luck, the Mamluks wouldn't realise the rest of his army was in the north, fighting traitors.

"Ready the army to march," he said, dismissing the others. He would start riding for Tabriz in the morning, but it would take a few days for the rest of the army to pack up camp and follow.

When the others had left, Hulagu stared at the map of the region, his mind working it all through.

Ten thousand men was not an insignificant number, but if the Mamluks learned that was all that stood between them and Mongol-conquered cities in Syria, they might go on the offensive. He needed something to scare them. The obvious answer made Hulagu uncomfortable.

He needed Temujin. He didn't understand the source of his son's abilities, but no one could deny its power. He had destroyed the walls of Aleppo in the space of a few heartbeats. Right now, Hulagu didn't care how it worked, or if his men were afraid. All that mattered was how it could be used against his enemies. With half a dozen like Temujin, he could wipe out the Mamluks in less than a year. Topple every wall, destroy every fortification, and then flood the streets with his warriors.

Temujin's fire had burned through stone as if it had been wet clay. Against men it would be even more devastating and send a clear message of his intent. Part of him hated the idea that he needed his son so badly, but Hulagu took comfort that at least he was loyal to the Mongol Empire.

CHAPTER 38
Temujin

No matter the consequences, Temujin would never again allow his father to use him as a weapon.

The destruction of Aleppo haunted him. The rational part of his mind said that he was not to blame. Part of him knew that without him being there, the siege engines would still have toppled the walls. People would still have been killed. But knowing that didn't help him sleep at night. He was haunted by screams, real and imagined, from the atrocities he'd witnessed.

In an attempt to exhaust himself and sleep without dreams, Temujin started taking long walks around Tabriz. The walks left him hungry, although that wasn't too surprising. His body had been left severely malnourished after what he'd done in Aleppo. A few seconds more and he would have died. Slowly but surely he was regaining weight and muscle with lots of food and regular exercise. Every day his reflection reminded him less of an old man.

The long walks also gave him time to think about what he was going to do next. Despite what he'd said to his father, Temujin had made no attempt to find others like him. More than one person wielding power like his would be disastrous. It would change the balance of warfare. Siege engines would become obsolete, and the army only there to invade a city once its defences were breached. Such power did not belong in the hands of someone like Hulagu Khan. Then again, his father's greatest enemy, the Sultan of Cairo, was no better. If Temujin had been born in Egypt, he knew the Sultan wouldn't hesitate to use the same destructive power against the Mongol Empire. All of which left him stuck in the middle, with no idea about what to do next.

Every day he passed hundreds of people in the streets, but not once did he see someone with eyes like his. There were some with a few flecks of different colours, but it was never absolute. It made him feel alone, despite always being surrounded by people.

Previously, he would have sought solace in food, but now it gave him little comfort. He visited a couple of his father's pleasure houses, and although he came away physically sated, the experiences made him lonely.

The only thing that helped was meditation. Spending hours wrapped in a cocoon of silence, in contemplation of the Eternal Fire, gave him perspective. Although his irrational fears faded, they didn't vanish and he remained unsettled.

Reyhan remained committed to his quest. He was determined to find out everything about the mysterious Kozan. However, the librarian had recently admitted that he was running out of places to look. Once he had scoured all of the books on warfare, religion, history and mysticism, he had delved into more obscure areas, seeking nuggets buried in random books. All of which left Temujin fumbling along without any guidance.

He had not dared to try anything since his nearly fatal incident. Temujin's only hope was to find the woman he'd seen in his dreams. But despite criss-crossing the city many times, he'd not run into her. After a few days of aimless searching, Temujin had begun to wonder if she'd been nothing more than a figment of his imagination.

After meditating on it, he believed that she had been real. She had found him, more than once. She would find him again. He needed to be patient and steadfast in his belief.

On the seventh day since returning to the city, Temujin rose shortly after dawn, meditated for an hour, ate breakfast and then left the palace to roam the streets. The Empress knew of his mission to find others like him, but he'd not told her the truth. As much as she loved him, Guyuk wasn't his mother, and Temujin knew her loyalty was primarily to her husband and the Mongol Empire. He was searching for other Kozan, but he had no intention of ever telling his father about them. He didn't want them to become weapons in his father's pointless war. If she knew what he was really doing, Temujin was confident he would find himself locked up in a cell.

By midday, his feet were beginning to ache. He paused in a small park to rest and eat in the shade of a copse of trees. Despite being early spring, the sun was already baking hot. As he wolfed down a bowl of rice and lamb stew from a street vendor's cart, Temujin wondered if he should stay in one place and let the woman find him.

A disturbance drew his attention. Other people in the park were being harassed by a beggar. The scrawny man, dressed in rags, had only one hand and a crooked back. His other arm was wrapped in bloody bandages, suggesting he'd lost the hand for being a thief. His lined skin was caked with dirt, and through the gaps in his shirt Temujin could see old scars on his back from a whip. The man's scraggly beard and shaggy hair were iron grey, and he had a grubby eyepatch over his right eye. His left was a deep brown and it sparkled with mischief. Despite his obvious troubles, the man cackled with delight while he rattled his wooden bowl at people. Just to get rid of him, many offered a coin.

As the beggar approached, Temujin wrinkled his nose at the rancid smell. He reached for a coin before he was asked. The man offered him a big smile and, much to Temujin's surprise, the beggar had a full set of teeth.

"Can you spare a coin for an old soldier, young master?" he asked. Temujin dropped a heavy coin into the beggar's bowl, and then he added a second coin. "Oh, that's very generous, thank you."

"You're welcome." From the smell, Temujin didn't think the man had bathed for at least a year.

The old man looked into the bowl, rattling the coins about. "Very generous, but surely a Kozan can afford more than that?"

"What did you say?" he asked, but the old beggar had scampered away. "Wait!" shouted Temujin.

The beggar ran out of the park towards the busy streets. If he got too far ahead, Temujin would never find him in the crowd.

Temujin sprinted after him, trying to close the distance between them. The sound of his footsteps made the old man glance over his shoulder. Panic swept across his face. After tucking away his bowl, he started to run faster.

"Wait! I have money!" said Temujin, hoping to appeal to the beggar's greed. Either the old man didn't hear, or didn't believe Temujin, as he dove into the flow of bodies. By the time Temujin reached the same spot, the beggar had disappeared into the crowd. He turned in all directions, but couldn't see him. Temujin thought the chase was over until he spotted groups of people recoiling from the beggar, creating a trail through the crowd. Temujin jogged after him, passing down one street and then along a narrow alley, before losing him at the next crossroads. When a wagon driver yelled at someone, he instinctively ran in that direction. Temujin was just in time to see the beggar disappear down a narrow side street.

The old man was tired. Temujin could hear him wheezing. The beggar slowed to a walk and then stopped to catch his breath, resting against a wall. They were alone.

"I just want to talk," said Temujin, trying not to scare him.

The old man spun about. When he saw Temujin blocking the alley, he pulled out a knife from within the folds of his ragged clothing.

"What do you want?" he screeched, waving the blade about. "You can't have the money back."

"I don't want it. Here, you can have more," said Temujin, producing a few more coins. "What's your name?"

The old man hesitated, surprised by the question. "Eraj," he finally said.

"Why did you call me a Kozan? Do you even know what it means?"

"Do you?" asked the old man.

He grinned at Temujin and then stood upright. The hunch disappeared and with a quick twisting motion, the bloody bandage fell away from his stump. Underneath was a normal hand with all of his fingers intact.

"You're a swindler," said Temujin.

"I'm more than that," said the beggar. Temujin noticed even his voice had changed, becoming rich and more cultured. The final surprise came when he took off his eyepatch, revealing one startling green eye. "I'm a Kozan."

"Enough," said a familiar voice. The woman from Temujin's dreams stepped out of a doorway. She was dressed in a pale blue dress, but he noticed her feet were bare. "Stop teasing him, Eraj."

"I've done my job, Kat. You talk to him," said Eraj, sauntering away. "Thanks for the donation, my Prince," he yelled, rattling his bowl.

"Come with me, please," said the woman, beckoning him towards the doorway. "We needed to be sure that you were alone. Did you know that you were being followed?"

"It must have been someone sent by my father. I don't even know your name," said Temujin, stalling for time.

"It's Katarina," she said with a faint smile. Now that he was face to face with her, Temujin heard a slight accent, and he thought some of her features were Slavic. "You don't have to worry. I won't hurt you."

Temujin hesitated but followed her through the door. Inside was a small courtyard with an old fountain at the centre. Dozens of pots around the edge contained bright flowers and herbs, filling the air with a rich, heady scent. A calico wandered around and Katarina paused to scratch the old cat behind the ear. The cat purred but quickly tired of being fussed and wandered off to lie down in the shade. The atmosphere was calm and peaceful. Temujin's apprehension faded away and he relaxed, confident that she didn't intend him any harm. He sat down on one of the benches in the courtyard to study his surroundings.

Through an open set of doors, he could see part of the building's interior. It was decorated with a range of peculiar items whose origins he couldn't identify. A lot of goods from across the world flowed through Tabriz, but what was on display was something entirely different. On the far wall hung a narrow black mask made of what he thought was painted wood. It looked ancient and one edge had rotted with age. On a pedestal sat a jade figurine of a peculiar serpent with wings and horns. Beside it were three busts of a woman at different ages. There were half a dozen paintings idly stacked against a wall. The one at the front was a partial nude. The artist had taken a few liberties, but he recognised the subject was Katarina. All of the paintings were portraits of her. From the ceiling hung a collection of colourful bone fans, dozens of gold necklaces, heavy with gemstones, and at least a hundred rings on a piece of leather cord. From just the small area he could see, the amount of wealth was significant. Temujin guessed it was only a portion of what was inside the house.

"Feel free to look around," said Katarina gesturing at the house. "I don't mind."

Temujin briefly stepped into the house and glanced around.

He saw a range of items that spoke of a life that had been well-lived. Someone who had travelled far beyond the borders of the Mongol Empire, to countries he knew nothing about and probably couldn't even name.

"You've lived here for a long time," said Temujin, retaking his seat.

Katarina smiled. "I see the Eternal Fire is gifting you with insight."

"It is, but I worked that out myself. So, what am I?"

"Before I tell you anything, I want you to make me a promise. If you refuse, then you have to leave and we'll never speak again." Her friendly smile had faded. "You must never again use the Fire as a weapon. You were incredibly lucky you didn't die last time. Even so, I want your promise."

"I was desperate, and it was a huge mistake," said Temujin. "I swear never again to use it as a weapon."

Katarina relaxed and her smile returned. "Good. So, what do you want to know?"

"Who are the Kozan?"

"We are the rarest of the rare. Do you know how special you are?"

"I don't understand," said Temujin.

"Most people have some discolouration, but about one in a million have eyes like ours. And out of them, maybe one in a million of those have the gift." Katarina sat forward, pinning him in place with her stare. "Temujin, until you came along, there were only six Kozan in the world. It has been this way for many, many years."

"It sounds lonely," he said, remembering how isolated he'd felt before.

"You get used to it," said Katarina. "I would suggest you make friends wherever you travel. That way, people are always pleased to see you and it feels like coming home. It helps with the long, quiet nights."

"What do the Kozan do?"

"I have a question for you first," said Katarina. "Do you intend to share your gifts with your father?"

Temujin shook his head. "I cannot. I told him I was coming to Tabriz to find others like me to fight his war, but that was a lie. Even if I knew what I was doing, I would never share them with him. It would tip the balance of power. The dream of my great-grandfather would become real, and the Mongol Empire would span the entire world."

Katarina leaned back against the wall and heaved a long sigh. She even closed her eyes for a moment and smiled. "I'm very pleased to hear you say that."

"Why?"

"If we wanted, the Kozan could rule the world. Who could stop us?" The Eternal Fire appeared in the palm of her hand for a moment before it vanished. "Some of our kind think we should take control. Lead nations and empires to a better tomorrow. Others believe it is not our place, and we should let people find their own way. For a long time, we have held each other in check, with three on either side of the line. When they pull one way, we pull in the opposite direction, to maintain balance. Your appearance has upset that, and I'm afraid it could mean all-out war."

A cold prickle ran down the back of Temujin's spine and a lump filled his throat. When something flickered on the periphery of his vision, Temujin slowly turned his head. Perched on the first-floor windowsill of the house was a familiar figure. It took him a moment to recognise Eraj. His skin was clean. His hair and beard had been brushed, and the rancid smell was absent. A small crossbow was casually held in Eraj's left hand, which he pointed at Temujin.

"The tip is poisoned," he said with a grin. "Venom from a deadly spider. It will stop your heart in seconds."

Eraj eased the bow away from the window and then disappeared inside the house.

"I'm sorry," said Katarina, startling Temujin by grabbing his hand. He'd been so intent on the crossbow he hadn't seen her move across the courtyard. As she sat down beside him, he noticed she smelled of jasmine and sandalwood.

"Why?"

"Imagine if your brother, Jumghur, had been a Kozan instead of you. What would happen?"

"He would burn down every city standing in the way of our father's army. He would scorch thousands of people to death, just for fun. It would be even worse if he had one of his black moods."

"Together, they would decimate all of Syria, then Arabia and flatten every building in Egypt. It would be a vicious bloodbath and tens of thousands would die."

"My father would rule over a dead world," said Temujin.

"You have tipped the balance," said Katarina. "Eraj, Teague and I have chosen to advise, guide and mostly observe. We are chroniclers of history. We do not interfere directly with the development of a nation or empire, even if we think it's evil and should be destroyed."

"Why? Why not help others?"

"Because all empires fall. It happened to the Greeks and the Romans. One day, it will happen to the Mongols as well."

Temujin expected to feel something. Regret. Anger. Loss. But there was nothing. Buried deep inside was a touch of relief. Men such as his father and uncles should not be allowed to rule.

"Besides, who are we to decide the fate of others? Our powers do not make us better than anyone else," Katarina said. "Just different."

"You mentioned there were six. What of the other three?"

Katarina grimaced. As she tucked a loose strand of hair behind one ear, he noticed she had seven gold earrings. The metal was plain, but each was etched with tiny symbols.

"They like chaos," said Eraj, coming out of the house. Thankfully he was no longer holding a crossbow. Instead he carried a glass of wine and a half empty bottle. The ragged clothing had been replaced with a loose white shirt, black trousers and boots. With a clean face, Eraj's features were more apparent. Temujin noted the peculiar angle of his eyes, the prominent jaw and sharp cheekbones. All of it indicated mixed heritage he couldn't unravel. "They interfere and make people into their puppets."

"They meddle," said Katarina. "And so we look for changes in the natural flow and seek to correct whatever they have altered. We cannot attack one another directly, and we do not operate in the open. Not even they would go that far."

With one simple, clumsy, strike he had destroyed a city's defences. If the Kozan went to war with each other, the damage would be catastrophic.

"So what happens now?" asked Temujin.

"That's up to you," said Katarina. "If you want, I will show you the fullness of your gifts. I will teach you how to defend yourself, so this doesn't happen again," she said, touching the narrow band of burned skin around his wrist.

"You were stupid and lucky," said Eraj.

"What about the others? Do they know about me?"

Eraj laughed. "Of course, and it's a good thing we found you first. They would have asked you to join them, and if you refused you'd already be dead."

"Unfortunately, what my blunt friend is saying is true," said Katarina. "Now that they know about you, it's likely they will still try to recruit you. You need to know how to fight."

"I thought we didn't fight each other?" said Temujin.

"Not in the open, but some of our gifts are more subtle than others," said Katarina with a smile. "You need to be ready."

They had only just met, and yet Temujin felt at ease in Katarina's company. He thought he could trust her, but was less certain about Eraj. He had the feeling the swindler would slit his throat if it was necessary. Across the courtyard, Eraj drained the last of the bottle and raised an eyebrow.

"Where do we start?" said Temujin.

"First, you need to do something for us," said Katarina, exchanging a look with Eraj. For once his cavalier attitude was absent and he had a grave expression. "And you're not going to like it."

Late that afternoon Temujin returned to the library. As usual, Reyhan was still buried up to his shoulders in books. The table was covered with an assortment of dusty tomes, scrolls and scribbled notes. There were more books stacked around the edge of the room, and a few lay open on the floor.

The ageing librarian was reading a book, but it was clear the subject wasn't that exciting. His face was propped up on one hand and his eyes kept glazing over.

"There you are," said Reyhan, giving himself a shake. "You look better. Healthier."

"Anything new?" asked Temujin.

Reyhan shook his head and closed the book in front of him. "I didn't want to admit it, but I think we've exhausted everything. I've not found anything of worth in the last two weeks."

"Is this all of it?" said Temujin, gesturing at the books on the table.

"I know that when it's all gathered together, it doesn't seem to amount to much," admitted the old man.

"It doesn't matter now," he said, trying to swallow the painful lump in his throat.

"Why not?"

"They found me. The Kozan," said Temujin. With barely a thought the Eternal Fire sprung to life, dancing above the palm of his outstretched hand. "They're going to teach me how to become one of them. No more fumbling around. I'll have a real teacher."

"That's wonderful," said Reyhan, "but what about all of this?" he said gesturing at the clutter in the room.

"If my father ever found someone else like me, this knowledge could change the course of the Mongol Empire."

Reyhan's face sank. "You're going to destroy it?"

"All of it. I must leave nothing behind. Not a single clue for him to follow." Temujin extinguished the Eternal Fire and drew a dagger from his belt. "I'm so sorry. I wish there was another way."

Reyhan had defended him in front of his father. He was the first person to say that Temujin was special. He'd been a friend and confidante. Without his guidance and brilliant mind, Temujin would not have unearthed a fraction of the clues about the Kozan. But he was also Temujin's responsibility. Reyhan's life had been placed in his hands. Even if he burned all of the books, it wouldn't be enough. His father had limitless resources and other copies of the same books might exist. With enough time Reyhan could recreate all of it, but without him, anyone else who tried wouldn't know where to start. They didn't have his knowledge or ability to read ancient languages.

He'd killed before, in the heat of battle, but he'd never planned a murder. He'd never killed someone who was a friend.

Temujin's hands shook as he approached Reyhan who, mercifully, closed his eyes and patiently waited for death.

CHAPTER 39
Kaivon

With fresh blood drying on his armour, Kaivon slipped off his horse and marched into the palace of Tabriz. He'd been in the north, investigating reports from Hulagu's spies, when they'd run into a group of Mongols from the Golden Horde.

The Khan was talking with his vizier, but he waved the man away as Kaivon approached. Rashid retreated to the far side of the room, but didn't leave.

"My Khan," said Kaivon, giving a deep bow.

"What's happened? Is that your blood?"

"No, it's from my men. We were attacked by a squad from the Golden Horde. They're all dead, but so are a third of my men." Both groups of warriors had been so surprised at the appearance of the other, they'd hesitated. It was Kaivon who had drawn his sword first, breaking the stalemate. What followed had been a vicious and bloodthirsty battle.

"Traitorous whore!" bellowed Hulagu, slamming his fists down on the table. The wood creaked, threatening to collapse. "You saw them? With your own eyes?"

"They were Berke's men. One of them even recognised me and used my name." It was a small lie, but it was highly possible one of them had been with them in Baghdad. Hulagu's fury

STEPHEN ARYAN   401

went from hot to ice cold. Some of the colour drained from his face and he became very still.

"You took no prisoners?" asked Rashid, keeping his voice low.

Kaivon shook his head. "The men were too angry."

"Where are the three princes?" said Hulagu. He appeared calm, but the air was charged with energy.

"Resting in their rooms, in the palace," said Rashid.

"Have them brought here," said the Khan.

Normally he would ask honoured guests to join him, but his tone was clear. If they refused to attend, the Kheshig were to drag them through the corridors.

Rashid hurried away, and seconds later, Kaivon heard the clatter of many Kheshig on the march.

"I need to attend to my men," said Kaivon, trying to excuse himself.

"You will stay." Hulagu's eyes were cold. Normally he would listen to suggestions, but today it was clear that he would not. He was the Khan and his word was law.

Kaivon bowed and moved to one side of the room to make space for visitors. The air crackled with the promise of violence. It was an effort not to smile.

Hulagu paced back and forth across the room. Kaivon stayed in one place and didn't fidget in case he drew the Khan's ire. He didn't want to be on the receiving end of the anger that was building up.

A short time later, the three princes were escorted into the room by half a dozen Kheshig and Rashid. Prince Ahmad was swearing at the masked bodyguards, who ignored the insults and shoved him forward.

"I will have your head," promised Ahmad.

"Lord Khan, what is the meaning of this?" asked Prince Yotaqan.

"Do you know this man?" asked Hulagu, gesturing at Kaivon.

"Yes, Lord Khan."

"And do you think he is an honourable man? Trustworthy?"

"He is," said Yotaqan, not seeing the jaws of the trap closing around him.

"Tell them what happened, General," said Hulagu.

Kaivon laid it out, simply and without embellishment. The surprise meeting. The vicious fight and the bloody aftermath. "They were carrying wealth and possessions they'd stolen from settlements in the north of Persia."

"They were obviously traitors," said Yotaqan. He remained calm, but his brothers had noticed that all of the Kheshig had drawn their swords. If the young prince was nervous, it didn't show. "My father will thank you, General, for killing them."

"There have also been a number of raids. Whole towns and villages razed. The people slaughtered, or sold into slavery. Is this also the work of traitors?" asked Hulagu.

Yotaqan shrugged. "I cannot say, Lord Khan. I have not seen those responsible. Do you have prisoners? Witnesses?"

Hulagu stared at the cocky young prince for a long time. Kaivon was certain the Khan would give the order to execute them. The warriors who had travelled south with them had already returned to the Golden Horde. Only the three princes had stayed behind in Tabriz, certain that their station and plausible deniability would protect them. They were spies and traitors to the Mongol Empire. Kaivon knew the words were on the tip of Hulagu's tongue.

Yotaqan appeared calm, but watching him closely Kaivon saw beads of sweat trickling down the sides of his face. His brothers were less practised at concealing their emotions. They were pale, shaking and one looked on the verge of tears, but Hulagu was not known for his compassion.

"Get out of my sight," hissed Hulagu, turning his back on the three princes.

Ahmad sagged against his brothers. Yotaqan finally wiped sweat from his brow. The room stank of fear sweat, and Kaivon thought someone had pissed themselves. The Kheshig stood aside as the three princes hurried from the room. Rashid and Kaivon turned to leave when the Khan spoke.

"Stay, General."

Rashid gave him a tight sympathetic smile. Before the doors were fully closed, Empress Guyuk came storming into the room. She smelled of smoke and her furious expression spoke of more bad news. Kaivon worked really hard not to grin at the possibility of another disaster.

"What is it now?" snapped Hulagu.

Normally, the Empress would not have tolerated being spoken to in such a tone of voice, but today she was distracted. She wrung her hands together and her eyes were distant.

"Guyuk. What's happened?" said the Khan, loud enough that his wife came out of her reverie.

"There's been a small fire in the library," said Guyuk. "All of the books in one room were destroyed." For her to bring such a minor issue to the Khan meant something else was going on. Hulagu folded his arms and waited. "It was Temujin. He killed the old librarian from Baghdad and destroyed all of his research."

Kaivon braced himself for a volcanic eruption of rage, but instead Hulagu stumbled backwards and sat down. The Khan looked genuinely shook to his core, but Kaivon didn't think it was only about his son's betrayal.

"Bring me Rashid," said Hulagu in a whisper.

Kaivon went into the corridor and found the vizier lurking outside.

"Don't do this," Guyuk was saying as Kaivon came back into the room, but Hulagu was ignoring her. "There must be another explanation."

"Time and again, I have listened to you." He spoke as if they were not there. Kaivon felt as if he were eavesdropping on a private conversation. "Like all my children, I gave him every opportunity, and yet he remained a disappointment. Finally, he found something of worth. A spark, that might make him useful, and this is how he repays my leniency."

"But–"

"No more," shouted Hulagu. His voice echoed around the room. He turned away from the Empress and Kaivon saw her wipe away tears. "Temujin is a traitor. He is to be declared an enemy of the Ilkhanate, and an outcast from the Mongol Empire. He is to be killed on sight. Whoever delivers his head will receive a significant reward. Send it to the four corners. Make sure he has nowhere to hide. Anyone found offering him shelter will be executed, along with their family and their home burned to the ground."

"As you command, my Khan," said Rashid, hurrying from the room.

"Leave us," said Hulagu, finally releasing him.

As Kaivon walked away, he heard the sound of raised voices until the Kheshig closed the door behind him. One of his biggest worries had resolved itself. Prince Temujin was now an outcast. He would never use his powers against the enemies of the Ilkhanate. Hulagu would have to wage war against the Mamluks, and the Golden Horde, in the traditional way. Only now he was fighting two enemies instead of one.

Between the inevitable civil war and the betrayal of the Khan's son, Kaivon found himself grinning. He smothered a laugh that was bubbling up until he was alone in his rooms, before finally letting it out.

For the first time since he'd entered the service of Hulagu Khan, the end of the Ilkhanate and freedom for Persia was a real possibility.

Kaivon and two other officers were in the stables, inspecting the horses, when a messenger entered in a rush. The man was red-faced, and his horse looked on the verge of collapse.

"Urgent message," he gasped. "The palace. Army defeated."

Kaivon took the scribbled note, recognised Rashid's handwriting and carefully read the contents. His hands trembled and he shook his head in denial.

"General?" asked one of the officers. Kaivon and the messenger exchanged a look. "Here," said Kaivon, passing the note to the other officers. It was better that they find out from him than someone else. Without waiting to see their reaction, Kaivon jumped onto his horse and rode hard for the palace.

By the time he arrived the news had spread. Every servant was panic-stricken, their eyes wide with terror. Even the steady Kheshig were nervous. As he handed off his horse to a groom, Kaivon was approached by a pair of bodyguards.

"Don't go in there," one of them said, which was surprising. "How bad is it?"

The Kheshig shook his head. "I've never seen him so angry."

Although it was dangerous, Kaivon knew he would never have another opportunity like this and he had to take advantage. "I appreciate the warning," he said, heading for the front door.

Inside, the corridors were abandoned. Any time he spotted a servant, they were running, trying to get to somewhere else as fast as possible without being noticed. When he made eye contact with one woman, she squeaked and ran in the opposite direction. Long before he reached the throne room, Kaivon heard the sound of raised voices.

Hulagu Khan was raging.

The pair of Kheshig standing guard at the door were petrified. They clearly wanted to be anywhere else, but could not abandon their posts. Something heavy smashed into the door with a crash. Inside the room Kaivon heard the sound of breaking glass. Red wine, or perhaps blood, trickled out from under the door. The Kheshig pretended not to notice. Neither one of them opened the door for him, not out of a lack of respect, but self-preservation. They didn't want to be noticed by the Khan.

After taking a deep breath, Kaivon pushed open the door and stepped inside.

The throne room was a mess.

The floor was littered with broken glass and there were patches of blood staining the tiles. He didn't know whose blood it was as there were no bodies, but there was enough spattered around for at least a couple of people. On his left, something had impacted a column so hard, it had shattered the stone and gouged out a chunk the size of his fist. Cracks ran from it in all directions, and blood had trickled down and then dried.

The throne had been shattered. The armrests broken into small chunks and the back was missing. He spotted it across the far side of the room. Someone's feet stuck out from underneath it in another pool of blood.

Hulagu stood in the middle of the room, screaming like a madman, with a mace in one hand. He swung the weapon at the throne again and again, breaking apart the stone seat before kicking the pieces. On the far side of the room he spotted Rashid, cowering behind a column. There was blood on his face and a gash on his cheek. All of the decoration on the walls had been ripped down and stomped on. Every trinket and gift had been ground into a fine dust.

Red-faced, covered in sweat and eyes bulging with fury, Hulagu threw the mace across the room. It barely missed Kaivon's head before hitting the wall. The only reason he didn't flinch was he hadn't seen it coming until it was too late. Exhausted, with his fury finally burned out, Hulagu collapsed on the steps leading up to the throne. His shoulders shook with rage as he tried to regain his breath. As Rashid crept out of the shadows, Hulagu finally noticed Kaivon was there.

The note Kaivon had received had been short. Hulagu's army had suffered a defeat, but he didn't know any more than that. Rather than ask, he simply waited in silence with the vizier. Both of them were balanced on the balls of their feet, ready to dodge any projectiles that were thrown in their direction.

"General Kitbuqa is dead," said Hulagu. His voice was hoarse from shouting and, perhaps, grief for his old friend. Kaivon noticed he said nothing about the thousands of men under Kitbuqa's command. "Tell him," said Hulagu, gesturing at the vizier.

"The General sacked Sidon and Tyre." Rashid paused, perhaps trying to find words that would soften the blow, but it was too late for that. "The Mamluks marched north in force, so General Kitbuqa travelled south to meet them. They fought at a place called Ain Jalut, where our warriors suffered a terrible defeat."

"They were slaughtered," said Hulagu, spitting out the words. "We have never been defeated before on the battlefield. Never."

Kaivon could hardly believe it. The expansion of the Mongol Empire had seemed inevitable, but now it had suffered a major defeat.

"They knew the bulk of our forces had withdrawn," said Rashid.

Kaivon put a hand to his mouth, feigning shock. "How?"

"You know how," said Hulagu. For a moment, Kaivon thought he knew the truth.

"We don't know for certain that it was the princes," said Rashid.

"They wouldn't," said Kaivon, covering up his relief.

"Who else could it be?" asked Hulagu. "Leave me."

"Please, my Khan, I beg of you," said Rashid. "Don't make any rash decisions."

"Get out!" roared the Khan. He scrabbled around for something to throw at his vizier, but thankfully there was nothing in reach. Rashid scuttled out of the room. Kaivon went with him, before he was hit in the head by some flying debris.

"What do you think he will do?" asked Kaivon.

Rashid wiped his face clean and looked at the blood on

his fingers. "I don't know, but I fear this is the beginning of something terrible."

The following morning, Kaivon and the rest of the city had their answer.

The streets of Tabriz were full of whispers, with groups of people standing around gossiping. He caught bits and pieces of what was being said, but he needed to see it for himself.

A large crowd of several hundred had gathered outside the palace. More were turning up all the time, filling the surrounding streets. Despite his rank and status, it took Kaivon some time to push through to the front. Those around him were talking in low voices, pointing and whispering behind their hands.

Tilting his head back, Kaivon stared up into the faces of the three princes from the Golden Horde. Each had been hung by his neck from the walls of the palace. They didn't smell yet, but their skin had already turned an unhealthy grey. Bloated tongues lolled from mouths, and the final expression on their faces was one of terror. All of them had suffered in their final moments.

It was a bold and clear message to the Golden Horde. Berke Khan would have spies in Tabriz. Kaivon didn't think it would be long before he received news about his sons. The only person he pitied was Prince Taraghai. His agony was yet to come.

Leaving the crowd and their whispers behind, Kaivon took a long walk through the city, stopping often to check that he was not being followed. The tea house was quiet so he was able to sit at a table outside in the shade. A short time later, his brother Karveh sat down opposite.

"What news?" asked Karveh, helping himself to some baklava.

Kaivon poured him a glass of tea and sat back in his chair. "Everything went exactly as planned. I sent a second messenger to the Sultan of Egypt."

Hulagu had already sent a letter, demanding that the Mamluks surrender before they suffered the same fate as the people of Iraq. It was intimidation and mind games, designed to spread fear. The Khan didn't expect the Sultan to actually give up without a fight. Kaivon's letter had included detailed information about Mongol troop numbers in Jerusalem, likely tactics and who was leading the warriors. The three princes might have leaked information to the Mamluks, but it was Kaivon's letter that had condemned Kitbuqa and his men to death. He regretted the death of the General, but he was still a Mongol and therefore the enemy.

"By now, I suspect the Mamluks will have retaken parts of Jerusalem. They may already be marching into Syria. Hulagu doesn't have enough men to stop them. They will be forced to rctrcat, giving up land they've only just conquered."

"Such a terrible shame," said Karveh, feigning tears. "And soon, he will be at war with the Golden Horde as well."

"Fighting wars on two different fronts. It will be a challenging time for the Ilkhanate, especially without Prince Temujin and his powers."

"And, sadly, the Great Khan has also gone to war with his brother, Ariq. The Mongol Empire is coming apart at the seams."

The two of them shared a smile as they watched people passing by on the street. Kaivon knew his brother was also imagining a time when Persia was free of its Mongol occupiers.

"It's a good start," said Kaivon, not wanting to spoil the mood, but they both knew this was only the beginning. "But there is still much to be done."

"Actually, I have some more good news," said his brother, slurping his tea. "I've made contact with another group. They're committed and have resources and skills that we don't. Apparently, they even have someone close to the Khan."

"Really?" said Kaivon, leaning forward. "Tell me more."

CHAPTER 40
Kokochin

A long and boring day passed in silence in the cells, and then a second day. At first, Kokochin thought it was all a ploy, but then she began to hear whispers. Even in the cells, news filtered through the guards and servants, from the surly woman who brought her a bowl of broth every day, to the guards on duty. Carried on the still air, she heard them talking about rumours of a civil war with the Golden Horde, dead princes hanging from the walls of the palace, and a terrible defeat in the south.

Deep in her cell, sounds carried from the streets above. Although she couldn't follow conversations, Kokochin heard snatches and the worried tone of many voices. The air was ripe with tension.

Despite her circumstances, she took comfort that the delay was not part of a mind game. She was simply a low priority, and Guyuk would deal with her when more pressing matters had been addressed. To keep herself busy, Kokochin exercised within the confines of her cell. She was used to training in a small space, and the cell became her House of Grace. Moving from one position to another, running through drills and imagining fights in her mind, she kept her joints and muscles loose. When she tired of that she meditated, trying to find the quiet place inside, so that she could face whatever was coming.

On the third morning, Kokochin heard the grinding of metal, and the thump of feet and she rose gracefully to greet her visitors. Empress Guyuk marched down the corridor followed by four Kheshig. With an irritated wave of her hand they stayed back, so that the Empress came the rest of the way by herself.

"I suspect even down here, you've heard bits of news," said the Empress, wrinkling her nose at the smell. At first it had bothered Kokochin, but after a day or so, she'd grown used to it.

"A few rumours."

"The Golden Horde has betrayed us and the Empire. They've been sending slaves to the Mamluks for years, shoring up their army. War is now inevitable. To make matters worse, there was an attempt on the life of the Khan's son, Abaqa."

Kokochin wanted to ask a question, but this was not a conversation. They were not in the sunny east wing of the palace, drinking tea. She was being told all of this for a specific reason.

"Eleven of his men gave their life to protect Abaqa, but thankfully he was uninjured."

Abaqa had always been kind to her when they'd spoken. She was glad that he had survived, but she didn't share this with the Empress.

"One of those responsible was captured alive. He refused to talk, but it was clear what he was and who had sent him. He was an Assassin."

"I thought they had been eliminated," said Kokochin, despite herself.

"So did I," said Guyuk, "but like other vermin, they found a way to survive. They fled to Egypt, and have been working with the Mamluks. It was the Sultan who sent the Assassins."

The Empress paused, waiting for Kokochin to say something. Having already spoken once, Kokochin bit the inside of her mouth to prevent another outburst. Instead she focused on her breathing and tried to remain calm.

"Ugh, the stench is unbearable. You will wash and then we will continue this conversation. Bring her," said Guyuk, gesturing at the Kheshig.

Kokochin was escorted back to her rooms and, once the guards were certain she couldn't escape, she was left alone to bathe and change into fresh clothing. Normally she would have languished in the bath, but today she merely scrubbed her skin until it was clean. A modest breakfast was delivered by a nervous servant, who stared as if she were a wild animal. Two Kheshig, armed with crossbows, stood behind Kokochin the whole time she ate.

An hour later, surrounded by four guards, Kokochin was marched through the hallways to another part of the palace she'd not visited before. Guests often stayed at the palace, senior figures from other parts of the Empire, visiting dignitaries and the like, but this was the first time she had seen their quarters. The rooms were lush but they went past them without stopping, to another corridor with bare walls and no decorations. They were for servants who belonged to the visitors. The rooms were modestly appointed, with few comforts. At present, all of them were empty and the whole area felt abandoned.

At the far end of the corridor, Empress Guyuk stood waiting with another pair of Kheshig. In front of her was a closed door, which immediately made Kokochin nervous.

Something jabbed her in the back. Turning her head, Kokochin saw one of the Kheshig had pressed the point of his sword into her spine. At Guyuk's signal all of the others drew their swords, which heightened her anxiety. Two of the bodyguards held her by the upper arms. Their fingers dug into her flesh hard enough to bruise, but she refused to cry out.

"I urge you to remain calm," said the Empress. Taking a key from her pocket, she unlocked the door and stepped back, giving Kokochin space to peer into the room.

The space within was less than a quarter of what she lived in, but it was still a nice room with comfortable furniture. The window would have been pleasant, if not for the recent addition of thick iron bars. She absorbed all of this in a blink of an eye, as her gaze was immediately drawn to the room's only occupant.

Layla.

She was sitting in a chair by the window, where rays of sunlight bathed her face. Her eyes were closed and she appeared to be basking in the heat like a cat. There were a few cuts and scrapes on her face, but otherwise she appeared unhurt. As Kokochin's heart lurched in her chest, the grip on her arms tightened. The guards had to lift her off the floor to stop her from running forward.

The disturbance drew Layla's attention and her eyes flicked open. Time stopped as they stared at one another. Kokochin immediately stopped wrestling. For a brief moment, she completely forgot all about everyone else. It was just the two of them, sitting in the sun. They'd spent whole afternoons like that, happily working in silence on their jewellery, lying in bed talking or practising moves in the House.

Layla was the most important person in the world, and there was nothing Kokochin wouldn't do for her. The ache in her heart was so fierce she took a step forward, pulling the Kheshig along with her. The huge weight dragging on her body snapped Kokochin back to the present.

"Calm, princess," said the familiar voice of Guyuk in her ear.

There were six Kheshig and two of them. The Empress herself was no threat. Taking out all of the bodyguards, in such a confined space, would be incredibly difficult. The only way would be to divide them, splitting their focus. The corridors were not too wide, so they wouldn't be able to come at her more than two abreast. Raising one eyebrow she opened her palms, pretending to surrender, but really she was hoping Layla understood what she was suggesting.

Very slowly, Layla shook her head. Kokochin knew there had to be a specific reason for Layla's refusal to fight. No matter how desperate her need, Kokochin knew she couldn't best all six Kheshig by herself. If she tried it would be a suicide, and then there would be no need for the Empress to keep Layla as a hostage.

As she was dragged away down the corridor, Kokochin fixed an image of Layla in her mind, and she tried to remember all of the good times they'd shared.

As she sat down to tea with the Empress in the lush surroundings of the east wing, Kokochin tried not to count all the ways she could kill Guyuk before the Kheshig shot her in the back. Two were standing behind her armed with loaded crossbows. There were two more on the far side of the room, blocking the other doorway, and one was standing two paces behind her to the right with a drawn sword.

If she moved really fast, she could jam the delicate two-pronged fruit fork into Guyuk's neck at least six times, before she was killed. It might even be worth it, just to see the look of surprise on her face.

"What are you smiling about?" said Guyuk, pouring herself some tea. There were no servants anywhere. The Empress had to serve herself and wasn't pleased about it.

"Why am I here?" asked Kokochin.

"I will ask the questions and you will answer. Do I need to resort to threats against your friend?" asked Guyuk.

"No."

"Good. I have no patience for such posturing. Tea?"

"Thank you, Empress," said Kokochin, holding up her cup.

"Let's start with a difficult question. Are you a member of the Order of Assassins?"

"No. I'm not," said Kokochin, which surprised the Empress. "I see no point in trying to deceive you. A lie might buy me some time, but I really don't want to end up on Elbuz's table."

"That man is grotesque." Guyuk shuddered in revulsion. "So, if not the Order, who do you both work for?"

"No one. Ourselves," she added, when Guyuk's frown returned. "I wanted to learn how to protect myself. I was tired of being scared to go out into the city by myself. Not long after I arrived, there was an incident with two men. I never wanted to feel like that again."

Guyuk didn't say anything, but it was clear she understood. Her gaze rested on one of the masked Kheshig for a moment before drifting away. "Have you killed anyone?"

"Yes," said Kokochin. She waited for the Empress to ask her for names, but for a time she said nothing.

"What did it feel like?" she eventually asked.

"I didn't enjoy it, if that's what you're asking."

"Then why do it?"

"Because it needed to be done, and there was no other way," said Kokochin.

"I'm glad to hear you say that," said Guyuk with a grin.

Even though she was in familiar surroundings, it felt as if Kokochin had walked into a bear trap. Only now was she starting to feel the steel teeth closing in.

"What do you want me to do?"

"You're going to put your new skills to good use. You will become my tool. I will point you at someone, and you will kill them."

"And what do I get in return?" asked Kokochin.

"Besides your life?"

"Yes."

"Nothing. But your friend, Layla, also continues to live. I'm sure you can imagine all manner of horrible things Elbuz will do to her if you refuse. Neither of us wants that to happen," said the Empress leaning across the table. "But let me be absolutely clear. If I believe you're lying to me, holding out in any way, or dragging your feet, I will give her to the butcher.

She will scream for weeks, and beg for death long before it finds her. And right before the end, she will come to hate you."

When she had first arrived in Tabriz, Kokochin had thought Guyuk generous. The Empress had taken Kokochin under her wing and honestly explained her position, but also the opportunity of her position. If not for her, Kokochin would never have gone out into the city to find her purpose.

In reality, there wasn't an ounce of compassion in the woman. She would slit her own mother's throat if it was required. Kokochin had never met a more ruthless and mercenary person in her life. Nothing was allowed to stand in the way of her ambition.

"I understand," said Kokochin, because she had no choice. Layla couldn't fight back, not yet at least, so she needed to buy some time. "What do you want me to do?"

Guyuk's cruel smile sent a shiver down her spine. "You must kill Temujin, the Khan's son."

CHAPTER 41
Hulagu

It had been almost a week since Hulagu's youngest son had betrayed him. And in all that time, despite the significant bounty upon his head, there had been no sign of Temujin.

Lounging on his new throne, Hulagu idly noted that the craftsman had done an excellent job of repairing the room. He couldn't see the smallest trace of where he'd smashed the servant's head into the pillar. The whole room was just as it had been before his spate of bad news.

Hulagu knew he was brooding but, given the circumstances, it was justifiable. Letting his gaze drift around the throne room, he took in the opulence. The tiled mosaic floor, the arched curved ceiling, and the vast painting down the left wall showing several of his recent conquests. Four Kheshig stood on duty inside the room, and four more beyond, but those in view were as lifeless as statues. Only the blinking of their eyes behind their masks gave him any indication that they were still alive.

"You look bored," said an unfamiliar voice.

On his left Hulagu saw a tall Persian man idly leaning against a pillar eating an apple. The doors had not opened. He had simply appeared. With a rasp of steel, the two Kheshig at the door drew their swords and ran towards the stranger.

Hulagu saw a blur of movement across the room and then the man was beside the pillar again, nibbling on his apple. The only difference was one of his hands was covered in blood. The two Kheshig dropped to their knees. One of them had a fist-sized hole in his chest. The other was upright, but his head was facing in the wrong direction.

The two bodyguards dropped to the ground.

One of the remaining Kheshig yanked open a door and called for aid. In less than a minute the intruder was surrounded by eight more Kheshig. Each one had a spear pointed at his throat. The only reason they didn't stab him to death was that Hulagu had raised a hand.

Despite his predicament, the man was at ease. He picked the apple clean and idly tossed the core into a brazier where it sizzled and turned black.

"Who are you?" said Hulagu.

"My name is Behrouz," said the Persian. His broad face was unremarkable, but it was his eyes that caught Hulagu's attention. The left was a deep brown, but the right was a cold and icy blue.

"What do you want?" said the Khan.

"I'm here to give you a demonstration, Lord Khan," said Behrouz with a wolfish grin.

One second he was leaning against the pillar, surrounded by a ring of steel, and the next his hands blurred through the air in front of his face. The steel of the spears crumbled to dust, until he was facing eight wooden staves. With a devilish grin, he disappeared and reappeared on the far side of the room.

The Kheshig drew their swords, but then waited for the order.

"Kill him," said Hulagu, just to see what would happen.

Behrouz laughed in delight as the bodyguards ran forward. Then he disappeared again, blurring into motion. Hulagu briefly saw something flickering at the corner of his vision, but by the time he'd turned towards it, Behrouz was already gone.

The intruder criss-crossed the room, again and again, moving around, over and sometimes through the Kheshig.

It was over in less than six heartbeats.

Behrouz stood on the far side of the room, spattered with blood from head to toe, with a plate of pastries in one hand. In the centre of the room were the corpses of eight Kheshig, all of them killed in a different way. One had been diced up into six pieces that slid apart to the floor. Another had completely lost his head as it tumbled from his shoulders. A third had been reduced to a desiccated skeleton dressed in armour, which broke apart when it hit the ground. Behrouz had swept through them faster than the eye could follow.

When the final chunk of bodyguard dropped to the ground, a deathly silence filled the throne room.

As he stared at the man, Hulagu felt a growing sense of unease, which he did his best to hide. "What are you?" he asked.

"I am a Kozan," said Behrouz with a bow. "And I am here to serve you, Lord Khan."

MAIN CHARACTERS

Hulagu Khan – *ruler of the Ilkhanate, brother of Kublai, Möngke and Ariq*

Kokochin – *The Blue Princess, the from Mongol tribe of the Bayaut and newest wife of Hulagu Khan*

Kaivon – *Persian General and former southern rebel*

Temujin – *Hulagu's youngest son, a disappointment to his father*

THE ILKHANATE AND ITS ALLIES

Guyuk – *First Wife of Hulagu Khan and Empress of the Ilkhanate*
Doquz – *Second Wife of Hulagu Khan, also known as the War Wife*
Rashid – *Vizier of the Ilkhanate, a powerful and very shrewd man*

Abaqa – *eldest son of Hulagu Khan and heir to the Ilkhanate*
Jumghur – *second eldest son of Hulagu Khan, a violent and impatient man*
Taraghai – *seventh son of Hulagu Khan, far more cunning than people realise*

Kitbuqa – *A General and close friend of Hulagu Khan, a Christian*
Nasir – *A clever Persian man and chief engineer for Hulagu Khan*

King David of Georgia – *has historic grievances against all Muslims*
Prince Bohemond of Antioch – *A Christian, also known as the Fair*
King Hethum of Cilician Armenia – *A Christian*

Karveh – *Kaivon's brother and a Persian rebel*
Layla – *a jeweller in Tabriz*
Ariana – *a healer in Tabriz*
Shirin – *owner of a tea shop in Tabriz*

Reyhan – *the chief librarian at Baghdad's central library*

THE GOLDEN HORDE

Berke Khan – *Ruler of the Golden Horde, the northwestern Khanate, cousin of Hulagu Khan*
Gurban – *Vizier to Berke Khan, a clever man loyal to his Khan*

Yotaqan – *a prince of the Golden Horde and the youngest son of Berke Khan*
Ahmad – *a prince of the Golden Horde and son of Berke Khan*
Tinibeg – *a prince of the Golden Horde and son of Berke Khan*

THE CHAGATAI KHANATE

Buqa-Temur – *Ruler of the Chagatai Khanate, the southeastern Khanate*

OTHER PROMINENT CHARACTERS

Kublai – *Grandson of Genghis Khan, fifth Great Khan of the Empire. Brother to Hulagu, Möngke and Ariq.*
Möngke – *Grandson of Genghis Khan, fifth Great Khan of the Empire. Brother to Kublai, Hulagu and Ariq.*
Ariq – *Grandson of Genghis Khan, fifth Great Khan of the Empire. Brother to Möngke, Hulagu and Kublai.*

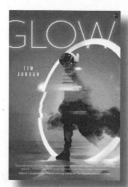

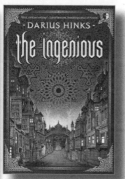

BLUEBIRD
CIEL PIERLOT

embedded
Dan Abnett

SWASHBUCKLERS
Dan Hanks

We are Angry Robot

LAST GOD STANDING
MICHAEL BOATMAN

WORLD RUNNING DOWN
AL HESS

STRANGERS
CHRIS PANATIER

angryrobotbooks.com

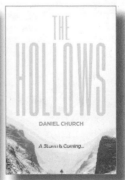

THE SINGULAR & EXTRAORDINARY TALE OF MIRROR & GOLIATH BY ISHBELLE BEE

THE CONTRARY TALE OF THE BUTTERFLY GIRL BY ISHBELLE BEE

THE HOLLOWS
DANIEL CHURCH
A Storm Is Coming...

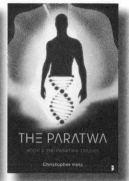

We are Angry Robot

angryrobotbooks.com